"Exploring th   s isn't a good idea.

Wait… what? Jack thought Viv was about to bring up the chemistry between them? He clearly thought of her in that way or this wouldn't be an issue.

"I was—"

"I don't like tension in my work space."

"And you think there's a problem between us?"

Why was her whisper suddenly husky like some seductress? She certainly wasn't trying to seduce him. Not that she'd mind.

"I think you drive me out of my mind." Jack took a half step closer. "I blame myself for my thoughts, but I blame you for making me want things I have no business wanting."

"I'm not trying to do anything to you. I'm attracted to you, but I know you're my boss and that's a line we can't cross, even if you were interested in me that way."

Jack muttered a curse, took a step forward and had her pinned between his hard chest and the wall.

"*If* I was interested?" he repeated with a laugh of disbelief. "Do I look like a man who isn't interested, Viv?"

* * *

The Heir's Unexpected Baby
is part of Mills & Boon Desire's No. 1 bestselling series, Billionaires and Babies: Powerful men… wrapped around their babies' little fingers.

THE HEIR'S
UNEXPECTED BABY

BY
JULES BENNETT

First Published in Great Britain 2017
By Mills & Boon, an imprint of HarperCollins*Publishers*
1 London Bridge Street, London, SE1 9GF

© 2017 Jules Bennett

ISBN: 978-0-263-92806-8

51-0217

Our policy is to use papers that are natural, renewable and recyclable products and made from wood grown in sustainable forests. The logging and manufacturing processes conform to the legal environmental regulations of the country of origin.

Printed and bound in Spain
by CPI, Barcelona

National bestselling author **Jules Bennett** has penned over forty contemporary romance novels. She lives in the Midwest with her high-school-sweetheart husband and their two kids. Jules can often be found on Twitter chatting with readers, and you can also connect with her via her website, www.julesbennett.com.

To everyone who has opened their homes
and hearts to foster children...
you are truly a blessing.

One

"What are you doing here so early?"

Jack Carson brushed past Vivianna Smith and stepped into her apartment, trying like hell not to touch her. Or breathe in that familiar jasmine scent. Or think of how sexy she looked in that pale pink suit.

Masochist. That's all he could chalk this up to. But he had a mission, damn it, and he needed his assistant's help to pull it off.

Wouldn't life be so much easier if Viv were only his assistant? He'd avoided the unwanted attraction for four years, yet the longer she worked for him, the more difficult that was proving to be. And lately, he'd been having dreams. Okay, fine. Fantasies. And she starred in every single one of them.

How the hell could he even have these thoughts about her? It was flat-out wrong, not to mention unprofessional.

"I need you to use that charm of yours and get more information." He turned to face her as she closed the door to her apartment. "You're going to have to dig deeper into the Parkers' lives."

Clint and Lily Parker were a young couple who had been killed two months ago in a robbery gone wrong. The perpetrators set the Parkers' house on fire. The only survivor was a sweet infant named Katie…a baby Viv now fostered.

The burn in his chest was still crippling. Jack wasn't going down the baby path, not even in his mind. He admired Viv for reaching out and helping a child, as she had so many times over the years. But babies weren't for him. They never could be if he wanted to keep his heart intact.

"You're positive the O'Sheas had something to do with that crime?" Vivianna asked, moving around him to head down the hall.

With no option but to follow her swaying hips, he fell in right behind her. He was human, and a guy. Where else could he look but those hips? She always had on those damn body-hugging skirts…he believed she referred to them as pencil skirts. Those curves would be the death of him.

"I know they did," he confirmed.

The infamous O'Shea family of Boston was always slipping around the law, ignoring the basic rules of human decency. Jack's main focus in life was bringing cocky bastards like that down. Every time he went against those believing they were above the law, he saw the person who had killed his wife and unborn child… and still ran free.

The O'Sheas might run a polished high-society auction house known around the globe, but he knew they were no better than common criminals. And Jack was about to prove to this arrogant family who was in charge. He would bring them down in a spectacular show of justice. And his ticket was the woman who fueled his every fantasy.

A year ago, Jack had set up the perfect bogus background for Viv. She was working only part-time for the notorious family, but that's all he needed for her to gain intel.

The FBI had sought him out, needing someone with his experience and resources to infiltrate the O'Sheas. Since Jack was the best in the business of investigating, of course they needed him. That wasn't vanity, either, just a fact. Jack could get things done when others couldn't.

The millions he'd made hadn't rolled in by him sitting back and delegating responsibilities. He'd worked his ass off, throwing himself into his work and opening Carson Enterprises when he got home from Afghanistan ten years ago.

He'd returned to find that he'd lost his entire family while he'd been overseas. What else had there been to live for other than seeking justice anywhere he could?

Since he'd already made a fortune, he often turned down jobs when they didn't appeal to him. But the O'Sheas were right in his wheelhouse. They had been in talks with the Parker couple about acquiring some of their antiques when the robbery happened. There wasn't a doubt in Jack's mind that this tight-lipped family knew what really went down that tragic night.

Viv went into the nursery. Heart clenching, Jack opted to wait in the hall—demons and all that.

He commended Viv for her love of children, the way she fostered with open arms. Over the time he'd known her, he'd seen her with various children, but never an infant. He couldn't get involved in any of that. The wounds he'd lived with for so long had never healed... probably never would.

Viv stepped back into the hall, Katie's head resting against her shoulder. "I need to drop her off at the sitter next door and get to work."

Viv was lucky that her next-door neighbor was a retired teacher and widow. She loved kids and took care of Viv's foster kids when she was working.

"I'm doing what I can, Jack." Her eyes held his and he hated how tired she looked. Beautiful, sexy as hell, but still tired. "They're already suspicious because of the missing data. If I press too hard, they'll know I'm not who I say I am."

Jack hadn't wanted to put her in this position. But he couldn't back down when he had a job to do. And that job wasn't staring at the V in her suit jacket as baby Katie tugged at the opening.

A flash of a white lacy bra taunted him, making him want to undo those few buttons to see if the lace...

Damn it. Get a grip.

She stepped forward, and Jack had to force himself to focus on her face. Which wasn't a hardship. Viv was part Native American. Her grandmother had been in the Sioux tribe, so Viv had inherited high cheekbones, long, dark hair and deep brown eyes. He'd seen more than one man do a double take her way...and each time, Jack had wanted to throat punch the stranger.

Guilt banded around his chest like a vise. He shouldn't be lusting after another woman. He'd had the love of his life; she was gone. Gone because he hadn't been there to protect her or their baby.

Getting drawn to Viv was just a by-product of working together for so long. She was the only woman he associated with, other than his housekeeper-slash-chef, Tilly. He admired Viv because she was strong, with an undertone of vulnerability. Add in her striking looks and perfectly shaped curves and it was only natural he be attracted to her. But he had to keep his emotions beneath the surface where he could control them.

"I'm on your side here," she told him with a soft smile, pulling him back to the moment. "Why don't you come over this evening and we can talk more."

"I have a conference call this evening with some clients in the UK."

Viv gave a slight nod. "Oh, okay. Then tomorrow? I'll make dinner and we can figure out our next step."

Dinner? With her and the baby? That all sounded so…domestic. He prided himself on keeping work in the office or in neutral territory. But he'd come here this morning to check on her…and he couldn't blame it all on work.

Damn it. The longer this case went on, the more protective he became—the more possessive.

"You can come to my place and I'll have my chef prepare something."

There. If Tilly was on hand, then maybe it wouldn't seem so family-like. Viv often fostered kids who had no place else to go. He had no idea why she'd never settled down and started a family of her own, when it was so obvious she loved caring for children. But that was none of his business. Just because they were associates didn't mean he had a right to pry into her life. Clearly, she didn't want to discuss such things or she would've brought them up.

"I can do tomorrow," she told him, her smile widening. "Katie and I would love to get out of the house.

I get off work around four, so I'll pick her up and be right over."

Jack hadn't had her over with a child before. On the rare occasions he and Viv got together outside the office, it was usually just the two of them. In the past couple years, ever since he started really noticing Vivianna as more than his assistant, he'd tried to keep their social interactions to a minimum.

"Any requests?" he asked.

Did her gaze just dart to his lips? She couldn't look at him with those dark eyes as if she wanted…

No. It didn't matter what she wanted, or what he wanted for that matter. Their relationship was business only. Period.

"Um…no requests." She shook her head, offered a smile. "Whatever you have will be fine."

Jack rubbed his damp palms against his jeans. He needed to get out of here. Between that telling look she'd thrown him, the precious baby still sleeping in her little pink onesie and his lack of sleep from working, his mind was throwing all sorts of impossible scenarios at him.

Jack crossed to the door and gripped the doorknob. He glanced over his shoulder as Viv closed in behind him. "Be careful, Viv. I don't want you to take unnecessary risks."

She shifted the sleeping baby and tipped her head. "You've taught me how to look out for myself. I promise I'll be fine. See you tomorrow."

Jack paused, soaking in the sight of her in that prim little suit, holding the baby. Definitely time to go before he forgot she actually worked for him and took what he'd wanted for months. He didn't need any more heartache or distractions in his life.

* * *

It was finally four o'clock and Viv couldn't wait to get out of her office at O'Shea's and go see Jack. Ridiculous, this infatuation she had with her boss. Clichés were definitely not her thing, yet she'd be diving headfirst into his sheets if he gave her the green light.

Sad. She was a sad woman hoping her boss would notice her. Like she had time for a torrid, steamy affair. She was caring for a child, an infant. There was nothing sexy about the haggard, overworked-mom look. But Viv would never give up fostering. She could still be a mother, yet not get too emotionally attached.

The heartache of knowing she'd never have her own children was somewhat pacified, yet the underlying hurt was never too far below the surface. But work kept her busy and her attentions focused elsewhere. It wasn't as if she didn't have a full load at the moment.

Viv started at O'Shea's part-time, which was perfect for her fostering schedule, not to mention that she still worked for Jack, as well. Being single, she had only a handful of people she could count on. Her parents were no longer around and she was an only child. She'd learned some time ago how to be independent, but even so, she needed some help when caring for a child and working outside the home.

Her quirky neighbor, Martha, was an adorable elderly lady who watched Katie most of the time, but when Viv was in a bind, she'd simply take Katie into the office. Well, her office with Jack.

Oh, she "worked" at O'Shea's, but that was only a cover created by Jack to get her on the inside, up close and personal. Her real employer was one sexy, rich investigator who couldn't move beyond his heartache to see there was still life out there.

If it wasn't work, he wasn't interested...which was the only reason he'd shown up so early at her house yesterday morning. The man had been through so much pain in his life, it was no wonder he was married to his job. He'd lost his mother when he'd been around nineteen, then he'd seen battle in war. His wife had been killed and he'd never known who his father was... Viv knew just enough details for her heart to break for him, but she wished he would try living again. She'd love to be the one to show him that not everything was harsh and cold...if he would only let her in.

Viv headed toward the back office of O'Shea's. Laney, the youngest O'Shea and the only female sibling, was out front dealing with a potential client. Since they had discovered some information had been leaked to the Feds, at least one member of the infamous family was here at all times...which made Viv's snooping a tad more difficult, considering she was here only about twenty hours per week.

Circling the antique desk that had been assigned to her in the office, she opened the top left drawer to find a pen. She wanted to jot down some items she needed to pick up from the store or she'd forget.

Katie was teething and the nights were getting longer and longer. Poor baby. She'd lost her parents and now she wasn't sleeping. Viv wanted to comfort the sweet girl while she was in her care.

All kids that came into Viv's home were precious, and they were all hard to say goodbye to. But Viv stayed strong for them. With this being her first baby, she worried how much more difficult it would be, both emotionally and logistically. She already had a demanding schedule, but she couldn't turn away this poor orphan who'd just lost both parents.

At the moment, Katie needed more pain reliever for her swollen gums, and Viv was out of nearly everything. Grocery shopping wasn't high on the priority list right now. Saving kids, helping Jack, trying to get Jack to notice her as more than a friend…would he ever? Her to-do list seemed to grow by the day.

Vivianna reached inside her desk for a pen and a slip of paper. She'd used this particular desk since coming here a year ago. During that time she'd earned the trust of the O'Sheas, and occasionally felt guilty about her act, but she wasn't naive. She'd heard the rumors around Boston. Anyone who delved into the art or auction world knew who the O'Sheas were. The terms *mafia* and *mob* seemed to follow them wherever they went.

Something brushed the top of her hand. Viv jerked back, bent down, but didn't see anything inside the drawer. If there was a spider in there tickling her skin there wouldn't be enough antibacterial gel to kill those horrendous germs.

She quickly reached back in for her pen and paper. And once again something brushed the back of her hand.

Viv reached for her cell phone and shone the light inside the drawer, fully expecting to see a family of hairy tarantulas.

When she bent down, she saw a sliver of paper sticking out…from the top of the drawer? Since Viv had used this desk for so long, she had no idea what that could be.

She listened. Laney and the client were still talking. Viv's desk sat in the corner, away from them, so the coast was clear. Pulling her chair over, she took a seat and bent to examine the underside of the desk. How had she not noticed anything before?

Gripping the paper between her thumb and index

finger, she tugged slightly. When it eased out further, she noticed some cursive writing she couldn't identify. Pulling a bit more, she felt something give. Putting her phone inside the drawer to shine upward, she reached with both hands. The board was loose.

Viv pulled slightly, careful to not make too much noise, but Laney and the client were now laughing. Perfect.

The board was a bit of a struggle, but it came loose. And a small book fell into the drawer.

Viv stared, curious about where it had come from and who'd hidden it in the desk. She quickly grabbed her purse from the bottom drawer and slid the book inside. She'd have to look at it later.

Grocery list forgotten—she could worry about that later—Viv grabbed her things. She belted her wrap coat and quickly hoisted her purse up onto her shoulder as she headed out the back door. The bitter wind cut right through her, but she was anxious to get to her car.

Once she settled into her older model car, Viv turned on her heated seat, locked the doors and pulled the small leather-bound book from her purse.

It didn't take her long to realize she'd struck gold. The author of this journal was none other than the late Patrick O'Shea. The patriarch of the Boston family Jack was hell-bent on bringing down. The family she'd been infiltrating for a year.

As she skimmed the pages, she knew when she got to Jack's house he'd devour this thing. She couldn't wait to get this to him, to show him she was valuable and actually had something concrete they might be able to use.

She flipped another page, then froze as she read the entry. Her blood chilled as each word sank in. There was no skimming this one. In fact, she read it twice to make sure she wasn't seeing things.

Heart in her throat, she knew there was no way Jack could ever see this journal. Everything he'd wanted to bring down the family was here…including the fact that Jack was Patrick's illegitimate son.

Two

Heels clicked on the hardwood, the echo growing louder as Viv approached. Jack came to his feet and turned toward the entryway of the patio room. He'd had his chef set up dinner out here so they could close all the French doors and have some privacy.

Jack sucked in a breath the second she came into view. The punch of lust to the gut was nothing new, though. More and more, when he saw her, she never failed to have a dramatic impact…an issue he'd have to deal with on his own.

Her pink suit jacket cut in at her narrow waist, the matching skirt fell just above her knee and her black heeled boots showcased just how long those legs truly were.

He'd traveled the world, both in the military and for pleasure, and had seen stunning women all over the globe. But Viv, who managed to embody innocence, class and a touch of sultriness, was one woman he couldn't get out of his mind.

Jack knew Viv would be gorgeous in anything she wore. That Native American heritage of hers set her apart from nearly every woman he knew. And the fact that she stood out in his mind only added to his guilt. He had to get a grip or he'd mess up their working relationship, and he refused to find another assistant. Viv was invaluable and they worked smoothly as a team.

And she was the only one he trusted to get inside the O'Sheas' inner sanctum and bring back information.

"Sorry I'm late." She blew out a breath, hugged little Katie closer to her chest. "She's been a little fussy and I'm pretty sure her teeth are bothering her."

Jack shoved his hands in his pockets. He had no experience with teething babies...not that he wouldn't have welcomed it once. But that chance was stolen from him the night his pregnant wife had been in the wrong place at the wrong time.

Working with Viv seriously hit his emotions from every single angle. Self-control was key to him not losing his ever-loving mind. And if he focused on the task at hand, at bringing down the O'Sheas, then nothing else mattered.

"I hope I didn't hold you up." Viv glanced at the table, her eyes wide. "Wow. You really went all out."

The yeast rolls, the turkey roulade with plum sauce, the roasted potatoes and veggies, wine...even pats of butter in the shape of doves. Tilly, his chef, housekeeper and wanna-be matchmaker, had gone a bit overboard. And Jack knew for a fact there was a homemade red velvet cheesecake waiting for them in the kitchen.

He gave a mental shrug. Tilly's attempts were all in

vain. Regardless of the fact that Jack had told her this dinner was strictly business, she clearly had ignored him and done her own thing…as usual.

Tilly had been his chef for nearly a decade and never missed a chance to set him up with a woman. Jack had turned down numerous blind dates she'd foisted on him. When he was ready, he could find his own damn date. Considering he was married to Carson Enterprises and dedicated to working for justice, he didn't have time to worry about dating or keeping a woman happy.

Jack glanced at the overly romantic table, then back to Viv. "I told Tilly this was a business dinner, but she's hell-bent on marrying me off."

Viv quirked a dark brow. "Well, this is already better than nearly every date I've been on. I'm still recovering from the last one."

Before Jack could ask what she meant, not that it was his business, Katie let out a cry. Viv patted her back and rocked back and forth, whispering comforting words in an attempt to calm the baby. Nothing seemed to be working, but he wasn't exactly an expert…nor would he ever be.

"I left the diaper bag up front where Tilly hung our coats. Could you grab it for me?"

Diaper bag. Sure. Maybe this meeting would have been better suited to a phone call. Viv had her hands full, technically working two jobs and caring for an eleven-month-old baby.

Jack refused to feel guilty as he headed to retrieve the diaper bag. Viv had been with him long enough and she was a strong woman. He wasn't worried she couldn't pull this off. He was *counting* on her to pull this off.

And that irritated him on a certain level. He hated relying on someone else to get the job done. He was a hands-on guy, so waiting for her to feed him information was not his idea of a dream job. But the FBI was counting on him to uncover something that would tie the O'Sheas to the crimes against the Parkers. Then they would have the open door to search the rest of their dealings.

The gray-and-white-patterned bag sat next to the accent table by the front door. Jack grabbed the strap and jerked the heavy bag up onto his shoulder. What the hell was in this thing? How could someone so small need so much stuff?

He started back down the hallway, but stopped short when Tilly stepped through the wide arched opening leading into the kitchen.

"Everything all right, Mr. Carson?"

Mr. Carson. She'd worked for him for nearly ten years and he'd given up trying to get her to call him by his first name. Tilly epitomized respect. Ironic, considering she didn't mind nosing right on into his love life…or lack thereof.

"Fine, Tilly. Thank you. Viv just needed her diaper bag."

Tilly smiled, the corners of her eyes creasing. "That little girl is lucky to have Ms. Smith in her life."

Jack nodded. "You're off duty from playing cupid tonight." And every other night.

A smile spread across her face, deepening the fan of wrinkles around her eyes. "I don't know what you're talking about," she claimed as she turned back to the kitchen. She stopped, threw a glance over her shoulder and added, "Just let me know when to serve the cheesecake for two."

"I'll serve it," he told her with a laugh. How could he not admire her determination, even if it was wasted? "Why don't you go on home?"

Her eyes all but sparkled. "Want to be alone? I get it. Consider me gone."

He wasn't going to correct her. Yes, he wanted to be alone with Viv, but not for the reasons Tilly assumed. She'd draw her own conclusions no matter what Jack said, so he wasn't wasting his breath. Besides, he never let Tilly in on his cases. Keeping his work to himself was the only way he managed to crack cases and find justice for the people he helped. The money was just a bonus.

Tilly argued that he was too busy traveling for work and making money to find a woman. She often hinted that all that money was a waste if he had nobody to spend it on.

As much as the thought of another woman in his life terrified him, Jack couldn't fault Tilly for her efforts. The woman's heart was in the right place—he just wished she'd give up. He'd had the love of his life once. That kind of love didn't happen twice.

As far as dating, well, he didn't want to worry about that, either. He was perfectly content with the way things were. Worrying about himself was enough.

But part of him, okay a huge part, worried about Viv when she was with the O'Sheas. He'd be a fool not to worry. So much for not getting personally involved.

Katie's cry pulled him away from his thoughts as he headed back onto the patio. Viv sat in one of the cushioned chairs at the table. She was muttering nurturing words and holding Katie in a cradle position.

Jack froze when he spotted the pale pink lace peeking from beneath Viv's suit jacket. *Mercy, not again.* Katie had a white-knuckled grip on the V and was pulling the material apart.

The lace was quite the contrast against Viv's dark

skin…skin he shouldn't be looking at and lace his fingers shouldn't be itching to trace.

Pull it together.

He adjusted the diaper bag on his shoulder and attempted to ignore the fact this woman loved lace lingerie.

"What do you need out of here?" he asked, unzipping the bag.

She lifted her head and every time those dark eyes clashed with his, he struggled to look away. She had a power she wasn't even aware of and he'd do good to remind himself she was off-limits.

"Just set it down. I can get it."

Setting the bag at her feet, he stepped back and took a seat across from her. Unfortunately, when she bent down to dig inside the bag, Katie's grip tightened and that V only widened. A little pink bow was nestled in the middle of her breasts.

Damn it all. How the hell could he conduct a "business" meeting like this?

"Just tell me what you're looking for."

He got to his feet and picked the bag up, forcing himself not to look her way. *Focus on the bag.* That was the only way they were going to get anywhere this evening.

"Oh, the pain reliever." Viv shifted Katie on her lap, then adjusted her controversial jacket. "It's a small pink-and-white bottle with a dropper lid."

What the hell was a dropper lid? He shuffled through diapers, wipes, jars of baby food, lotion, a stuffed doll…

"Sorry. The outside pouch. I put it in there so it would be easily accessible."

Of course she had.

Jack finally pulled out the right thing and handed it

to her. With his hands on his hips, he stood back and watched as Katie settled back against Viv's arm.

"It's okay, sweetheart." Viv put the medicine in her mouth, then seemed to be rubbing it on Katie's gums. "You'll feel better in just a minute."

Viv had brought Katie into his office a couple times when her neighbor wasn't available to babysit. During those occasions, Jack found a reason to step out for the day. Being near this combination of beautiful woman and enchanting baby was like getting smacked in the face with all he'd lost…his family being the sole reason he was determined to bring down those who kept skirting the law.

As Jack watched Viv console a fussy Katie, he couldn't help but wonder what his life would've been like had his wife lived. He tried not to go there in his mind, but sometimes that just wasn't possible.

"Sorry." Viv looked up at him with a soft smile. "Why don't you go ahead and eat. I'd hate to hold you up any longer."

Thankful for the chance to focus on something else, Jack started filling both of their plates. "How was today? Did you work with Laney?"

Laney O'Shea, the baby of the clan, was now engaged to Ryker Barrett, right-hand man and family enforcer. The two were expecting their first child in the summer and Jack hated the jealousy that rolled through him. People like that shouldn't get to experience the happiness that had been robbed from him.

"What?" she looked up at him, then back to the baby. "Oh, yeah. Laney was there all day."

"Any interesting clients?" he asked. "Did Ryker or her brothers stop in?"

Viv eased the baby up onto her shoulder, patting her

back in an attempt to calm her. "Ryker dropped by and brought Laney lunch. He's been pretty territorial and protective of her since she got pregnant."

Gritting his teeth, Jack set her full plate in front of her. "Did he do anything else? Use the computers, make a call?"

"No. He was actually in and out in about ten minutes." Viv looked down to her plate. "There's no way I'll eat all of this."

"Eat what you want. Tilly takes any leftovers to the homeless shelter by her house. She actually always makes extra and takes it there anyway."

Viv stilled, her hand resting on Katie's back. "That's so sweet."

Jack shrugged. "She's got a big heart and she doesn't mind using my money to help others."

Katie's cries had calmed. Either the meds had kicked in or the poor thing was exhausted from crying.

Viv picked up her fork and stabbed one roasted potato. "And what about you? I'd say your heart is big or you wouldn't let her use your money for such things."

"I have no problem helping anyone when I see the need." He stared across the table, realizing she hadn't looked at him since mentioning work and was now trying to steer the conversation into another territory. "I grew up with a single mother who worked hard to make sure we never wanted for anything. I figure she struggled raising me alone. I would often hear her crying at night when she thought I was asleep."

Jack stopped, not wanting to dig too far into his suppressed memories. The past could easily cripple him, pull him down. The only thing he could use his past for was to propel him forward, to always remember where he came from. And he'd never forget the mother who sacrificed so much.

He pulled in a breath, determined to get back on track. "What happened today at the office?"

Her fork clattered to the plate, but she quickly picked it back up and shrugged. "Nothing. Just the same daily routine."

Again, the lack of eye contact. He'd known Viv long enough, hell, he'd been a soldier and investigator long enough, to know when someone was lying. What was going on?

Slowly, without taking his eyes off her, he leaned forward in his seat. "What happened today?" he repeated, slower this time until she finally looked directly at him.

"Jack, I'm telling you what happened." Now she held his eyes. Katie had fallen asleep and lay across Viv's arm, curled into Viv's body. "We were busy this morning with a new client and Laney handled that. I stayed in the back and logged inventory for the spring auction."

He listened, easing back in his cushioned seat. Why was he doubting her? He'd never second-guessed her before and she was his most trusted ally in this quest. He wouldn't have put her in this position if he didn't trust her completely.

"And then Ryker came with lunch," she went on. Her eyes darted down to the sleeping baby. "After that it was slow for about an hour and Laney and I ended up in the office talking baby things. She knows I foster and she had some questions."

"Like what?" He literally wanted every detail of what went on in that office. The key to his case was in there and he was not going to rest until every possible avenue was explored.

Viv shrugged. "She was asking about different milestones at different ages. But I've never had an infant until now. My foster children have always been older. The youngest I'd had was three."

Jack knew why Viv's taking Katie in deviated from her normal pattern of only fostering older children. One, she'd worked with the Parkers when they'd come into O'Shea's so she had a mild connection. According to Viv, she'd even played with little Katie during one of their visits.

Two, she knew the system was overloaded. Because she was certified to take in children, and since she was more than aware of the tragic situation, she'd actually asked to foster Katie.

"About an hour before we closed, an elderly lady came in and wanted to discuss some pieces she wanted to sell. She claimed they were from her honeymoon in Rome and thought they were valuable art."

Intrigued, Jack tipped his head. "What were they?"

Viv picked up her fork and took a bite of her potato. "I'm not sure. She had some pictures, but didn't want to bring the actual pieces without talking to Laney first."

That all sounded like a typical, boring day. A day that didn't help him one bit. But something was off. Viv had literally frozen when he'd first mentioned her workday at O'Shea's, then she wouldn't look at him.

"You're sure that's all?" he asked.

She shifted Katie to the other arm, which only aided in pulling her jacket open a bit more when Katie's hand got caught in the V. Viv did readjust the gap, but not before he was awarded another view of the swell of her breast.

"I'm just stressed," she assured him with a smile. "Katie is teething and the auction is going to be here before we know it. Working at O'Shea's isn't just me snooping and eavesdropping. They expect me to actually do a job, so it's tiresome at times."

Not to mention all the work she was doing for him. She was technically a single mother working two part-time jobs. But that part-time added up and when he was constantly meeting her outside of business hours, that didn't help. Damn it, he was ready to wrap this case up and let the justice system take care of this mob family. But he had to be patient. It was a trait he hated, yet it was necessary in his line of work.

With Katie resting peacefully, Viv continued to eat. Jack didn't press the topic again. He didn't know if he was just reading too much into her actions or if she was truly just stressed, but he wasn't about to add more to her plate.

"They don't suspect you, right?"

Viv took a sip of her wine. "They suspect everyone who's been in and out of that office. But, not me specifically. I'm careful, Jack."

Why was his name on her lips like a tight ball of lust hitting his gut? He couldn't afford the distraction—especially when it came to his damn assistant.

When this case was over, he'd head to his villa in Italy. He could relax, find a woman to spend a meaningless night with. He clearly was not thinking straight and he blamed everything on being overworked and sexually frustrated.

"There is a new shipment of paintings coming in on Monday," Viv went on, oblivious to the turn in his thoughts. "I'm supposed to be off, but I thought I'd see if I could come in and just tell them I'd like some extra hours."

Jack curled his fingers around the tumbler of bourbon and considered her idea. "I wouldn't. They already know someone is leaking information. If you ask for extra time, that could be a red flag. I need you to do everything as you always had before."

Viv nodded. "I guess that makes sense. I just wish there was more I could do."

Taking a hearty, warm gulp of his favorite twenty-year bourbon, Jack wished there was more to be done. But he wasn't inside, and using Viv as his eyes and ears was the only thing he could do at this point.

"I'd rather you explore the Parkers' angle," he told her, easing back in his seat and glancing at the sleeping baby. "You have the perfect lead-in, especially when you're with Laney. Continue to talk about Katie, discuss how she's adjusting, throw in the loss of her parents and you've opened up the floor."

Viv pushed her plate back, wrapped both arms around the baby and pursed her lips. "That could work. Laney and I tend to always discuss the baby when we're not talking about the auction."

"Now's the time. That's the angle we need to work. If we can find out more about the night they were killed, I know it will circle us right back to the O'Sheas."

Jack didn't care what the initial charges were. This corrupt family had plenty of crimes they could be pinned with. But first he needed concrete evidence that proved the O'Sheas weren't so squeaky clean.

No matter who was in charge now that Patriarch Patrick O'Shea had passed, this family was into illegals so deep, there was no way they could've gotten out in such a short time.

"I'll be there from eight to noon tomorrow," she reminded him, as if he didn't have her schedule memorized down to the very last second. "I need to take

Katie to the doctor for a checkup, so I'll text you when I leave work."

When Katie started to stir, Viv came to her feet. Rocking gently back and forth, Viv patted the baby's back in an attempt to calm her once again. Jack watched as she instantly went into mother mode. Viv was the most giving person he'd ever known. A born nurturer. He'd checked her background thoroughly before hiring her, so he knew she'd never married or had kids. He'd seen quite a bit of hospitalizations when she'd been young, but she'd never mentioned an illness, so he never asked. He could've easily found out, but he'd snooped enough and didn't want to betray her trust at this point. Honesty was of the utmost importance to him and he expected it to be a two-way street.

"I should get her home," Viv stated. "She needs to rest and I need to get my own downtime or I'll be of no use to anyone."

Viv wasn't a superhero, though she was a working foster mother juggling two jobs and carrying a colossal lie on her shoulders, so that was pretty much the same thing. Jack set his napkin on the table and rose to stand in front of her.

"Why don't you see if your neighbor can watch Katie for a few hours extra each day so you can relax?" he suggested. "I'll pay for it if that's an issue."

Viv's brows shot up. "I don't care about the money, Jack. The reason I became a foster mother was to care for children who don't have anyone. Pawning Katie off on my neighbor just so I can nap will never be an option."

"That's not what I meant," he retorted, though she'd made him look uncaring, which was not the case. He cared...too much. "If you don't look out for yourself, how do you expect to do everything else?"

Her lids lowered, her breath came out on a deep sigh. She shook her head before meeting his gaze. "Everything I do is for those I care about. This child, you. I have no family, Jack, so I work to fill a void. When I stop working, when I stop caring for those around me, I start to think. I don't want the down time. I can't mentally afford it. Do you get what I'm saying?"

Jack swallowed the lump in his throat. How could she put his thoughts, his emotions, into such perfect terms? It was like they lived a parallel life, and he desperately wanted to know what made her this way. Why did she use work as her coping mechanism?

He'd already known she had no family. He of all people understood the need to connect with something in life and he clung to work...apparently so did she. He'd never heard her so passionate about it before, but he understood the ache, the emptiness that needed to be filled.

"You're talking to the workaholic," he told her, trying to lighten the intensity of the mood. "I just wanted to make sure you were taken care of, as well."

Shoulders squared, she tipped her head. "I assure you, I'm fine. But I do need to get home and I promise I'll text you tomorrow. We'll get this," she assured him. "We've come this far, we'll make it the rest of the way."

Jack helped her with the diaper bag, then assisted her with her coat and Katie's coat—which was no easy feat, considering she was still asleep.

Once Viv was gone, Jack leaned against the front door and stared into the empty two-story foyer. Yeah, he understood perfectly about not having anyone. He'd bought this massive home in Beacon Hill after his wife died. He couldn't stay in the small cottage he'd bought for her, the place where they'd planned to start their family. While he'd wanted to burn the cottage to the ground, he ended up selling it to a young newlywed couple who had the same dreams he'd once had.

He'd moved on, made more money than he knew what to do with and when he started looking for a permanent residence, he knew he wanted something large...something he'd never be able to fill with a family. He wanted the space so it didn't feel like the walls were closing in on him.

Some might say he was flashing, living in a huge house all by himself, but he didn't care. His cars, his vacation home in the mountains, the two homes overseas, they were all material things he'd give up in a second to have someone in his life.

No. Not someone. His wife.

Yet lately, when he would think of someone to share his wealth with, Viv kept popping up. He wanted to scrub that image from his mind because thinking of another woman was surely a betrayal to Carly...right?

As he headed down the hall and passed the kitchen, he instantly remembered the cheesecake. If Tilly came back in the morning and saw that none of it had been eaten, she'd be disappointed.

Easy fix. He'd be gone before she came in and he'd take it to the office with him.

Or he could take it somewhere else.

Viv claimed she didn't need anyone to look after her, but that was a lie. And Jack would take on the role in the name of business...because that's all he had time for in his life.

Whatever notions he had in his head about Viv, he had to remember she was his assistant. She could never be anything else.

Three

With Katie turning one next week, Viv had decided that the baby's shots were going to have to happen on her half day at O'Shea's.

Now that the doctor's visit was—mercifully—over, Viv was convinced the shots had hurt her more than they'd hurt Katie. Viv had just walked into her apartment, dumped the diaper bag next to the sofa and put Katie in her Pack 'n Play when someone knocked on her door.

She couldn't suppress the groan that escaped her. She was soaked to the bone from the chilly rain. All she wanted to do was strip off her wet suit and get into her cozy pajamas. Viv had been able to shield Katie from the elements by wrapping her inside her coat and holding Katie's favorite blanket over the tot's head. Now Viv needed to get that blanket into the dryer or there would be hell to pay come bedtime.

The pounding on the door persisted. What were the

odds she could ignore her unwanted guest? If she lived in a house, maybe, but in an apartment building she couldn't have her neighbors put out.

"Vivianna?" Jack's voice boomed and Viv realized her wish to pretend no one was out there had just vanished.

She crossed the floor, her shoes squishing. She wasn't even going to glance at her reflection in the mirror next to the door. The drowned-rat look wasn't becoming on anyone.

Flicking the lock, Viv opened the door. Of course Jack didn't have one drop of rain on him. The large black umbrella he held at his side was dripping.

"You're…"

"Soaked," she finished. "I know. Come on in."

She stood back so he didn't have to brush against her as he stepped inside. Katie made noises and clapped when she spotted Jack. Inwardly, Viv tended to have that same reaction, but she wasn't too keen on the fact that he was seeing her look so haggard and frumpy.

She'd really been confident this morning when she'd left for work in her gray pencil skirt and fitted, pale yellow sweater. She'd even taken extra time with her hair, since Katie had slept in. Now Viv must look like all she'd done this morning was shower…with her clothes on.

She was so over this winter weather. One day it snowed, the next it rained. Spring couldn't come soon enough. But it was only February, meaning Valentine's Day was fast approaching. A holiday she could totally live without.

"I brought this for you."

Katie eyed the dish in his hand. She'd been too preoccupied with her looks to realize he held food.

Glorious food. She didn't even care if that domed plate held a bologna sandwich, her stomach growled at the sight. She'd skipped lunch because she'd left work late and had barely made it to Katie's appointment.

"Whatever it is, thank you," she said, taking the covered plate. She headed toward the kitchen, cringing as her shoes made the most unpleasant noises.

Of all the times Jack could see her, of all the times he *had* seen her, this was not her best moment. She set the dish on the counter and pulled the lid off. A laugh escaped her.

"Cheesecake?" she asked, turning to glance over her shoulder.

Jacked shrugged out of his suit jacket and hung it on the hook by the door…as if he'd done so a thousand times. Seeing a man's jacket hanging next to hers did funny things to her belly. Her eyes locked on the two pieces beside each other, and she didn't want to dwell on it too long, but couldn't get over the fact that this simple gesture seemed so intimate.

But he wasn't staying, he was visiting, for pity's sake. For a second, though, she wanted to pretend. He looked good in his all-black suit, with that rich, dark hair. He'd brought her cheesecake when she looked like a mess, and he didn't seem appalled by her appearance. If he wasn't the world's most perfect man, then one didn't exist.

Would he ever see her as more than an ally? As more than his assistant?

She hadn't missed the way he'd sneaked a peek at her cleavage last night. He was a guy; they all did it. But when she'd caught his gaze on her, everything inside her had warmed, tingled. Because he hadn't just looked and glanced away. No, there had been a hunger in his eyes she hadn't seen before.

"What are you doing here so early in the day?" she asked, turning to lean back against the counter. "Not that four o'clock is early, but you tend to work much later than this."

"I had a meeting today not far from here, so I thought I'd come by to see what happened at O'Shea's today."

Katie clanged her blocks together and squealed as she flung them out of her Pack 'n Play. Viv ignored them. This toss and fetch was an endless game and one she wasn't going to get sucked into.

"I need to get out of these wet clothes," she stated. "Can we talk after?"

His eyes raked over her wet body. Jack never needed words to get his point across. This powerful man had such a hold on her emotions, and he had no idea.

All this was her problem, she knew, but did he ever think of her outside of work? Not that she'd ever know. Jack's personal life was never on the table for discussion. She knew of Tilly, his right-hand woman, but that was all. Anyone else in Jack's life was there only because of work. To Viv's knowledge, he didn't even date...or if he did, he was extremely discreet.

"I'll wait in here," he finally told her.

Viv tiptoed through her kitchen and out into the hallway toward her bedroom. Once inside, she shut the door, thankful for the few moments to herself. She hadn't expected him to just show up, with carbs and calories no less, so she was even more taken aback than usual.

Before the O'Shea case, Jack had never showed up at her apartment. He'd texted and called after hours, but all pertaining to work. Granted, his recent home visits also centered around work, but he'd seriously stepped up his game in an attempt to bring the notorious family down.

Viv closed her eyes and pulled in a shaky breath. The fact that Patrick O'Shea's journal was hidden in her closet weighed heavily on her mind. Guilt, anxiety, fear…they all consumed her, making her question her next move.

She hadn't been lying when she said she had no one in her life. Keeping a relationship with Jack, no matter how platonic, was imperative.

She needed to tell him what she'd learned, but how did she do that without hurting him? The FBI trusted Jack, was counting on him, and he was counting on her. He sought justice like he needed it to live, so telling him about her discovery would cloud his judgment…and hurt him in a way that would alter their relationship.

She didn't want to hurt him, and finding out Patrick O'Shea was his father would most certainly destroy Jack. Still, he deserved to know. The question was, when should she tell him?

Viv made quick work of ridding herself of her wet clothes and shoes. She wasn't telling him today. She couldn't. There would be a right time, just…not now. Hopefully, a break in the case would come soon. Then she could give the journal to him and let him decide what to do with the information.

She didn't bother drying her hair, just twisted it up into a messy bun. After throwing on a pair of yoga pants and an off-the-shoulder sweatshirt, she headed back out into the living room.

Jack still remained closer to the kitchen than the living room. His gaze was directed across the open space at Katie, who was oblivious as she chewed on the fingers of her plush doll.

"Let's cut into that cheesecake and talk," Viv suggested. She needed something to occupy her hands, her mind, other than the journal in the other room and the unnerving effect Jack's presence had on her. "How did your meeting go?"

He didn't answer her. He never even looked her way.

"Do you think she knows the significant people in her life are gone?" he murmured, almost as if his thoughts had traveled out into the open without his knowledge. "I mean, she seems happy with you, but is she aware of the void?"

Viv thought of that often since Katie had come to live with her. The older kids she had fostered obviously knew all too well the reality of why they were in foster care. But sweet little Katie would have no idea why her world was suddenly so different.

"She says 'Mama' over and over, but I'm not sure if she's just babbling or actually asking for her. But I'm certain she notices the absence." Viv crossed her arms, stood beside Jack and watched his face. "Are you okay?"

He blinked as if waking from a trance. "It's been a long couple months. That's all."

When he turned to her, Viv stepped back. That intense gaze landed directly on hers and she had no idea what to do with the emotions stirring within her, from the guilt and anxiety over when and how to tell him about the journal, to the tension and chemistry that couldn't be ignored. It seemed unlikely she was the only one who felt the air crackling between them, yet Jack was in total control and never let on that he thought of her in any other way than simply his assistant.

But he'd shown up on her doorstep with red velvet cheesecake his chef had made.

"Tell me about your meeting."

He shook his head. "Later. I want to know what happened with you today."

"Not much," she admitted, then held up a hand to stop him when he opened his mouth. "But I overheard Laney and Braden talking. They said the FBI hadn't contacted them in a few days, but they were keeping their guard up. Braden told Laney not to erase any records and that he had nothing to hide in regards to the Parkers."

Jack's eyes held hers, but he said nothing. She wasn't delivering case-breaking news, but she had to tell him everything she'd heard, learned…except for the the piece of evidence that was burning a hole in her conscience.

"Something else happen?" he asked.

Viv pulled herself from her thoughts. Those midnight eyes still penetrated her, as if he were trying to read her thoughts…as if he *could* read her thoughts.

"Not today, but Braden said Mac was flying in on Monday and he'd be in the office all next week."

"Why?"

Viv shrugged. "They didn't say, but I'm working three full days next week and I'll find out then."

Jack raked a hand down his face and blew out a breath. "This is so damn frustrating. For years they flaunted their lifestyle in the face of law enforcement. Luckily, I work for myself and I don't have to stick so close to the rules."

Viv didn't want to see him struggle, didn't like that she'd found so little for him to go on. "I tried to engage Laney in conversation about the babies, but a client called and she was pulled away. Then I had to leave for Katie's doctor's appointment."

Jack shoved his hands in his pockets and glanced

at the ceiling. Watching him battle with this frustration was more difficult than Viv had thought it would be. But she had to keep the journal to herself for now. Everything—absolutely everything, from his life to this case—would change in the matter of seconds as soon as he learned about it.

"You're in my office tomorrow." He regrouped and focused his attention back on her. "I want both of us to go over every bit of intel we have on this family. Maybe there's some tiny nugget of information we're missing. Something that can put us on the right track. I want you ready for next week, when everyone is here."

He was getting desperate, yet she understood his need to protect his reputation as being the best. Unfortunately, the journal she'd discovered wasn't the master key to solving this equation, and she had nothing else.

"Tell the Feds that all the players will be available next week," she went on, hoping to give him something useful, to buy them a bit more time. "With everyone at the office, something must be going on, or else they're worried about this investigation."

Jack leaned a shoulder against the wall and pinned her with his stare. "Maybe they have an idea who's been leaking the information."

The thought sent a shiver up her spine. Taking this job had been risky, but she'd agreed to let Jack create a solid cover for her. She'd put her life in his hands... literally, if all those rumors surrounding the O'Sheas were true. But Viv hadn't been afraid. Jack wouldn't let anything happen to her.

"I'm not getting that vibe," she replied as she moved into the kitchen. "Do you want a piece of this cheesecake or not, because if I eat the entire thing, I won't fit into my pencil skirts."

His eyes traveled the length of her body. How in the world did that man evoke more emotions and glorious sensations with one look than some men did with foreplay? Seriously. How did Jack make her want him so much, so deeply, when he wasn't even trying?

"Your figure is just fine, with or without the cheesecake."

Viv turned away, because that sultry tone of his sent a combination of shivers and thrills darting through her. Add in the way he'd assessed her body—such as it was, clad in yoga pants and a sweatshirt—and she wondered if maybe she'd pegged him wrong for not showing any interest and keeping his emotions all closed off.

Katie let out a squeal, breaking the tension. She seemed quite content to sit and play with her toys for a bit. Thankfully, her pain reliever had kicked in fast after the shots.

Once Viv had generous pieces of the decadent dessert on a couple saucers, she crossed to her two-seater table in the breakfast nook. Well, technically it was her breakfast nook, dining room and home office, depending on the time of day. Her apartment wasn't big, but it suited her needs. She rarely had guests unless it was foster children, so she didn't require a grand table. Besides, the place was close to Jack's office and the rent was perfect.

Though right now she did feel a little inadequate, remembering how amazing Jack's patio had been. He most likely had an exquisite dining room and an eat-in kitchen, yet he'd still set up dinner on his screened-in sunroom. Just the little bit she'd seen of his house had left her in awe. The rich wood, the clean lines of the furniture, that grand entryway with a masculine yet impressive chandelier suspended from the second floor were worthy of a magazine. Her entire apartment could fit into that foyer alone.

Jack either had a perfect eye for detail and decor or he'd hired someone to tastefully, expensively decorate his mansion. He took a seat across from her, but her round table proved to be smaller than she'd thought when his knees bumped hers. Why did his every single action get her body all tingly and jittery? This was Jack. Her boss. Her very sexy, very single, very mysterious boss. Other than the fact that he was a widower, never dated and had served in the military, she didn't know much else about his personal life…but oh, how she wanted to.

He scooped up a bite. "Tilly will be thrilled we're getting to this."

"Trust me, I'm more thrilled." Viv wasn't going to even think about calories right now. Turning down red velvet cheesecake would be a sin. "She's going to be happier to know you came to my apartment."

His eyes caught hers. "For business."

Right. Business. What else would he want from her?

"Still, she seems ready to make sure you have a woman in your life."

When he remained silent, Viv kept going. She would crack his shell at some point. Over the past couple years she'd worked for him, he'd not volunteered any information unless it pertained to a case. And the only reason Viv knew about his mother was that he always referred to her in the past tense. His father was never mentioned.

And Viv would've assumed Jack was a regular single guy had Tilly not slipped and said something about his "late wife." That had been at the office. One sharp look from Jack and the woman's lips were still sealed to this day.

"I don't know how your dating life has been—"

"Nonexistent."

Viv swallowed. She'd assumed as much…but why? He was, well, hot. He had money, not that a bank account made a man, but it wasn't like he couldn't get a woman. Maybe he just didn't want to. Maybe he had some other reason for being married to his work and ignoring the world around him.

"I really should consider going that route, because I've had some doozies."

Doozies? Way to sound classy, Viv.

Jack took another bite, obviously not feeling so chatty about his own personal life. Whatever. She was chatty enough for both of them, especially when she was a bit nervous. And between the attraction and the journal only a couple rooms away, she had plenty of unease spiraling through her.

"One time, I had a guy who offered me dinner and a movie."

"Predictable," Jack muttered.

"I can handle predictable," she added with a laugh. "It was the expectations he had for the evening. Cooking me a frozen pizza and binge-watching old movies wasn't my idea of a night out. He was shocked when I made an excuse to leave. He seriously thought…"

Jack laid his fork down and narrowed his eyes. "You're kidding? Tell me you didn't."

Viv tipped her head. "I do have standards, Jack. It takes more than a frozen pizza to get me into bed."

Those bright eyes held hers, then dipped to her mouth before traveling back up. "What does it take?"

Four

Where the hell had that question come from?

This was why Jack had always refused to get personally involved with anyone. Yet here he was, asking his *assistant* what it took to get her into bed.

Clearly the case, and working so closely with this breathtaking woman, was making him delirious.

"Well—"

"No." Jack held up his hand. "Don't answer that."

Viv quirked a brow, taunting him with a teasing smile. "You're sure?"

There could be no flirting, no unwanted attraction. Too much was at stake—the case, his sanity.

When he remained silent, she laughed. "We'll just say that it takes more than a lame dinner and a black-and-white movie."

Jack laughed with her. He couldn't help himself. "Any man who doesn't pull out all the stops for you is an idiot."

She tipped her head again, pursing her lips. "You never do that."

Easing back in his seat, Jack met Viv's eyes across the small table. "Laugh? No, I don't."

She crossed her arms and rested her elbows on the table. "Why not? What do you do for fun?"

"Stakeouts."

She rolled her eyes just as Katie let out a cry. "I'm serious," she stated as she rose to her feet.

Jack watched as she maneuvered through the living room to Katie. The little girl instantly extended her arms to reach for Viv. Jack turned away. All this... familial life was digging into that past wound, threatening to tear it wide open.

Some might say he was hard, uncaring, detached. Whatever it took to stay sane, to stay on top of his game, to help bring criminals down—to find justice... Jack didn't care what label he was given.

He concentrated on taking the empty plates to the kitchen and placing them in the sink. Resting his hands on the edge of the counter, he pulled in a breath. He shouldn't have come by. Venturing into Viv's world, into her damn apartment, was not smart.

In his defense, he'd been close and she hadn't texted, and he wanted to bring the dessert, so he'd broken his own rule of not getting into someone else's personal space. Time to head back home, where he could hide in his office, drink his bourbon and contemplate his next move. He was done waiting around for the O'Sheas to slip up.

When he turned, he found Viv standing close to him...too close. So near he could see the dark flecks in her eyes.

"Something wrong?" she asked, her brows drawn in.

Katie pulled on Viv's still-damp hair. All that gorgeous, silky, midnight-black hair. He'd be lying to himself if he pretended he hadn't envisioned that mass spread out over his navy sheets. When had this woman gone from assistant to starring in his fantasies? Lately, the line between professional and personal was becoming more and more blurry.

Even from the start, when he'd interviewed her, he hadn't denied her beauty. But after a few years of working together closely, and especially this past year, the dreams were becoming more frequent. Forget the fact that he vowed never to open himself up again; he was a professional having extremely unprofessional thoughts.

"I'll let you get on with your evening," he told her, ignoring the worried look on her face. She need not be concerned about him. His emotions had been murdered along with his wife, years ago. "I'll be sure to tell Tilly you enjoyed her dessert."

Viv seemed as if she wanted to say something else, but finally nodded and stepped aside to let him through. "If she wants to bake anything else and send it my way, she's more than welcome. I have a sweet tooth."

"I'm aware." Jack nodded toward the bowl of chocolate candy on the counter. "Your desk at work has a matching bowl."

Viv shrugged as Katie continued to pull on her hair. "I won't apologize for my snacks."

If those snacks were what kept that body all curvy and mesmerizing in skirts, then he'd buy her a full year's supply.

No, damn it, he wouldn't. Admiring her body wasn't his job as her boss. He had to get the hell out of here before he made an absolute fool of himself. Sitting at her little table, watching her with Katie…it was all too much. She smelled too damn good and had that rumpled, sexy look down pat. The rain she'd been caught in hadn't done a thing to diminish her beauty.

If circumstances were different—if he wasn't a jaded widower, her boss and her protector on this job—then maybe he'd seduce her. Maybe then he'd exorcise her right out of his system.

"Why are you looking at me like that?" she asked.

He still hadn't moved, even though she'd made an opening for him to pass. Jack stepped forward, his eyes on hers.

"I've never seen you out of your professional element. I just…"

"What?"

Hell, he didn't know. Wanted to touch her? Kiss her? To know if either of those would compare to his detailed thoughts of having her in his bed?

Viv shifted Katie in her arms, reached out and placed her hand on his shoulder. Jack stilled. Such a simple touch shouldn't evoke instant bedroom fantasies.

"Everything will work out with this case," she assured him. "We're getting closer. I just know it."

Yes. Let her think his moment of becoming a mute, staring fool had to do with stress from the case. The last thing he needed was for her to believe he was attracted to her. Hell, if she thought that, who knew what would happen?

Wait. He knew exactly what would happen…which was why he had to get out of here before he turned his thoughts into actions.

"I'll see you in the morning."

With that, he got the hell out. Maybe the chilly rain would cool him off and draw his thoughts back to the job—and not his assistant splayed across his bed.

* * *

The rain had stopped, but had quickly turned to snow. As if in tune with the crappy, depressing weather, Viv's morning had gone downhill fast.

First her blow-dryer had gone kaput after about one minute of drying her hair. Then Katie had a blowout in her diaper, so that called for a change of every single item of clothing, from her onesie to her shoes. How did babies have that much in them that they could ruin an entire outfit?

To top everything off, Martha was sick and unable to babysit. Lovely. But nothing Viv couldn't manage.

She had thrown her wet hair in a side braid and changed Katie into something fresh. Unfortunately, there was no backup sitter. So here she was, wrestling the diaper bag, a sack of toys and Katie into the office. At least she was with Jack today and not at O'Shea's.

After Jack left her apartment last night, she couldn't help but reflect on their conversation…or the way he'd looked at her. The dynamics had silently shifted between them. She wasn't sure what had changed, what he'd been thinking or why he'd been staring at her like he wanted…well, her.

The shiver racing through her body had nothing to do with the February arctic breeze and everything to do with the possibilities swirling through her mind.

Maybe it was the fact that Valentine's Day was next week. Perhaps all the hearts and cupids in the storefronts were messing with her mind. When was the last time she'd actually had a valentine?

If Jack was having thoughts of her, would he ever act on them? Would he make a move, or was he that removed from the emotional world that he'd keep everything professional between them?

What if she weren't his assistant? Would that change the game?

So many questions. Thankfully, Viv had Katie to think about, and her first birthday was next week, which could cancel out any Valentine's Day celebration. Not that Viv had dates lined up, but now she had an excuse to ignore the day not created for single women.

Warmth enveloped her as she stepped inside the office. The inviting brownstone had once been Jack's apartment, before he turned it into a permanent office. The place was cozy, yet professional, with neutral colors and leather sofas. It felt more like a home than a workplace. Viv didn't mind bringing Katie here because she could easily section her off from the front area, where clients might be.

Once the door closed behind them, she breathed a sigh of relief and dropped her bags to the floor. If nothing else, by the end of her time with Katie, Viv would have toned arms.

She didn't want to think about giving Katie up to her adoptive family. Letting go of any child was always a bittersweet moment, but Katie was special.

Viv had never met the parents of any of her other foster kids. But she'd met with the Parkers on more than one occasion. She and Katie shared a unique bond Viv couldn't deny, but she would have to continue to guard her heart or she'd be crushed in the end. Not being able to have children of her own was a bitter pill to swallow, so getting too attached to Katie would only cause her more heartache.

Jack came out of his office and glanced at the mess at Viv's feet. "What's wrong?"

Holding a bundled-up Katie, Viv merely shrugged. "It's been a crazy morning of trying to get ready and learning Martha wasn't able to watch Katie. That snow is coming down pretty fast and I have no sitter."

He wasted no time in crossing to her and bending to retrieve her bags. "You could've taken the day off."

"There's too much work to do," Viv stated, as she wrestled the hat and coat off Katie.

Gripping her bags, Jack headed toward the back, where her office was located. "We could've phoned or emailed," he called over his shoulder. "I'm not that much of a slave driver that I expect you to take her out in this mess."

This wasn't the first time she'd had to bring Katie, so Viv had invested in a small play yard for her office. This way the door could stay closed, and there was an entertaining area for Katie to explore while Viv worked. The brownstone had two spacious bedrooms that Jack had converted into offices. He also happened to keep a sofa in his office that converted to a bed…which she knew he often used instead of going home.

Viv sat Katie in the designated kid area in the corner and turned to take off her own coat. Jack had set the bags on the long accent table against the back wall and was closing the distance between them.

Why did her boss have to smell so good? And why did she have to be tortured by it?

"I expect you to tell me when you need a break."

Viv untied her wrap coat and draped it across the back of her desk chair. Smoothing her silk blouse down over her pencil skirt, she attempted to calm her nerves. She'd lain awake most of the night worried about that journal.

Correction. She'd read the journal the first half of the night, then had stared into the darkness the other half, terrified of Jack's reaction once he discovered the truth.

From the veiled hints penned in Patrick O'Shea's neat hand, Jack was indeed the patriarch's son. Jack's mother had wanted to keep their affair a secret. Though, according to the timeline, Patrick and Jack's mother had been an item shortly after Patrick lost his wife.

Most likely the man had turned to her only for comfort. But according to the journal, he'd been torn up over not having his son in his life. The reasons seemed valid enough. Jack's mother didn't want her child to be exposed to the O'Shea lifestyle, and she worried what would happen if Jack were given the infamous last name. The affair wasn't created out of love, but from Patrick's tone, Viv could tell he cared for her.

Regardless of Patrick's past feelings or intentions, Jack wouldn't care. He'd be furious learning who his family was. All this time he'd thought he had nobody, but the family he was hell-bent on bringing down shared the same blood.

Every time he mentioned his mother, Catherine Carson, his tone held pure affection and adoration. Jack was a loyal man, which was why the pain he'd endured too often had hardened him. He was protecting himself.

"Sit down."

Viv jerked back. "Excuse me?"

Jack reached around her, turning her chair until it bumped the backs of her knees. When he curled his hands around her shoulders, she stilled. Oh, those hands were powerful as they pushed her into the seat. His eyes never left hers as he loomed over her.

"If you exhaust yourself to the point you can't work, you're no good to me."

Viv shivered, from her damp hair, from his stare… from his low tone that resembled anger, though there was concern in those eyes staring back at her.

"I'm off tomorrow," she reminded him. "I can rest up then. But if I needed a day off, I would've told you."

His gaze flickered to Katie, then back. This wasn't the first time she'd noticed how uncomfortable he seemed around the little girl.

"Does this bother you? Her being here?"

Jack shook his head. "Of course not. I'm just not experienced with babies, that's all."

She knew he had no kids of his own, and he was an only child, so it made sense that he was nervous. But there was almost a level of sadness there—an emotion she recognized all too well.

"What's got you so nervous?" she asked.

Jack eased to his full height, crossed his arms over his chest and stared down at her. The intimidating stance might work on some, but Viv saw right through him. She wasn't a stranger to defense mechanisms herself.

"I need to answer a couple of emails, then we can start working," he stated, obviously changing the subject.

Viv slowly came to her feet, not at all surprised when he didn't back up. "I never took you for someone who runs away from confrontation."

Jack's eyes swept over her, then up again to meet her gaze. "I never run from anything."

"No?" she retorted. "You're married to your job, you don't date and the sight of a child has you twitching. I'd say you're running from several things."

Viv ignored his sneer. Sometimes people just needed to be called out on things. Perhaps not her boss, but she couldn't stand her curiosity anymore. She'd worked for him so long, yet he never, ever opened up. How did anyone live so closed off for that long? It was like he bounced between the office and his mansion. What did he do at home in that empty, sprawling house?

He traveled for work, always alone, but that was all the man did. Living a robotic life with very little meaningful interaction sounded so hollow, so depressing.

"Not everyone is so open with their personal lives, Viv."

Why did her name sound so sexy coming through those kissable lips?

"When was the last time *you* dated?" he added, quirking a dark brow as if he'd bested her.

"The day before Katie came to live with me." There. That should wipe that smirk off his face. "And you?"

The muscles in his jaw ticked. "Instead of digging into my personal life, why don't we dig in to work?"

Viv shrugged. "Fine with me. I need to get Katie settled and give her a snack. Go send your emails."

When she turned to ease her chair back, Jack's hand curled around her arm. Viv glanced from his strong fingers over her silk blouse up to his eyes.

"You may want to rethink giving me commands." That low, throaty tone washed over her, the warmth from his touch piercing right through to her heart. "And always remember who's in charge."

Oh, he could be "in charge" of her any time he wanted. But now would be a good time to keep her mouth shut. Apparently she'd hit her mark. If the hunger in his eyes was any indication, Jack wasn't thinking of her as just his assistant anymore.

Good. It was time he was as uncomfortable as she was, because she'd been keeping her sexual frustrations in check for too long.

He released her, but didn't step back. "Be ready in twenty minutes."

Viv nodded, letting him think he could throw his weight around. Fine. Whatever. This was his office, he was her boss, but they both knew she'd knocked him off his game earlier.

Jack took a step back and shoved his hands into his pockets. "Call the deli on the corner and have lunch delivered at noon. I want—"

"A Reuben with half the corned beef, no pickle on the side, no chips and a piece of carrot cake."

When he raised his brows and smiled, Viv added, "This isn't our first lunch stuck in the office."

Katie started screaming, "Up, up, up."

Viv laughed. "Sorry. Her new word apparently is *up*."

Brushing past Jack, Viv approached the Pack 'n Play. Those sweet little arms stretched toward her. Katie clearly needed the comfort that only human contact could provide. Viv understood that yearning.

After settling Katie onto her hip, Viv turned back to Jack, who remained exactly where she'd left him. "I'll be ready in a few minutes. She just needs some love right now."

The muscle in his jaw ticked again. "Does she do that often? Want you to hold her?"

Katie rested her head on Viv's shoulder. Viv knew of nothing sweeter than to be a comfort for a grieving child. Even if there was no possible way Katie understood the grief, she understood the void.

"She seems to be clingier than when she first came." Viv wrapped her arms around the little girl, holding her firmly against her chest. "It's almost like she realizes now that certain people aren't coming back into her life."

Viv was extremely careful never to say *mommy* or *daddy*. She didn't want to trigger any painful emotions in Katie. But at the same time, Viv hated acting as if the Parkers had never been part of the child's life. Hopefully, the family that adopted Katie would tell her about the amazing parents she'd had.

Jack eased around the desk, but didn't get too close to her as he kept his eyes on Katie. "I will bring them down," he vowed. "It won't bring her parents back, but there will be justice."

The conviction in his voice, the anger flaring in his eyes, brought on a fresh wave of guilt. How could she help him bring down his own family? Would he want to bring them down if he knew the truth?

Pulling herself together, Viv crossed the office to the table. As would anyone experienced with children, she used a one-hand grab to find snacks in the diaper bag.

"Just give me a few minutes," she told him. "Then I'll be ready."

She continued to shuffle items until Jack left the room. Once he was gone, Viv closed her eyes, resting her forehead against Katie's. Because at the root of all this chaos, the lies, the unknowns…the fear, there was an innocent child who deserved to be Viv's top priority. Every action, every decision right now revolved around Katie and her welfare. The journal, the secret—none of that mattered in the grand scheme of things. Viv would put Katie ahead of her own needs, her own wishes and even what was morally right, if need be.

Even if it cost everything with Jack once he realized she'd lied and withheld the ultimate secret.

Five

Jack eased back in the leather club chair opposite Viv's desk as she reached for yet more pieces of candy from her little glass dish. He wondered if she even realized she was doing so. She scrolled through the items on her computer screen with one hand, and used the other for snacking.

He could watch her eat candy all day. His body tightened as her tongue darted out to catch a stray piece of chocolate on her bottom lip. Why was he so turned on by such a simple movement? He knew why—because it was Viv.

"The notes I have copies of are all clean," she stated softly. Katie finally had fallen asleep in her Pack 'n Play after lunch, so they had to talk quietly. "There's no red flags on shipments, nothing that looks suspicious in the days leading up to the Parkers' deaths. On the evening of the robbery, Ryker and Laney were out to dinner with Braden and Zara. Mac and Jenna were in Florida at the Miami location. They haven't deviated from their stories even once."

Jack eased forward, resting his elbows on his knees and raking his hands through his hair. "I'm going to call a meeting with Braden."

Viv jerked around in her seat. "What?"

He saw no other way. Jack had already put the pressure on Ryker, the family henchman. If that didn't work to Jack's satisfaction, he'd go straight to the top, and that meant the oldest of the O'Sheas.

"You can't do that," she went on. "They'll know who you are if you go to them."

"It's a chance I'm willing to take."

Viv leaned her forearms on her desk as her worried gaze held his. "You were at Braden's house with me for the Christmas party. Then you surprised them just a couple months ago with a visit. You think he won't start putting all this together?"

The Christmas party. As if Jack could forget. Viv had worn some emerald-green dress that hugged every damn curve she owned, and that memory had haunted his dreams, sleeping and awake, ever since. He'd been her faux date so he could get inside and eavesdrop. Not that he thought some epic family secrets would be revealed, but he wasn't letting the opportunity pass him by...and he sure as hell wasn't letting another man take his place.

Jealousy was an unwelcome bastard.

"That was months ago," he told her. "Besides, I had a full beard then and my hair was longer. And when I approached them after, I didn't look like the same man. They have no clue. They know now I'm onto them, but they don't realize I was the guy at the party with you."

He often changed his appearance, even in minor

ways, because the average person didn't look beneath the surface. With all the people milling about, Jack was confident nobody would remember him from the Christmas party...not when he'd been overshadowed by Vivianna's beauty. He'd also been sure to make himself scarce the times she'd chatted with the key players. This had certainly not been his first time sneaking around and altering his identity.

"And what are you going to say?" she demanded in a harsh whisper. "You can't very well ask him to spill all his illegal doings."

Jack wondered if she had any idea that her eyes widened when she grew angry, that one of her brows arched higher than the other.

"I've done this a long time," he assured her. "Trust me."

Viv closed her eyes, reaching up to rub her forehead. Glancing at his watch, he was surprised to see that they'd been at this for quite a while. Katie had been asleep for over an hour, and judging by the dark circles under her eyes, Jack guessed it had been a while since Viv had actually had a restful night's sleep herself.

"Go in my office and lie down."

Viv lifted her head, smoothing her hair behind her ear. Her braid had started unraveling, giving her that sexy, tousled look. As if she needed to look sexier.

"You're exhausted and she's asleep. I promise I'll come get you when she wakes."

Because he'd have no clue what to do with a baby, and attempting to learn now would not be wise for the sake of his sanity.

Viv shook her head. "I'm fine."

Not surprising that she refused, but he wasn't about to let her win this fight...or any other, for that matter.

"Thirty minutes," he stated. "The couch is more than comfortable."

"You're speaking from experience?" She tipped her head to the side, knowing very well he slept in his office on occasion.

"I'm not asking, Viv. I'm telling you."

She rubbed her temples, as she'd done several times in the past twenty minutes, and Jack wondered if her head ached from her hair being pulled back or because she'd been staring at her computer screen.

Pulling her braid over her shoulder, she reached up and jerked the rubber band out. After threading her fingers through the strands to loosen them, she gave her head a shake. There was no way he could take his eyes off her now. The simple move was just as sultry and seductive as a striptease. All that long, rich hair spilling down her back, the groan that slipped through her lips had his own body stirring. Again.

"Viv."

Damn, that had come out like a growl.

Her eyes snapped to his. They'd worked countless hours in her office, but this was the first time he'd locked the main door so they wouldn't be interrupted. This was also the first time they'd closed her office door, but that was for Katie's sake. Still, being so confined with Vivianna, knowing the crackling sexual tension wasn't going anywhere, Jack was having a difficult time focusing.

He rubbed his index finger against his thumb, practically feeling all that hair wrapped around his hand as he tugged on it…from behind.

Raking a hand down his face, Jack finally came to his feet. "Actually, head on home. We're not getting anywhere, and I'm going to call Braden anyway and arrange a meeting."

Viv continued to look up at him. All that hair spread around her, those midnight eyes wide… His body stirred again.

"Why are you angry?"

More like sexually frustrated.

Jack shoved his hands in his pockets. "I'm not angry with you. There's so much at stake here and I refuse to let those bastards get the best of me."

Katie made a whimpering sound and Jack realized he hadn't even tried to keep his voice down. Viv's gaze darted in the baby's direction, then back to Jack.

"They won't," she told him. "But don't be so hell-bent on destruction that you don't find the truth."

"What the hell does that mean?" he demanded in a harsh whisper.

Viv circled her desk to stand before him. "I'm just as eager to learn what happened to the Parkers as you are, but what if the O'Sheas truly had nothing to do with their murders?"

This was the first Jack had heard her even mention any doubts. Where were they coming from?

Viv smoothed her hair behind her shoulders. "Listen, I know you and the Feds want to nail the O'Sheas. I understand. I just really don't know that they had anything to do with that night."

Jack gritted his teeth. "If you're getting soft because you're working there—"

"I'm not getting soft." As if to prove her point, she tipped her chin and narrowed her eyes. "If anything, I'm getting to know them a bit better, and I can honestly say I just don't see it."

Jack couldn't believe this. He threw his hands in the

air. "Most criminals don't go around with a sign announcing their offenses. Of course they're going to be friendly toward you so you're not apprehensive. And why the sudden change of heart? You never questioned my suspicions before."

She said nothing, just kept staring at him as if she wasn't sure how to respond…or as if she knew something he didn't. His radar wasn't often off the mark. Why would Viv come to the defense of such seasoned criminals?

"Did one of them threaten you?" he murmured, taking a step closer to her.

"What? No, of course not."

She gripped his elbow and squeezed. A simple gesture any friend would use when trying to get his attention. Still, the touch from Viv was anything but friendly…at least in his own mind.

"Listen, I'm just saying they definitely had their share of, shall we say, questionable transactions in the past." Viv offered him a sweet smile. "But with Braden in charge now, I know they are trying to keep things on the up and up."

Viv clearly wanted to see the best in this family. Perhaps it was because Laney was pregnant and Viv felt protective—one woman to another. Jack wasn't quite sure, but he'd done this work long enough that he refused to be sidetracked by the family's sudden need to walk on the right side of the law.

He reached for Viv's hand on his arm. Sliding it between his, he held her still, ignoring the way her eyes widened in surprise.

"I need you, Viv." In ways he couldn't even let himself believe. "You're my eyes and ears on the inside.

You can't get caught up in this family when we're on the brink of shutting them down."

When she trembled, Jack gripped her hand tighter. She closed her eyes and pulled in a breath. Black lashes fanned out against her tanned skin. What was she so worried about?

"Is it because Laney is expecting?" he asked. "Is that what has you upset?"

Viv shook her head, lifting her lids to meet his eyes. "No. Well, that does bother me, but I just worry not everything is as it seems."

"Is there something you need to tell me?"

Katie belted out a cry, which had Viv jerking her hand away and heading toward the baby. And just like that the moment was gone. What was Viv hiding? He turned and saw that she had entered her comfort zone as she wrapped her arms around Katie and swayed back and forth.

Viv's hair lay in waves down her back, shifting as she moved. She seemed to be humming in an attempt to sooth Katie's cries. Jack watched, wondering again why Viv had never pursued a family of her own. Maybe it was time he dug a little deeper into his assistant's personal life. After all, she was so determined to dive into his.

Days off were absolutely glorious. To have a day off from both jobs was even more splendid. Viv actually welcomed lounging in her pj's and getting caught up on housework. She'd gladly take wielding a toilet wand over volleying back and forth between a rumored mob family and the sexy boss she was hiding the truth from.

Katie crawled behind her as they headed down the

hallway. With the baby still in her footed pajamas, her knees would occasionally slip on the hardwood, but she'd push herself right back up and continue on.

Viv didn't want to think about how she'd bounce back once this case wrapped up. Eventually Jack would learn the truth, in turn he'd hate her and at best she'd be fired. The fact she'd kept something so personal, so life altering from Jack would tear him apart. Plus, on top of the inevitable, the O'Sheas would likely learn she'd been spying. And Katie would find her forever home.

Viv pushed the negative thoughts away before they could consume her.

"Up, up, up."

Glancing over her shoulder, Viv laughed at Katie, who now sat at the end of the hall outside her bedroom. With her arms extended, she wiggled her little fingers back and forth and continued to demand, "Up."

Just as she started back down the hall to get Katie, Viv's cell chimed from the kitchen. She quickly scooped Katie up and played airplane as she ran the short distance to the galley-style kitchen. Braden's number lit up, instantly giving Viv's heart a few extra beats.

The new family patriarch for the O'Sheas had never been anything but kind to her, but she still worried at the random call. It wasn't typical of him to contact her when she was off, and with everything going on, she certainly didn't want to draw attention to herself.

Katie pulled on Viv's loose ponytail as she swiped her finger across the screen. "Hello?"

"Vivianna. I need you to come in to the office early on Tuesday."

That stern voice boomed through the line, reminding her of her father. Len Smith never let his children get out of line, except when Viv had wanted to leave home and live in a big city. But that was not a subject she wanted to think about right now.

"Of course," she replied, tipping her head when Katie reached for the cell. "Is one hour early enough?"

"That will be fine. The FBI needs to question all employees again." Braden blew out a sigh, as if echoing her own feelings. Fear also crawled up her spine, causing shivers. "It's a nuisance, but necessary to get them to back off. I apologize for putting you out. You've been an exemplary employee."

Well, either he didn't suspect her of anything or he was a really great actor trying to trap her.

"It's no bother at all," she replied. Katie lunged for the phone once more and Viv eased her back down to the floor. "I don't mind answering more questions."

Katie grabbed hold of Viv's plaid pajama bottoms and started her chant once again. "Up, up, up."

Braden laughed. "Sounds like you're busy, so I won't keep you."

The O'Sheas might be ruthless and known for their less-than-legal business dealings, but nobody could ever say they weren't a loving family. Family meant everything to them. And with Braden's wife and sister expecting babies, he apparently was in tune with little ones.

"I'll be there at eight on Tuesday," she told him, smiling down at Katie, who continued to tug, her tiny chin now quivering. "See you then."

She'd kept her voice steady, she hoped, while talking to him, but a new worry crept in. What if the FBI had found something? The Feds knew she was a plant; Jack was very thorough with keeping his contacts informed. Still, if they were questioning the whole office, maybe they were about to crack this case.

And then what? What would Jack do? The journal

was completely personal, so there was no need for the Feds to know about it at all. But she was the only living person who knew the truth. It was her moral duty to tell him, whether the case was blown open or not.

Katie started fussing, rubbing her eyes and biting down hard on her gums. Viv set the phone back on the counter and reached for her. It was getting later in the day, but Katie had been up nearly all night with teething pain. Viv would give anything if those teeth would just pop through and let Katie have some rest. Poor thing was turning one in a week and Viv wanted to plan a fun celebration, even if it was just the two of them.

"It's all right, sweetheart." Viv ran her hand up and down Katie's back as she headed toward the nursery. "Let's rock a bit and see if we can get you to rest."

Three hours, no sleep and an empty bottle of pain reliever later, Viv needed reinforcements. The bottle of medicine had only one dose left when she'd pulled it from the cabinet, but thankfully, she kept a spare in the diaper bag.

With Katie on her hip, Viv frantically searched her apartment. Where on earth could it be? She always kept it right by the front door so this didn't happen.

Katie's screams were getting worse and Viv's frustration level was soaring. How could she be so irresponsible and misplace the bag with the backup medicine in it? She'd put her spare bottle in the bag when she took Katie to the office yesterday and…

Oh, no. Viv's heart sank. The diaper bag was at the office. She'd completely forgotten it in her haste to get out of the confined space with Jack.

She could throw on clothes and run to the drugstore two blocks away, but she truly hated to take Katie out in this weather. She glanced at the clock hanging above her bookshelf and noted that it was much later than she'd thought. She really had only one option if there was any hope of sleep tonight.

Six

Jack felt like a complete fool. His instincts had gotten him through combat; he'd managed to make enough business deals in the past decade to make him a millionaire; he spoke Italian and Portuguese and owned homes in both countries. Yet as he stood outside Viv's apartment door with diaper bag in hand, along with a sack of extra items from the store, he cursed under his breath.

He should've just brought the bag Viv had requested and not gone the extra mile. The last thing he needed was her reading too much into his actions. He was having a hard enough time justifying them to himself. He'd come damn close to kissing her in her office yesterday so he needed to calm down and reassess exactly what he needed to focus on…and it wasn't his assistant.

A middle-aged woman walked by and stopped at the next door. She threw him a soft smile, causing her eyes to wrinkle in the corners.

"You're here for Vivianna?" she asked.

Jack nodded. "You must be Martha."

He'd never met the babysitter before, but he knew she lived just on the other side of Viv. Jack shifted the diaper and drugstore bags into one hand and stepped forward to take Martha's bag of groceries.

"Let me," he offered, not letting her argue. "I'll carry them inside."

"But you have your own load."

Jack flashed her a smile. "Then you better unlock your door so I can go in and set yours down. My mother raised a gentleman."

She fished out her key and threw a glance over her shoulder as she turned the knob. "I like you. Are you here to take Viv out? That girl never gets out except to work."

Jack secured the large brown grocery bag against his chest as he followed Martha into her apartment, which was the same layout as Viv's. Martha decorated quite a bit differently, though. There wasn't a shelf or stationary surface that didn't have a knickknack on it. The porcelain cats, ducks, random shot glasses from around the world…there was just so much to take in at once. How the hell did anyone watch a child here? Breakables were everywhere.

"I'm returning the diaper bag she left at work," Jack finally replied, once he got past the chaos of the place.

Martha motioned for him to set the bag on the dining table. "That's a shame. I was hoping some fine-looking young man was going to take her out on the town. I'd gladly watch Katie, if that were the case."

The naughty twinkle in the woman's eye had him inching toward the door. The last thing he needed was a meddling neighbor trying to play Cupid. He was getting along just fine on his own.

Who said money didn't buy happiness? He was happy, damn it.

When this was all over, he decided, he wouldn't vacation at his villa in Italy. He was buying a whole new house for a getaway. He'd always loved the beauty of Amsterdam. Maybe he'd go there and look into real estate.

"I'll let her know you're available." Jack started through the open door, but the woman wasn't done with him yet.

"The weather is getting bad out there." She wiggled her brows. "If you need to stay for a bit, just have Viv run Katie over."

Was this lady for real? Jack merely smiled with a nod and got the hell out. That was the babysitter? Jack needed to have a talk with Viv about this. Not that he had any say over whom she preferred to have babysit, and Katie sure as hell wasn't his kid, but Martha seemed a bit too eager to get a man alone with Viv.

How many other men had she tried to set Viv up with?

The thought irritated Jack as he pounded on her door. He had no right to be jealous, but damn it, he couldn't help where his thoughts instantly went. The idea of some faceless bastard—

The door jerked open. It took Jack a moment to fully assess everything before him. Viv's hair was half up, half down…and not in a stylish way. More like Katie had yanked on it in a fit kind of way.

Gone was her typical pencil skirt and silk blouse. She'd donned plaid pants—were those flannel?—and a long-sleeved T-shirt that was a bit damp in the chest region. And she wasn't wearing a bra. Maybe having Katie stay next door with the crazy neighbor was the safest option, after all.

"Thank God you're here." Viv blew out an exhausted breath. "She's been screaming for the past fifteen minutes. Sorry to bother you, but I figured you'd still be at the office this late."

The screamer in question turned from Viv's shoulder to look straight at Jack. Her little eyes were red and puffy, and drool covered her chin. Her blond curls were in disarray. The two females before him looked as if they'd been through a battle.

Jack stepped in and immediately put the diaper bag on the table just inside the door. Without asking, because he recalled from the last time, he reached into the front pocket and pulled out the pain reliever.

Katie let out a cry, and Viv grabbed the bottle from his hand. "I can't thank you enough. I really didn't want to get her out in this weather, and I can't believe I left the bag at the office. What kind of foster parent am I?"

She struggled with the lid and holding a fussy baby. Jack eased the medicine from her hands and twisted it open. "You're the best foster parent."

Tears welled in Viv's eyes. "She's been miserable and I couldn't do anything to help."

He understood that helpless feeling all too well.

As Viv administered the medicine, Jack shrugged out of his coat and hung it over the back of one of two kitchenette chairs. Then he returned to the accent table and started pulling things from the drugstore sack.

"What are you doing?" Viv asked.

Feeling like a fool at the moment.

"I didn't want you to run out of pain reliever tonight, so I brought a few backups."

He stacked the various boxes on the table, because he didn't know which brand was the best and had bought two boxes of each.

"A few?" she asked with a slight laugh. "That will last me forever. Maybe you should be a foster parent. Clearly, you plan ahead better than I do."

She had no clue that associating the word *parent* with him was literally like a knife to his chest. She didn't know, because he'd never told her.

When Viv swiped at her damp eyes, Jack nearly reached for her. And what good would come from that? What did he intend to do once he touched her? Console her? Tell her everything would be all right? He sucked at consoling, to be honest. He wanted to, damn it. She made him want to try. He hated that she obviously felt inadequate and second-guessed herself.

Katie whimpered a bit more and Viv patted her back, bouncing softly in an attempt to calm her. "I'm sorry you had to stop here on your way home," Viv told him, then blew a stray strand of hair from her eyes. "I'm even sorrier I'm a complete wreck."

"You're not a wreck. You look like a woman who's putting the needs of a child first." Which made her even sexier. "Never apologize for caring."

Viv kissed Katie on the forehead and smoothed back her unruly curls. "I just hate to see her in pain. Teething is no joke. We were up most of last night, then she was fine this morning and I managed to get my cleaning done."

He might not be able to do much, but Jack knew of one thing that would hopefully put a smile on her face. He reached for the last item in the bag.

Viv gasped as he held up her favorite candy. "I think I love you."

Jack froze. Viv's eyes widened. "I mean, thank you," she quickly added. "You don't know how low my stash was running, and these are the name brand. I always buy the generic."

Yeah, he'd seen the empty bags in her office, which was just one of the reasons he wanted her to have the real thing.

Jack tore the package open and crossed toward her kitchen. He dumped the candy into her glass bowl and tossed the empty sack.

"I met your neighbor," he commented, leaning back against the counter. "Does she always try to set you up with a booty call?"

Viv's eyes widened. Her hand, which she had been rubbing up and down Katie's spine, stilled. "Excuse me?"

Shrugging, Jack went on. "She was all too eager for me to let you know she'd watch Katie if I wanted to take you out, or if we wanted to stay in, since the roads are getting bad."

Viv closed her eyes and wrinkled her nose. "Please tell me she didn't really say that."

Jack bit the inside of his cheek to suppress his grin. "Do you think I would make that up?"

When she finally opened her eyes, she looked everywhere but directly at him. Vivianna was sexy as hell and adorable all at the same time…and that invisible string pulling him toward her kept getting shorter and shorter. There wasn't a damn thing he could do to stop it. He hadn't felt the stirrings of desire for another woman in years.

"She's tried to set me up on dates so many times, but this is a first."

Viv shifted Katie in her arms. Apparently, the medicine had started kicking in, because the infant had one fist in her mouth and was playfully tugging Viv's fallen hair with her free hand.

"In her defense, she was married to her high school

sweetheart for forty years. He passed from a heart attack a couple of years ago." Viv moved into the living
area and started to put Katie in her Pack 'n Play. Having other ideas, Katie merely clung to her. "She's always looking for someone for me because she thinks
I'm unhappy alone."

Jack navigated around the half wall separating the
kitchen from the family room. "And are you unhappy
alone?"

Finally, those dark eyes met his. "I'm not alone. I
have Katie."

He came to a stop within a foot of her. "And when
she's gone? Will you still be happy?"

Viv tipped her chin. "I'm always sad to see my foster kids leave. Saying goodbye to Katie will be harder
to deal with because I'm so close to the story. But if
you're asking if I need a man in my life to make me
happy, the answer is no."

"What does make you happy?"

Why was he asking? Jack wondered. He should get
his coat on and get the hell out. The roads weren't getting any better and…what other reasoning did he need?
He was getting too cozy with his assistant.

"Right now?" She raised her brows and smiled. "A
shower. If you'd watch Katie for me for just five minutes, I will put in all the extra hours you want and you
won't even have to pay me."

Watch Katie? Jack would rather hand over his no-
limit credit card and send Viv on a trip to Rodeo Drive.
Not because he didn't like children. Quite the opposite.
But there was that fear that had been ingrained in him
a decade ago. He'd been so hyped up on the idea of becoming a father, and then when that dream vanished,
he'd forced himself to shut down that side of his mind.

"It's okay." Viv shook her head with a wave of her hand when he remained silent. "I just appreciate you bringing the bag and all the backups, especially the candy. Having her medicine is clearly more important than my hygiene at the moment."

He was such a jerk. Here he was worried about his fears, when Viv was constantly putting everyone's needs ahead of her own. From being an incredible foster mother to Katie, to working at—no, excelling at—two jobs because of him, the woman was a marvel. And all she wanted was a damn shower.

"Go shower. I'll watch her."

Viv's eyes widened in surprise, mimicking his own feelings. The offer was out of his mouth before he could talk himself out of it, but he wasn't sorry. The second her shock wore off, her entire face softened and her smile warmed something deep within him… something he'd thought he buried with his wife and unborn child.

He thought Viv might argue or tell him not to worry about it, but she quickly handed Katie over and muttered a thank-you as she dashed down the hallway.

Gripping the child beneath her arms, Jack looked into her baby blue eyes. The irony that she'd lost her parents and he'd lost his own child was not wasted on him. But it wasn't like he was going to be in Katie's life permanently. Still, holding her didn't make him miserable. In some strange way he couldn't explain, having her in his arms was rather therapeutic.

Katie smiled as drool ran down her chin and dripped onto his hand. Even that didn't turn him off. When he tucked her against his side, he felt a bit awkward. But the way she kept her eyes on him, as if she fully trusted him, had his heart stirring.

He hoped like hell Viv stuck to that five-minute plan because he wasn't sure how much longer his emotions or his sanity could hold out against the power of this innocent infant.

Viv felt human again. She'd managed a quick shower, hair washing included, and she'd brushed her teeth. She'd been mortified that Jack had to see her so...so blah. There had been no way around it, though. She'd needed the bag and she'd known he would be at the office.

The fact that he'd brought her the name-brand candy had her wondering if he was reaching out to her on a personal level. Obviously, but why?

Viv wasn't going to dig too deep into this, because even if Jack was trying to become personal, she was harboring a colossal secret. Pulling in a deep breath as she tugged her tank top over her head, Viv realized this case might never be solved. Would she have to hide the truth from Jack forever? But he deserved to know, even though it might ruin his quest for justice...and her chance at a deeper connection with him.

Worry coiled low in her belly. She didn't like secrets and she'd never been a liar before.

Well, until she became a spy for Jack and started working for the O'Sheas. Her moral compass had never been so screwed up in her life.

As she came down the hall, she wondered how long she should give herself before she told him. Each day that passed only added more layers to her guilt. But before she could give herself a time line, the sight in the living room stopped her every thought.

Jack was the sexiest man she'd ever met and reduced her insides to mush every time he entered the room.

But seeing him cuddling a sleeping baby might just be the ovary buster.

Nestled in the crook of his arm, Katie seemed perfectly content to catch some much-needed rest against Jack's broad chest. And Viv was a tad jealous.

"I'm sorry," she whispered as she crossed the room. "I tried to hurry."

Jack's eyes met hers, then traveled down her body. Every part of her tingled just as if he'd touched her. Perhaps she should've put on more than a pair of sleep shorts and a tank, but she'd been in a rush and grabbed the first thing she came across.

"She was out almost as soon as you walked away," he stated, glancing back down at Katie. "Now what do I do with her?"

Inching closer, Viv brushed against his arm as she stood on her tiptoes to look down on Katie. Such a precious little girl, one who trusted so easily. Viv didn't want Jack to leave just yet, but she wasn't sure if he wanted to continue to hold the sleeping baby.

"Are you hungry?" Viv asked, looking back up at him. "I could make dinner for us. But if you want to get home, I totally understand. Nothing I make would compare to Tilly's cooking."

A smile flirted around the corners of his mouth. "I can stay. She isn't cooking tonight. I actually threatened to give her the week off, because she's about as subtle as your neighbor and wanted you to come back for dinner…and breakfast."

Viv couldn't help the images of all the possibilities surrounding that scenario that popped into her head. But she'd never spend the night in Jack's bed—especially after she revealed the truth.

"Then maybe Martha and Tilly shouldn't meet," she

stated as she moved around him. "Would you mind holding the baby for a bit longer while I get dinner ready?"

Jack's lips thinned as he stared at Katie. "Not one bit."

There was a sadness to his tone, one Viv wanted to explore but had no right to. She had bigger problems… like cooking a dinner that a millionaire would find appealing. She had a feeling microwave mac 'n cheese wouldn't make the greatest impression.

Viv tried to block out the image of Jack holding a baby in her living room while she made dinner. There was so much wrapped in this moment—fear, hope, nervousness, sexual tension. All she could do now was concentrate on cooking. Later, she'd sort out her emotions—and decide when to come clean to Jack about his birth father.

Seven

Jack held Katie while Viv ate her simple meal of hamburger, baked potato and salad. She had protested, but Jack had insisted, gentleman that he was. Or maybe he'd just taken pity on her after witnessing her tears and frustration earlier. She was so grateful he was here—not that she should get used to having him around.

Once she was done, Viv crossed to the living room, where Jack sat on her hand-me-down sofa. He looked so out of place with that designer suit, groomed hair and a baby sleeping across his chest. Still, he looked perfectly at home, too. How cruel of her heart to cling to such a ridiculous fantasy.

Viv eased the still-sleeping baby from his arms so he could get up and go eat.

"I never dreamed she'd sleep this long," Viv muttered. "I'm just going to lay her down in her room. I'll be right back."

Viv had gotten his plate ready and poured him a glass

of iced tea, which was all she had unless he wanted whole milk or water. Definitely nothing like the dinner he'd served her at his house. But she wasn't ashamed of how she lived. She wasn't a billionaire, but she rocked the thousandaire title pretty well.

As long as she had enough funds to keep fostering and caring for children who had nobody else, she didn't care how padded her bank account was. A trip to Tahiti would be nice, but was definitely not a necessity.

Viv took her time laying Katie down in the white crib she'd found in a secondhand shop and repainted. The yellow bedding was cheery, yet calm, quite the opposite of Viv's nerves.

The stress of the secret was weighing on her. The fear of the unknown, the future, scared her more than anything. But she had to remain quiet for now…all the more motivation to help Jack clear up this case sooner rather than later.

Darkness had long since settled in, causing the tiny night-light to kick on in Katie's room. Viv gave the baby one last glance before pulling in a deep breath and tiptoeing away. After being up all night and agitated all afternoon, Katie would sleep until morning, she hoped.

Viv backed out of the room, pulling the door closed. Jack's strong hands gripped her arms just as she was about to turn.

"Sorry." His whispered word by the side of her cheek sent shivers through her. His firm touch on her bare arms nearly had her leaning back against his chest. "I didn't want you to trip over me."

Viv turned, but Jack didn't take a step back. So close. He was so close, yet with just the soft glow from the kitchen light and the small lamp in the living room, she could barely make out his expression.

"I need to get going," he told her. "I just wanted to thank you for dinner. Tilly is the only one who cooks for me, so this was a nice change."

Viv refused to believe a man who'd traveled the globe, both for business and pleasure, was impressed by a meal she'd thrown together.

"Actually, before you go, could we just talk?"

She didn't want him to leave.

Jack tipped his head. "I don't think that's a good idea."

Viv stepped away from the door so she didn't wake Katie. "Why isn't it a good idea?"

He moved in front of her, raking a hand over his hair, ruffling it, reminding her of the unkempt way he'd worn it when they'd first met. The man could seriously shave his head or grow his hair long and still have just as much sex appeal.

His eyes narrowed. "Exploring this tension between us isn't a good idea."

Wait…what? He thought she was about to bring up the chemistry between them?

First of all, she wasn't that brave. Second, he clearly thought of her in that way or it wouldn't be an issue. Part of her wanted to jump up and down, but the realistic side remembered the damning journal in her bedroom.

She'd just wanted him to stay so she'd have some company. Okay, that was a lie. She wanted him here so they could talk about something that maybe wasn't only work. Perhaps if he would just slide into personal territory even once, maybe he'd see she was more than an assistant. She was a woman with a desire for her boss.

"I was—"

"I don't like tension in my work space," Jack continued. His broad shoulders blocked the light from the living area.

"And you think there's a problem between us?"

Why did she suddenly sound husky, like some seductress? She certainly wasn't trying to seduce him. Not that it would be a hardship.

"I think you drive me out of my mind." Jack took a half step closer, towering over her and doing nothing to slow her rapid heartbeat. "I blame myself for my thoughts, but I blame you for making me want things I have no business wanting."

Viv's breath caught in her throat. He'd never made such bold statements before. She'd caught him looking, but he'd never, ever been this audacious. She'd be lying if she denied the sudden thrill of knowing he couldn't ignore his feelings. All this time she'd thought he was made of stone. Clearly, this man was all flesh and blood. And sending her smoldering looks from mere inches away.

"I'm not trying to do anything to you," she murmured. "I'm attracted to you, but I know you're my boss and that's a line we can't cross, even if you were interested in me that way."

Jack muttered a curse, took a step forward and had her pinned between his hard chest and the wall. He propped one hand next to her head as he leaned in.

"*If* I was interested?" he repeated with a laugh of disbelief. "Do I look like a man who isn't interested, Viv?"

She bit the inside of her cheek. Treading this unfamiliar territory was not how she thought the evening would go down. She needed to tell him about the journal… That would squelch any interest he had. But now wasn't the time.

Jack placed his other hand on the opposite side of her head. He didn't touch her, but there was barely enough air moving between them in that miniscule gap.

"Just one taste," he whispered. "You should stop me now."

He didn't give her an option to answer before his mouth covered hers…not that she would've protested. She'd waited too long for this moment and she was going to savor each and every touch.

But the kiss remained his only touch. He didn't rush, didn't force. He didn't need to. The slow, sensual way his mouth moved over hers instantly had her wanting more.

He lifted his head slightly, just enough to change the angle before capturing her lips beneath his again. Viv couldn't hold back. She didn't have the willpower Jack apparently possessed.

She lifted her hands to his shoulders as he nipped at her lips. When he shifted slightly, bringing their bodies flush against each other, Viv let out a groan. If he'd offered to take her to her room right now, she wouldn't have objected.

Jack left her mouth to trail kisses along her jawline. Before she could stop herself, his name escaped her lips in a whispered plea.

He stilled beneath her touch and slowly lifted his head. When their eyes connected, there was enough of a glow for her to see he was done. His pained expression was back, the torment he inflicted on himself so evident from his thinned lips and the creases between his brows.

"Jack," she muttered once again. "You don't have to stop."

His hands fell to his sides as he took a step back. A chill enveloped her and she knew that self-erected wall was back in place.

"I need to go."

She didn't get a word in before he turned on his heel. In moments, the front door opened and closed, leaving her feeling even worse than before the kiss.

Viv slid down the wall, pulled her knees to her chest and dropped her head. Why did he have to kiss her? If she'd known he was going to have instant regrets, she would've preferred he leave her alone. Now all she could feel were his lips. He'd touched her nowhere else, but her entire body still hummed.

And from his reaction, she knew he would never touch her again.

Tears burned in her eyes. She'd practically inhaled her boss, then begged him not to stop. How the hell would she ever show her face at work tomorrow?

"If you have nothing to hide, then meeting me won't be a problem."

Jack's gloved hand gripped his steering wheel. Frustration rolled through him from all angles, especially concerning that kiss he'd experienced an hour ago. He could still taste her.

But now his anger shifted from himself to Ryker Barrett. This was one tough guy to crack, but Jack was tougher. He wasn't intimidated by the mob family's thug.

"Meeting you would be a waste of my time," Ryker replied.

"On the contrary," Jack countered. "You can't dodge the fact you all are the key suspects in the Parkers' murders."

"Nothing to dodge. Do you honestly believe we'd steal the items we wanted to auction? Pretty hard to pull that off, even for us."

Jack hated this man. Hated the way he blew off the

fact the Feds were swarming all around the O'Sheas. Either they were that arrogant or they truly had nothing to hide. Jack refused to believe this family had turned so lily-white after Patrick's passing.

The patriarch was notorious for getting deals done, no matter the cost. He'd been careful, had the right people in his back pocket and had never even gotten so much as a parking ticket.

And Jack would be the one to bring them all down.

"Come by the coffee shop next to my office tomorrow at eight," Ryker finally grunted.

Jack hung up and tossed the phone onto the leather passenger seat. Snow continued to fall and here he sat outside Viv's apartment. He'd battled whether to go back in and apologize, then he'd opted to call Ryker and set up a meeting instead. He wasn't worried about meeting with him, especially in a public place. The O'Sheas—and their henchman—were playing it smart now, anyway. They knew they were being watched and didn't want to bring more attention to themselves.

Jack would start with Ryker, then move to Braden, Mac, anyone who would talk and give Jack the lead he needed to crack this damn case.

It was getting late and he still had a call to make with one of his clients in the UK, to go over some security detail he was sending a team to cover. A simple job that would pay an easy seven figures. It was the one aspect of his life where he could maintain control and keep his sanity intact.

Because kissing the hell out of Viv had cost him everything.

He never showed weakness, never let his guard down, but he had done both with her. He'd gotten too damn cozy holding Katie while waiting on Viv to cook dinner. This wasn't some suburban family setting, yet it had sure felt that way to him.

Beyond the whole domestic feel of the evening, Viv had come out from her shower smelling like lilacs and innocence. They were both damn lucky all he did was kiss her. He'd at least held on to that last thread of control by not putting his hands all over her…but damn, how he'd wanted to.

She was his assistant. The only woman, other than Tilly, he'd let into his life on any level since his wife had passed.

Jack knew his wife would've wanted him to move on. That wasn't the issue. The issue was the pain he'd gone through when he'd lost her. Every single damn day since her murder, he'd had to live with the fact that he hadn't been there to protect her. Did he want to open himself up to even the slightest risk of that happening again?

No. He had business dealings all over the world, clients who demanded his full attention. There was no woman who would understand, not even Viv. Besides, he was a much different man than he'd been a decade ago. Life had blindsided him and left him to pick up each shattered piece. He hadn't even had the energy to put all the shards back together. Instead he'd opted for a fresh start, completely revamping his future goals.

Never once had seducing his assistant been on his list.

Jack put his SUV in gear and pulled from the curb. He had to put some distance between him and Viv. Had to get his head on straight so he could come out on top during tomorrow's meeting. And he had to forget the way Viv had kissed him back with total abandon and want. Because he knew if he went back up to her apartment to apologize now, they'd end up taking a step he wasn't sure he'd ever be ready for.

Eight

She hadn't had a good glass of wine in so long, but Viv was rewarding herself tonight. Katie had fallen asleep without incident. Martha said there had been no issues during the day, and Katie had two teeth popping through. Viv nearly wept with relief at the sight of those little white points.

She'd gone into O'Shea's earlier in the day. Even though it was Saturday, they were getting ready for the spring auction and there was a constant stream of data to be inputted.

Viv had left the office early and done some birthday shopping for Katie. She was turning only one and would never remember this time in her life, but Viv wanted to make the day special. She'd never had a foster child at birthday time before and she may have gone a bit overboard. Her credit card had definitely taken a hit, but she didn't care.

Once Katie had gone down, Viv had relaxed with a

bubble bath. The lavender lotion she'd applied afterward had instantly calmed the rest of her nerves.

She hadn't heard from Jack since he'd kissed her and bolted out the door. His silence spoke volumes, though. For a man who checked in with her almost hourly, he'd gone off the grid, most likely to analyze his actions. Knowing Jack, he was going to come back with some quick, stern apology and expect to move on like nothing had happened. He would shut down once again if she didn't do something to make him realize that the kiss had not been a mistake.

If it had been, she wouldn't still be tingling and reliving every glorious detail.

Viv settled back against her pile of pillows, propped her feet on her bed and reached for the book on her nightstand. Armed with a glass of wine and a good novel, she didn't care what went on for the next hour or so. She was taking this time for herself.

With the snow blowing around outside, being cozy in her apartment was the perfect setting for getting lost in a good book. Unfortunately, she'd started this one so long ago she'd have to start over to refresh her memory.

Viv had just opened the hardback when she heard a thump. She glanced to the video monitor screen on her nightstand. Katie hadn't moved one inch since being laid down. Viv strained to hear another sound, figuring it must be one of her neighbors.

Just as she dismissed the noise, she heard it again. Sounded like someone was at her front door. Viv quickly set her glass and book on the nightstand, grabbed her phone and the monitor and tiptoed across the hall to Katie's bedroom. If someone was trying to get in, she wanted to be in the same room as the baby.

Her building had security, but nothing like the fingerprint scanner at Jack's office and his home. Her heart beat too fast as possible scenarios flooded her mind. Was someone trying to get in? Was this related to the case she was working on from both sides?

It was too late for visitors and the only people who ever dropped by her place were Jack and Martha. Viv didn't figure either of them would be attempting to get in to her apartment.

Viv heard a creak, very faint. She couldn't just open the door and look, because if someone was there, they could hurt her and take Katie. Right now, Viv needed to stay with the baby.

She dialed Jack and willed him to answer and not still be sulking about their intense kiss.

He answered on the second ring. "Viv."

"I think someone is in my apartment," she whispered. She kept her eyes glued to the crack beneath the bedroom door, praying she wouldn't see a shadow.

"Don't move," he said, his tone suddenly alert. "I'll be there in five minutes."

In other words, a lifetime.

"Don't hang up," he told her. "Keep this line open while I drive so I know you're okay."

Beneath the bold, firm command, Viv caught an underlying sense of fear.

"Don't be reckless," she whispered. "The roads are—"

"Damn the roads," he growled. "Talk to me. Where are you and Katie in the apartment?"

"I came into her room."

She heard another faint thump and squeezed her eyes shut. She'd never been one to rely on someone else to get her out of a jam, but this was different. Fear gripped her as she stood by the crib, clutching the phone and watching the door. She'd at least turned the simple lock when she'd come in.

"Viv."

"I'm here."

"Don't talk anymore," he ordered. "I'm almost at your street."

Still minutes from getting in to her apartment. But just knowing he was close, knowing he was on the other end of the line, was a comfort.

Thankfully, Katie slept on, unaware of any turmoil.

Viv hadn't heard anything in the past couple minutes, but she wasn't ready to step out of the room and leave Katie yet.

"I just parked and I'm heading inside."

He already knew the building code and the code to her apartment. Viv waited, hearing random clicks and footsteps through her cell phone.

He was in her building and she was going to be just fine. But was someone out there waiting for him?

"Be careful," she whispered.

Then she heard a few beeps seconds before her apartment door opened.

"The door was closed and I don't see anyone in here."

The heavy weight lifted from her shoulders as she tucked the monitor under her arm and quietly stepped from Katie's bedroom. Jack stood at the end of the hall, filling the opening with his broad shoulders. She'd never seen a more beautiful sight in all her life.

And it struck her that her first instinct had been to call him and not 911. Jack was the only protection, only security she wanted.

With the monitor and phone clutched to her chest, she moved on into her bedroom and dumped them on the bed. The wine and the book remained on the table where she'd left them what seemed like hours ago.

Wrapping her arms around her waist, she tipped her head down and drew in a shaky breath. Strong hands gripped her shoulders and Jack pulled her against his firm chest.

"You're fine now."

She nodded, afraid to speak. His heartbeat at her back was nearly as frantic as her own.

"Sorry I bothered you so late," she muttered.

"I would've been pissed had you not."

She turned, not caring how utterly unprofessional this entire scenario was, and wrapped her arms around his neck.

"Give me just a minute," she murmured against his chest. "I just…need to get my heart rate back under control."

When his arms circled her, tugging her tighter against him, Viv melted right into his embrace. The woodsy cologne he always used filled her senses. The warmth from his touch had her nerves settling. Just knowing she'd called and he'd beat feet to get here had her heart swelling.

"Thank you." Viv eased back to look up into his eyes. "I probably should've called 911, but I thought of you and then I heard another noise. I just dialed your number without thinking and didn't know who else to—"

Jack placed a finger over her lips. "I'm always your first call. Always."

Viv nodded, never taking her eyes off his. She noticed then that she wasn't the one trembling now. Every part of him, from his hand touching her face to his body pressed against hers, had a slight tremor.

Curling her fingers around his wrist, Viv pulled his hand away. "Are you all right?"

"Of course I am."

The words came out on a huff, as if she were asking an absurd question. But worry was etched all over his face. The drawn brows, the thin lips. Jack had been just as scared, maybe more, than she had been.

"You're shaking."

"Adrenaline." He kept her close, his gaze on her face. "It's not often I get a phone call after midnight unless it's business, and even then I'm expecting it."

She noticed then that this was quite possibly the first time she'd ever seen him sporting something other than an Italian-cut suit. He wore jeans and a long-sleeved black T-shirt. He hadn't even bothered with a coat.

And she was even more aware of how little she wore, considering she'd gotten ready for bed. Suddenly her silk tap shorts and matching pink tank seemed like nothing. The thin material was barely a barrier between them.

Viv took a step back, hating how her body cooled instantly once away from his touch. "Um…sorry you came for nothing. I think I'll be fine now."

Jack's eyes raked over her. "I'm not leaving."

Heart in her throat, Viv crossed her arms over her chest—the only defense she had, given the nearly sheer material and no bra. "It's fine, Jack. I'm sure it was a neighbor and my mind just played tricks on me. I'm sorry I dragged you out in this weather."

"Never apologize and never call me second when you need someone." He took a step forward, closing the gap between them. "I'm staying on the couch tonight."

"But—"

"I'm not asking your permission." He glanced around

her bedroom, his eyes landing on the nightstand with her wine and book. "Pretend I'm not here."

Viv snorted. As if that were even a possibility.

Once again, he was visually sampling her—and he wasn't hiding the fact. Having Jack on her couch all night would ensure one thing…there was no way in hell she'd get one wink of sleep.

Nine

Jack was used to sleeping in random places. The military had instilled that ability in him from the get-go. Then, when he'd started doing surveillance, he spent many nights holed up in his car or a van with video equipment. While he might have eight bedrooms, in his home here and villas in two other countries, he wasn't pampered and didn't need the finest accommodations. He was comfortable anywhere.

Or so he thought.

Viv's sofa smelled like flowers, like her. And he could possibly get beyond that, but every time he tried to close his eyes, images of her in that damn silky pajama number flooded his mind.

Hell, he didn't even need to close his eyes to see that glorious view.

And how much of a jerk was he, sitting here fantasizing about her, when she'd been scared out of her mind earlier. When she'd called him, Jack hadn't even thought. There hadn't been time. The fear in her tone, the way she whispered that she needed him, had absolutely gutted him…and thrown him back ten years.

Letting anyone else get hurt, or worse, on his watch again was not an option. Especially someone he cared about. And he did care about Viv—more than he would ever admit.

Jack dropped his head back against the cushion and stared into the darkness. Viv was only a few walls away, still wearing that outfit that dreams were made of. How much willpower did a man have?

Part of him wanted to ignore the fact that she was his assistant, and to go take what they both wanted. The boss part of him knew there would be no turning back—and the boundaries he'd so carefully constructed would be permanently blurred.

Did he really want to risk that for one night?

Before Jack could think too much, he came to his feet. Hell, yes, he wanted to risk it. If anything, he'd learned to take what he wanted out of life…and he wanted Vivianna Smith.

She'd stared at the same page, the same paragraph, for the past fifteen minutes. She'd downed her wine immediately, because she'd needed something to calm her nerves…nerves that had nothing to do with the scare she'd had earlier and everything to do with the man keeping guard in her living room.

That whole protective nature of his was such a turn-on, as if she needed more reasons to want him. So far the only flaw she'd discovered was his inability to let anyone behind the wall he'd erected around himself.

But after the way he'd kissed her, the way he'd looked at her and proved to be a white knight, Viv wasn't letting her desire go. She had to know if there was more passion in him where that came from.

Her mind made up, she set the book on the nightstand next to her empty glass. Just as she rose to her feet, there was a creak outside her bedroom. A second later, the door eased open.

Viv stood next to her bed, eyes locked on Jack filling her doorway. The small accent lamp on her nightstand was the only thing illuminating the space. Jack raked his gaze over her as he'd done earlier...as if he couldn't get enough. She was counting on just that.

"What took you so long?" she asked. "I was coming to you."

He stayed in the doorway, but Viv wasn't deterred. She knew he'd come this far and wasn't about to leave. She remained by the bed, because there was no way she was going to cross that space now. The next move was his.

"This is it," he murmured, stepping over the threshold. "Tonight has nothing to do with tomorrow."

If that's what he chose to believe, whatever. She knew better, but she wasn't about to argue, not when she was so turned on she was about ready to pounce on him.

"What changed your mind?"

He stalked closer, until they were toe to toe and she had to tilt her head to look into his eyes. "Does it matter?"

In the grand scheme of things maybe, but right this second? No.

Anticipation had her stomach quivering. Now that he was in her bedroom, Viv really wished he'd do something rather than stand so close with no contact. Throw her down on the bed, for starters.

Jack's fingertips traveled up her bare arms, across her collarbone, before slowly sliding the straps of her tank out of the way.

"Do you always wear sexy silk things to bed?" His eyes remained on the task of undressing her as he spoke.

"Yes."

He eased the thin material down until the tank pooled around her waist. Instinctively, her body arched, reacting to the cooler air and the anticipation of his touch. He was slowly killing her.

"If you don't move faster, I'm going to take over."

Jack's eyes darted to hers. "I've waited for this. I'm going to take in every single second."

He'd waited? For how long?

Before she could analyze his statement too much, Jack hooked his thumbs in the bunched material around her waist and slid everything lower. When he crouched down, she lifted one foot, then the other, until she was completely bared to him.

If any other man was at her feet, Viv would think him submissive, but she knew better with Jack. He was in control at all times.

Jack curled his fingers around her ankles, then pushed his way up her body, over her hips to the dip in her waist, until he was on his feet again. Viv let out a moan when he finally palmed her breasts.

"You're so responsive."

Now wouldn't be the time to tell him she'd never been this responsive to another man. She'd never ached for a man like this before. Viv wanted to see him, too, all of him. She reached for the hem of his shirt and jerked it up. Jack released her long enough to whip the garment over his head and toss it aside. Keeping his eyes locked on hers, he quickly rid himself of his jeans and boxer briefs, until he stood before her in all his glorious masculinity.

"I'm not—"

Her thoughts were lost as he snaked his arms around her waist and pulled her against his body. His mouth crashed down onto hers as if every shred of his control had snapped.

The backs of her knees hit the edge of her bed. Jack followed her down, never breaking away from her. The weight of his body pressing her into the duvet was a welcome sensation. She'd dreamed of this moment, never thinking he'd be in her bed. In her imagination they'd always been in one of the rooms of his grand home.

Jack pulled his lips from hers as he looked down into her eyes. He rested his elbows on either side of her head, smoothing her hair away from her face.

"Be sure."

Viv bent her knees, sliding her ankles around his waist and locking them behind his back. When he closed his eyes and pulled in a deep breath, she stilled. Realization hit her.

"You don't have protection, do you?" she asked.

He shook his head. "I clearly didn't plan this when I left."

"I don't keep anything here."

The corners of his mouth tipped up. "On one hand that makes me happy. On the other hand, I'm dying."

Viv wasn't the most sexually active woman and pregnancy wasn't an option with her history. But now was definitely not the time to start verbally going through her medical chart.

"I'm clean," she told him. "And you don't have to worry about pregnancy."

His eyes turned darker as he lowered his lids once again. Before she could question him, he slid his mouth across hers and murmured, "I'm clean, too."

Viv tightened her grip around his waist, urging him to take what they both were so desperate for.

The second he joined their bodies, he locked his eyes on hers. This was what she'd been waiting for. This man, this moment.

Viv arched into him, her fingers gripping his shoulders as he set the pace. Jack captured her mouth, nipping at her lips over and over as his hips met hers. He reached down, curling his hand around the back of her knee and lifting just enough for her to feel even more sensations rushing through her.

Viv tore her mouth from his the second her body started to climb. She squeezed her eyes shut, not wanting him to see just how affected she was by the intensity of their passion.

Jack's lips on the side of her neck, drifting down to her sensitive breast, was all she needed to peak. Her body clenched around him as she cried out. He jerked against her, his own body stilling as he followed her into oblivion.

Moments later, Viv continued to tremble. Jack kissed her once more, then rested his forehead against hers. His heart beat harshly against her chest and she wanted desperately to know what he was thinking. Then again, the silence of the moment was perfect. She could relish the fact that she'd made love with the one man she'd wanted for years. He'd come to her because he'd been unable to fight the attraction any longer.

Could he just walk away after this? Could he be satisfied with just one night and then go on as if this didn't alter their lives?

Viv turned her head aside as guilt and fear trickled through the euphoric state she'd been floating in.

The journal was behind her closet door. The key to Jack's past was only feet away. She'd been looking for the right time to talk to him, but this certainly wasn't it.

"You were right earlier," he murmured against the side of her neck. He rolled slightly so his weight wasn't directly on her, but he kept an arm around her waist. "I was scared when you called. It's not an emotion I connect with or have often."

Viv jerked her thoughts from the journal and shifted to face him.

"My wife died when I was overseas, and I wasn't there to protect her." He held Viv's gaze as his thumb stroked her abdomen. "She was in the wrong place at the wrong time. I know I may not have been with her even if I had been stateside, but knowing I was so far…"

Viv slid her palm over his stubbled cheek. "You don't have to explain why you were afraid. I know your wife died while you were overseas. I didn't know specifics, though. You aren't to blame. You have come to grips with that, right?"

Jack eased away and rose to his feet, instantly leaving her chilled. When he started gathering his clothes, Viv knew he was holding true to his word. What just happened was all he would give. There would be no opening up and sharing past stories now.

And how could she expect him to reveal a part of himself, when she held such a damning secret?

"I'll be on the sofa."

His parting words left her cold. She wished he would have just gone home, because what had taken place in her bed hadn't drawn them closer together at all. If anything, she felt more distanced than ever.

Ten

Jack glared across the coffee shop, willing Ryker Barrett to step through the etched glass doors. After last night, Jack wasn't in a great mood, which was perfect for a meeting with the man who knew all the O'Sheas' secrets.

Sipping his black coffee, Jack tried to ignore the ache in his chest. Last night had been everything he'd wanted, everything he hadn't known he'd been missing. But there was no way anything could ever come from hooking up with Viv. She was all about taking care of children, and he refused to allow himself the luxury of even entertaining the idea of a family life.

He'd had sex. He certainly wasn't looking for holy matrimony. Once was enough. The risk of going through such heartache again wasn't something he was on board with. Besides, no permanent relationship could come from an affair with his assistant, even if he were looking for something long term.

Which was why he'd found himself hightailing it from her apartment before she and Katie woke. He'd gone back to his Beacon Hill home to change, dodged all questions from Tilly and had made it out to Bean House, hopefully in time to catch Ryker.

Jack had done enough surveillance to know the man frequented this coffee shop next to the O'Shea offices. He wasn't surprised that Ryker had picked this neutral territory for their meeting.

Jack waited nearly twenty minutes before he spotted the man in the dark leather jacket, with coal-black hair and a menacing look in his eyes. Ryker Barrett was exactly what he portrayed: mysterious and standoffish, and exuding a go-to-hell attitude.

Well, too bad. Jack was eager to get this little pow-wow started.

After Ryker placed his order, Jack stepped to the end of the counter and met the man's gaze, relieved not to see recognition there.

"Get your coffee and meet me over in the corner."

He didn't wait for Ryker to answer. Even though Jack had been at the O'Sheas' Christmas party, he hadn't spoken to Ryker that night, so it was unlikely the family's right-hand man would link him to Viv.

Just as Jack took a seat, Ryker came to stand on the other side of the table. Coffee cup in hand, he glared down at him.

"You can sit or stand, but you may not want everyone to hear our conversation." Jack wasn't in the mood for games.

Ryker sipped his coffee, then slid the wooden chair out and casually dropped into it. He glanced around the café as if he didn't have a care in the world. Arrogant jerk. Jack wanted to reach across the table and punch the smug look off his face.

"I've already told you everything, which is more than you deserve." Ryker flung an arm across the chair beside him and set his cup on the table. "You have two minutes."

Jack knew if he wanted to get to the bottom of this case once and for all, he'd have to take a different approach. "I'm willing to work with you to find out who committed the crime against the Parkers," he said grudgingly.

There was a ring of truth to the saying about keeping your enemies closer, even if Jack hated every second of it.

"And why would I want to work with you?" Ryker countered.

Jack shrugged, leaning forward on his elbows. "Because you want to clear the O'Shea name and I want to find out who made an orphan out of an innocent child."

Even though Jack had a gut feeling he was looking at the main suspect. But if he could work closely with Ryker, and Viv kept digging at the office, there was no way they could miss the truth.

"You've been hell-bent on pinning this on us," Ryker stated. "Why the change now?"

"I'm determined to get to the truth. You can either work with me or get out of my way."

Ryker's dark eyes narrowed. "Threatening me isn't your smartest move."

Jack couldn't help but smile. "That wasn't a threat. That was a promise."

Determined to keep the upper hand, Jack pushed himself to his feet. "Talk it over with your friends and let me know."

Gripping his to-go paper cup, Jack headed out the café door and into the brisk February air. There wasn't a doubt in his mind he'd be contacted by Ryker or another member of the O'Shea clan in short order. If they were truly going legit in the legal sense—and Jack wasn't so sure about that—then they'd want to work to clear their name and get the Feds off their backs.

Jack sipped his hot coffee as he made his way to his SUV. He'd head into the office, because he wasn't in the mood to go home and face Tilly. After he'd spent the night at Viv's apartment, there was no way Tilly wouldn't know something was up. She'd caught him sneaking in this morning and he'd dodged her questions, but he couldn't forever.

First, he had to come to grips with what had happened last night before he could even attempt to make excuses to his nosy, yet loving, chef and maid.

Logically, he knew he shouldn't have slept with Viv, but there was no way he could've avoided her forever. The more he worked with her, the more he wanted her. The physical aspect he could deal with, and thoroughly enjoy. It was everything else that came after the sex that had him questioning what the hell he was doing.

Like why he was still thinking of her. Thinking of the way her hair had spilled around him, the way she'd looked at him with hope, as if their one night could lead to something more.

Jack climbed in behind the wheel of his SUV and brought the engine to life. He'd been up front with Viv, telling her that he was unable to give more, and she'd agreed. But her face as he'd dressed and left the room said differently.

They both needed time apart. Unfortunately, that

wasn't possible, since they were working so closely together. Jack had to keep the upper hand on his emotions or he'd find himself falling deeper for Viv. And that was a heartache he couldn't afford to revisit.

He'd avoided her for two days.

Viv sat behind her antique mahogany desk and willed her door to open. She'd come in and gone straight to her own office like she did every morning she was scheduled to work with Jack. But this morning was unlike any other. This was her first day back to work after sleeping with her boss.

The phrase sounded so clichéd and tacky, but there was no sugarcoating the truth. He'd left her bed before she'd fully recovered, and spent the night on the sofa, then slipped out before she was up for the day. Clearly, he meant what he'd said about one night being all he could give.

Viv would be lying if she didn't admit she'd hoped he'd change his mind. Did he feel anything at all toward her? Was a one-night stand all he wanted? The man was so closed off, she honestly had no clue.

In his defense, he hadn't lied to her.

Viv dropped her face into her hands as guilt consumed her. Jack may have had sex with her and left, but at least he'd been totally up-front with her. As opposed to Viv, who was still hiding a secret that would completely change his life and everything he thought to be true.

The timing hadn't been right, then their attraction had snowballed and they'd slept together. Now here she sat, half in love with her boss and trying to help him bring down the family that was his by birthright.

From this point on, nothing would be easy. Not her feelings, not her actions…absolutely nothing.

Viv jumped when her cell rang. Glancing to the ID on the screen, she quickly slid her finger across to answer.

"Hello."

As if her heart wasn't already beating fast enough, now she waited to see what the social worker wanted. If it was time to say goodbye to Katie, then she'd have to let the precious baby go. But Viv wasn't ready.

"Vivianna, I hope this is a good time."

"Of course." It wasn't like she was actually working. "What can I do for you?"

"I'm calling with a question that I'd like you to take your time to consider."

Viv eased back in her leather chair and crossed her legs. "All right." Smoothing her pencil skirt down her thigh, she gripped her cell in anticipation.

"Before you took Katie in, you had expressed interest in full adoption. Is that still an avenue you'd like to explore, or are you content with fostering? I'd like to make it clear that Katie has no other family members."

Hope blossomed in Viv's chest. Being a parent had been a dream she never thought she'd reach. She'd put her forms in to adopt because she did want a family. She'd thought someday she'd be okay with erasing that distance between her and the foster children she helped, but honestly hadn't known if that day would ever come. Was Katie the one to be part of her family?

To know she could fully adopt a baby so sweet, so perfect… Viv was almost afraid to get too excited.

"Adopting is definitely an option," she replied, unable to hide her smile. "But I have questions and concerns."

"Of course. I'm happy to answer anything. Would you like to take some time to think, to fully process what this means? There are so many things to consider. Cost, time, paperwork. You're a fostering veteran, so you've already gone through a great deal of the process."

Viv came to her feet just as her office door opened. Of course Jack would decide to barge in now. She held up a finger and he nodded as he sauntered over and took a seat in the leather club chair across from her desk.

Viv turned her back to him and concentrated on the view out the window. Snow swirled around, piling on top of the three inches that had already been dumped on Saturday.

"I'm definitely interested in talking with you further," Viv stated, well aware that Jack was likely hanging on her every word. "Why don't I call you in a day or two? Maybe by then I'll have my questions all made out and we can go over everything at once."

"Perfect. And Vivianna, there's no pressure here. We can find a home for Katie. I just thought you would be the best candidate for her."

Viv blinked as tears burned her eyes. "Thank you. I'll be in touch."

She disconnected the call and held on to her phone as she crossed her arms. Adopting Katie would be a dream come true. The little girl she'd come to love and care for could possibly be hers forever. Her heart swelled nearly to bursting.

"Viv?"

Jack's voice pulled her from her daydream. Composing herself, she turned to face him, thankful the desk still sat between them as a barrier. She could handle only so much at once.

"Everything all right?" His eyes held hers and he frowned. "You're crying."

Viv swiped at the stray tear that had escaped. "Everything is fine. What did you need?"

"First I need to know why that call has you upset."

Viv leaned over her desk chair and placed her phone back on her calendar. "Nothing that has to do with work."

Slowly, he pushed himself to his feet, never taking his eyes off her. "Is this how things are going to be?"

"You mean a professional relationship?" she asked, crossing her arms. "Isn't that exactly what you decided on? I'm just following orders like a good assistant."

Jack rounded the desk, those green eyes never wavering from hers. He came to stand toe to toe with her, forcing her to tip her head back. Viv didn't step away, but nerves spiraled through her.

"Don't make things difficult," he growled. "When I see you upset, I have to know why."

"And you have no right to ask." Oh, how she wanted to share this news with him, but after he'd all but sprinted from her bed, she just couldn't expose herself to any more hurt and rejection. "My personal life has nothing to do with you. Now, I'll ask again. What did you barge in here for?"

The muscles in his jaw ticked. "I spoke with Ryker on Saturday. I offered to work with him in order to solve this case."

Now Viv did step back, mostly from shock. "What? What did he say?"

Shoving his hands in the pockets of his Italian suit, Jack shrugged. "We battled back and forth. I left before he could turn me down, but I'm sure he'll think about it. He'll discuss the offer with Braden and Mac, and with Mac coming into town, one of them will reach out to me."

"You think they'll agree to work with you?"

"I have no idea, but I'm not giving up and I had to find a new tack."

Viv closed her eyes. If he knew about the journal, perhaps he could approach them in a different way. Maybe they'd be more willing to speak if they knew Jack was family.

But first and foremost, Jack was an investigator and security specialist. He was still the enemy, according to the O'Sheas. So for now, the journal and the secrets would remain locked safely in her closet.

"I'm going in early tomorrow to talk to the Feds," Viv told him. "I know everyone will be at the office."

"There's nothing to be nervous about." Jack reached for her, then dropped his hand before he could make contact. "They haven't discovered anything to incriminate you."

Oh, but *she* had. Something much more life-altering than clues that might solve a mysterious case.

"I told you about the files I copied," she countered. "That was months ago and I haven't taken anything else, but the O'Sheas are convinced someone on the inside is betraying them."

"The Feds won't ask you anything that will be damning in front of Braden or Mac."

Jack did reach for her now. His hands curled around her shoulders and she couldn't help but stiffen at his touch.

"I don't want you worried. I'll take care of you."

Viv laughed. "Right. For the case, I know." She shrugged away from his touch. "I have work to do."

Jack fisted his hands at his sides. "And ignoring the other night is part of that?"

Oh, that was rich coming from him. "Says the man who couldn't get out of my bed and dressed fast enough."

Eleven

There was no way to avoid this conversation, but Jack just wished like hell he didn't have to see that hurt in her eyes. How was he protecting her when he was the one causing her pain and frustration? He should've kept his damn hands to himself. But the slippery slope he'd been clinging to for months had become too much.

"Don't do this."

"What?" she asked, tilting her chin in defiance. "Call you out on the truth?"

"Damn it, Viv." Jack raked his fingers through his hair. Propping his hands on his hips, he forced his eyes to stay on hers. "You're everything I used to want."

Great, now he'd exposed a portion of himself. Letting anyone see that side of his heart wasn't an option, but the words hovered in the air between them and he wished like hell he could snatch them back.

Viv's brows dipped as she frowned. "I don't even know what that means."

He'd come this far. Viv deserved the truth after the way he'd blurted out half of it.

"As you know, my wife died while I was overseas."

He hated thinking about that time in his life, let alone talking about it. Yet somehow he felt the need to open up to Viv about it for the second time.

Other than Tilly, Viv had been in his life the longest since his darkest hour. If anyone deserved to be let in, it was her. Besides, he prided himself on being truthful whenever possible.

Viv had always been an open book, never pushing for more in return. Her loyalty, her honesty and her commitment to stand by him even during his moody days were humbling…and that was the only reason he was opening up to her. It had nothing to do with the fact he'd felt a connection while he'd been in her bed. That connection couldn't go any deeper and she would understand why soon enough.

"My wife was shopping when a robber decided to randomly open fire. He turned the gun on himself before the cops arrived."

Jack swallowed, turning away when moisture gathered in Viv's expressive brown eyes.

"She was shopping for baby furniture," he whispered, when his own emotions threatened to take hold.

Viv's audible intake of breath pulled his focus back to her. "I wasn't there with her. I only had one month left in the service and I was getting out, because we were planning the family we always wanted."

"Jack."

Viv reached for him…and he let her. Perhaps he needed the contact, or maybe he was just a glutton for punishment, because he wanted more of her touch whether it was the right thing to do or not.

She took his hands, squeezing them in hers as she stared up at him. "I don't even know what to say."

Tears spilled down her cheeks. He'd never had someone shed a tear for him before, never let anyone get close enough to care.

"I know that pain," she whispered. "Losing what you want more than anything in this world."

He opened his mouth to question her, because there was definitely a story there, but she kept going as if she hadn't just alluded to a dark past of her own.

"But you're the strongest person I've ever known. Don't you want to move on and take back what was stolen from you?"

Jack gritted his teeth. "I want to bring down criminals who skirt the law and believe they're above reproach."

She let his hands drop as she reached up to frame his face. "And what about your personal life?"

When she stared at him in such a caring way, Jack realized that, their passionate night of sex aside, she got him. She understood him because she had her own demons.

"I opened myself up once, Viv." He gripped her wrists and eased them away from his face. "I won't make that mistake again. I've chosen to devote my life to seeking justice."

"Even at the cost of your own happiness?"

Jack let go and stepped back. "I have homes in three countries, so much work I'm turning clients away and I'm about to bring down the biggest Mafia family Boston has ever seen. How could I not be happy?"

The corners of Viv's mouth tipped in a sad smile. "The fact you equate happiness with material things tells me all I need to know."

She pulled her office chair out and took a seat. Jiggling the mouse on her computer, she brought her screen to life. "I have some emails to sort through. Go ahead and close the door on your way out."

Jack stared at the back of her head for a split second before he whirled her chair back around. Leaning down, he curled his fingers around the arms. Her eyes widened in shock as he jerked the chair even closer, so their faces were only a breath apart.

"I warned you once about dismissing me," he murmured against her mouth. "Just because I refuse to commit doesn't mean I don't still crave you."

He crushed his mouth to hers, damning himself for letting his emotions guide his actions. Reaching up to grip his hair, she didn't hesitate in opening for him.

Encircling Viv's waist with his hands, Jack hauled her up against him. Without breaking contact, he shifted until he was leaning against the edge of her desk and she stood between his legs.

One taste wouldn't be enough. He'd known that the moment he'd stepped into her bedroom. He was doomed to repeat the performance, and he didn't give a damn if they did it right here in her office.

A chime interrupted erotic thoughts of Viv spread out on her desk, begging. He wanted to ignore the cell in his pocket, but business always came first.

Viv tore her mouth from his, taking a step back and smoothing her skirt down. Shoving her hair behind her ears, she turned to face the window, as if she were ashamed.

He'd have to deal with that later. He'd wanted a kiss, and damn it, he wasn't going to deny himself anymore when she wanted it, too. Jack pulled the cell from his pocket and answered without looking at the screen.

"Jack Carson."

"Jack, Braden O'Shea. I hear you're looking to work together."

In an instant, Jack's back straightened. "Braden."

Viv jerked around, eyes wide. Jack had to ignore the swollen lips he'd just tasted. His body was still revved up from having her plastered against him. Her curves were something he couldn't deny himself...and that was going to have to be addressed sooner rather than later.

"I'll meet with you on my terms," Braden stated.

"Depends on the terms," Jack retorted. He wasn't about to hand over control so easily.

"You can come by our main office on Friday after we close. We're a bit busy this week."

Yeah, with the Feds breathing down your neck.

"Friday it is," Jack agreed. "See you then."

"One more thing."

Jack gripped the phone, pinning Viv with his gaze as he listened. "What's that?"

"If you try to play both sides, you'll regret it."

Jack laughed. "Threats don't work on me. You'd do best to remember that."

He disconnected the call, making sure Braden knew full well going into this little meeting who was in charge.

"He threatened you?" Viv whispered.

Jack slid the cell back into his pocket and waved a hand. "We came to an understanding."

Viv wrapped her arms around her abdomen. "If you get hurt..."

"I'm fine. This all will come to an end soon."

Pursing her lips, Viv glanced down at the floor. She was a confident woman, one of the qualities he found so damn sexy, but something was wrong.

"About earlier—"

She jerked her eyes back up to his. "Don't apologize."

"Fair enough, since I wasn't going to." He reached out, palming her face with his hand. He stroked her full bottom lip. "I want you in my bed. *My* bed. I won't make excuses or promises. You're what I crave and I intend to have you again."

She swiped the tip of her tongue across her lip, catching the pad of his thumb and sending another jolt of arousal through him.

"Maybe I want more than just to be the one to scratch your itch."

Jack laughed as he hauled her against his body once again. "Honey, you're not just scratching an itch. I've had that before."

"So what am I?" she pressed.

"You need a label? Can't this just be simple?"

Viv laughed in turn. "No, it can't."

Jack pulled in a deep breath, careful to choose his next words wisely. "I can't name this, Viv. What we have…I've never done this before. You're my assistant, my friend."

"Your lover."

He nodded. "That's what I'm offering, no more."

She cocked her head with a quirk of her brow. "Is everything a business deal with you?"

"There's no other way to live."

Viv stared back, silence heavy in the narrow gap between them. "There's every other way to live. Happiness, building on your dreams, raising a family."

And all that had been robbed from him, making him detach from ever wanting such luxuries again.

"Looks like I only scratched that itch, after all," she murmured. "I have goals I'm moving toward and I won't let anyone get in my way…no matter how much I may care for him."

Viv turned away and circled her desk as she headed out of her office. That jasmine scent clung all around him, mocking him with the promise of a woman he'd had, but never would again. And he had nobody to blame but himself.

Twelve

Viv sank into the desk chair in her office at O'Shea's. After an hour of answering questions from the Feds, with Braden, Mac, Ryker and Laney all present, her nerves were shot and she needed a moment to herself.

She was still reeling from the emotional roller coaster she was on with Jack. One minute he was telling her no, the next he was kissing her as if he needed her more than air. She wanted him, that was never in question. But she'd also come to realize she deserved more than an occasional romp whenever *he* wanted…which was exactly the tacky proposal he'd delivered.

Katie's adoption was another emotional standoff Viv found herself in. Her first instinct was to say absolutely yes, but that was the selfish side of her. She wanted to truly think about this from every angle. Viv had lain awake most of the night worrying if she could provide the best environment for Katie to grow up in.

She lived in an apartment, with no yard for a child to play. She was a single parent, and Katie deserved two.

But Katie was comfortable with her. They were already a team in the short time they'd been together. Letting Katie go to another family would be crushing, not just for Viv, but possibly for the baby, too. Even though she was just shy of a year old, Katie had already experienced enough trauma in her life. Stability was essential for children.

Approaching footsteps had Viv snapping out of her reverie. Braden.

"You have a second?"

As if she'd tell him no. Viv nodded and came to her feet.

"Sit down." He motioned with his hand as he crossed to the accent chair across from her desk. "I appreciate you coming in early and going over the Feds' questions with me. They have a tendency to be redundant, trying to get us to slip up."

"I have nothing to hide." Lie of the century. "So there's no slipping up."

He gave a clipped nod as he crossed his ankle over his knee. "Loyalty is of the utmost importance in our line of work. We appreciate you hanging in there through this past year. It's been a bit of a rocky road."

Viv offered a smile, despite her stomach clenching in knots. "I need the job and I value family. Working here is a perfect fit for my lifestyle."

Braden laced his fingers over his abdomen and held her in place with those intense green eyes of his. "How is the foster situation going with Katie?"

As tightly as her lies were woven, she always had to prepare a quick response in her head before she delivered it. One misplaced word or action could be detrimental to not only her, but Jack, as well. Despite whatever was going on with them personally, she would never jeopardize his work.

Viv let out a sigh. No way was she going to reveal the fact she might be adopting Katie, either.

"It's going really well. Katie has adjusted and I'm planning a little cake and a fun outing for her birthday next week. If the weather cooperates we'll go sledding."

"Bring her out to the estate. We have plenty of room and slopes."

Viv stilled, hoping her smile didn't falter. She'd been to Braden's home only once, for the Christmas party where Jack had insisted on being her date, albeit in disguise.

If she was invited to their house again, clearly they continued to trust her and didn't suspect a thing. Yet Viv couldn't help but wonder if any of them even knew that journal existed. Most likely not. She'd found it shoved in the secret compartment in the top of her desk...a desk they'd assigned her to.

Unless it had been a plant. Would she be pulled into some downward spiral by failing a test?

Paranoia was not her best quality, yet she couldn't help but look at this scenario from every possible angle. That's the only way she could be prepared for the fall-out.

"I may take you up on that," she replied. "I know she's only turning one, but I want her first birthday to be special."

"She's lucky to have you." Braden eased forward in his seat, planting his elbows on his knees. "I'd like to ask you something."

Why did she have to be so on edge? He was just a

man. A powerful, mysterious man who might or might not be on his way to prison.

"What's that?"

"Would you consider coming on here full-time?"

Shocked, she shifted in her seat. Definitely not what she thought he was going to ask. Not that she had a clue as to what he'd been thinking, but never once did she consider they'd want her here more often.

"I know you have Katie to think about, as well, but we'd be more than happy to accommodate you if you need to bring her in every now and then." Braden's chiseled face broke out into a wide smile, softening his harsh features. "It's not like this place won't be filled with babies soon enough, anyway."

With his own wife and sister expecting, Braden was definitely immersed in the baby world. This was one area he was going to get a crash course in very shortly.

"How soon do you need my answer?" She'd have to discuss this with Jack, and see if it was even possible for Martha to watch Katie more often.

"Laney would like to start working from home more, so you'd be picking up a little of her work, plus Zara and I would be coming in to take up the slack, as well. If you could just let me know in the next few weeks."

Hopefully, in that time the case would be wrapped up and she wouldn't be here. Part of her couldn't help the guilt that settled heavily in her chest. Over the past year, she'd gotten to know the O'Sheas. No matter the rumors surrounding them, or how Jack felt about them, she truly believed they wanted to move forward and just focus on auctions and growing their family. They might obtain some of their items through less than legal ways, but they weren't hardened criminals. Or murderers.

Patrick O'Shea may have done things differently, but Viv would bet just about anything that Braden, Mac and Ryker had nothing to do with the Parkers' deaths. Still, there was no evidence either way.

"I'll think about it," she assured him. "Katie is my top priority right now, so I need to do what's best for her."

Braden came to his feet. "I wouldn't expect any less from you. I'll let you get back to work. We have the final inventory list coming in this morning. I believe there are seventy-two pieces for you to input."

Viv nodded with a smile. "I'll be looking for the email."

Once she was alone, she blew out a breath and rubbed her temples. If she were a drinking woman, she'd take a whole bottle of something strong right about now. But she was a simple girl, and a scented bubble bath and a good book would do the trick... Too bad she had no time for the mental breakdown she deserved.

And at the heart of everything going on was Jack. He'd gotten her into this impossible situation with the O'Sheas, he'd turned her emotional life inside out and he'd left her wanting more. She'd walk through fire for that frustrating man and he was willing to settle for a romp in the sack.

Some fantasies weren't meant to be fulfilled. She just wished she could get the image of him in her bed out of her mind. Each time she lay down, she felt him, ached for him. And she didn't know if she'd ever get over that need.

Tilly had the week off, but she'd come by and prepared food to keep him going and promised to leave him alone. She was either worried he'd starve or she was nosy…and he knew the answer.

She'd given him a wink and told him she'd made more cheesecake. Damn it, the woman knew his plans for the night and he hadn't even said a word. Which was why their relationship was utterly perfect.

Still, she could make all the cheesecakes she wanted, could throw him that knowing grin and think she knew what he was up to during his personal time, but she had no idea.

In all honesty, he couldn't grasp his own thoughts lately, not when it came to Viv and all the unwanted emotions she'd conjured up.

Tonight, though, he'd called her to his house because of business. No other reason. He wouldn't even let his mind go down the path toward anything personal. He'd offered her all he had to give; she'd turned him away. They wanted completely opposite things in life, which he'd known going in. But that didn't stop him from wanting her.

Jack downed the rest of his whiskey just as his doorbell rang. He slammed his tumbler onto his desk and headed down the curved staircase. The exterior lights shone on Viv, revealing her shape through the etched-glass door. There was no mistaking that luscious figure. His hands itched to touch her intimately. Hell, he'd been aching for her since he'd left her bed days ago.

As soon as he used his fingerprint on the security panel and opened the door, he knew the possibility of having her tonight wasn't on the table. Not that Katie on her hip was the issue, because she'd fall asleep eventually, but Viv's eyes narrowed on his a half second before she pushed her way into his foyer.

"Good evening to you, too," he muttered as he closed the door.

"You demand I come by after work and won't tell me why." She slid the hood off Katie's head and Jack reached over and eased the baby from Viv's arms. "So I rushed to pick her up and get here, thinking something was wrong, but as I'm driving in this hellacious weather, I realize nothing is wrong and you're just being you."

Jack unfastened Katie's coat as Viv jerked her own off and flung it over the banister. She took Katie back, then removed her coat and tossed it there, as well.

"So, now that we're here, what could you possibly want that you couldn't text or call about?"

Jack crossed his arms and didn't even try to hide the smile that spread across his face. Was now a bad time to tell her how damn hot she looked when she got worked up? Because this fire and passion shooting from her was seriously turning him on.

Damn it. He didn't need to be more turned on by her. He needed to cool it. She wanted things he'd given up on. And she deserved every bit of what she worked for. He just wished she'd give in to what they both wanted while she was on the path to her dreams.

"What's the smirk for?" she asked, her eyes narrowing even more.

"I've never seen you so…"

"What? Frazzled? Losing my sanity? Confused and terrified all at the same time?"

Jack closed the space between them, instantly regretting that he hadn't taken better care to protect her. She was fine physically, but he should've seen that this entire process would take its toll on her emotionally. Not to mention the fact that she was a single mother. She gave to everyone but herself, always and in all ways.

"Something happen?" he asked, searching her eyes for the hint of tears. If she shed any, he'd be a goner. He could handle anything but the vulnerability of a woman, especially this woman. The instant tears came onto the scene, he was ready to slay any proverbial dragons on her behalf, even if that meant himself. And he'd hurt her, he knew that, but he was trying like hell to never do it again.

"Just the Feds in today, questioning me again."

"I listened to the audio. You did amazing."

He'd been so damn proud of her for sounding so confident, giving the same answers she'd given time and time again. But with the Feds still working the case, things would look suspicious if Viv wasn't questioned just as much as the rest of the staff and family at O'Shea's. He and Viv had gone over her story and background so much before she'd ever started working for them, there was no way she would flub up. He'd made sure she was mentally armed before going into enemy territory to do his battle.

And that still pissed him off. He hated placing her inside, knowing she was getting tangled up in that corrupt family. The sooner he could bring them down, the better off they'd all be. At this point, he was itching for them to screw up and just get a parking ticket—anything to open up the field to investigate every aspect of their lives.

Katie struggled in Viv's arms and Viv eased her down onto the floor. Jack watched as the infant pulled herself up, holding on to Viv's legs. She gripped the hem of Viv's pencil skirt and started glancing around the unfamiliar territory.

Yeah, his house wasn't kid friendly.

"So what was so important?"

He focused back on the woman before him, the woman he shouldn't want, but did, almost as much as he wanted to solve this case.

"You're moving in here with me."

Thirteen

Viv laughed, sure she'd heard him wrong. "Nice try. What do you really want and where is our chaperone?"

Jack rested his hand on the newel post and leveled his stare at her. "Tilly is on vacation for the next several days and you are moving in. It's not up for debate."

Who the hell did he think he was?

"I don't know what plan you have in that overactive mind of yours, but I can't move in here." She pointed down to Katie, who had started crawling around the hardwood floor of the foyer. "We're a team."

"Move her in, too," Jack stated, as if things were that simple.

Viv shook her head and crossed her arms. "What has gotten into you? I turn down your oh-so-romantic proposal of sleeping with you at your beck and call, so now you're trying to overcompensate by having us live together?"

"Damn it, no." He blew out a breath and rubbed his

hand over the back of his neck. "I think you'd be safer here. If Braden were to piece things together or get a hint that we're working together... It's just too risky. You've already heard suspicious noises at your apartment. Next time I may be too late to help."

Viv nodded, fully in agreement about the safety issues. "I can work from home for you, so why jump to the conclusion that I'd be safer here?"

"First of all, the security in your building is ridiculous."

Viv rolled her eyes and crossed to the entryway to the formal living room. Katie was off exploring and Viv knew from experience that she needed to keep her eyes on the active child.

"You have to have a code to enter my building. I'm perfectly safe. I'm sure a neighbor was moving furniture or something and I just overreacted."

When Katie started crawling toward the stone fireplace, Viv intervened. The last thing she needed was the baby climbing up onto the hearth and falling. As if sensing the end to her fun, Katie turned and speed-crawled toward the low coffee table. Thankfully, there was just a variety of classic novels on display and nothing breakable.

When Viv turned toward the wide, arched doorway, Jack met her gaze. Leaning against the frame, he had his arms crossed and that look on his face that said he wasn't in the mood to argue. *Welcome to the club.* She wasn't too keen on having been summoned here to have this insane conversation.

"If there was nothing else, we'll head back home. I've never been a fan of driving in this crazy weather."

Didn't matter that she'd lived here for years, she still

didn't like navigating the narrow Boston streets when they were snow covered.

"We need to talk, so if you want to go home tonight, I can drive you, or I can take you home in the morning."

Viv glanced at Katie as she pulled herself up with the help of the coffee table. Maybe Viv could lower her blood pressure if she counted backward from one hundred. She doubted it, and she didn't have the time. Jack seemed to be under the impression that she would just do anything he commanded.

"You should know me well enough to understand I don't do demands." Viv circled the table and took a seat on the leather sofa. The thing looked like nobody had ever sat there, which was probably true, considering Jack wasn't the most social of butterflies. "I'm safe where I am, but I will agree to not go into your office until this is all over. That's the compromise."

Jack pushed off the door frame and stalked toward her, his eyes never wavering. When he stood only inches from her, Viv smiled.

"Intimidation may work on your adversaries, but I'm not afraid of you."

Turned on, reliving every moment of their night together in vivid detail, but not afraid.

"I won't let you get hurt. And if Braden figures all of this out…"

Jack's growl sent shivers through her. Knowing what she did about his past, about the crippling loss he'd suffered, was the only reason she wasn't grabbing Katie and leaving. He was scared…for her. How could she be angry about that?

Still, she wouldn't be bullied into staying here. For her own sanity, she couldn't. She was half in love with him, and being under the same roof, faux playing house, was not an option.

"I'm not going to get hurt," she informed him. "Actually, I was offered a full-time position at O'Shea's."

"When was this?"

"Today." Viv peered over her shoulder just in time to see Katie heading back to the fireplace. "Braden came in and talked to me after the Feds left."

Katie protested when Viv picked her up. Jack's house was definitely a bachelor pad. Yet another reason they wouldn't be staying here.

"And what did you tell him?"

Viv pulled off her bangle and handed it to Katie. Promptly, the gold bracelet went into the infant's mouth, but at least she wouldn't choke on it. Jewelry, the new teething ring for on-the-go mommies.

"I said I'd think about it and get back to him."

Exhaustion set in and Viv went back to the unused sofa and sank down. She slid her shoes off, not because she was staying, but because there was only so long she could be "on." She'd reached her limit for the day.

"I explained that I needed to think about what was best for Katie, but I knew I needed to talk to you, as well."

Jack came to sit next to her. Resting his elbows on his knees, he leaned forward and stared across the room. "I don't like this," he murmured.

Confused, Viv shifted in her seat, tucking Katie into the crook of her arm. "I thought you'd jump on board. Having me there every day would give us the leverage we need."

"I think they know something."

Viv shook her head. "I don't agree."

Jack's dark brows rose. "And why is that? Because you've become so chummy with them?"

The hurt in his tone made her feel guilty. She certainly had plenty to feel guilty about, but not because she'd gotten to know the notorious family on a personal level. She wanted justice for whoever killed Katie's parents, but didn't happen to think it was her fake employer.

"I don't want to argue with you."

Viv started to rise when Jack placed his hand on her knee.

"Stay."

The simple command had her stilling beneath his touch. Jack had a way of looking at her that made her want to obey his every word, and that irritated her. She couldn't let herself get swept into his world. He didn't want her there on a personal level and she had a damning secret that would blow everything out of the water.

Inevitably, the situation would come to a head, and she knew for a fact they'd both be hurt in the end. "I'll take the full-time position," she told him. "It's the smart move. I can work from home in the evenings for you, plus I'll be alone some if I'm a regular employee there. This will bring us closer to solving the case, I know it."

Jack blew out a sigh and shook his head. "I don't like it, Viv. If you find something incriminating, you can't take it. They may not suspect you yet, but this is a test. If anything at all happens, you'll be to blame."

Katie wiggled down once again, taking Viv's bangle with her. "I'm aware of that. I won't do anything to raise a red flag."

Viv knew where all the security cameras were, knew nearly all the passwords to various accounts and she'd be the contact people would speak to if she was the only one there.

The irony in all this? She'd been completely innocent in her actions when she'd stumbled upon Patrick's journal. When she actually tried to snoop, she'd discovered very little. She'd copied those files in the hopes something would be in them, but no such luck.

Which only went to confirm her own suspicions about the O'Sheas being exactly who they claimed to be.

"I want to know your every move, every contact, even what you eat for lunch."

Viv laughed. "Don't you think that's a bit much?"

He leveled his gaze at her. "Where your safety is concerned? It's not enough."

Shivers slid through her at his throaty tone. That whole dominating, protective trait was the sexiest part about him…and he had a whole lot of sexy going on. There was no way she could be this close, inhaling his masculine scent, and not recall exactly how he felt with his weight pressed against her. The way his hands had traveled over her body was a memory she'd carry forever. Even though he hadn't stayed in her bed, their intimacy was one of the best moments of her life.

She needed to leave. Unless they were strictly discussing business, she needed to keep her distance, because she only wanted him more, and she had no right to.

Every part of her wanted to tell him about that journal, but trumping her need to be truthful was the guilt she felt about being the one to hurt him. And knowing who his father was would destroy him. His passion for justice would come second to the cold, hard truth of his paternity.

Jack jumped up from the sofa and sprinted across the room. Viv came to her feet in time to see him grab Katie before she could climb onto the stone hearth.

Great. She'd been fantasizing about her boss and totally ignored Katie's safety. If that wasn't a sign she needed to get her priorities straight, she didn't know what was.

"Nice try, speedy." Jack scooped Katie up and did some mock airplane moves around the room. Frozen in place, Viv could only take in the sight. He would've been a great father. His protective side was obvious, but this playful side was something she hadn't seen. Jack would've put his family first, above all else. He might be a big shot in the industry and moving into global territory of security and investigating, but the smile on his face right now told her everything she needed to know.

The man wanted a family. He didn't want to be as closed off and hard as he came across. She'd witnessed his caring nature time and time again. And watching him right now had Viv's heart tumbling in her chest. Jack would be the perfect husband, father. He'd be the fiercest protector and greatest provider.

There was no denying the fact, now that she'd fallen face-first in love with Jack Carson. She'd tried to dodge her deeper emotions, hoping she was just physically infatuated. But no. She admired everything about him, and at this point, being with him would never be an option.

Tears pricked her eyes. Blinking them away didn't help as they slid down her cheeks. She swiped at the dampness with the back of her hand and pushed her hair behind her shoulders.

As Jack spun around, he zeroed in on her and stilled. Pulling Katie close to his chest, he strode over to Viv.

"She's fine," he assured her.

Viv nodded, emotions too thick in her throat to form words.

"What is it?" he pressed, patting Katie's back.

His large hand covered Katie's entire pink floral jumper. Such a strong man who'd had so much taken from him, and Viv was only adding to his heartache… only he had no idea.

Another round of tears hit and she didn't even try to hide them. She needed to tell him the truth. Viv loved him and he deserved to know. In the face of her feelings, this case was nothing.

Jack's free arm wrapped around her shoulders as he pulled her to his side. Viv instantly rested her head on his shoulder, even though she had no right to. Seeking comfort from the man she was lying to was hypocritical, at best.

"Jack, I—"

Katie reached out and fisted a handful of Viv's hair.

"No, no." Jack twisted his body, pulling Viv slightly to the side. "She's a grabber. Apparently, everything goes into her mouth."

Viv squeezed her eyes shut. The words weren't coming. She'd just fully confessed to herself that she loved him, and here she was, ready to tell him a secret that would destroy him. Why did life have to be so complicated?

"What were you saying?" he asked.

"I'm sorry," Viv sniffed in an attempt to compose herself. "I guess I'm just tired from work and trying to figure out what to do for Katie's party."

"I'll help plan the party. Tell me what to do."

Viv laughed, the room blurring before her from the moisture in her eyes. "You plan first-birthday parties often?"

Jack glanced down at her, his crooked smile melting her heart. "Never, but how hard can it be? She's one. She has no expectations yet."

"I know." Viv moved from his hold, because it was so easy to lean on him, to draw from his power and strength. "I just want her to have the best."

"She will. I'll make sure of it." Jack glanced at Katie, who was toying with the tiny button holding down the collar of his dress shirt. "Right, speedy? You'll have the biggest cake and a roomful of presents—"

"Let's not get carried away," Viv interrupted. "My apartment isn't that big."

She smoothed her silk blouse back in place and dabbed beneath her eyes, sure her mascara had run against her splotchy skin. If there was ever an Ugly Crier award, she'd win hands down.

Of course, if she weren't waging such an epic internal battle, then there wouldn't be an issue.

"Stay here tonight," Jack told her, looking back her way. "You're exhausted."

Viv shook her head. "I'm fine. Besides, there's only a few diapers left in my bag and Katie doesn't have the stuffed animal she hugs when she falls asleep."

The intensity of his gaze warmed her. The man inside who had loved and lost was still there. Would he ever make a full appearance? Would he ever let down that guard again and open himself up to a relationship?

She hurt for him. She hurt for the life he'd been through and the truth he'd yet to discover. She loved this man, wanted more than anything to be with him, but she couldn't form the words.

"Don't look at me like that, Viv."

"I see the truth," she whispered. "I know you want more and you just won't let yourself feel."

His jaw clenched. "I can't afford to feel. Not anymore."

"Then I'll be living in my own apartment and working from there." Viv reached for Katie, who protested and reached back for Jack. "We're going home, sweetie."

Turning from Jack and those mesmerizing eyes, Viv made her way to the foyer. He fell in step behind her, but she ignored him as she busied herself getting her and Katie's coats on.

"I want to know when you're home."

Viv picked Katie up, securing her on her hip. "You don't have that luxury, considering I'm only your assistant."

She circled around him and jerked the door open. "I'll see you in the office—actually, I won't, because I'll be working from home—"

Jack's hand flattened on the door, slamming it shut and closing out the cold air. She whirled around, but before she could say a word, he kissed her hard and fast before he released her.

"You're more than my assistant, so quit throwing that in my face," he commanded. "You will tell me when you reach home because I care. Damn it, Viv. I care too much and that's the problem."

When he said things like that he made it damn near impossible to stay angry.

Reaching behind her, she turned the knob. "It's only a problem for one of us."

Fourteen

Four days had passed without any real contact from Viv. Without hearing her laugh, her soft tone of voice. Without seeing those expressive eyes as she watched him when she thought he wasn't looking.

Four. Days.

Evidently, Viv was holding her ground and not having anything to do with him if it didn't involve work. She'd been only emailing or texting. He hadn't even heard her voice over the phone. Fine. He could handle this switch.

But he didn't like it. He hated every moment that had passed without her. Damn it, he missed her.

He'd noticed a void by the end of day one. A hole in his life that only Viv filled. When had she become so important, so permanent in his life, that he was miserable without her?

The office was boring as hell and it smelled…not like her jasmine scent. Her cheery yellow-and-white office mocked him every time he passed by. He finally closed the door on the second day.

But having her work from home was the smart move to make. Wasn't it? He wanted her safe, out of harm's way as much as was possible with this messed-up case.

Now, after four days of not seeing her face, Jack stood at her apartment door with an insane amount of shopping bags—he'd left the boxes in his car. Katie's birthday was today and Viv had texted him that she was doing a cake and maybe taking her sledding in the park. There was no way in hell Jack was going to ignore that invitation.

Because not only had he missed Viv, he'd missed Katie. He wasn't quite sure when he'd become attached to the innocent girl, but he couldn't wait to wish her a happy birthday.

As he gripped the bags, he wondered if he'd done too much. What was the protocol for buying presents when a child was in temporary housing after being orphaned? In Jack's opinion, there was no maximum amount...as he'd just proved with his no-limit credit card.

The neighbor's door opened and Jack groaned inwardly, pasting a smile on his face as he turned to see Martha poke her head out.

"Oh, nice to see you again," she said with a wide smile. Her eyes darted to the bags in his hands. "Are those for Katie? That is one spoiled little girl."

He wasn't about to mention the dollhouse or the motorized convertible toddler car he'd left in his SUV.

"You only turn one once, right?"

Viv's door opened, saving him from further conversation with the nosy babysitter.

"Jack. Come on in." Viv peeked out the door and

waved to Martha. "Thanks again for the stuffed elephant. She loves it. I'll bring you some cake in a bit."

Her neighbor winked. "Take your time."

Ushering Viv back in, Jack threw Martha a nod and followed her. Once they were inside, Viv closed the door with a giggle.

When she laughed her beauty was like nothing he'd ever seen. She was absolutely breathtaking. With her hair down around her shoulders, a simple cream sweater hugging her every curve, Viv was the quintessential girl next door, but she was as complex as any woman he'd ever known.

And he wanted her. The attempt to get her to move in with him was legit; he was worried about her safety. But he wanted her under his roof where he could keep his eyes—and his hands—on her.

Damn it. He shouldn't want this. Yet there was no way he could stop the ache, the need.

"I've never seen anyone scare you." She continued laughing. "Yet you're afraid of my elderly neighbor."

Jack didn't reply. There was no denying the truth. That woman terrified him.

He glanced around the open apartment. A bundle of pink balloons lay on the small dinette table, while white and pink streamers were twisted around every stationary object. Two cakes sat on the kitchen counter, a small one with a large purple *1* in the middle and a larger one that was pink with white-and-purple polka dots.

"You've been busy," he commented, setting the bags down.

Her eyes darted to the load he'd carried in. "I hope all of that is not for Katie."

"I actually have more in the car," he told her, feeling like a fool when her eyes widened. Perhaps he had gone too far, but whatever. He wasn't sorry and he still believed Katie deserved everything and more. "I had a problem choosing just one item."

"Jack." Viv closed her eyes and sighed before meeting his gaze again. "Go get the rest."

Stunned, Jack tilted his head, narrowing his eyes at her. "You're not angry?"

"Does it matter?" she laughed.

"Not really. Once I got to the store and the clerk started showing me all the new things that had arrived, I just kept adding to my pile. Honestly, if I'd had more room in my car, I would've bought more."

Viv's hand went to her forehead and she began rubbing her temples. "I don't know why I'm surprised, but…okay. Just go get the stuff and I'll get Katie into her birthday outfit."

Jack darted out the door and made quick trips, grateful not to get caught by Martha again. He was nearly out of breath by the time he'd carried everything into Viv's apartment. Obviously, he needed to up his workout routine. He'd been a little preoccupied lately to get in all the miles and lifting he was used to.

As he closed the door the final time, he realized his purchases had pretty much overtaken her apartment. Wrapped boxes in various colors, with thick bows, littered the living area; the bags he'd brought in first circled the dining table. Between all the variegated shades of pink, there was no denying this was a little girl's birthday party.

Katie came crawling out of the bedroom wearing a polka-dot top with some ruffles around the hem. She seemed to match the theme of the newly decorated apartment. He may have gone overboard monetarily, but Viv had seriously thought this out and wanted something special for the little girl.

Viv stood over Katie, reached down and took her hands. Suddenly, Katie was on her feet, wobbling toward Jack.

His heart swelled. How could he be so excited to see her learning to walk? He wasn't invested in her... was he?

No. Absolutely not. She wasn't staying with Viv. One day, probably soon, Katie would move on to the family that would give her a forever home.

Still, he couldn't help but smile. He wasn't completely detached from emotions.

"When did she start this?" he asked.

Before he realized his actions, Jack found himself squatting down and reaching for Katie. That wide, two-toothed smile tugged at strings he thought had been severed years ago. This sweet child didn't have a care in the world. How could he not smile back? How could he even think of anything going on in the outside world when she was teetering toward him, those bright blue eyes locked on his?

"She started a week or so ago, but she's getting stronger."

Viv let one of Katie's hands go and Jack took hold. Together they walked toward the dining area. The image of a family hit him hard and he attempted to tamp it down, but damn it, this was everything he'd wanted. A woman like Viv was exactly what he'd be looking for if he wanted a family. She was perfect in the way she cared for Katie, the way she was sexy and sweet, the way her cheeks flushed when he caught her looking at him. She'd called him first when she'd been scared, so she trusted him to protect her. At one time that's all it would've taken for him to get her and keep her in his bed, his life.

But that man was gone. His dreams had been murdered. There would never be a future with Viv. His sexy assistant would have to remain just that. And working with her day in and day out was wearing on him.

Somewhere along the way, though, his wants had changed, and they looked too much like everything Viv was offering.

Was it even possible to have that life he'd once wanted? After ten years of grieving, of burying himself in work and building his empire, could he actually put a personal life back in place?

Katie let out a squeal. "Up, up, up."

Jack didn't hesitate and didn't even question who Katie was requesting pick her up. He merely reached down and swung her into his arms. The weight of her little body, the slender arm that rested behind his neck... There was something so special, so perfect about her.

And maybe he could slowly ease back into the idea of having his own family one day. He knew his wife would've wanted him to move on.

"I've never done this before," Viv stated. "Should we just let her dive in to her cake first?"

Jack laughed. "I don't think there's a rule here."

Pulling out one of the chairs, he took a seat and situated Katie on his lap. "Bring her cake over and let's see what she does."

Viv's eyes widened. "She's going to get you filthy. Put her in her high chair."

Jack shrugged. "We'll be fine. I have other dress shirts."

He maneuvered his arms around Katie so he could fold up his sleeves while Viv went to get the cake. She placed one white candle in the top and set the confection in front of Katie.

"Hold her arms back while I light this."

Viv pulled out a lighter and lit the candle. With a smile, she pulled her cell from the pocket of her jeans and held it up. "Should we sing?" she asked.

"Sure."

Jack started "Happy Birthday" and didn't feel silly at all, sitting in a sea of pink. If anything, he felt...hopeful. Damn it. He deserved to have this. He *wanted* to have this.

While Viv sang and snapped pictures with her phone, Jack motioned for Katie to blow out the flame. Of course she had no clue what was going on. Jack met Viv's eyes, the smile on her face making something inside his heart clench. Before he could assess the emotion, she leaned toward the candle. Together, they blew it out.

Jack reached out and slid his finger along the icing. He showed the glob to Katie, then took one of her hands and guided it toward the cake.

And that was all he needed to do. She dived in to the white cake and colorful icing with both hands, bringing fistfuls of the clumpy mess to her mouth. She rubbed her hair, rubbed his pants, turned and smeared some across his lips.

Viv laughed, still snapping pictures.

Jack licked his lips. "This is really good. You made this?"

"I did. I'm not much of a baker, but I figured I could handle a simple cake recipe."

Viv set her phone down and went to get napkins—pink-and-white polka-dot ones, of course.

"About the other day—"

She shook her head, cutting him off. "I don't want to discuss it. Forget about it."

Surprised at her flippant response, Jack eased the cake closer to Katie before meeting Viv's intense stare. "Isn't that supposed to be my line? I wanted to forget everything, but I can't."

"For now, let's focus on Katie." She smiled, warming him in places he thought would always be cold, empty. "And discuss where you think I can possibly keep all the toys you bought."

He didn't want to discuss toys. He wanted to discuss how he'd ached for her since he'd last seen her. He wanted to discuss how he'd handled the situation poorly.

But mostly he wanted to discuss how they could erase this sexual tension between them, which was more prominent than ever. And he had a feeling there was only one way.

Fifteen

Jack discarded his dress shirt straight into the trash. It wasn't even worth having Tilly take it to the cleaners at this point. The icing appeared to be permanently embedded, which was just fine. He honestly didn't recall when he'd had a better time…at least not in the past ten years.

His dress pants weren't faring much better, but he couldn't exactly walk around in his black boxer briefs and light gray T-shirt. He'd scrubbed out as much of the pink icing as he could, but only managed to grind it in more. Tilly would scold him, but whatever. His tailor in Italy wouldn't mind making a new suit.

Viv had taken a sugar-loaded one-year-old back to the bath. Poor Katie could barely keep her eyes open, but her ringlets had been dripping icing and she needed a good scrubbing.

While he was alone, Jack attempted to tidy up, but he was wondering if he should just buy Viv a new condo. It would take days to get her tiny apartment looking like it once did. Granted, with all the purchases he'd made, the living area would look like the toy department at Saks as long as Katie lived here.

Unwelcome emotions suddenly clogged his throat. He'd gotten attached to the innocent child, when he'd told himself he wouldn't. But only a heartless person could look in that sweet baby's face and not feel a connection. She demanded affection and damn if he didn't want to give her everything. Toys were one thing, but he wanted her to have the perfect family. That would mean leaving...which would destroy Viv. Hell, he was beginning to think it might destroy him, too.

He'd give Viv the world and her every desire if he were in a better place. She deserved to have everything handed to her. More than anything, he wanted to be that man who could do that. But he couldn't risk the pain to his already battered heart.

Attempting to focus on things he could actually control, Jack took a trash bag and started gathering up the wrapping paper and empty boxes. Once that was done, he piled the toys on one side of the living room. When he turned back to the dining area and kitchen, he groaned inwardly. There was no way that was going to come clean without something akin to a pressure washer.

When Viv stepped into the living area, she glanced around and let out a laugh. "We survived."

Jack took in her disheveled hair, ends damp from the bath and a glob of icing dangling on one side. She'd stripped off her sweater and now wore a simple white tank that hugged her breasts and dipped in at her waist. As messy as her appearance was, Jack wanted his hands on her. Now that he knew the way her silken skin felt beneath his palms, his need for her was all-consuming.

But after this family moment they'd just shared, seducing her wouldn't be the wisest decision. Everything from this day was temporary: Katie, Viv, Jack, the party, the appearance of domestic bliss.

"Why don't you go shower and I'll figure something out in the kitchen."

Shaking her head, Viv crossed to the chaos on the table. "I'll clean this up. You didn't come over to get assaulted by a birthday cake. You can head home."

She threw him a glance over her shoulder. "Where's your shirt?"

"Trash."

Her eyes widened. "I can wash it for you. There's no need to just throw away a good shirt."

He shrugged. "I have more at home."

Viv rolled her eyes and focused on gathering everything inside the plastic tablecloth she'd laid out. "I'm not going to offer to wash your pants."

Jack couldn't hold back the smile. "If you want me to take them off, just ask."

Flirting was dangerous, but he could control himself. He'd help her clean up and then be on his way. It was getting late, but where else did he have to be? Nobody was at home, and for the first time in years, he didn't want to go back to that empty place where his own breathing echoed in the halls.

"Keep your pants on and help clean if you insist on staying," she said with a laugh. "Just grab a garbage bag and hold it open."

Jack pulled another bag from the roll beneath her sink and shook it out, holding it in front of her. When she turned with the bundled tablecloth and pieces of mashed cake, she tripped, sending the whole gooey mess onto his chest.

Her eyes immediately went to his. "I'm so sorry," she gasped.

Jack dropped the sack on the hardwood floor, scooped up a hefty amount of icing with his hand and flung it. The glob landed just at the scoop of her tank, disappearing into her cleavage.

Her eyes narrowed, but the glimmer of mischief there warned him this war had just begun. He quickly picked up the discarded bag and held it out as a shield, but not before she scooped up another chunk of hot-pink icing and smashed it into the side of his head.

As he reached down for more discarded cake, Viv ran toward the living area, her hands stretched out in front of her. "Okay. Truce."

The wide smile, the brightness in her eyes… Even smeared with cake—especially smeared with cake—she looked sexy as hell.

"I don't think so," he stated, stalking toward her. "You got me twice. I owe you one."

"Jack, it's in my shirt," she argued, taking another step back until she hit the side of the sofa. "We're even. I didn't intend the first attack—I tripped."

He jerked one hand out to grab her arm, pulling her against him, then smeared the icing over her chest with the other. Slowly, he stroked that exposed skin just above her tank, keeping his eyes locked on hers. Viv shuddered beneath his touch.

"You're not…playing fair," she murmured.

Jack snaked his arm around her waist. Trailing his fingers up to her mouth, he spread the last of the icing across her lips.

"I'm not playing at all, Viv."

Tipping his head down, Jack held her close as he slid the tip of his tongue over the icing just below her collarbone. Her breath hitched, so he did it again.

"Jack."

The way she whispered his name set off a fire inside him he didn't know existed. Gripping her hips, Jack aligned her body perfectly with his.

"You drive me crazy," he muttered against her lips. "I tried to ignore you, ignore this. Damn it, Viv, I want you."

Her fingers threaded through his hair, urging him closer, and it was all he could do to not rip her clothes off and take her to the floor.

"Then have me."

She covered his lips with hers, demanding he turn his words into actions. No problem. He slid his hand inside the back of her tank, palming her bare skin. Her body arched against his as she tore her mouth away and started licking the icing off his jawline, his neck. His body was strung so tight, but he didn't want just a quickie.

"I want more than just your bed tonight," he told her.

Viv lifted her head and smiled. "Then maybe we should start with a shower, where I can thoroughly clean you."

Every part of Jack's body tightened as he lifted her off her feet and headed toward the hallway. Viv wrapped her legs around his waist.

"Go to the bathroom in my bedroom," she whispered in his ear. "My shower is huge."

Anticipation gnawed at him as he turned the corner to her room. The second he set her on her feet, he grabbed the hem of her tank and yanked it over her head. Icing and cake crumbs covered her lacy white bra. Jack wasted no time in bending down to lick every last bit, until she gripped his shoulders and trembled beneath him.

Reaching behind her, he flicked the closure of her bra until it sprang free. She flung it aside.

Jack fisted his T-shirt and slid it over his head, sending it to the floor. Her eyes raked his chest before she reached for his pants. Jack glanced down, watching as she continued to undress him. Those delicate hands shook as she eased the zipper down.

He toed off his shoes and kicked away his pants.

"I want you in that shower now," he growled. "So if you don't want to go in with your pants on, I suggest you take them off."

Her eyes widened as she quickly went to work, and within seconds she was gloriously naked before him. Jack reached for her, seizing her by her waist. He backed her into the bathroom, keeping his eyes on hers.

"I've never had a food fight before," he told her. "I better be thorough with the cleanup."

Viv reached between them, covering him with a gentle stroke of her hand. "I like a man who's thorough."

Mercy, she was going to be the death of him. There was nothing sexier than a woman who took charge and knew what she wanted.

The corner shower had two glass walls and a rain head. Jack opened the door and reached in to turn the water on, testing the temperature before stepping in and pulling her with him. He positioned her directly beneath the spray, smoothing her hair away from her face.

Droplets dotted her skin. Jack's hands roamed up and down her sides, needing to feel every bit of her.

"Tell me what you want," she murmured.

He spun her around until her back hit the tiled wall. "Every inch of you."

Sliding his hand between her legs, he stroked her. Viv's head tipped back, her eyes lowered. Every time he touched her, she shook with need—a need he completely understood.

Her hips pumped against his hand and Jack couldn't take his eyes off her. There was nothing more erotic than a woman about to come undone at his touch...*this* woman. She was different than any other, an epiphany he'd come to so recently, he was still reeling from the shock to his system.

Viv panted as she turned her head to the side, squeezing her eyes shut. Water trickled over her flushed skin, catching on her lips a second before she slid her tongue out to wipe it away.

The moment her body tightened, Jack captured those lips. He hadn't been kidding when he'd said he wanted every single inch of her. He swallowed her groan as she gripped his biceps. Having her cling to him was everything right now.

When she finally stilled and pulled away, she blinked against the water and met his gaze. When she bit that swollen bottom lip, Jack removed his hand and reached up to frame her face.

"Whatever you're thinking, leave it." He kissed her fast, hard. "It's just us here. Nothing else matters."

Wasn't that what she'd been trying to get him to see? She'd been urging him to live again, to find happiness again. Part of him, a part he'd just revived, desperately wanted to risk his sanity for that happiness. He wanted to know what taking a chance on a relationship would do.

Tears filled her eyes. "I need to—"

He nipped at her lips. "I need *you*. Nothing else right now."

Her brows drew in as she studied him. Her hesitation had worry spearing deep inside him. "Are you having second thoughts?" he asked.

"No." She shook her head and reached up to grip his wrists. "No. I'm just…nothing. I want this, I want you. Are you sure? Because the way you left the other day…"

"Right now, right here, this is all that matters." He couldn't express his feelings, was still struggling to come to grips with them himself. "I need you, Viv."

Admitting that was a leap for him. He never needed anyone, ever. But Viv was his. She had been for a while and he was finally realizing just how much he ached for her…and not just physically.

Her arms circled his neck and her ankle locked behind his knee. "Then take me."

Jack lifted her against the wall, pinning her in place with his body. She wrapped her legs around his waist and began to rock her hips against his.

Staring at him from beneath thick, dark lashes dotted with water, she whispered, "Make me yours again."

How could he deny the lady?

Jack gripped her hips and joined their bodies. With no barrier between them, he stilled, taking just a second to bask in everything Vivianna. She was utterly perfect and she was completely his.

With an arch of her back and a moan, Viv urged him to move. She closed her eyes and bit down on her lip as he complied, but he was having no part of that. If she was going to be his, then she was going to damn well know it.

"Look at me," he commanded.

Her dark eyes locked on to his. Jack kept one hand firmly on her hip and gripped her jaw with the other before crushing his mouth onto hers. He craved more.

She was like a drug and he couldn't get enough. Would he ever?

Her knees dug into his waist as Viv pressed even closer. The warm spray beat all around them and Jack knew he'd never take another shower without imagining her thrusting her body against his with total abandon.

Viv's body quickened and she gripped his shoulders. He eased back, needing to see her come undone again.

She held his gaze as her body tightened around him, thrusting him into his own release. He didn't look away, couldn't if he wanted to. Viv's expressive eyes most likely mirrored his own. So many unspoken emotions…

Jack clenched his teeth, fighting the urge to say something. Any confessions stemming from feelings during sex were not smart. Later, when they were lying in bed, he'd say what he needed to, what she deserved to hear.

When her body went lax, Jack rested his forehead against hers as he came down from his own release.

"Jack—"

He kissed her. Whatever she was about to say would have to wait. Right now, he was reeling from the fact he was falling for a woman, the first in over a decade. And he had no idea how the hell that would fit into the life he'd created…a life he'd intended to live alone.

Sixteen

He'd wrapped her in a thick bath towel and carefully laid her in bed before climbing in beside her—as if this was part of their daily routine.

Viv blinked back the tears, thankful for the darkness. His feelings for her had changed. Somewhere along the way, he'd started falling for her. She'd seen it in his eyes, tasted it on his lips and felt it with every single touch.

There was so much he didn't know, so much he deserved to know. She had to stop being such a coward and just tell him, reveal the most damning secret. But the words wouldn't come. Viv lay in the crook of his arm, her hand resting directly over his heart. "I can't have children," she whispered into the darkness.

As if that was the only secret she'd been keeping from him. Nerves spiraled through her as the inevitable conversation hung in the air. But this was at least one truth she didn't mind sharing. The reality of never having her own children had caused an open wound so deep inside her, she hadn't revealed it to anyone. She wanted to with Jack. She wanted to share everything… but the lie that she'd held on to for weeks would likely be the hurdle they could never jump together.

"Have you tried?" he asked. He stroked her shoulder with his thumb, sending a shiver through her.

Viv pulled in a shaky breath. "I'm infertile. I was sick when I was younger. The choice was never mine."

He squeezed her tighter against his side, turning to kiss her forehead. "That's why you foster."

Wrapping her arm around his waist, Viv nodded. "I don't have to give up my yearning for children, and I can help many. Fostering is the best fit for me. I'm single, so it would be more difficult to raise a child on my own."

As she explained her reasoning, the heaviest weight she'd ever known crushed her chest.

"You're an amazing woman, Viv."

She didn't want his praise, and she sure as hell didn't deserve it.

"I'm actually thinking of adopting Katie. I was asked and I…I think I'm going to move ahead with the process."

The idea both thrilled and terrified her. She was so excited to be a mother, and sweet Katie was an angel. But could she do it on her own? At least with fostering she had gaps between children, could decide when she was ready to open her home again. She could keep her heart from getting involved—though with Katie she was already a goner. But adoption was permanent and Viv wanted to make sure Katie was getting the best life possible. Would one parent be enough?

Jack shifted to lie on his side, facing her. "I can't

think of anything better for you or her. She's lucky to have you."

"I want to give her everything," Viv confessed. "I just don't want to make a mistake."

Jack's soft laugh filled the room. "You wouldn't make a mistake. When you come into anyone's life, they're better for it. Katie... Me..."

Viv's heart clenched. "Jack—"

"I need to tell you that you mean more than—" He broke off with a muttered curse before continuing on. "Damn it, I want this, Viv. I want to see where this will go, how we can make this work. I can't promise anything. Hell, this is all still new to me, but I know when I'm not with you—"

"Stop."

She couldn't listen to his declaration. Once he knew everything, every last part that she had to share, then he could decide...and Viv knew in her gut that he wouldn't feel the same. Still, she had to tell him. This wasn't about the case anymore, this was about family. If they were going to have any chance at being a couple, a family with Katie, he needed the truth now.

In the glow from the baby monitor, she found it hard to look at him. But she couldn't wait another minute. The dynamics in their relationship had shifted immensely and as much as she wanted to wait for the right time, she knew in her heart such a moment didn't exist.

It was now or never.

"I—I've learned something about the case," she whispered, tears threatening to clog her throat.

Jack propped his head on his hand and stared down at her. "When? Today?"

"A few weeks ago." She closed her eyes. "I didn't know how to tell you."

"Weeks?" he repeated. "What don't you know how to tell me? Damn it, Viv, I need to know everything. Don't worry about how to break news to me."

Silence settled between them and already the wall separating them was being erected. She'd been building it brick by brick the second she'd opted to keep that journal hidden.

"How the hell could anything you discover be upsetting to me?" he went on. "What could you possibly have learned?"

Viv never wanted to be the one to destroy Jack. His need for justice overrode everything in his life. She knew he had to have all the facts. But even now, on the brink of blowing this case, she couldn't tell him.

She rolled over, flicked on the lamp and headed to her closet. Without a word, she reached up to the top shelf and pulled down the leather journal. She'd read it front to back, twice. She knew the secrets Patrick O'Shea had kept, knew more than just Jack being his son. She'd read about how his children wanted him to go in a more legal direction, but he'd been hanging on to contacts he couldn't cut ties with.

Turning back around, she met Jack's gaze. Those green eyes pierced her from across the room. He glanced at the book she held.

She'd never been more vulnerable in her entire life. Viv stood before Jack wearing absolutely nothing…except the truth clutched in her hands. Completely bared to him, Viv willed herself to push through this, to do the right thing.

With her arm extended, she walked to his side of the bed and handed it to him. Jack kept his eyes on her as he took the journal.

Finally, he shifted his focus to the leather-bound

book in his lap. He opened the cover, immediately seeing Patrick O'Shea's name.

Jack jerked his attention back to her. "You've had this for how long?"

Viv swallowed against the guilt, the remorse. There was no going back now. "Too long," she whispered.

Unable to look at his face, coward that she was, Viv grabbed her robe from atop the comforter and jerked it on before heading to the antique trunk at the end of her bed. She took a seat, facing away from Jack. Twisting her hands in her lap, she imagined each word he was reading. She knew where the bombshell was located within the pages; he had a few more to go.

Each time he turned another, Viv cringed.

Jack's audible gasp gutted her. Still, she couldn't face him.

"You read this."

His accusing tone was like a slap. "Yes."

"And you didn't think I deserved to know this bastard was my father?"

Viv came to her feet, tightened the belt on her robe and turned to face him. The pages lay open, Patrick's dark penmanship mocking her.

"Of course you needed to know," she said, knowing she had no right to feel wounded. "I wanted to tell you the second I found it. But I—"

"What?" he demanded as he jerked the sheet aside and came to his feet. He reached for his boxer briefs from the floor and tugged them on. "You got too close with the family and shifted your loyalties?"

Stunned he'd even think that, Viv shook her head. "No. Never. I never shifted my loyalties to them. I may believe in my heart they're innocent, but I am on your side, Jack."

His laugh mocked her. "Really? I'd hate to see if you were my enemy. How the hell do I even know this journal is real? It could've been a plant. Did you ever think of that?"

Viv nodded. "I've thought of this from every perspective. But I wasn't snooping when I found it. The one time I was actually just doing my job, I stumbled upon it."

In a rush, she explained how it was caught in her desk, but the way it was wedged in, she truly didn't believe it had been placed there to trick her.

"Conveniently, it was *your* desk," he replied in that dry, disbelieving tone. "So why now? You waited until we'd grown closer for what? Because you thought it would soften the blow somehow?"

"No," she whispered. "I just…I couldn't keep it from you any longer. I'm falling for you and—"

"Don't say it," he demanded. When he started gathering the rest of his clothes, Viv's heart sank. He wasn't even going to stick around to hear her defense…not that she hadn't seen this coming. "Don't even try to tell me that you love me, or any other feelings you're having. At this point, what you want, what you feel, is irrelevant."

He stepped into his pants, shrugged his T-shirt on, then grabbed the journal. "You know how much this case means to me. You're the only person I've confided every damn thing to. I've confessed my fears to you because I knew you understood from being on the inside."

The disappointment in his tone was worse than the rage. He'd trusted her. He'd placed her on this particular case because he knew she'd always been loyal and honest.

She'd failed him.

"I can't take back what I did," she explained, crossing her arms over her chest. "I was scared when I first found it, worried I was being set up to see what I'd do with it. But as I read on, I figured there was no way the O'Sheas knew you were their half sibling. Braden would've confronted you. So then I tried to find the right time to tell you."

"The second you found it was the time," Jack countered, narrowing his eyes at her. Only moments ago those eyes had held her in place with passion and signs of love. "But you clearly chose the team you're on. And it's not mine."

Katie's cry blared through the monitor. Viv jumped from the unexpected intrusion, then glanced at the screen. Katie turned, grabbed her favorite blanket and quieted down.

Jack sat on the edge of the bed to pull on his socks and shoes. "Everything you've learned, from the journal and otherwise, needs to stay with you until this case is wrapped up. Clearly, you'll need to stay at O'Shea's, because the Feds are counting on you, but I no longer need you to do work for me."

He didn't look at her as he delivered the toneless speech. Cutting her out of his life was that quick, that final. As much as she wished he'd listen to her reasoning, she knew Jack wasn't that man. He saw things as black-and-white, and his once-glossy perception of her had been tainted. Quite possibly, his need for justice had been tarnished, as well. How could he take down the only family he had left?

As much as it hurt to let him walk away angry, she truly had no choice. He needed to think, and she needed to let him go. She loved him, more than she thought possible. But for now, she'd keep things professional—and live with the gaping hole he'd left in her heart.

She hoped in time he'd come around, hoped he'd realize that she loved him and had done everything to protect him.

"Do you want me to stay on with the O'Sheas full-time?" she asked.

Jack's mocking laugh rang out as he rose to his feet. "I'll text you the name and phone number of the contact from the FBI. You can direct all of your questions to him from here on out. I'll have your things from your office sent over."

With the leather journal in hand, he headed toward the bedroom door. He stilled at the threshold and threw a heartbreaking look over his shoulder.

"This isn't how I planned the night to end." His eyes held her in place from across the room. "And to think I nearly let my guard down and told you how I truly felt."

By the time she processed exactly what that veiled statement meant, he was gone.

Viv clutched the V in her robe as she sank to her knees. Tears gathered and fell as she struggled with the reality that Jack had fallen for her. He didn't need to say those exact words; he'd shown her.

Swiping at her eyes, she glanced at the monitor. Sweet Katie slept peacefully now. Viv had done the right thing in finally telling him. It didn't matter what her heart wanted, all that mattered now was that child and giving her the best life.

But that didn't mean Viv would let go of what she'd found with Jack without a fight.

Sometimes seeking comfort is the only way to get through the mourning process. I had no idea a child would come from our intimacy. As much as I want to be part of his life, I respect Catherine Carson's wishes. I came into her life, offering nothing, so the least I can do is stand by her in a silent manner and support her from a distance.

It kills me. Goes against everything I stand for. I take what I want, what's mine. And this little boy with green eyes like my own is mine.

Sending checks isn't the same, but he will want for nothing.

Jack stared at the words, hating every single one of them. At this point he even questioned his loyalty to his own mother. She'd lied to him by remaining silent. She'd never once hinted that his father was the notorious Patrick O'Shea, but here it was, in plain sight.

Easing back in his leather office chair, Jack stared at the open pages, willing them to rewrite history. He didn't want to be the son of such a criminal. He'd done nothing these past ten years but take down jerks like him.

Yet here he sat, at a crossroads, and he had no idea how the hell to move forward. What direction did he take at this point? Did he confess to the Feds that he was too close to the case now? Did he go to Braden, Mac and Laney and tell them…

What? What would he say? "Congratulations, it's a boy"? Somehow that didn't sound right. There was no "right" way to go about this, yet Jack had to make a decision and he needed to make it fast.

He swiped a hand over his face, instantly smelling something floral. Jasmine. The shower he'd taken with Viv had left its mark on him. There was no escaping her.

The idea that she'd had this information for weeks tore him up. He'd lost sleep over the case, had gone to the enemy, had quizzed her over and over. Yet she had remained silent.

He'd slid right into her world, trying like hell to remain closed off, but where Viv was concerned, he hadn't had a choice. Everything about her drew him in, from the way she took in foster children to the way she called him out when he was being difficult.

She had curves that any man would beg to touch, and he'd done so much more. He literally craved her, ached for her. How did he just turn that off?

And sweet Katie had gotten into his heart, too. How could he ignore that emotion? An innocent baby had stolen his heart when he wasn't looking.

But Viv made him smile, made him want… Made him realize there was enough life left in him to do exactly what he'd intended, and that was to have a family of his own.

She'd helped him in a sense, but in the end, she'd destroyed him. If she cared for him the way she claimed, she would have come to him first.

Falling for Viv wasn't what hurt. Knowing she didn't trust him with the truth cut him so deeply, he didn't know if he'd ever recover from the wound.

But there was only one thing he could do at this point. The Feds didn't need to know about Jack's biological connection to the O'Sheas—at least Viv was right in that area. They only wanted Jack's help with proving or disproving the theory that the family had something to do with the Parkers' deaths.

Uncovering the truth about his past, his family, was more important to Jack than any damn case.

For once in his life, something was coming before work.

When he glanced at the antique clock on the corner of his desk, he realized time had literally slipped away from him. It was nearly six in the morning. He'd left

Viv's house so late, then come straight to his home office and bottle of twenty-year-old bourbon. He'd read Patrick's damn journal cover to cover, trying to make sense of it all.

Jack had no doubt this book was legit, and he highly doubted the rest of the O'Sheas—*his siblings*—knew anything about their father's deepest secrets.

Tapping the edge of his desk, he continued to glare at the black ink. He'd wait a bit longer before making the call. A call that could change his entire future.

Jack tipped back the rest of the bourbon in his tumbler. His thoughts drifted to Viv again, and he damned himself for ever letting her into his life.

He cursed himself further for still wanting the hell out of her.

But that was something he'd have to address later... after he met with his newfound brother.

Seventeen

Neutral ground was always his first choice, but for this little meeting, Jack had agreed to go to O'Shea's. Mac was still in town and Jack wanted to meet him and Braden together. He wanted to go through this story only one time, though he knew that wasn't likely.

Jack entered the offices an hour before they officially opened. He'd been up all night and called promptly at seven. Braden had agreed to the emergency meeting, though Jack could tell the tycoon wasn't too thrilled with the demand. Too damn bad. Jack's life had spiraled into a cursed mess in the past twelve hours and he was done getting smacked in the face by fate.

He figured the only way to get them all together was to tell them he had information about their father. Which was the truth.

Clad in a black dress shirt and black pants, Braden stepped out of the back. Jack couldn't stop the punch to the gut as he stared into the man's green eyes. The same shade he saw every morning in the mirror. How had he never noticed the resemblance?

Because there had been no reason to until now.

"This better be good, Carson." Braden motioned for him to follow. "Come on back. Mac is here and Laney will be along shortly."

And where Laney was, Ryker was. Arrogant prick.

Jack clutched the journal in his hand and headed toward the back. He expected to feel a little fear, if he were being honest with himself, but right now all he wanted to do was get this over with. The odds of losing control were in his favor; after all, this meeting was going to be four against one. But he'd gone against odds before. Jack never backed away from a challenge. Besides, he held the journal—of which he'd made copies—and he also had more ties with law enforcement than the O'Sheas could ever hope to have.

Jack stepped through the doorway to the back office and met Mac's angry stare. With a clipped nod in greeting, Jack surveyed the rest of the space. He hadn't been in this part of O'Shea's before. He knew from Viv's description that the mahogany desk in the corner was hers.

Bringing Viv into his thoughts right now would not help him get through this meeting. He needed to focus 100 percent on what was about to happen, because this journal didn't affect just his life—he was getting ready to drop a bomb directly onto the people he'd despised for so long.

Ruining them had to take a backseat to the truth. He wanted them to know exactly what he'd discovered.

And after reading Patrick's words, Jack had a gut feeling he might be trying to bring down the wrong individuals. His father—it still hurt to think of Patrick O'Shea in those terms—had been the one who'd needed to be brought to justice for his past crimes. Braden, Mac and Laney were all guilty by association, but they'd pleaded their innocence in this case all along. Ryker… well, he brooded and threatened, but he'd maintained his story, as well. Perhaps Viv had been right all along. Maybe this family was innocent and were only hypothetically guilty because of their notorious name.

"What couldn't wait?" Braden asked as he took a seat behind the oversize desk in the middle of the room. "It must be something big for you to agree to come here."

The journal felt heavy in his hand. "I've stumbled upon some information."

And he'd thought hard about how to admit where it came from. He might be feeling hurt and betrayed by Viv, but he wasn't about to out her in front of this family. Even he wasn't that big of a jerk.

"There's no easy way to do this," he admitted as he crossed into the room and laid the journal at Braden's fingertips. "This was your father's."

Mac, who'd been silently leaning against the desk, glanced down to the leather book. "How did you get this?" he asked, turning his focus back to Jack.

"That's not important. What's important is what is inside." Jack swallowed, but he kept his features taut. "Halfway in, you'll see a date flagged—June 30."

Braden blew out a sigh, as if he'd rather be anywhere else than talking with Jack barely after sunrise. Well, Jack would rather be anywhere else, as well, but there was no escaping the inevitable.

Keeping his eyes on Braden, Jack propped his hands on his hips and waited. Moments later, the man slid the open pages to his brother.

"Where the hell did you get this?" Braden demanded. "I suppose you believe you're the son?"

Jack nodded. "I know I am. Catherine Carson was my mother. Patrick refers to her often, and my mother never told me who my father was. I know we were taken care of, because when I turned eighteen, I received a lump sum of money. There's no way it came from my mother, who worked in a flower shop."

Mac held the journal in his hand and gestured with it. "So because you find this out of the blue, and the time line adds up, you just assume—"

Jack held out his palms. "I'm not assuming. I'm willing to get a DNA test."

Mac set the journal back on the desk and eyed his brother.

"Sorry I'm late." Laney swept in, Ryker right on her heels. She tugged her coat off as she glanced between Jack, Mac and Braden. "What did I miss?"

"Here." Braden held out the journal, open to the page that changed Jack's life.

Ryker took the book and read with Laney. Her gasp filled the room, but he just grunted out a laugh.

Ryker took Laney's coat and folded it over the back of a leather chair. "Where did you find this?" he asked.

"He won't say," Mac stated.

Jack wasn't about to let the power slip through his fingers. "Where I found it doesn't matter. Is that Patrick's writing?"

Laney nodded. "Yes. How do we know you're the son he's talking about?"

She eased down into the seat and leaned against her coat, her hand covering her swollen abdomen. "All this time Dad knew he had another child out there and didn't say a word," she murmured. "I bet that tore him up inside."

Jack gritted his teeth. He didn't care what it did to the old bastard. The man was a crooked liar. He'd done vile things to innocent people.

"Your eyes," Laney stated, looking back up at Jack.

He nodded. The eyes clearly told the truth. Everyone in this room, save for Ryker, had the same shade of green eyes.

"That doesn't mean a thing," Ryker snarled. "If you're trying to get money—"

Jack laughed. "Don't be absurd. I couldn't care less about your money. I'm here for the truth."

"You're here with a new approach to try to pin a crime on us we didn't commit," Braden stated.

Jack shrugged. "I could use this information to my favor if I wanted. But I'm starting to believe you."

All eyes turned to him. Yeah, the revelation was just as shocking to him as it was to them. He didn't want to admit he was wrong—who did? But he wasn't going to make excuses for his actions. He'd gone on his instincts and past scenarios, and believed he was working the right angle.

"This is all too coincidental." Mac rose to his full height, crossing his arms over his chest. "Suddenly our long-lost brother comes in and wants to help us save the day against the big, bad Feds."

Jack's cell vibrated in his pocket. Nothing was as important as this, so he ignored it. Again, he was putting his personal life ahead of work.

"I didn't say I believe you completely," he retorted. "I'm willing to work together, and if that clears your name, then so be it."

"What exactly do you want from this meeting?"

Braden asked, narrowing his eyes and leaning back in his chair. "You expect us to welcome you to family gatherings or reveal our deepest secrets?"

Jack glanced around the room. Ryker and Mac seemed to be angry, Braden still skeptical, while Laney looked at him as if she wanted to reach out and hug him, but was afraid. So many mixed emotions, so many lies swirling between them, and Jack was trying to set straight as many as he possibly could.

"I don't expect to be trusted, by any means," he stated, glancing back at Braden. "I wouldn't believe me if I were in your shoes. I wanted to present you with what I'd found. The journal is yours to keep. I made copies."

Braden closed the book and tapped his fingers on the leather cover. "I'd still be interested in knowing how this fell into your hands."

The same way everything else lately had fallen into his hands...by chance. Viv had entered his life when he hadn't been looking, just like the journal.

"I have a large reach," he replied. "Same as you. I doubt you give up your informants."

There was no way he'd ever give up Viv's name. No matter what happened between them on a personal level, Jack cared for her, and he'd never want to see her hurt. She'd come to work for him when she'd needed a job, and he'd thrown her into the lion's den. She'd never complained, but had stuck by his side and worked double duty.

And when she'd discovered a journal that uncovered a lie over three decades old, she'd panicked. Jack would be a jerk not to realize that she'd been scared, that she'd been trying to protect him while he finished this case. She knew the amount of time and mental effort he'd put into seeking justice.

And as furious and hurt as he was that she'd kept something so pivotal from him, he'd have to be blind not to see her reasoning.

"You don't have to give up your informant," Braden stated, shifting Jack's focus back to the present. "I know you and Viv have been working together. I've known for some time."

Keeping his cool, refusing to show any sign of affirmation, Jack merely asked, "And what makes you think this?"

Braden shrugged and came to his feet. "She's the likely candidate, but Laney didn't want to believe Viv would turn on us. She's the only reason we kept Viv here."

Jack flashed Laney a glance. The sadness in her eyes proved how much this family had come to care for Viv. Damn it, this was a debacle of epic proportions, because he, too, cared for her. Too much.

"Leave Viv out of this," Jack stated. There was no reason to try to hide the facts or treat them like fools. "She worked for me, but she's no longer in my employment."

"Relax," Mac interjected. "We also kept her here because we have nothing to hide. We know the Feds want to pin the Parkers' tragedy on us. If you want to stop snooping around and actually work together, maybe we can find the guilty parties and clear our name."

Jack tried to process everything happening. First and foremost, Viv's true identity had been discovered long ago and they'd still kept her on. They could've done anything to her, given the rumors surrounding the family. But now that Jack was getting a glimpse inside their lives, inside Patrick's journal, he was starting to see that maybe this family wasn't all death and destruction.

"So you're agreeing to work together?" he asked, taken aback.

"The truth goes both ways," Braden said. "We don't trust easily, but if you want to do this, then we're all-in."

Jack needed Viv, he realized. She had ties to this family that he didn't, and they obviously respected her.

Damn it, that wasn't the only reason he needed her. He missed her, and it had been only hours since he'd seen her, touched her.

But the O'Sheas wanted to work together to clear their name. Jack wanted justice for the Parkers...justice he'd never been able to deliver on behalf of his wife and unborn child.

His family.

And he might have another chance at a family yet. Viv had made a mistake, but she wasn't malicious.

"I'd say with our combined resources, we can solve this case together," Jack agreed. He had to focus on this moment, and deal with his personal life later.

"Get that DNA test," Braden demanded. "I see it, though. I know the truth just by looking at you. What my father wrote may be shocking, but it's the truth. Eyes aside, you've got the O'Shea attitude."

Jack didn't want to have the O'Shea name tacked on to his life. In his line of work, he couldn't afford it. But at the same time, he wanted a family of his own. Only time would tell if this group would be his or not. He wasn't quite ready to cozy up to the idea of holiday dinners or family portraits.

"I'll have it done, but the result stays inside this room." He glanced around at the people who were family by biology...nothing more. "I have a business, a reputation to protect."

Braden smirked. "Can't be associated with the notorious family? I get it. No problem."

Mac glanced at his watch. "I need to pick Jenna up at the airport. She caught an early-morning flight."

Braden nodded. "Go ahead. We'll discuss a game plan and I'll fill you in later."

Once Mac stepped out, Jack and Braden sat down at the desk. He wanted to solve this damn case the FBI had entrusted him with. His priorities had shifted, but he was still keeping his guard up, as he suspected Braden was, too.

"I'm going to go out front and get the store ready to open," Laney stated. "I'll keep this door shut for privacy."

Ryker pulled up a chair beside Braden, his dark eyes narrowing in on Jack. "You need to talk to Viv before we get started?"

Jack shook his head. "No. She has nothing to do with this anymore." But even as he said the words, he knew they weren't true.

"I don't know what's going on between the two of you, but—"

"No, you don't." Jack settled back in his chair as he cut off Braden's words. "Now, let's get to work."

Jack pushed Viv out of his mind so he could concentrate on this all-important meeting.

Too bad he couldn't push her out of his heart.

Eighteen

Martha was all too eager to watch Katie for the evening, but Viv assured her she wouldn't be long. Valentine's Day sucked, and heading to Jack's house was just salt in the wound. But she had things that needed to be said. Once she got all this off her chest, maybe...

No. She wouldn't feel any better. She'd still feel empty inside, but she had to tell him how she felt and had to defend herself. Added to that, she needed to return all these presents.

She'd piled the ridiculous toys he'd bought into her car. Where on earth would she house a tiny sports car, anyway? Katie didn't need such extravagant gifts and Viv was doing her best to cut all ties with Jack. That was what he'd wanted, after all.

He'd made it perfectly clear that she was of no use to him any longer. But she knew he still cared for her. He wouldn't be so hurt if he didn't care. Plus, she'd seen the way he looked at her, felt how perfectly he'd touched her. They shared a bond whether he wanted it or not. Viv just wished that was enough to get them back where they needed to be. She'd give anything to be able to turn back the clock and hand him that journal the second she'd discovered it.

But she'd made the best decision at the time. At least she thought she had. Hindsight and all that.

Viv pulled in a breath as she tugged her coat tighter around her neck. The snow would not let up. This would be a great night for all those lovers to stay indoors.

She cursed Valentine's Day again as she rang the bell at Jack's Beacon Hill home.

In moments, the wide door swung open and Tilly greeted her with a smile. "Honey, come on in. It's freezing out there."

Viv stepped into the foyer, forcing herself not to look around the house for the man she'd dreamed about all night. She needed to drop the toys off and leave. That's all. Now that she was here in his domain, she couldn't talk to him. What would be the point? He was so furious with her. He hadn't spoken to her or reached out to her at all since he'd left her bed.

"I can't stay," Viv informed Tilly. She needed to get out of here. "I have some things in my car that belong to Jack."

Tilly's brows rose. "Oh, well. I'll go get him—"

"No!" Viv didn't mean to shout, but she didn't want to make this evening any more unbearable than necessary. "I mean, I can carry them in."

Tilly tipped her head to the side, reaching out to grab Viv's hands. Her warm touch threatened to break Viv. She was already so close to an emotional breakdown... she just didn't have time for one.

"I don't know what happened with you guys," Tilly

started. "But he's a grouchy bear. I can't get him to eat. He stays in his office and only asks me to bring him more bourbon. I've seen him like this just one other time."

When his wife died. The words hovered in the air as if she'd said them.

Viv swallowed the tears clogging her throat. "It's all my fault," she whispered.

"I'm sure it can be fixed." The elderly woman wrapped her arm around Viv and squeezed. "Go talk to him."

Viv shook her head. "He's angry, and rightfully so. I just think it's best if I drop off all these things and be on my way."

Tilly eased back and patted Viv's hands. "His wife was taken from him too soon. You're the first woman I've ever seen him interested in since that time. Are you sure you want to throw all of that away because you're afraid?"

Viv closed her eyes. Was she willing to risk more humiliation and rejection?

"He's upstairs in his study." Tilly took a step back and gestured toward the grand stairway. "I'll be finishing up in the kitchen before I go. You can bring the toys into the foyer and take off, or you can do what you know in your heart is the right thing. Either way, I'll be leaving shortly."

Tilly headed down the hall to the kitchen.

Viv's chest was heavy as she eyed the steps. She'd never been upstairs, but she wasn't going to let this moment pass her by. She'd say her piece, put the ball in his court, then be gone.

If he truly wanted to sever all ties, then at least she'd know she'd done her part.

Viv gripped the carved newel post and willed her legs to carry her up the steps. Nerves threatened to take over, to force her to turn back around and get out. But Jack was facing one of the most difficult situations of his life and he was justified in his feelings toward her. She couldn't apologize enough, but she wasn't going to miss the chance to say it one last time.

The wide hallway was dark, except for the dim light shining beneath one closed door. Viv pulled in a shaky breath and crossed the distance. She tapped lightly on the door with her knuckles.

"Go away, Tilly. I'm fine."

He didn't sound fine. He sounded…crushed.

Viv didn't knock again, but merely turned the knob and pushed the door open. He was already angry at her. Barging in on his personal space was nothing compared to what she'd done.

"Tilly, I…"

He glanced up from behind his desk, the words dying on his lips as he met her gaze across the room. Viv's heart beat heavily against her chest. She clutched the knob for support as she remained frozen in place.

"I came by to return the toys," she stated. "I, um, well, Tilly said you were up here and…"

The way he sat unmoving, without saying a word, had her nerves spiraling out of control. But she'd come this far and she was going to get this out.

"I know you hate me." She eased forward, one slow step at a time, across the expansive office. "You have every right and I don't blame you. But when I found that journal, I was stunned. My immediate thought was to get it straight to you, but then I realized what that truth would do to you. You think of nothing but justice. When

I learned about your wife and child, I understood how deep your need for justice went. You've been trying to bring the O'Sheas down for so long and I didn't want to be the one to crush you."

Motionless, Jack stared at her. The bottle of bourbon sat on the corner of his desk, and he clutched an empty tumbler in his hand. Was he drunk? Was he even listening?

"I kept it hidden, waiting for the right time, hoping the case would wrap up and I could present it to you. I wanted you to be able to separate work from this bombshell because I knew the case was so important."

She stopped at his desk. Tugging the tie on her coat a little tighter, she wished she had something else to do with her shaky hands. Those green eyes held her in place, pinning her with an unreadable expression.

"But then the timing didn't matter," she went on, biting her bottom lip to prevent the trembling. She attempted to tamp down the tears, but her eyes filled. "I started falling for you. The attraction I'd had for so long turned into something I didn't expect."

Jack came to his feet, setting his glass aside. "Viv—"

"No, let me get this out, then I'll go."

She didn't want him to kick her out, not until she explained herself and apologized the proper way.

"When my feelings got stronger, I cursed the day I found that journal. I didn't want to know that truth, didn't want to carry it around with me, to hold such a burden. I knew it would hurt you no matter when I told you. But I didn't want to be that person, Jack. I didn't want to be the one who had to drop this bomb into your life."

Viv swiped at the tear that slid down her cheek. "I'm sorry I lied. I'm sorry I kept something so vital from you. But at the time, I thought I was doing the right thing by saving you heartache."

Viv took a step back, blinking the moisture from her eyes. "I'm sorry," she whispered. "That's…that's all I wanted to say."

She spun on her heel, more than ready to get out of this room, this house. The ache of seeing him again spread through her and she had no idea how the hell she was going to recover, but she had no choice. She would get through this, in time…she hoped. A little girl was depending on her.

Firm hands gripped her, hauling her back against his chest. "Don't go."

Viv's heart slammed against her chest. "I can't stay, Jack. I've said all I need to say."

He spun her around to face him. The intensity of his gaze had never been so powerful, so raw.

"Well, I haven't said all I need to, and you're going to listen."

She nodded. He deserved to say whatever he wanted, and the hell he was about to throw at her was completely justified.

Jack stepped aside and pointed to the chaise in front of the wall of books. On any other day, she'd marvel at the entire wall of hardbacks, but since she would never be here again, she'd have to just commit the scene to memory.

"Sit down."

Viv shouldn't have been surprised at his aggressive tone, but, well…she was. Without a word, she crossed and took a seat, sliding her fingers along the velvety arm of the chair.

"I've thought about nothing else since I saw that journal," he began, pacing like a caged animal. "My father was a criminal, I've been working to destroy my half siblings, only to find they are legit, and the woman I trusted most lied to my face."

Viv glanced down to the ends of her coat ties. She toyed with a single dangling thread.

"No, you don't get to look away."

She glanced up to find him standing before her. Hands on his hips, he glared down at her.

"You came to me. Now you're going to listen."

She glanced at the bottle on his desk. "How much have you had to drink?" she asked.

Jack snorted. "Not enough to dull the pain, but I'm not drunk."

Viv bit her lips, nerves dancing in her belly, because she had no clue what he was about to tell her. And he was right. She'd come to him, so she would listen.

"Braden and I have come up with a plan and I've gone to the Feds with it. They don't need to know any more than the fact Braden and I are working together. They trust me and they know I'll find the people responsible for this crime."

Viv nodded, glad for that at least. Maybe if he and Braden did this together, Jack would slowly ease into the idea that the O'Sheas weren't monsters.

"That's great," she told him. "I'm happy for you."

He raked a hand over his face and stared up at the ceiling. Only the Tiffany lamp on his desk cast any light in the room. But she saw the pain in his eyes, sensed the frustration rolling off him. She'd hurt him, but he still cared. She felt it.

"I only want what's best for you," she went on. "I know it doesn't seem like that, but I do."

"That's the other thing that has haunted me." He spread his feet wide, crossed his arms and pinned her with that sultry gaze. "I've looked at this from every angle. Mine, yours. I want to push you out of my life for hurting me."

"I understand and I don't blame you." Guilt fueled another round of tears. "I'll just go."

She'd started to stand, when Jack's hands came down on her shoulders and forced her back down.

"You're staying right here." Viv didn't know what to say, especially when Jack squatted down in front of her. "I'm not done talking."

"I get that you're hurting, but we've said everything." She had to get out of here. "Let me unload my car and I'll be out of your life for good."

Jack dropped his head, blew out a breath before looking back up into her eyes. "I don't want you gone, Viv."

Hope slammed into her. "What?"

He reached up and gripped her hands. "I'm upset, yes, but I understand why you did what you did. Hell, I don't know that I'd have done things differently had I been in your position."

Viv blinked, sure she'd heard him wrong.

"When I was torn over what to do about approaching Braden and Mac, I caught a glimpse into what you must have gone through. And that was for people I didn't particularly care about. I know you care about me, so I can only guess how much that tore you up."

Viv pulled her hands from his and stood, causing him to rise, as well. "No. Don't forgive me, Jack. That's not why I'm here. I just—I wanted you to accept my apology. I know we can't go back to where we were. I don't deserve it."

She shoved her hands inside her coat pockets. "I need to get back home."

"Will you just stop?" he demanded, when she started to move past him.

Standing shoulder to shoulder with Jack, she froze, not glancing to her left, where he stood a breath away.

"Damn it, Viv. You love me. Why are you doing this? I'm trying to forgive you. I'm trying to tell you that I'm sorry, too, for thinking the worst. For not listening to your side from the beginning."

Air caught in her lungs as she turned fully toward him. "What?"

"You love me," he said softly, smiling this time. "I know you do or you wouldn't have been so upset about the journal."

She closed her eyes. "You're sorry," she whispered. "I hurt you and you're apologizing. You had every right to—"

He slammed his mouth down onto hers, gripping her wrists at her sides. Jack wasn't gentle, wasn't slow. He consumed her as if he were claiming her all over again. Jack nipped at her lips before easing back to look her in the eyes. "I may not like what you did," he murmured. "But I understand why you did it. And don't bother fighting me or telling me you don't love me, because that won't work at all with my plans."

"What are your plans? To kiss me like you love me, when you know exactly how I feel?"

He laughed, easing her arms behind her back to draw her arched body into his. "Oh, but Viv. I do love you. And that's why I was so hurt."

Viv's heart quickened as she stared up into his eyes. "You what?"

His mouth quirked. "I can admit when I was wrong and I can admit that I love you. I knew I was falling for you, but when I left your apartment, I realized it was love. Someone I didn't care about couldn't get close enough to make it hurt so bad."

Viv closed her eyes. "I never wanted to hurt you. I wanted the exact opposite."

"I know." He nipped at her lips again. "I know you didn't want to hurt me."

Jack pulled back, stared down at her, making her wonder what was going to happen next. Where they would go from here. *He loves me.* The words swirled in her head, her heart. She'd never expected him to return her feelings, never thought he'd forgive her, let alone love her.

"I'm waiting."

Viv narrowed her eyes. "For what?"

He leaned into her, causing her body to arch even further into his. He continued to hold her arms behind her back and Viv ached for his touch, sans clothes.

"For you to tell me you love me. I want the words."

Viv licked her lips, pleased when his eyes watched her mouth. "I love you, Jack. I'm sorry I hurt you. I'm sorry I ever made you doubt my loyalty. But I love you more than I've ever loved anyone in my life."

He started for her mouth again, but Viv turned her head. "Wait."

"What?"

She glanced back. "If you love me, why were you holed up here worrying Tilly to death?"

"I was in a pissy mood about how to approach you," he confessed. "I was coming to your place tomorrow, but I was working through my plan of action to get you back."

Viv raised her brows. "And what was the plan you'd concocted?"

Jack released her hands and immediately went for

the tie on her coat. After he peeled the garment off and sent it to the floor, he tugged at the closure on her jeans.

"My plan was to strip you naked, have my way with you and tie you to my bed until you believed me."

Arousal shot through her. "You can still do all those things, but I'm going to have to text Martha first and tell her I'll be a little later than I thought."

Jack gripped the V of her button-up shirt and jerked, sending buttons flying across the room. "I have a feeling she won't mind."

Viv tipped her head back as Jack feasted on her neck, then made his way down to her chest. She'd text Martha…in a bit.

Epilogue

One year later...

"Happy Birthday to you," the whole crew sang.

"Hard to believe she's two already," Jack stated, as Viv helped Katie blow out the two little purple candles on her three-tiered cake. Maybe he'd gone overboard when he ordered the cake, but he did tell Viv she could handle everything else.

"Time flies once you become a parent." Braden held his own baby, Michael, who was six months old now. "I can't believe all the things this little guy is doing on his own already. He's army crawling across the house. Zara went nuts and baby gates are everywhere."

"They're not everywhere," Zara chimed in, sliding a party hat over Braden's head.

"I don't want a hat," he grumbled. "It has a ballerina on it."

"It's not your party," Zara stated, as she patted the side of his face.

"Who wants cake?" Viv announced. "We have plenty and we'll all be eating it for the next week."

She sent Jack a look and a wink. He'd never thought he'd find love again, but everything was different with Viv. She was perfect for him and had come into his life at exactly the right time.

After he'd discovered he was actually an O'Shea, Jack and Braden had worked around the clock to clear their name. It ended up that some wannabe gang members had botched the robbery and tried to cover their tracks. Once Jack had gotten the proper intel, it took only one stakeout to bring down the criminals.

And after all this time, the O'Sheas were completely legit. Braden hadn't been lying; the family had cut ties with all illegal dealings. Their worldwide auction house was more lucrative than ever. It had taken some time, but Jack and his new siblings were all meshing perfectly together. Jack had wasted no time in marrying Viv and they'd adopted Katie together. They were in the process of adopting another child. He and Viv both wanted a large family and he was more than ready to fill up his large home. Tilly was overjoyed, of course.

As Viv passed out pieces of cake, Katie played with her own layer of purple icing and pink cake.

"More, Mommy." Katie held up her sippy cup with one hand and shoved icing in her mouth with the other.

"I'll get it," Jack said, taking the sticky cup. "You're a messy monster."

Katie smiled at him, her purple teeth flashing. "Wuv you, Daddy."

Those words never failed to make his heart clench. As a man who had thought he'd lost everything, he was beyond blessed with Katie, Viv and the O'Sheas. He literally had every single thing he'd ever wanted at his fingertips.

As he filled Katie's cup with juice, Mac let out a whistle. "While we're all here, I have an announcement."

Jenna stepped close to his side and smiled. Mac wrapped an arm around her, pulling her in tight.

"We're having a baby," he yelled.

Laney squealed, rushing for Jenna and enveloping her in a hug. Ryker stepped up and smacked Mac on the back with one hand, while he held his baby girl on his other arm.

All these kids... Jack smiled as he twisted the lid back on the cup. "Looks like there will be a whole new generation of O'Sheas," he proclaimed, crossing back to the dining area. "Just when I thought my house was big enough to host this family..."

"We're going to need a compound if we keep wanting to have family events," Zara said with a laugh. "I'm okay with that, since we plan on having more."

More O'Sheas. At one time that thought would've angered Jack, but now...well, he couldn't be happier.

He threw a glance at Viv, who mouthed, *"I love you."* He sent her a wink and knew he was the luckiest man alive...and that included being an O'Shea.

* * * * *

Logan McLaughlin was perfection under her hands.

Trinity wanted more. And took it.

Tilting her head, she deepened the kiss and he countered instantly, swirling his tongue forward to find hers, heightening the roar of hunger pounding through her veins. His mouth. God, the things it was doing to her. The things it could do.

And then all at once, his lips disappeared and she swayed forward, desperate to get them back on hers. Instead, he leaned in and nuzzled her ear.

"How'd I do?" he murmured. "Close enough to what you were going for?"

Trinity laughed, because what else could she do? "Yeah. That was perfect."

He'd been on to her scheme the entire time. Of course. What had she thought, that a man with commitment and white picket fences written all over him might actually go for a woman like her, who'd turned her independence into a shield? That he'd been as into the kiss as she had, almost forgetting it wasn't real?

Never in a million years would they make sense together—unless it was fake.

This was a great place for goodbye. But for some reason, Trinity was having a very difficult time taking her hands off her partner.

* * *

From Enemies to Expecting
is part of the Love and Lipstick series—For four female executives, mixing business with pleasure leads to love!

FROM ENEMIES TO EXPECTING

BY
KAT CANTRELL

First Published in Great Britain 2017
By Mills & Boon, an imprint of HarperCollins*Publishers*
1 London Bridge Street, London, SE1 9GF

© 2017 Kat Cantrell

ISBN: 978-0-263-92806-8

51-0217

Our policy is to use papers that are natural, renewable and recyclable products and made from wood grown in sustainable forests. The logging and manufacturing processes conform to the legal environmental regulations of the country of origin.

Printed and bound in Spain
by CPI, Barcelona

USA TODAY bestselling author **Kat Cantrell** read her first Mills & Boon novel in third grade and has been scribbling in notebooks since she learned to spell. She's a Mills & Boon So You Think You Can Write winner and a Romance Writers of America Golden Heart® Award finalist. Kat, her husband and their two boys live in North Texas.

One

Logan McLaughlin hated losing. So of course the fates had gifted him with the worst team in the history of major league baseball. Losing had become an art form, one the Dallas Mustangs seemed determined to master. Short of cleaning house and starting over with a new roster, Logan had run out of ideas to help his ball club out of their slump.

Being the team's owner and general manager should be right up his alley. Logan's dad had run a billion-dollar company with ease and finesse for thirty years. Surely Logan had inherited a little of Duncan McLaughlin's business prowess along with a love of baseball and his dad's dot-com fortune?

Ticket sales for the Mustangs' home games said otherwise. A losing streak a mile long was the only reason Logan had agreed to the ridiculous idea his publicist had put forth, otherwise, he'd never have darkened the door of a reality game show. As last-ditch efforts went, this one took the cake.

But, as his publicist informed him, Logan had run out of charity golf tournaments, and they hadn't helped drive ticket sales anyway. Short of winning games—which he was working on, via some intricate and slow trade agreements—he needed to get public support for his team another way. Now.

Exec-ution's set teemed with people. Logan stood in the corner nursing a cup of very bad coffee because it was that or rip off someone's head due to caffeine withdrawal. He should have stopped at Starbucks on the way to the studio, but who would have thought that an outfit that asked its contestants to be on the set at 5:00 a.m. wouldn't have decent coffee? He was stuck in hell with crap in a cup.

"Logan McLaughlin." A pretty staffer with an iPad in the crook of her elbow let her gaze flit over the other contestants until she zeroed in on him standing well out of the fray. "Care to take a seat? We're about to begin filming."

"No, thanks. I'll stand," he declined smoothly with a ready smile to counter his refusal.

Chairs were for small people; at six-four, 220, Logan hadn't fit in most chairs since eleventh grade. Plus, he liked being able to see the big picture at a glance.

A soft-looking middle-aged man in a suit nodded at Logan. "Thought I recognized you. I'm a Yankees fan from way back. Used to watch you pitch, what, ten years ago?"

"Something like that," Logan agreed easily.

The Yankees had let him go eight years ago, but who was counting when the career he'd poured his heart and soul into ended in a failed Tommy John surgery? His elbow still ached occasionally, just in case he didn't have enough reminders that his days on the mound were over.

"Man, you were great. Sorry about the arm." The man shook his head. "Shame you can't get any of your starters shaped up. The Mustangs could use a guy with your skill."

Yeah. Shame. Logan nodded his thanks. He tossed his crap in a cup into a trash can and crossed his arms over the void in his chest that owning a baseball team hadn't filled. It was getting harder and harder to convince himself that his glory days were not behind him.

Winning games. Ticket sales. Merchandise sales. These were things that would fix that void. And when he won *Exec-ution*, sports news outlets would have something to do with his name besides dragging it through the mud.

The staffer called a few more people to take seats around the boardroom table. A photograph of the downtown Dallas skyline peeked through the faux window behind the table. Crew members buzzed around the cameras, and a few tech guys sat behind glass in a control room, wearing headsets. The host of the show sat at the head of the table, hands carefully laced in front him, with perfectly coiffed hair and a bogus TV smile.

"Let's have a good show!" The staffer melted away, and Well-Coiffed Guy launched into his spiel.

"Hi, everyone! I'm Rob Moore, your host for *Exec-ution*, where executives compete in two-person teams in an entrepreneurial challenge designed to showcase the ability to run a business. The winners get one hundred thousand dollars for charity. Losers? Executed!"

Logan rolled his eyes as the host smacked the table with his trademark chopping motion. So cheesy.

A commotion caught everyone's attention. A dark-haired woman strode onto the set with the pretty staffer dogging her heels.

Logan promptly forgot about the smarmy host and fake boardroom in favor of watching the real show—the dark-haired woman walking.

She moved liked an outfielder with a batter's home run in the works: fast, purposeful and determined not to let that ball go over the wall. Maybe she could teach his guys a few things about how to hustle.

The closer she got, the more interesting she became. A wide stripe of pink ran down the left side of her hair. The right side had been shorn close to her head in an asymmetrical cut that made Logan feel off-kilter all at once. Or maybe that was due to her thick, black Cleopatra-style eye makeup, which was far sexier than it should be.

She had everyone's attention exactly where she wanted it—on her. A woman dressed in a slim-fit, shocking pink suit cut low enough to allow her very nice breasts to peek out clearly expected people to notice her.

"Sorry I'm late," she offered the host. Her throaty voice thrummed through Logan in a way he hadn't been *thrummed* in a very long time. Not since his pitching days, when baseball groupies had been thick on the ground, which he'd taken advantage of far less than he could have.

This lady in pink had the full package, and then some. For some other guy.

Logan avoided packaged women like the plague, as they often came with nasty surprises once you unwrapped them. He liked his women simple, unaffected and open, a younger version of the best woman he knew—his mom.

Didn't mean he couldn't appreciate a gorgeous woman with a sexy voice.

Pink Lady drew even with Logan, electing to stand despite open seats at the table and ice-pick heels on her feet that couldn't be comfortable.

"I tried to explain that we'd already started filming," the staffer told Rob Moore in a hushed voice that carried across the whole set. "She barged in anyway."

"It's okay," the host said with a crafty smile. He waltzed over to them, his gaze cutting back and forth between Logan and the lady in pink at his side. "Oh, I like this. Very nice. Bad girl meets all-American boy. The viewers will love it."

"Love what?" Logan glanced down at his blue Mustangs T-shirt and jeans and then at the dark-haired woman. Moore's comment sank in. "You want us to be teammates? I don't think so."

That was not happening. But Moore had already moved on to the next couple, both of whom looked relieved with their matches.

The sinking feeling in Logan's stomach bottomed out. Pink Lady had crossed her arms under her spectacular breasts, shoving them upward so that they strained against the fabric of her suit. He averted his eyes as she started tapping out a staccato rhythm with one stiletto.

"What's wrong with being my teammate?" Her agitation pushed her voice up a notch. "You don't think I have any business savvy because of the tongue piercing. That's crap and you know it."

A...*tongue* piercing? Instantly, he envisioned exactly what skills a woman with a steel bar through her tongue might have. And they all centered on being naked. With her mouth on his flesh as she pleasured him.

Dragging his thoughts out of the gutter took entirely too much will. That's why he liked unassuming, unsexy, *uneverything* women.

"I didn't even notice that," he informed her truthfully and tried to stop himself from catching a glimpse of the piercing. "My objections have nothing to do with you."

That part was patently false. It had everything to do with the fact that she had *distraction* written all over her. He'd have to get a new teammate, no question.

For God knew what reason, she laughed, and that did a hell of lot more than *thrum* in Logan's gut.

"I have a BS meter with new batteries," she said. "Look around, honey. Everyone else has been paired. Can we get with the program?"

Logan peered down at his new teammate's fingernail, which had landed in the dead center of his chest. Then he glanced back up at her incredibly disturbing eyes. They were a shade of ice blue that seemed so much more stark and unique than they should, probably because of her eye makeup.

"I'm with the program." He reeled back the curl of awareness that her finger had aroused. "The question is, are you? I wasn't late."

"Five a.m. is an ungodly hour, and I was only fifteen minutes late. You can't hold that against me."

Yeah, actually he could. *He'd* been on time and so had everyone else. But since it did appear as if all the other teams had been set, he sighed. "Fine. You're forgiven. What did you say your industry is again?"

"I didn't. What did you say your name is again?"

The point wasn't lost on him. He'd completely abandoned civility with this pink curveball, and his mama had taught him better than that. He stuck out a hand. "Logan McLaughlin. Owner and general manager of the Dallas Mustangs."

"Sports is your thing, I see. The lack of dress-up clothes threw me." She glanced at his Mustangs shirt, and then slipped her hand in his for what should have been a perfunctory shake.

The moment her palm slid against his, a shock zinged up his arm, arrowing straight for his groin. He let it ride because it was that powerful and, God, he hadn't felt anything like it in ages. Her eyelids drifted downward a touch, and she peeked up at him from under her lashes, clearly affected by it as well.

"I own suits," he muttered, loath to release her and completely aware that he should have ended the handshake at least thirty seconds ago. "I'd rather go naked than wear one."

What was he *doing*?

Get a grip, McLaughlin. This woman was the polar opposite of his type, and flirting with her could only lead to disaster, especially since they were supposed to be focused on winning. Unfortunately, he had a feeling the disaster train had already pulled out of the station.

"Naked is my favorite, too." Her voice had dropped back into the throatiness he much preferred. That was not going to work, either. "Trinity Forrester. Yes, as in the holy trinity, the chick in *The Matrix* and the river. I've heard all the jokes, so save them."

"I guess I'm not allowed to ask if you're overly religious, then."

She smiled, leaning in close enough to share a whiff of her exotic scent that of course only added to her allure.

"If you do, you get my standard answer. 'Any man

in a ten-foot radius is expected to treat me like a god-dess. You can get started worshipping me any time.'"

Oh, she'd like that, wouldn't she? His eyes narrowed.

If they were going to be teammates, they had to get a few things straight. No flirting. No throaty voices coupled with come-hither glances. Logan called the shots, and Ms. I've Heard All the Jokes had better be able to keep up. Sexy heels were optional.

The cameras had captured every word of the exchange. So far, so good.

The more the cameras tuned in to Trinity, the more times the producers would overlay her name and Fyra Cosmetics on the screen. You couldn't buy better advertising than that, and Fyra needed all the positive press it could get.

Trinity Forrester would get that press come hell or high water. Nothing could be allowed to happen to her company, the one she and her three best friends from college had built from a concept and a dream. Thanks to an internal saboteur, Fyra was struggling. As the chief marketing officer, Trinity took the negative publicity personally. It was her job to stop the hemorrhaging. *Exec-ution* was step one in that plan.

Otherwise, she'd be in her office hard at work on the campaign for Formula-47, the new product they'd hoped to launch in the next couple of weeks.

Mr. McLaughlin still had her hand in his as if he might not let go. Perfect. The more enthralled he was, the easier it would be to take charge. Men never paid attention to her unless they wanted to get her into the sack, mostly because that was the way she preferred it. Sex was the only thing she'd ever found worth doing with a man.

She smiled at Logan for good measure. He had good ole Texas boy baked into his DNA. Toss in his longish brown hair that constantly fell in his face and his casual clothes, and yeah, Logan McLaughlin was the epitome of the all-American type. Also known as a nice guy.

Nice guys were always hiding something not so nice, and she'd learned her lesson a long time ago when it came to trusting men—don't. A surprise pregnancy in her early twenties had cured her of happily-ever-after dreams when the father of her baby took off, and then a miscarriage convinced her she wasn't mother material anyway.

"Mr. McLaughlin," she murmured. "Perhaps you'd give me my hand back so we can get to work?"

He dropped it like he'd discovered a live copperhead in his grip and cleared his throat. "Yeah. Good idea."

They retrieved a sealed envelope from the show's host, and Logan followed Trinity to an area with an easel and large pad of paper for brainstorming. Her fingers itched to mark up those pristine white pages with diagrams. If that didn't jump-start her missing muse, nothing would. Though she'd tried a lot of things.

The cameraman wedged into the small area with them, still rolling. Perfect. She'd have to come up with more outrageous things to do, just to ensure the editors had plenty to work with. Coming in late had been a stroke of brilliance. And McLaughlin's face when she'd informed him he couldn't hold fifteen minutes against her…priceless. He was obviously a rule follower. Shame.

He tore open the envelope and pulled out the contents, scanning it quickly. "We have to run a lemonade stand in Klyde Warren Park. Whichever team makes the most money wins the task and avoids execution."

"Excellent." Rubbing her hands together, she then quickly sketched out her vision for the stand, filling in small details like cross-hatching to indicate shadowing. "Orange will be the best color to paint the booth. Good contrast against green, assuming we'll be in the grassy part of the park."

Her partner loomed at her shoulder, breathing down her neck as he stretched one muscular arm out to stab the pad. "What is this?"

"A sign. That says Trinity's Lemonade."

What did the man bathe in that smelled so…manly? The clean, citrusy notes spread through her senses and caught the attention of her erogenous zones, none of which had gotten the memo that she did not go for Texas boys who looked like they lived outdoors.

The man owned a sports team, for God's sake. He'd probably need a dictionary to hold a conversation over drinks, which would no doubt include beer and a hundred TVs with a different game on each one. She and Logan were ill matched for a reality game show, let alone outside one, his rock-hard pecs aside. Her fingertip still tingled from when she'd poked him, not at all prepared for the body she'd discovered under that blue T-shirt.

"Why would we call it Trinity's Lemonade, exactly?" he asked, his deep voice rumbling in her ear. "Logan's Lemonade sounds better. Starts with the same letter."

"It's alliterative, you mean," she supplied sweetly. "I understand the dynamics of appealing to the public better than you do, honey. So let's stick with our strengths, shall we?"

She stroked a few more lines across her work of art and then yelped as her partner spun her around to face him. His mouth firmed into a flat line and he towered over her even in her five-inch Stuart Weitzman sandals. Trinity was used to looking men in the eye, and the fact that she couldn't do that with Logan McLaughlin put her on edge.

"You've done a really good job of not mentioning your strengths, *darling*," he threw in sarcastically. "I run a multimillion-dollar sports franchise. What do you do, Ms. Forrester?"

"Haven't I mentioned it?" she tossed off casually when she knew good and well she hadn't—on purpose. The moment a man like him heard the word *cosmetics*, he'd make more snap judgments and she'd had enough of that.

At this point, though, she needed to impress upon him that she was in her sweet spot. "I'm the CMO at Fyra."

Blandly, he surveyed her. "The makeup company?"

"The very same. So now we're all caught up," she informed him brightly. "Marketing is my gig. Yours is figuring out which guy can hit the ball hardest. When we have a task that requires balls, I'll let you be in charge."

This lemonade stand graphic was the first inspired thing she'd done in weeks, which was frankly depressing. Her muse had deserted her, which was alarming enough in and of itself, but the timing was horrific. Fyra planned to launch its premier product in the next ninety days. Fortunately, no one knew she'd run dry in the creativity department. It wasn't like she could tell her business partners that she had a mental block when it came to Formula-47. They were counting on her.

His mouth tipped up in a slow smile that didn't fool her for a second. "In case you've forgotten, we're partners. That means all tasks require balls, specifically mine. Shove over and let's do this together."

Nice. Not only had he called her on her double entendre, he'd done it with a style she grudgingly appreciated. Which was the only reason she stepped a half inch to the right, graciously offering him room at the pad.

His arm jostled hers as he took way more space than she'd intended. The man was a solid wall of muscle, with wide shoulders and lean hips, and yeah, of course she'd noticed how well his jeans hugged the curve of his rear. That part of Logan McLaughlin was a gift to women everywhere, and she'd gotten in her share of ogling.

Without a word, he picked up his own marker and crossed out "Trinity's Lemonade," then scrawled, "McLemonade" across the sign. Oh, God. That was perfect. How dare he be the one to come up with it?

Scowling, she crossed her arms and in the process made sure to throw an elbow into his ribs. Which promptly glanced off as if she'd hit a brick wall. And now her elbow hurt.

"Fine," she ground out. "We'll go with yours. But the booth will be orange."

He shrugged, shouldering her deliberately. "I didn't have an issue with that."

The man was intolerable. Nowhere near the nice guy she'd pegged him as, and once he opened his mouth, totally unattractive. Or at least that was what she was telling herself.

"Oh, yeah? So the stuff you do have issues with— that's all getting the McLaughlin veto?" Standing her ground shouldn't be this hard, but heels coupled with the immovable mountain snugged next to her body threw her off, and not solely because it was impossible to think through the shooting pangs of awareness that she couldn't seem to get under control.

Instead of glaring, his expression smoothed out and he took a deep breath.

"Let's start over." He extended his hand.

Because he'd piqued her curiosity, she took it and he swallowed her palm with his. Little frissons of awareness seeped into her skin at the contact.

"I'm Logan McLaughlin. I run a baseball team and our ticket sales suck. My publicist insisted that this game show would be a good way to get some eyes on the team, so here I am. Any help I can get toward that goal is appreciated."

His clear hazel eyes held hers, and his sincerity bled through her, tripping her pulse unexpectedly. Well, jeez. Honesty. What would the man think of next?

"Hi," she said because that seemed to be all her throat could summon as they stared at each other, intensity burning through her. "I'm, um, Trinity Forrester. I sell cosmetics alongside three women I love dearly. Our company stepped in a negative publicity hole, so *my* publicist came up with the brilliant idea to stick me on a TV show. I'm…not so sure that was a good move."

That made Logan laugh, and the rich sound of it wound through her with warmth that was so nice, her knees weakened. Weakness under any circumstances was not acceptable. But hardening herself against him took way more effort than it should have.

Was it so wrong to let a man like him affect her? Sure he was insufferable, pigheaded and way too virtuous for her tastes, but he had a gorgeous body, a nice smile and longish hair made for a woman's fingers. He couldn't be all bad.

"Oddly enough, I was thinking the same thing," he admitted, his eyes crinkling at the corners. "But I've changed my mind. I think we can help each other if we work together. Willing to give it a shot?"

Guess that was her answer about what else he had up his sleeve—he was going to be pleasant instead of an obstinate jackass. Strictly to mess with her head, most likely.

But she needed to work with him to benefit both of their goals. She bit her tongue and slipped her hand from his. "I can give that a shot."

They put their heads together, and true to his word, Logan listened to her ideas. She considered it a plus when he laughed at her jokes. No one had to know she secretly reveled in it.

By the end of the afternoon, they'd amassed a solid four hundred dollars and change with their McLemonade booth. God knew how. They'd fought over everything: how much to charge, where to set up, how much lemonade to put in the cups. Apparently, Mr. Nice Guy only made an appearance when he wanted something, then vanished once he got into the thick of things.

Finally, the show's producer asked them to pack up and head to the studio so they could wrap up the day's shooting. They drove separate cars to the set and met up again in the fake boardroom.

This time, Trinity grabbed a seat. An entire day on her feet, most of it on grass while wearing stilettos, was not doing her body any favors.

"Welcome back, everyone!" Rob Moore called, and the teams gathered around the table.

Logan stood at the back and Trinity pretended like she didn't notice the vacant seat by her side. All the other teammates sat next to each other. Fine by her. She and her partner got on like oil and water and had only figured out how to work together because they'd had to.

"We've tallied all the sales, and I must say, this was an impressive group of teams." The host beamed at them. "But the winners are Mitch Shaughnessy and John Roberts!"

Disappointed, Trinity clapped politely as the winning team high-fived each other and jogged to the head of the table to claim the giant check made out to St. Jude Children's Hospital. That was the important thing—the money was going to a good cause.

"The winning team's proceeds were…" Rob Moore paused for dramatic effect. "Four hundred and twenty-eight dollars. Impressive!"

Oh, dear God. They'd lost by a measly twenty-five dollars? She thought about banging her head on the table, but that wouldn't put the cameras on her face with a nice graphic overlay stating her company's name. But what if there was a way to get some additional airtime? The cameras were still rolling, panning the losers as the host launched into his trademark parting comments.

"Fire up the electric chair, boys," he cried. "We've got some executions to perform!"

This was the cheesiest part of the show, which she'd hoped to avoid. She had a good idea how to do that and get some cameras on her at the same time.

Pushing her chair backward with a sharp crack, she bolted to her feet and charged over to her partner, poking her finger in his chest with a bit more force than she'd intended. But she'd gotten the cameraman's attention, and that was all that mattered.

"This is all your fault, McLaughlin. We would have won if it wasn't for you."

His gaze narrowed, and he reached up to forcibly remove her finger from his person. "What are you talking about? This ship started sinking the second we were paired. Bad girl meets all-American boy. *Please.* What they should have called us was train meets wreck."

That struck her as such a perfect way to describe the day that she almost laughed, but she bit it back. She could admire his wit later, over a glass of wine as she celebrated the fact that she never had to see him again. "You know what your problem is?"

"I've got no doubt you're about to tell me," he offered and crossed his arms in the pose that she'd tried—and failed—to ignore all day. When he did that, his biceps bunched up under his shirt sleeves, screaming to be touched. She just wanted to feel one once. Was that so much to ask?

"Someone needs to. Otherwise, you'd walk around with that rule book shoved up your…butt," she amended, lest the producers cut the whole exchange due to her potty mouth. "Some rules are made to be broken. That's why we lost. Apply for sainthood on your own time."

His expression heated and not in a good way. "Are you saying I'm a Goody Two-shoes?"

"If the shoe fits, wear it," she suggested sweetly. "And that's not even the worst of your problems."

He rolled his eyes, fire shooting from his gaze, and she almost caved, because he was really pissed and while she wanted the cameras on them, she also felt like crap for poking at him. But when he got hot and bothered, he lost all his filters and focused on nothing but her.

That, she liked.

"Oh, I've gotta hear this. Please, enlighten me."

"You're attracted to me and you can't stand it." That

was like the pot calling the kettle black, though she scarcely wanted to admit that to herself, let alone out loud.

"I'm sorry, what?"

"You heard me."

Her finger ended up back on his chest. Oops. It was hard and delicious and there was something super hot about how immovable he was. Logan was solid, the kind of guy who might actually stick around when unexpected challenges cropped up. Sometimes a girl needed a strong shoulder. He had two.

"I heard you," he growled and went to smack away her finger—she'd assumed—but he crushed her palm to his chest, holding it captive with his hand. "What I meant was, that's the craziest thing you've said so far today."

The cameraman had zoomed in on their discussion. She noted the lens from the corner of her eye and nearly smiled.

You couldn't buy this kind of exposure. This time tomorrow—with her help—this clip would go viral: *Two executives melt down on the set of a reality TV show.* Viewers would see a strong woman not taking any crap from her male partner. As long as they spelled Fyra correctly, it should amp up the positive publicity and counter the negative.

"Get ready for more crazy, because not only are you attracted to me, you can't stop thinking about what it would be like to kiss me. Admit it. You're curious about the tongue piercing."

"Of course I am," he bit out, fuzzing her brain at the same time.

He was? Fascinated, she zeroed in on him, and yeah, there was a whole lot more than agitation in his expression. Logan McLaughlin, official Boy Scout of major league baseball, had never kissed a woman with a tongue piercing. And he wanted to.

Heat and a thick awareness flooded all the places between them. His heart thumped under her palm, strong but erratic, which perfectly mirrored the stuff going on under her own skin.

"What red-blooded male wouldn't be curious," he murmured. "When there's only one reason to have a steel bar through your tongue—to pleasure a man."

His eyelids shuttered for a beat, and when he opened them, his eyes held so much wicked intent, her pulse bobbled. Caught in his hot gaze, she swayed toward him, her hand fisting his shirt. "One way to find—"

His mouth captured hers before she'd fully registered him moving. And then all rational thought drained from her mind as Logan kissed her. The TV set melted away, the fascinated onlookers disappeared—none of it registered as he yanked her into his embrace.

Exactly where she wanted to be.

Logan McLaughlin was perfection under her hands, because *yes*, he was that hard all over. His back alone qualified as a work of art, defined with peaks and valleys that she hadn't ever felt on a man before. Imagine that. Something new to be discovered on a male body.

She wanted more. And took it.

Tilting her head, she deepened the kiss, and he countered instantly, swirling his tongue forward to find hers, taking command of the kiss, heightening the roar of hunger pounding through her veins. *His mouth.* God, the things it was doing to her. The things it could do.

And then all at once, his lips disappeared and she swayed forward, desperate to get them back on hers. Instead, he leaned in and nuzzled her ear.

"How'd I do?" he murmured. "Close enough to what you were going for?"

Trinity laughed, because what else could she do? "Yeah. That was perfect."

He'd been on to her scheme the entire time. Of course. What had she thought, that a man with commitment and white picket fences written all over him might actually go for a woman like her, who'd turned her independence into a shield? That he'd been as into the kiss as she had?

Never in a million years would they make sense together—unless it was fake.

This was a great place for goodbye. But for some reason, Trinity was having a very difficult time taking her hands off her partner.

Two

The next morning, Trinity entered the five-story glass-and-steel building that housed the cosmetics company she'd helped build with her marketing savvy and love of all things feminine. She still got a thrill out of the modern design and purple accents she and her three partners had selected, and the location just north of downtown Dallas was perfect for a single woman who owned an amazing condo in the heart of the city.

Cass had been making noises about moving the company to Austin. Trinity kept her mouth shut because Fyra's CEO had a very good reason for wanting to do so—her husband, Gage, lived there and they were expecting a baby together. Trinity didn't have anything against Austin, per se. But it was yet another example of something she had no control over. She hated anything that smacked of lack of control.

Plus, what was wrong with Gage moving his company to Dallas? Both CEOs ran large companies with lots of employees. Just because Gage was the man in the equation, why did that mean he automatically won the battle?

Trinity strode toward her office to the sounds of hoots and clapping. She took a moment to grin and wave. Obviously the footage of her kiss with Logan had made the rounds. The game show itself wouldn't air until later in the week, but she'd charmed the producer out of a clip of the kiss, starting it on its viral journey by posting it to her own social media accounts and tagging everyone she knew to share it.

Trinity wasn't one for leaving things to chance.

Cass had scheduled a meeting for first thing this morning, probably to get the full scoop. Humming, Trinity grabbed coffee and dug around until she found her iPad in her shoulder bag, then strolled to the conference room where Cass stood at the head of the table.

"Hey," Trinity called and repeated her greeting to Fyra's CFO, Alex Edgewood, and then to Dr. Harper Livingston-Gates, the chief science officer, whose faces appeared in split screen on a TV mounted on the wall. Both of them were participating in the meeting virtually since they'd abandoned Dallas the moment their husbands crooked their fingers.

Trinity sank into a seat and mentally slapped herself for being unkind.

Alex was pregnant with twins and on bed rest, so it made sense that she lived in Washington, DC, with her husband, Phillip, a United States senator. Harper's husband worked in Zurich, and Trinity didn't blame her for wanting to be in the same bed with a man as hot as Dr. Dante Gates, especially since they'd just figured out they were in love after being friends for over a decade.

Maybe Trinity was a little jealous that everyone else

had such an easy time with normal female things like falling for a great guy and having his support during pregnancy. And none of them had suffered a horrendous miscarriage that had left them feeling defective. Well, so what? Trinity had other great stuff in her life, like more men than she could shake a stick at.

Except lately, great men had been pretty scarce. The pitfalls of turning thirty. Made you think more about the definition of "great," and pseudo–frat boys with Peter Pan syndrome were not it. Unfortunately, that seemed to be the type she met at her usual haunts, which was fine for the short term.

She just wished she knew why that didn't feel like enough anymore.

Cass started off with a sly smile. "You and your reality show partner got pretty chummy. Do tell."

"All for the cameras, hon," Trinity assured her. God, what was with that pang in her gut? The kiss had been fake. On both sides—never mind that she'd liked how real it felt. "We were both interested in getting additional coverage. It worked."

Alex and Harper both murmured their disappointment that the story wasn't juicier.

"I know we've turned dissecting our love lives into a regular boardroom agenda item, but let's move on," Trinity insisted smoothly. "I'm sure Cass didn't call this meeting to talk about my partner on a reality game show."

"Actually, I did," Cass corrected. "We've got a publicity issue that's at the top of everyone's mind right now. After the mess with the leak and then the FDA approval fiasco, sales went into the toilet. We've got new problems daily as articles keep popping up in what feels to me like a smear campaign."

Felt that way to Trinity, too. Which was why it pissed her off so much. This was her territory. Her company. And someone was after it.

"Yeah, I'm aware. That's why I did the show, remember?"

"I'm not sure it's enough." Cass frowned. "I approved it since the publicist suggested it, but we need to move forward with launching Formula-47. When can you schedule time to present the marketing plan?"

"Next Monday?" Trinity suggested and started calculating exactly how screwed she was…since the campaign didn't exist. *Very* would be the precise amount of screwed.

It wasn't anyone's fault but hers, but then she'd never had a creative dry spell like this one, and she couldn't even commiserate with her friends. Recent personal events for all three ladies had driven a wedge between them, with Trinity on the wrong side of the married mom division.

Trinity hated it. She was happy for her friends, but sad that they'd all chosen lives so different from the ones they'd had. So different from the one she'd mapped out for herself. And she was pretty sure that was why her creativity had completely abandoned her when she needed it most.

The sketching she'd done on that pristine white pad while Logan peered over her shoulder had been a welcome flood of ingenuity. Maybe the medium was the key—she'd run out at lunch and pick up one of those easels. It could work.

She could totally get her muse to make an appearance, work straight through and have a brilliant campaign by Monday morning. Especially if the publicity from *Exec-ution* worked like it was supposed to. With that load off her mind, then she could concentrate on turning Formula-47 into a powerhouse wrinkle and scar cream that would put Fyra at the top of the industry.

Cass nodded and shifted focus to numbers, so Alex took the lead on that, while Trinity sank down in her seat to let her mind wander in hopes of jogging something passable from her subconscious. Didn't happen, but she had almost a week. No problem.

The easel and pad did not turn into a magic bullet. Neither did the marathon brainstorming session she called to generate ideas from her creative team. At four o'clock, she sent Melinda, Fyra's receptionist, to the office supply store to get a dozen more blank pads. The remains of the two Trinity had purchased at lunch lay in ripped and crumpled pieces on her office floor. She might have stabbed a couple of the papers with her Louboutin heels, but only because big jagged holes improved the package design she'd started on.

She didn't even have a product name, which meant she had no business trying to design the packaging. Her creative process required building blocks, and the name always came first, but she'd been desperate to make *some* kind of progress. Formula-47 would be Fyra's premier product and as the CMO, Trinity should and would take on the heaviest lifting. Her creative team had enough on their plates with managing the rest of Fyra's marketing juggernaut while she buried herself in this mess.

Melinda poked her head in the door. "I've got your pads. Also, Lara from Gianni Publicity Group is here. She doesn't have an appointment. Shall I send her away?"

The publicist. Great. That was exactly what Trinity needed right now—a reminder that Cass had hired an outside firm to do Trinity's job. And Lara's big contribution thus far had landed Trinity in the arms of a do-gooder Texas boy who kissed like a wicked fantasy.

Logan McLaughlin was a name she should have forgotten by now. For God knew what reason, it still rattled around in her head, heating up places that shouldn't be heating at the thought of a rugged, lean-hipped outdoorsy guy who wasn't her type.

She sighed. "No, it's okay. I'll see her."

Lara Gianni rushed into the office, long hair streaming behind her as the chic woman grabbed Trinity by the shoulders and kissed both cheeks, Italian style. "You brilliant, brilliant lady. Logan McLaughlin is *magnifico*."

"Back off. I saw him first," Trinity said drily. Was the woman reading minds now? "Why is he magnificent again? Please tell me it's because you've got good news."

The publicist laughed. "The best. Your video has already been shared over half a million times, and the response? Amazing. People love you two together. The comments are priceless. Love on the set of a TV show is brilliant marketing."

"Wait a minute. Love on a TV show? It was an entrepreneurial game show, not *The Bachelor*." The look on Lara's face gave Trinity a very bad feeling. "The public was supposed to see the name Fyra and think positive thoughts about it. That's how you sold the idea to us."

"That was before you went in a whole different direction. One I love! You're truly brilliant."

Yeah, that part was clear. What wasn't clear was what the hell Lara was talking about. "I didn't go in a different direction. We lost the game and I had to do something extra. I kissed my partner. Voilà, now Fyra is all over social media."

"No." Lara shook her head. "*You* are all over social media. They like the romance you unwittingly created. I would highly recommend continuing it."

Trinity's stomach dropped into her shoes. "Continue what? There's no romance. It was one kiss."

A hot kiss. If she'd watched the footage a couple of dozen times before she'd posted it, no one had to know.

Lara shrugged. "I suggest you figure out how to make it into more than a kiss. It doesn't have to be a real relationship so long as you get yourself photographed with Logan McLaughlin. A lot. While kissing and making goo-goo eyes at each other."

The logic of it warred with the insanity. A fake relationship strictly for publicity? She couldn't. *He* wouldn't. Yet…how was that so different than a fake kiss for the same reason? Logan had jumped on that deal like a starving dog on a steak. Maybe he'd be *really* good at pretending they were a hot-and-heavy couple.

The thought unleashed a shiver that nearly unglued her. The side benefits of such an arrangement held many interesting possibilities that she could not ignore, like enticing a nice guy into a walk on the wild side. How much fun would it be to corrupt the hell out of the all-American boy, especially on camera?

No. A long-term fake relationship was a whole lot different than one fake kiss. Her acting skills weren't that good. Except all at once, she couldn't figure out if she'd be feigning she was into him…or pretending she wasn't.

"No way. I can't do something like that."

Lara's brow furrowed as she pulled out her phone

and tapped a few times, then held it out to display a nearly all-red pie chart. "That's the click-through rate from your video to Fyra's website."

All the blood drained from Trinity's head. Seventy-five percent. *Seventy-five percent.* The click-through rate of her most successful social media campaign ever was 12 percent.

In the wake of the smear tactics someone had launched against Fyra, she couldn't afford to pass up this idea.

Looked like she'd be paying Mr. McLaughlin a visit. Tomorrow. *Hello, new boyfriend.*

Myra slapped the printed spreadsheet on Logan's desk and didn't bother to hide her smirk. "Told you that reality show would work."

Yes, it had. He didn't need his publicist to point out the double-digit increase in ticket sales. The Mustangs' entire front office had been buzzing about it since he'd walked in this morning. And he had Trinity Forrester, CMO, to thank.

Who would have thought that sizzling kiss would pay such huge dividends?

Duncan McLaughlin had never done *that* to get customers to open their wallets, but in Logan's defense, it hadn't been his idea. Yet he'd gotten on board with it pretty dang fast, at least once he'd realized the hot woman he'd been salivating over was not coming on to him. She'd simply found one last way to get the camera on them. As tactics went, he could find little to complain about.

Other than the fact that one bad-girl kiss later, he'd come to the uncomfortable realization that he could not wipe the feel of that tongue piercing from his memory.

His admin, Lisa, popped into his office, eyes wide. "Um, boss? You have a visitor. Ms. Forrester?"

Well, well. He leaned back in his chair as Myra's expression veered between intrigued and very intrigued. Logan had a feeling his own face might be doing something similar, so he schooled it before nodding to Lisa. "You can send her in. Thanks, Myra. I'll get back to you."

And then everything in the world of baseball ceased to exist as Trinity waltzed into his office, her off-kilter hair throwing him into a tailspin. God, how was that so sexy? On her, it was one more in-your-face reminder that she was a force to be reckoned with.

Today's outfit consisted of a deep purple suit with a micro skirt, black stockings that made her legs look a mile long and silver ankle breakers that he'd like better on his bedroom floor.

"Thanks for seeing me on short notice," she said.

That throaty voice. He'd underrated what it did to him when the sound slid down his spine. His blood woke up and sluiced through his veins in a rush that made him feel alive—only being on the mound had ever replicated that feeling.

Why her? Of all people? He'd *always* been on the lookout for a simple, uncomplicated woman who listened to country music and planned picnics. A nice woman to settle down with, who could have his babies and be the love of his life. That was how his dad had done it. That was how Logan wanted to do it. The fact that he'd yet to meet his fictional perfect lady was neither here nor there—she was out there somewhere.

And her name was not Trinity. He should not be attracted to her.

All at once, he remembered his manners and rose to

his feet, palm outstretched toward the love seat near the window that overlooked the ballpark, his favorite spot in the whole stadium as long as there wasn't a game in progress. Then it was the dugout until the bitter end.

Most general managers sat in an air-conditioned luxury box, but his players were slugging it out on the field, and in August, it wasn't unusual for the temperature to hit 110. The senior McLaughlin had regularly hit the trenches alongside his employees. Logan could do the same.

Instead of taking the offered seat, Trinity slid a steamy once-over all the way down his body. "You're wearing a suit. What was it you said about those?"

I'd rather go naked.

The unspoken quote hung in the air between them, dissolving into a dense awareness that answered one lingering question on his mind since that kiss—whether or not he misremembered how deeply she'd gotten under his skin with all her innuendo.

He'd recalled it perfectly.

"I'm being a grown-up today," he croaked and cleared his throat.

"Oh, yeah, I once thought about being one of those for Halloween." She shrugged with a smile that he felt in his gut. "By the way, I like you in a suit."

"What can I do for you, Ms. Forrester?"

The sooner he got her out of his office, the sooner he could get back to work. Or take a cold shower. The last thing he should do was give her an advantage, or she'd railroad him into doing her bidding before he'd fully surfaced from being whacked upside the head by all the pheromones.

"You can call me Trinity." She jerked her chin toward the desk, flinging the dark swath of hair into motion.

She hadn't colored it today, strictly to throw him off, no doubt. "Talk to me about your numbers."

He glanced at the spreadsheet Myra had thrown at him to give himself a half second. What was she fishing for? "I'm happy with the results of the viral video and hopeful that when the show airs, the upward trend will continue. How about your numbers?"

"Fantastic. So good, in fact, I'm here with a proposal."

The way she said it brought to mind closed doors, a secret rendezvous and a solid block of time to explore just how good that bar through her tongue would feel on his body. If that ever happened, she'd completely ruin him for all other women, no doubt.

His body tightened in anticipation. *Let's find out*, it begged.

"I'm listening," he said when what he should have said was *there's the door*.

"My target customers loved the video of us together. My publicist thinks we should take advantage of it and start a public relationship. Pretend that we're dating after meeting on the show."

"That's the worst idea I've ever heard. We'd kill each other before anyone believed we were a couple."

His mind ignored his instant denial and latched on to the idea, turning it over. The timing of the video coincided with the increase in ticket sales too neatly to be a fluke. What would it hurt to capitalize on the momentum?

It could hurt *a lot*. His major objection had nothing to do with the brilliance of the idea and everything to do with his illogical reaction to her every time she got within breathing distance.

And then last night, she hadn't even been in the room

when he'd let himself envision a bedtime story about finishing that kiss with her legs wrapped around his waist. Yeah, she might be the star in his current shower fantasies. It wasn't a felony. Except he'd never in a million years have guessed that today would bring her back into his orbit, especially not this way.

Her gaze glittered with calculation. "Actually, the worst idea you'd ever heard was the one where we got paired on that stupid game show. But we made that work. *Together*. It was a team effort, and we almost won. Just think what we can accomplish with a concerted effort to exploit the public's thirst for celebrity couples. I'm offering you my complete attention to boost your ticket sales."

Her negotiation skills hit all the right notes, buttering him up, stressing the goal. Worst of all? He had an urge to say yes, simply to find out what her complete attention looked like.

Was it distasteful to use this opportunity to sate his curiosity about Trinity? A better question was how long he could do it and keep his hands off her. Not long—either he'd make good on the urge to strangle her or he'd provoke her until she kissed him again.

This idea got worse and worse the longer he thought about it.

"How do you even know I'm single?" he countered. "Maybe I've got the perfect girlfriend already and I—"

"Please don't insult me, McLaughlin." She snorted. "Or yourself. You couldn't have cut the sexual tension between us with a meat cleaver. If you do have a girlfriend and you can still kiss me like that, you're not the man I assume you are."

He scowled, and not just because of her excellent point.

"I get it now." He nodded sagely. "This is a ploy to earn yourself some more camera time. Attend a few Mustangs games where the general manager's hot girl-friend would most definitely be a subject of interest."

Boldly, she contemplated him, not at all bothered by his half-assed accusations. "What if it is? Does that automatically make it a bad idea? My reasons for liking this plan have nothing to do with the reasons you should agree. Ticket sales are the only thing that matters."

Wow. He shook his head. When you called a spade a spade with Trinity Forrester, she turned over a full house. "Let me make sure I've got this straight. You're suggesting we manufacture a relationship. Date each other, be seen at some events. And the public is going to approve of this by spending a lot of money?"

"We're going to help them do that with ad campaigns heavily laced with click bait. But, yeah. Get your publicist involved. Talk to your marketing people. Let's make it a party and get some eyes on our individual brands."

Not only did everything she was saying make sense, she had a unique way of presenting it that appealed to him. That alone ruffled his nerves. "How exactly are we going to date and manage to be civil to each other?"

Like that was the biggest issue.

"Who said we were?" Her blue eyes glowed as she caught his gaze. "Part of what sizzles about us is the way we clash. It translates really well on camera. Didn't you watch the clip?"

He might have watched the video a few times, and there wasn't a good way to pretend she was wrong. Nor could he forget how arguing with her had exploded into the heat of that kiss. "So not only are we supposed to fake date, but we're also supposed to have knock-down, drag-out fights in public, too?"

That was way over the line. Logan and his temper were old enemies, and bad decisions followed when he allowed his emotions off the leash. He'd left his hothead days behind him when he bought the Mustangs. A team owner had to play it cool, and thus far, he'd call his newfound calm a success.

Until Trinity.

She was the only person of his acquaintance who threatened his composure on a minute-by-minute basis.

She shrugged. "Let me be clear. I'll do whatever it takes to get you to agree to this. If you want me to be nice and sweet and smile at your fans, I will."

Waltzing closer, she let her fingers trail down the front of his shirt, reminding him of the last time she'd done that—right before he'd tested out kissing a woman with a bar through her tongue.

As if she'd read his mind, her gaze instantly caught fire and swept him with a thousand licks of heat as she let her eyes wander down his body in a slow perusal that almost had him squirming. But he had far more control over his body than that—any athlete worth his salt had enormous discipline. Losing his pitching arm hadn't become an excuse to sit on the couch and get fat.

"Logan," she murmured throatily, splattering his control to hell and back as his lower half went hard. "If you want me to wear leather and carry around a whip because you like the bad-girl persona that *Execution* coated me with, I would be happy to oblige. Tell me what it will take."

Now that was an interesting proposition. His imagination took off at a brisk trot, and it was nearly impossible to rein it back in. "We'd have to make it look real."

Guess it was too late to pretend he wasn't considering it.

"Sure. Lots of public kissing. Affection. Lots of making up after a good fight. Maybe you pop the question at an event with a huge diamond ring that sparkles."

Not for a thousand percent increase in ticket sales would he do something so sacred unless he meant it. "I'm not proposing to you no matter how fake it is. That's reserved for the future Mrs. McLaughlin. She deserves to be the only one to have that experience."

Something flashed in her gaze. Longing, maybe. But it was gone before he could process it and her expression hardened. "Fair enough. You play this however you want."

"You realize we have to spend time together doing things. You're going to have to pretend to like baseball. No glazed eyes when I wax poetical about Nolan Ryan."

Actually, he might do that on occasion just for fun.

"Only if you listen with rapt attention when I mention Estée Lauder," she countered with a sly smile. "I need you. Make me an offer."

"I'll think about it."

He didn't have to. There was no way he could say no. The part he had to think about was how deep this fake relationship would ultimately go. How deep he'd be willing to admit he wanted it to go. And whether he could, in fact, hold on to both his temper and his sanity while dating Trinity Forrester.

She swept from his office on a cloud of femininity and something spicy that he suspected he'd smell in his sleep for a long time to come.

Before he could remind himself of the million and one reasons it was a dangerous, horrible idea, he texted her: I'm in.

Three

Trinity sat on Logan's text message for two days. Mostly because she had no idea what to do with a fake boyfriend. Boyfriends of any sort vexed her on the whole, but one she wasn't sleeping with broke all kinds of new ground.

What did you *do* with a man outside of bed?

Should she hit a club with him? Stand at the red rope and hope someone took pictures? That seemed too chancy, and frankly, the idea of Logan McLaughlin at a techno bar with lots of smoke and pulsing lights made her laugh. And he'd probably laugh at her if she suggested it.

While it might lead to an argument that would be delicious on camera, they'd have to actually be in public for that to generate maximum publicity. She couldn't think of anything that *would* work, though. Her lack of creativity lately was bleeding into the social arena as well, and it was bothersome. Almost as bothersome as the fact that she had a marketing presentation to give to her friends and business partners on Monday and it still didn't exist.

Formula-47 used nanotechnology to heal scars and reduce wrinkles. There were thousands of ways to market such a brilliant product. She should have two presentations by now.

That's what she had to focus on, not the two-word text message from Logan McLaughlin.

I'm in. Nothing else. No *let's meet for coffee and hash this out*. No *here are my conditions and expectations*. What? Was she supposed to do all the dirty work and organize everything? He had a stake in this, too.

By Thursday, she was ready to bite off the head of the next person who poked their toe into her office. When her phone beeped, she nearly shut it off. But then she saw Logan's name blinking at her. Eyes narrowed, she thumbed up the text message.

Charity gala tomorrow night. Guaranteed to have lots of cameras and press. Formal dress. Pick you up at 8.

Men. Logan had his share of nerve, assuming she could pull a formal ensemble together in less than thirty-six hours, not to mention she'd have to beg Franco for a last-minute appointment to get her hair done. Her regular nail girl was out of town, too. Trinity groaned and pushed back from her desk to go spend the rest of the afternoon shopping for the perfect dress to drive a man wild.

Logan McLaughlin totally deserved to spend the entire evening in the most painful state possible for springing this on her at the last minute. And if she secretly wanted to kiss him for getting her out from behind her desk and away from the reminders that her career might be circling the drain—she'd keep that to herself.

Miraculously, Franco had a cancellation, he personally found a replacement nail technician for her, and the most amazing dress fell into her lap. Logan might get a pass after all, but strictly because he'd stepped up when it counted.

When Logan knocked on the door of Trinity's penthouse loft in the Arts District, she was dressed and ready to go. Except for her lipstick. She swiped on a layer of Bohemian Rhapsody with a lip brush and dropped both into her clutch.

It was a ritual she'd always performed back when she'd dated more. Wait until he knocked and then apply lipstick, which left the guy on her doorstep for precisely the right amount of time. Enough that he'd start to wonder if maybe she wasn't dressed yet and was even at this moment throwing on clothes. Never hurt to dangle a visual in front of a man.

And then she would open the door to give him the real visual—her, dressed to the hilt in this smashing and sexy dress with cutout sides that displayed all her best features.

Except when she opened the door to Logan…in a tux…her tongue went numb and she dropped her clutch. Which he picked up for her.

Good God, did that man clean up well. The suit from the other day? Merely an appetizer to the main course of this gorgeous hunk of masculinity in a tuxedo that had clearly been custom-made for him.

Thank all that was holy that he didn't dress like that on a daily basis. The luxurious dark fabric spread across his shoulders, emphasizing the broad, dense build she shouldn't like as much as she did. Logan was too big. Too solid. Too…squeaky clean.

But the pièce de résistance was the single long-stemmed pink rose that he held out to her.

"Pink?" She took it and held it to her nose, trying not to be pleased but failing. A whole bouquet would have been overkill and completely unnecessary given that they weren't really dating.

One rose was classy. And well played.

"You wore a pink suit on the show," he said gruffly with a shrug and ran his now vacant fingers through his hair, sweeping it away from his face. "The association with that color and you is pretty much stuck in my head."

Her insides melted. She didn't know what to do with that or the best behavior vibe wafting from him. It was almost as if he'd lectured himself on the way over to remember he had a reputation for being a nice guy and maybe he should act like one.

She cleared her throat. "Thank you."

"Are you ready to go?"

Her brows rose. After three hours at the salon today, that was his comment? This sedate, boring version of Logan needed to vacate the premises, pronto, or they'd never heat it up enough for anyone to care about taking their picture.

"Don't I look ready to go?"

It would not kill him to compliment her dress. Her hair. Her punctuality. Something.

"You look like you should be spread across the floor of a Mexican restaurant," he said bluntly, with a once-over that totally contradicted his words. His gaze was more *I want to rip that dress off you* than *I want to eat tacos.*

Her hackles rose as she glanced down at her mosaic tile dress that nipped in so far at the waist it was almost two pieces. The large cutouts left her waist and hips bare, which meant when they danced, his palms would be on her bare skin. Something more along the lines of *thank you* would be highly appropriate here.

Was his vision impaired? She looked good. It wasn't arrogance. It was a fact, because she paid attention to details. If there was anything she knew how to market, it was herself.

"Well, don't hold back, honey. Tell me how you really feel about a dress that took me all day to find and set me back six grand."

"It's a little…risqué for a charity fund-raiser, don't you think?" His faint scowl told her he'd already decided the answer was yes.

"Considering Kendall Jenner wore the same dress with a different color scheme to the Met Gala, no," she countered and willed her temper back, because they hadn't even left yet. An argument now wouldn't benefit anyone, since there were no cameras around, never mind that she'd been trying to provoke him.

"I don't know who that is, but odds are good she'll never be dating me. You are. Maybe you could find a wrap?"

Hands on her bare hips, she contemplated her fake boyfriend, who was about to learn exactly how little that role entitled him to. "What's that supposed to mean? I'm not allowed to be myself because I'm dating the world's biggest Goody Two-shoes?"

His scowl grew some teeth. "Clearly we need to establish some guidelines to this…relationship. Partnership. Whatever it is. Ground rules are obviously a must."

Yeah, that was a day late and a dollar short. Honestly, she'd been a little surprised he'd agreed to this idea with no parameters.

She clapped enthusiastically. "Yay! I *love* rules."

Rules were going to go over about as well as the notion of a *wrap*. She was not putting a single thread on top of this Versace masterpiece, and he could eat his rule book. Though she was a little curious what rules he might throw down.

So she could break them all.

"Lose the sarcasm or this is going to be a very long night."

Her brows arched involuntarily. "That was always going to be true, and I'd rather lose the dress than the sarcasm."

"That can be arranged." The heat dialed up a notch as his gaze strayed to the straps around her neck that held the dress on her body.

"You wouldn't dare."

More's the pity. There was no way he'd actually strip her out of this dress simply to get his way.

Was there?

"Rule number one. Never dare me, Trinity," he said with so much wicked in his voice that she nearly pushed him on it, strictly to find out how good he was at undressing a woman in formal wear.

All at once, flashes of an ad campaign spilled into her head. A man sliding a dress off a woman and the woman stopping him before he reveals her scar. Cut to a shot of Formula-47 that would be called…

The rest blurred, sliding away before she could visualize the ending. But it was a start. And more than she'd had in a long time.

Holy hell. Where had that come from? Better yet,

could she get more of it if she told Logan to get lost so she could work?

Torn, she eyed him and swore. She'd agreed to do this fake relationship deal, and as she'd been telling herself all week, he had a stake, too. They had places to go and people to let photograph them. Lots of fake kissing to engage in—which she would deny to her grave she looked forward to.

She tapped her temple. "I dare say even I can remember that rule."

Seemed like a dare was pretty close to how she'd gotten him to kiss her the first time.

"Good. We can discuss the rest of the rules on the way. Grab your wrap so we can go."

"Counterproposal. You remember that this is a partnership and I don't answer to you," she shot back. "The whole point is to get eyes on us. This dress is guaranteed to be on a hundred fashion blogs by morning, and to be honest, your love life could use spicing up."

She'd done her homework on Logan McLaughlin, and the mice he normally dated barely registered a blip in the social media sphere. Photographs of him with a woman on his arm were rare in the first place, but the few she'd found—*please*. Either he liked invisible, unassuming women or his vision really *was* impaired.

He crossed his arms. "What's that supposed to mean?"

She almost grinned at his echo of her earlier comment, but only because things were starting to get interesting. Finally. "It means you're boring, darling. One of your players is dating a supermodel who posed for *Playboy*, and he gets more love in the press than anyone else on your team. Take a lesson."

"I'm aware." Logan's back teeth ground together. "I've asked him stop seeing her. It's distasteful."

"Oh, honey." She shook her head. That spine needed unstarching in the worst way, and she definitely had a lot of ideas on how to accomplish *that*. "Thank God you've hooked up with me. Now you listen. We're going to go to this charity deal, I'm not going to wear a wrap and we're going to sizzle. That's the only rule you need."

Logan regretted getting a limo the moment Trinity Forrester spilled into the interior. If he'd driven his own car, he could have occupied himself with the steering wheel. The lack of a place to put his hands hadn't been a factor on the way over. Now? There was entirely too much female skin right there within touching distance.

And God above, the will it took to stop himself from reaching out was monumental.

She smelled both divine and like the kind of sin that would put a man on his knees in a confessional before dawn. The paradox was driving him insane. And they hadn't even pulled away from the curb yet.

A butterfly tattoo flashed at her wrist. It had been covered before, and he was not happy about how much he liked it. He watched as she arranged her long skirt to let her sexy shoes peek out. The heels, of course, resembled ice picks, and only tiny straps held them to her feet, making him wonder how they actually stayed on.

Even her toes were sexy.

"Rules," he growled because he needed some. "Are—"

"Made to be broken?" she filled in sweetly.

The limo shuttled toward what promised to be a very long evening fraught with frustration and tension, most of it sexual, followed by a morning explaining to everyone he knew that he had not, in fact, lost his mind when he'd selected his companion for the evening.

"Rules are necessary so I—we—don't forget what we're doing here." Though he suspected she wasn't dealing with issues in that respect the same way he was. "Without rules, the world descends into chaos."

"Maybe your world does. Mine just gets more interesting."

"Case in point. The most important rule we need to establish is that behind closed doors, we're not a couple. Only in public. And it's not real."

The cockeyed gaze she shot him was further enhanced by her swirly makeup. Less Cleopatra today and more Picasso. It was very distracting.

"I kind of thought all that was a given."

"Well, that's why it's important to lay it out ahead of time. So there's no confusion." That way, there was no end-of-the-evening mix-up at the door where she invited him in for a drink, which was really code for sex, and he'd struggle to remember why he was supposed to say no.

Rules gave him that out.

And really, *this is all fake* was the only rule he needed. She apparently needed a few more, but he'd lost the battle over her outrageous dress and didn't expect he'd win any others—not tonight, anyway. He'd be a hell of lot more specific the next time they appeared in public together.

Rule number two—dress like a woman dating a billionaire who owned a wholesome sports team.

In all actuality, he'd never imagined such a dress existed. Her whole back was bare, dipping low enough to give a guy a tempting glimpse of her rounded bottom. The front wasn't much better, cinching in at the waist to reveal wide panels of her trim waist and abs, and rising over her breasts to cover her to her collarbone. Oddly, the lack of cleavage made his mouth water to unclasp the catch at the back of her neck and let the fabric spill to her hips to reveal the hard nipples tenting the fabric.

He could not get out of this vehicle fast enough.

The limo snaked toward the hotel where the charity ball was being held. When it was their turn to emerge, he got out first and held out a hand to her. He would not have been shocked if she'd refused, but this was it, their first appearance in public together since the kiss clip went viral, and they needed to make it work.

Her hand disappeared into his and he helped her from the limo, happy that she hadn't chosen this moment for their first public fight. Photographers lined the ropes on both sides of the entrance. Instead of beelining for the door like he normally did whenever someone with a camera was around, he paused and slipped an arm around Trinity. His date, for better or worse.

He nearly groaned as his fingertips hit the silky expanse of skin at her hip bone. She might as well be wearing a swimsuit for all the coverage the dress provided. It would take no effort at all to slide his hand inside the fabric and keep going, because there was no way she was wearing underwear. He had the strongest urge to verify.

"Smile," she hissed and snuggled into his embrace far too cozily.

Easy for her to say. She wasn't fighting an erection.

So far, the enormous effort associated with this plan far outweighed the benefit.

A million flashes proved him wrong. More people clamored at the rope than Logan would have ever credited, and every one of them had a lens aimed in his direction. Other couples walked into the building with zero fanfare. Completely ignored.

"Told you this dress would be the ticket," Trinity murmured out of the side of her mouth. "Trust me next time. Kiss me."

"What? Now?"

"What did I just say, Logan?" She smiled up at him, but the curve of her lips was strictly for the audience, because her gaze glittered with challenge. "Don't make me dare you."

He rolled his eyes and laid a chaste kiss on her lips that shouldn't have pumped up the erection in his pants as much as it did. But the score of flashes in his peripheral vision told him her instincts had been dead-on. So he didn't complain. Out loud.

He'd had enough of the spots dancing before his eyes and steered Trinity through the crowd and into the hall, refusing to think about how disappointing that brief kiss had been.

"What is this shindig again?" she asked, eyeing the decorations with enthusiasm.

"It's to benefit Roost, a foundation that helps families relocate and rebuild after a natural disaster. I'm on the board. I took my father's place."

His dad had established the foundation a year before his unexpected death, and Logan had gladly stepped in as the head of the board. It meant something to him to continue Duncan McLaughlin's legacy.

Of course the real heroes were the people doing the heavy lifting; Logan just funneled money into the coffers and ensured Roost's logo appeared regularly during baseball games. Occasionally, he showed up at a fancy deal like this one and gave a speech.

Her gaze cut to him and held far more appreciation than it should. "I've heard of Roost. I didn't know you were involved in it. It's a cause you're passionate about or is this just a family obligation?"

The offhand question dug at him, tripping more than a few wires inside. "Why can't it be both?"

She shrugged one bare shoulder. "I guess it can be. Just seems to me that if you're going to champion a cause, it should be your own. Not your father's."

"My father was my role model. I would do well to emulate him. So would a lot of people."

"Of course." But he didn't mistake her comment as agreement, and it did nothing to cool his suddenly boiling temper. "And you'd also do well to be yourself instead of a carbon copy of someone else. A philosophy you might guess I readily subscribe to."

A lecture on individuality from the woman with a tongue piercing was not on the agenda for the evening. Neither was a dissection of his desire to follow in his father's footsteps. "I'm happy with who I am, thanks. Roost is important to me. Have you seen what a house looks like after a tornado tears through it? It's my pleasure to drum up support for people who have lost everything."

"I'll write you a check later," she murmured as several people picked that moment to ask for an introduction to his date. "It's the least I can do."

"You're already doing the least you can," he commented under his breath and dived into the social minutiae required at such an event before she could come up with what would no doubt be a cutting rebuttal.

It was nice to win one occasionally.

Trinity chatted up the curious guests with ease, clearly in her element, while Logan thought seriously about leaving early. Wearing a tux ranked about last on his list of fun things to do, followed shortly by eating in a formal setting. As a member of the board, he had the dubious privilege of being seated at the head table, where all eyes stayed trained on him and his flashy date.

His uncomfortable awareness of her dimmed not at all as they worked their way through steak and asparagus that probably tasted great when it wasn't flavored by visions of whirling a woman into the shadows to see just how naked she was under that dress.

When the band struck up a slow jazz number, Trinity's hand snaked beneath the table to squeeze his thigh. He avoided jumping like a teenager, but just barely.

"What?" he muttered.

"Ask me to dance, ding-dong," she shot back in a whisper.

He checked his ninth or tenth eye roll of the evening and stood to offer her his hand. "Would you do me the honor, Ms. Forrester?"

She didn't bother to check her own eye roll as she let him help her to her feet. "Are you trying to sound ninety, or does it come automatically?"

"I never come automatically." He cursed. That had slipped out and probably told her far too much about his mental state.

"I'll keep that in mind." She sounded like she was trying not to laugh.

They walked out on the dance floor and his hands drifted into place at her waist as if he'd done it a thousand times. Which, theoretically, he had—if you counted all the times he'd done it in his mind since opening the door earlier that evening.

She felt so good that his fingers spread across her skin without any prompting on his part, but he couldn't help wanting more contact. The point was to give the appearance that they were into each other. He just wished it wasn't so easy to fake that part.

Unlike earlier, no crush of cameras clamored to capture their every move, but there were still plenty of eyes on them, which meant they had to make it look good. It helped that she moved in sync with him as they danced, a shocking turn of events. If anything, he'd have expected her to try to lead, to boss him around—anything other than the fluidity they fell into instantly, as if they'd danced before.

She peered up at him from under her lashes and smiled, which hit him with the approximate force of a fighter jet at Mach 5. Apparently she wasn't on board with the respectable distance he'd put between them, because she scooted closer, deliberately brushing his body with hers as she swayed.

It took far too long to unstick his tongue from the roof of his mouth. He was thirty-five years old, for crying out loud, and had certainly bedded a few hot women. Of course that had been a fair number of years ago, before he started looking for the future Mrs. McLaughlin.

"So," he said inanely. "Here we are."

One of the pitfalls of a fake relationship—they had to pretend they actually had things to talk about.

"Mmm, yes, we are here," she agreed easily.

Her hands meandered under his tux jacket to cup his butt, which she then fingered suggestively. Every drop of blood in his body drained into his groin, and his brain fuzzed.

"Um, what are you doing?" he choked out. "Are there cameras on us that I can't see?"

"Nope. I'm just naturally handsy. And curious." Her blue eyes glowed in the low ballroom light. "How can

I fake being hot and heavy with you if I don't actually know what your butt feels like when I grab it?"

He groaned as he envisioned the scenario under which she might be grabbing his butt—as she cried his name in her throaty voice, urging him on as he drove her to a blistering climax, for example. Or maybe as he pinned her to the wall and took her standing up. Or, his personal favorite, as she knelt before him and pleasured him with her hot mouth, sliding that tongue piercing across his flesh.

His vision grayed for a second, and he might have lost the feeling in his legs.

"Do I get the same courtesy?" he muttered, thoroughly impressed with himself that he wasn't laid out on the floor. "Because there's a lot of you I haven't grabbed yet, either."

They were so close, her laugh vibrated through his tight groin.

"What are you going to do if I say yes?"

"This." It was close enough to a dare that he locked gazes with her and slid two fingers under the fabric of her dress to caress one bare globe of her rounded bottom. No panties, as he'd guessed.

The temperature shot up as heat flushed through his body.

And then it was no longer a point to be proven, but an exploration of the woman he'd been angling to get his hands on all night.

God, she felt amazing, like warm silk. Heat flared in her expression, winnowing through his blood until he couldn't stop himself from pressing closer, desperately seeking more of her, questing for relief from the needy ache she'd induced.

"I don't recall actually saying yes," she said. Instantly he withdrew, a millisecond from spitting out an apology, when she grinned. "But I wasn't saying no, either."

"Make up your mind, woman," he growled.

"I'm not the one who laid down the ground rules. Wasn't there something about none of this being real?" She shimmied her hips in a practiced rhythm against his painful erection. "That feels pretty real to me. Are you sure *I'm* the one who can't make up her mind?"

She'd baited him on purpose. Probably had deliberately worn this dress with the easily accessible butt cheeks to drive him insane. This was exactly the reason he should have said no to this ridiculous fake relationship. Trinity Forrester was too bold, too exotic, too... *sensual* for a man who just wanted a nice girl to come home to at the end of a long day.

Nice girls didn't constantly make him think about getting naked.

"Why do you have to make everything about sex?" he grumbled. "Can't we just dance?"

And now he sounded exactly like what she'd accused him of: a Goody Two-shoes. A ninety-year-old. A stickler for rules.

That was not who he was. This woman had been manipulating him all night, and he was done with it. He'd agreed to this fake relationship but he hadn't agreed to let her run roughshod over him.

That stopped now.

"Me?" She had the audacity to feign surprise. "I've never so much as uttered the word *sex* one time."

"You don't have to. It wafts from your pores." Eyes narrowed, he spun her around until he could dance her off the marble floor and into the shadows at the back of the room.

She had reasons for why she was so overtly sexy, so in-your-face with her asymmetrical hair and tongue piercing, and none of them were because she was a free spirit who reveled in her individuality.

She was hiding something behind her shock value.

Let's just see how you handle a man who has your number, Ms. Forrester.

Before she could blink, he had her trapped against the wall, his body pressing hard against hers. Exactly where he wanted to be, every nerve primed to sink into her.

More than that…he wanted to expose her secrets in the same way she'd peeled back his need to be like his father.

"Cameras?" She peered around his shoulder in anticipation.

"No idea." He tipped up her chin, guiding her attention back where it belonged. "I'm just curious about whether kissing you feels as good as I remember."

Her expression heated as she zeroed in on him, ignoring the crowd. "Well, that doesn't sound like it's in the rules according to Logan."

"It's number three," he corrected silkily. "When a woman has been begging you for something all night, you give it to her."

And exactly like the first time he'd kissed her, he couldn't stop himself from caving to the blinding need to have her mouth under his. Their lips connected, and instantly, he parted hers to savagely seek her taste.

It exploded on his tongue. Back and forth, give and take, he kissed her with every ounce of pent-up longing and passion and frustration that he'd been battling since the moment she'd slid into his limo. Since before that. Since that first kiss.

He wanted to strip her raw and tunnel under her outrageous appeal in hopes of tempering it somehow.

The cool hardness of the steel rod through her tongue skated along his hot tongue, and yes, the contrast and the sheer uniqueness of the sensation was as affecting as he remembered. More so. Because there were no cameras on them this time and he didn't have to think about decorum if he didn't feel like it.

He didn't feel like it.

They'd be so hot together. He wouldn't have to think about anything but pleasure. She'd tell him what she wanted, take it, give it back tenfold, and there'd be nothing but miles of skin and Trinity's laugh.

Her hands were everywhere, in his hair and caressing his face, against his back.

He returned the favor, groaning deep in his chest as he slid both hands beneath the fabric of her dress to take as much of her bare bottom into his palms as would fit. Which wasn't much, because the stupid wall was in the way. He eased up his full-body press enough to go deeper, and that got a moan out of her that was like music to his ears.

"You're stopping," she murmured. "Don't stop."

He groaned. Again. Oh, yes, it would be so easy to wedge his hand between her legs and continue his exploration of the secrets under that dress. But they were in public, with other couples taking advantage of the shadows a mere few feet away.

He'd never been so tempted to throw caution to the wind.

"If I touch you like that, I want to be someplace where you don't have to be quiet," he advised her. His name tearing from her throat as she came over and over again would be perfect.

She smiled and nipped at his lips with hers, rolling her hips against his erection. "Trust me when I say I have a lot of practice letting a man pleasure me in places where noise isn't kosher."

He sucked in a breath. He so did not need to hear that. Too late. His mind started filling in the blanks, calculating how wild and insane an affair he and Trinity could actually indulge in and still stick to the rules—after all, they weren't behind closed doors.

His body nearly made the decision for him, straining toward her in eager anticipation.

No. He had more control than this. He could not let her drag him under her spell. No matter how slick and ready she must be. No matter how much he ached to find out if she was as turned on as he was. "You've never done that with me. I seriously doubt you could keep it together."

"Only one way to find out."

"That's not going to work this time." He shook his head. The only reason it wouldn't was because he seriously feared that if he gave in, she'd suck him so far down into her bad-girl fantasy that he wouldn't ever be able to cut himself free.

And he needed to be disentangled if he ever hoped to find something real.

Four

The sketches refused to come together.

Trinity threw down her pencil and let her head drop into her hands. A whole Saturday wasted on the premise of the ad campaign she'd glimpsed in her mind while with Logan last night. Wisps of it had floated through her consciousness while they'd been dancing. Then when he'd kissed her—it was like her entire body had woken up from a hundred-year sleep.

Glorious, wonderful inspiration flowed like lava. And then the man had flooded her, pushing out everything but him as he lit her up with his mouth. His hands had done a good job igniting sparks, too.

When he forgot to be a stick in the mud, Logan McLaughlin set her on fire.

Coaxing him out of his all-American shell had become somewhat of a favorite pastime. She hadn't gotten him there yet, not all the way, but he'd veered much farther toward the dark side than she'd have expected.

No more fantasies about teaching him everything she knew.

Back to work.

Instead of beating her head against the brick wall of her creativity, she checked a few of her social media accounts, where she'd reposted several of the better pictures from last night. A few shares. Nothing had gone viral like the video from the show. Of course, the majority of the photos circulating this morning were the posed ones in front of the limo where she'd practically had to order Logan to kiss her. The pictures were nice. Sweet. Not enough to generate a buzz in her stomach, so she held little hope they would generate much of a buzz with the public, either.

If only someone had captured Logan's hand down her dress as he kissed her within an iota of stripping her naked—*that* would have burned up the web. But alas, no one with a camera had been in shooting distance of those shadows, apparently. Shame. They'd have to do better next time, be more deliberate about their choice of locales.

Shadows.

What if… She picked up her pencil and sketched a quick drawing of two silhouettes engaged in a very hot kiss. Ad copy could go something like, *With Formula-47, you don't have to stay in the shadows. Because it fixes your scars.*

Eh. That wasn't exactly award-winning stuff, especially if she had to explain the concept. If only she could come up with a name, the rest would definitely fall into place. She had until Monday. And then the only things that would fall if she didn't have her act together were the faces of her friends and business partners, who were expecting a marketing presentation designed to sell the living daylights out of their signature product.

So, this was not helping. Maybe if she could generate a better showing for her brand-new fake relationship, some of the pressure would be off and her muse would get with the program.

Palming her phone, she sent Logan a text message asking if he was free tonight before the little voices could start laughing at her feeble attempts to make excuses for wanting to see him. Yeah, she'd had fun last night after figuring out that the key to everything was getting him hot and bothered. It wasn't a crime to admit she'd rather press those buttons than sit here failing at being brilliant for the rest of her Saturday.

The return message came back instantly.

It's the ninth inning, so I can jet in a couple of hours. What did you have in mind?

Crap. Should have thought that through a little better. What she had in mind and what was feasible to actually do in a crowd were two different things, despite what she'd told Logan last night about her public exploits. But it was only fair that she come up with an event since he'd done the work last night.

Something that didn't require hours to get ready would be great. And necessary, since it was already four o'clock. Something public, where she could goad him into a fight, preferably, because that seemed to have worked the first time to get so many shares.

Nada.

It wasn't like she never did social stuff. But for so long, she'd done them with her friends, met interesting men wherever they ended up, and then gone home with one if she was in the mood. Or not, as the case had been lately. And her friends had all gotten married, leaving her at loose ends and restless.

Married friends might be a saving grace right this minute.

There was nothing to do but ping Cass and ask if she and Gage were by some miracle in Dallas today instead of Austin and if they had plans. Maybe the CEO of Fyra might be up for a double date, and there would be the added benefit of having two more social powerhouses with her, since both Cass and Gage regularly made the society columns in both of the cities they frequented.

Cass texted her back almost immediately.

We have invitations to a party in Deep Ellum to benefit Children's Advocacy Center, but we're skipping due to all the smoke and loud music. Baby on board, as Gage likes to remind me. You want to go in our place?

Trinity did a victory dance. Looked like she'd be taking Logan to a club after all, and the timing was perfect. She texted him to pick her up at eight, then shut her laptop lid so she didn't have to stare at the blank screen any longer.

Humming, she took a shower, then did her makeup. Harper had just come up with a really great new eye shadow that she'd asked everyone to test. The deep emerald color matched Trinity's mood and had a touch of sparkle, perfect for a dark venue. She poured herself into a faux leather catsuit in black with a silver chain ring belt and donned six-inch platform heels that complemented the outfit but didn't totally scream *dominatrix*.

Logan's expression when she opened the door later said that he didn't quite get the distinction.

"No." He shook his head and shut his eyes for a beat. "I'm not going anywhere with you dressed like a cross between Catwoman and Lady Gaga."

That was such a ludicrous statement, she actually glanced down. "Are you kidding? Lady Gaga would laugh at how tame these shoes are. Also, we're not having this argument every time, are we?"

"Apparently." He crossed his arms over his Dallas Mustangs T-shirt, bunching up his biceps in the way that drove her mad. Because she still hadn't gotten her hands on them, not properly. "Until you get the memo that I'm a conservative, God-fearing baseball team owner who sells hot dogs, foam fingers and memories, not bondage equipment."

"Honey, you're about as conservative as a Ferrari." And twice as sexy. He was a little windblown, as if he'd driven from the stadium in Arlington with the windows open. "No one who kisses a woman like you do could ever be described as tame."

Windblown Logan was delicious. Almost as much as tuxedo-clad Logan. Maybe more. The tux had lent him an almost inaccessible air, too beautiful to mar, but today he had a ready-to-rumble look that said he'd throw down if she pushed. And she was in the mood to push.

"Tame and conservative are not the same thing," he said with a once-over that had enough bite that her lady parts perked up. "Kissing you directly benefits my goals. You wearing that outfit does not."

She crossed her arms to mimic him and let a slow smile spill over her face. "I'm not changing. We're going to a club in Deep Ellum. I guarantee you I will blend in. You won't."

"Good. Then we'll attract more attention if we don't blend." Without asking, he barged into her condo like a bull with the red cape in his sights, then whirled in the marble entryway. "Which direction is your bedroom?"

"Well, if I'd known that's all it took to get you there, I'd have worn this outfit the first day."

He scowled. "Stop being dense. You're wearing different clothes. I need to find your closet."

"Oh, that's a terrible reason to be in a woman's bedroom. Just curious, are you going to wrestle me out of this outfit?" Leaning on the open door frame, she contemplated him and pointed down the hall. "Because if the answer's yes, my bedroom is that way."

"Fantastic."

And then, without any warning, he swung her up into his arms as if she weighed no more than a child, slammed the door shut with his foot and carried her to her bedroom. Her pulse tripled as the hard planes of his torso cradled her body. God, he was as solid and strong as she'd always imagined, but he held her gently, as if he didn't want to break her. If she hadn't already been snuggled into his embrace, her weak knees might have put her on the floor.

Even though she knew he'd only done it to avoid the rest of the argument, the gesture was so…gallant. As many men as had crossed her threshold, not one had ever treated her like she was delicate, and honestly, she'd have shown every last one of them the door if they had.

There was something about Logan and his old-fashioned streak that hit her between the eyes, almost as if he refused to see her as a sex object, no matter how she regarded herself. It shouldn't be so affecting. But there it was.

He deposited her on the bed without a word and strode to her closet, throwing wide the doors without hesitation, as if he'd dressed many a woman in his day. And maybe he had.

Oh, hell. She kind of wanted to see what he'd pick out.

"Here." He came out of the closet with a pair of 7 for All Mankind jeans and a simple black T-shirt that she wore to spin class sometimes. "Put this on."

She couldn't help it. She laughed. "So we can be twins?"

He threw the clothes on the bed and hunted around in her drawers until he found a bra and panties, both black, which was an interesting attention to detail she appreciated, completely against her will. When was the last time a man paid *that* much attention to her?

Handing her the undergarments, he stared down at her on the bed. "No. So I can see the real you underneath all of your deflections."

The earnestness in his expression froze her lungs and dried up every scrap of amusement in this situation. "What do you mean, the real me? This is as real as I get."

Before she could move, breathe, blink, he knelt on the bed and grabbed one foot, slowly unbuckling her platform sandal. Transfixed, she watched, too curious where he was headed to stop him.

"In public, it's not real. Behind closed doors, we're not anything but two people who don't know each other. All bets are off. I want to see what you're hiding underneath all of this outlandishness."

Oh, God. He was serious. And so intent that it bobbled her pulse. But she was nothing if not voraciously attracted to new experiences. What was the worst thing that could happen? Her pulse thumped as he tossed the first shoe over his shoulder. His gorgeous hazel eyes did not have an ounce of hesitation in them.

"By all means, strip away." She granted him permission to continue with a wave of her hand as if it didn't matter, but that would be a lie.

This was far from the first time a man had undressed her. But the way he was doing it tripped a hundred sensors in her chest, warning her it wasn't going to be like any of those other times.

Despite the heavy awareness spreading across her skin, this wasn't about sex, and neither of them was confused about that. It was about something else. A quest for knowledge.

She'd always considered herself an open book, but as he dropped the other shoe to her hardwood floor, she suddenly wondered if he'd sense all the dark and personal corners of herself that she'd never shared with anyone.

The brokenness inside wasn't something she liked to think about.

And that made her want to slam the book shut.

But it was too late. He peeled the catsuit from her shoulders and dragged it to her waist, his gaze locked on to hers, never straying to the skin he was revealing. Somehow, that made the act of him undressing her *more* sensuous.

She'd expected him to look, to ogle her naked body, because come on. He *was* a man, as red-blooded as any she'd ever met, and he had pulled out a bra and panties. He knew she didn't have anything on under this outfit.

Carefully, he lifted her hips and kept going, unwrapping her so slowly that her throat burned. When she twisted to release the fabric from under her legs, his fingertips grazed the brilliant green ivy tattoo twining around her thigh. She could feel the question in his touch, and her muscles quivered.

"It leads to the garden of Eden," she murmured as he laid her bodysuit aside. "Or so the story goes."

His gaze cut to her eyes.

"What's the real story?" he asked quietly. Unobtrusively. Sincerely, as if he really did want to know who she was.

"Ivy is hearty. It climbs. The vine grows little feet and will cling to almost any surface until it's taller than the structure it's climbing on. That resonates with me."

"You're tenacious." He nodded and slid the panties over her legs and trailed his thumb across the tattoo as he settled them into place. "That's a good quality."

She shrugged, mystified why he'd picked that word from the concept she'd thrown out. She'd always thought of it as survival and then domination of her surroundings, because it was that or be trampled underfoot. Ivy was one of those plants that when you stumbled over ruins, it would still be thriving. Maybe even overtaking the entire structure.

The butterfly tattoo on her wrist had meaning to her as well. Everything she'd done to decorate her body had significance. She wasn't sure how much she liked that he'd immediately dug that out of her.

His thumb continued stroking her thigh, and she got very aware of his hands on her very fast. "Your thumb is a little low. The garden is underneath those panties you just put on me."

"Are you asking me to touch you?" His voice was rough with a need that thrilled her. "Because that is very against the rules."

"Make some new ones," she said and let the challenge roll through the space between them, of which there was way too much for her taste. Maybe this hadn't been about sex at the start, but it could be now. It *should* be. "I'm just going to ignore them all anyway. I'm very good at being bad."

To demonstrate, she slid her fingertips up his leg to brush his groin, but just as she was about to curl her palm around his shaft, he grabbed her hand, removing it forcibly.

"Why do you do that?" he said point-blank, holding her hand in his as far away from his body as he could.

"Do what?" She stared at him, desperately trying to figure out where she'd miscalculated. He wanted her, and there was no way he could lie about it when she'd felt the evidence herself. "Refuse to pull punches when I want something? I'm not going to apologize. I like sex."

"No, you don't. You like control, and seduction is how you get it." He stared right back. "It amuses you to lead a man around, and sex keeps him occupied so he doesn't dig too far down into places he's not welcome."

Shock made her hand go limp. "I don't do that."

She did. She so did.

How the hell had he figured that out when they hadn't even slept together yet?

"You do. You flirt and wear outrageous clothes and advertise your availability purely as a distraction. What are you afraid I'm going to find out?"

That she longed to be the kind of woman a man wanted to stay with. Since she wasn't, she might as well get something out of a man's company. Orgasms worked for her.

She tossed her hair. "I'm not the one who's afraid, McLaughlin. It bothers you that you're so attracted to me. That's why you want me in boring clothes, so you can keep pretending you don't have a secret desire to do all sorts of wicked things to me. Things you know I'd like. You're throwing all of this in my face because you're the one who needs a distraction. Stop being such a Goody Two-shoes and take what you want."

"What I want is for you to put these clothes on so we can go." The catch in his voice said he wasn't as unaffected as he'd like her to believe. "Good sex stems from intimacy. Connection. I like to have that with someone I'm sleeping with."

I want to see the real you.

He'd meant it. That hadn't been a ploy to get her out of an outfit he'd hated.

And all at once, she wanted to give it to him. To have this thing between them be real. She could confess all her secrets, tell him how he made her feel feminine for the first time in a long time. He wouldn't care that she couldn't have babies; he'd like her for her.

They'd have something between them besides sex.

That's when her fantasy dried up and blew away. What did she know about how to be in a real relationship? Nothing, obviously, or she'd have figured out how to keep Neil around once she'd told him she'd conceived.

Dutifully, she let Logan hook her bra into place and raised her arms so he could pull the T-shirt over her head, suddenly grateful for the cover. She felt oddly exposed, as if the sheer act of informing her that he was stripping away her shields along with her outfit could actually accomplish it.

And she had enough appreciation for the psychology behind his assessment to be a little freaked that he'd come up with such a tactic. Enough that she let him pull her from the bed so he could slide her jeans over her hips and then button them, fully concealing her. It marked the first time in her life that a man had dressed her, only for her to wind up more naked than when she'd worn nothing.

The appreciation shining in Logan's eyes as he laced his fingers with hers put a different kind of heat low in her belly. This barely-make-a-blip outfit had more effect than the in-your-face sexy one. For Logan, at least. What was she supposed to *do* with him?

"You're a beautiful woman, Trinity." He stated it like a fact, but that didn't decrease the potency in the slightest. "Dressed like this, you make so much more of an impact, because it allows you to be the star instead of the outfit."

Her knees did go weak at that, but she locked them. Now was not the time to get mushy over Logan McLaughlin. No time was good for that. This was all fake and designed to go his way so he could control his image. Nothing more.

She had to remember the most important rule— none of this was real. That was the reason he hadn't undressed her and used it as an excuse to cop a feel or ogle her. He wasn't attracted to her other than at a base level, and only then because it was involuntary physiology, not the connection he was looking for.

Good. She didn't want that. Not with Logan, not with any man.

Except maybe she did, and she did not like that he'd uncovered a longing she'd had no idea was there. A longing she had no business indulging in, because she didn't work like other women, couldn't. Her body wasn't made for pregnancy, and her ability to trust the opposite gender didn't exist. She had to stop this nonsense cold.

"Maybe I like my clothes to be the star," she muttered, and to her mortification, tears pricked at her eyelids. What in the hell was this man doing to her?

A better question was, why was she letting him?

"Wearing this outfit will get us the top spot on people's social media feeds, I guarantee it," he said mildly. "Do me one last favor and wear the shoes, though. I like it when you're tall enough for me to put my arm around you."

Oh, really?

The tears coupled with the unexpected exposure and longings that shouldn't even be a factor put her in a dangerous mood. "I call BS. You like these shoes because you have secret bad-girl fantasies."

He rolled his eyes. "It's not a stretch to say I like sexy shoes on a woman. I readily admit to that."

That set her back. The man was honest to a fault, and it kept throwing her off. He was supposed to lie to her and act like an ass and pull immature ghosting routines where he pretended his phone was off when she tried to reach him.

Maybe he'd already lied to her. Like when he said he wanted intimacy instead of sex. Or was he actually lying to himself about what he wanted?

"If I wear the shoes," she murmured throatily, "do I get a reward?"

Suspicion clouded his expression. "Like what? A gold star?"

She shrugged. "Maybe you take me to the bathroom in the club and see how far your hand goes down these jeans. Or didn't you notice how tiny these panties are on me?"

"I noticed," he said shortly and ran a hand through his hair, a habit she'd started to clue in meant he felt uncomfortable. "Trust me, I'm not that much of a good guy."

News to her. "Tell me. Would it be so bad to let your bad boy out to play occasionally?"

His eyes narrowed. "Yes, it would."

When he didn't elaborate, her curiosity went through

the roof. So he wasn't denying that he had a wild streak. Interesting. Because if he had denied it, she'd have called him on that, too. No man who put his hands down a woman's dress in a crowded ballroom with scarcely a glance around could claim he'd never done anything like that before.

Seemed like Logan might be hiding behind his public persona, too. What would he be like if she stripped him of his conservative armor?

Suddenly, she was ready to get him out in public, where she could flirt and seduce and provoke him into putting his hands on her again without fear. Because behind closed doors, it wasn't real. She had to get out of here before she forgot they weren't a couple with an interest in getting to know each other beneath the surface.

By ten o'clock, Logan had a pounding headache that beat against his temples in perfect time to the garbage being pumped out of the speakers at the Deep Ellum club Trinity had dragged him to.

The Mustangs had lost today—again—and what he should really be doing was combing through his roster—again—to see where he could make improvements.

As a whole, the team's manager had point on the fine details, but he had to work with the talent Logan gave him. It was the general manager's job to get the right guys onto the field for the best price. Bang for the buck was key when it came to the financials of a ball team. Managing money should come easily considering his DNA, but it didn't. He had to work at it.

So instead of crunching numbers and looking at possible trade angles, Logan leaned against the bar nursing a light beer that wasn't fit for unclogging a drain. The view was nice, though. Trinity perched on a bar stool, clutching a highball, one jeans-clad leg entwined with his. She'd done that a while back in a seriously sexy *back off, ladies* move that had raised his eyebrows, but he kind of loved it.

They couldn't exactly talk due to the music, yet the contact created a sense of intimacy he'd never have expected. As a result, he'd been sporting a semi in his pants since the moment her leg had snaked possessively around his.

All right, the fact that she was wearing jeans and a T-shirt that he'd personally put on her body might have a little more to do with the hard-on. When he'd said he wanted to see the real her, he hadn't expected to like it so much, or to discover a burning desire to uncover more. He'd barely scratched the surface of what lay beneath Trinity's outrageous exterior. And that thirst for knowledge was at least 50 percent of the reason he was still here.

The bump in ticket sales was the other fifty. Myra couldn't control her glee earlier when she'd phoned him in the dugout to say that today's game had hit an all-time high for attendance. Which unfortunately wasn't saying much, but it was saying *something*.

There was definitely room to get some more press, though.

And he needed to do it before his skull split in two.

A photographer had been circulating near the front of the club, and he bided his time until he saw her headed toward the bar. From the corner of his eye, he tracked her progress until she was close enough to guarantee she wouldn't miss it if he tossed her a great shot.

Logan plucked the highball from Trinity's grasp. Before she could squawk, he swiveled her stool and cupped her face in both hands, bringing it up to his. Their lips connected.

It should have been a token kiss, just show. But this was Trinity, and she didn't hesitate to open her mouth. That steel piercing slid hard across his tongue, sensitizing him all the way to the bottoms of his feet. Her arms raced down his back. She flattened her palms against it and shoved, grinding his erection straight into her center, hard enough to put stars across his vision.

God, yes, more of that. Aching, fiery need exploded between them, and he wrapped a hand around her thigh dangerously close to the ivy tattoo under her jeans, hauling her leg higher on his hip. The angle opened her wider and the stool was just the right height to make everything feel unbelievably good.

Deepening the kiss shouldn't have been so effortless, but she was as into it as he was, her moans vibrating her chest against his, or maybe that was the thump of the bass jarring them both. Whatever it was, this was the hottest kiss he'd ever participated in.

The music wasn't loud enough to cover the hoots of the surrounding partygoers, though, and somehow it filtered through his head that he'd more than accomplished his goal of laying a photo-worthy kiss on his date. And publicity was the only reason to be doing it. The only logical reason, anyway, and the only one he'd admit to.

With far more reluctance than he'd like, he ended the kiss and pulled away, but Trinity was having none of that. She threaded her fingers through his hair, pressed against his neck and nuzzled his nose with hers, brushing their lips together, and suddenly they were kissing again.

But this time, it was a slow slide into an intense web of awareness. Everything faded and time stopped as he tasted heaven. The floodgates of his body opened, welcoming her in. This was connection, the kind he'd said he wanted. It was so much more than a kiss, and he craved it like he craved blood to his heart.

This was what it was like to kiss the woman behind the curtain. No barriers. He'd been looking for the essence of Trinity and he'd found it. More importantly, she'd given it to him. It spread through him, warm, thick, sweet, and it was so right that it became a part of him instantly, as if she had always been there.

One of her hot hands slipped under the hem of his shirt, scrabbling at his waist as if she'd slide off the stool if she didn't hold on. He totally understood that. Because he was careening down a slippery slope as well, hitting a hundred miles an hour with no brakes.

And that's what finally snapped him out of it.

When he'd told her he wanted intimacy, he'd expected her to balk. It was supposed to put another barrier between them, a reminder that he wanted a home and hearth kind of woman, not one who threatened to incinerate every bone in his body.

This time, when he pulled back, she let him go, her arms falling into her lap. She blinked, reorienting herself, apparently as befuddled as he was by what had just happened.

"Did she get the shot?" Trinity murmured, and instantly it was business as usual.

"She better have."

If not, he was done with this farce. There was no way he could keep this up. Because it was starting to feel way too real even when they weren't behind closed doors.

When Logan's phone rang at 8:00 a.m., *Mom* was the last name he expected to see flashing on the screen.

He groaned and put a pillow over his head, but it still felt like each chime of the ringtone cut straight through his temples. He knocked the phone onto the bed without looking and dragged it under the pillow. "Don't you have church?"

"Hello to you, too." His mother was way too chipper for a Sunday morning. "I'm about to leave, yes. You should come with me."

"I have a game today," he reminded her, which she should know, since she had box seats and came to most home games. When he was free, he didn't mind taking his mom to the church she'd attended with his dad for over thirty years. He hated that she had to go by herself now.

"Judging by the pictures your grandmother forwarded me, you'd do better to come with me to church," his mother said and he could hear her raised eyebrows in her tone. "Who is this woman you were kissing like you wanted to swallow her whole?"

"Trinity Forrester." He could not have this conversation at 8:00 a.m. on a Sunday. Or any time on any day, for that matter. How did he live in a world where Grandma got her mitts on photos posted to the internet and tattled to his mother about them? "And it was just a kiss."

It was so not just a kiss, and odds were the photographer had captured the scene at the club last night at the height of the frenzy. Logan hadn't seen the pictures yet, but they must have been really good if they warranted an early-morning call regarding the subject of his eternal soul.

"Would it be too much to ask if I could meet her? Since you're seriously involved and everything?"

Logan groaned. "Mom, I'm not marrying her. We're just…dating."

"That's not what the caption says."

He sat up, knocking the pillow to the floor. "What? What does it say?"

"'Billionaire owner of the Dallas Mustangs celebrates as Fyra Cosmetics executive says yes to his proposal.'" She cleared her throat. "That's verbatim. I'm reading it straight off my screen."

Since he didn't need any more invitations to church, he bit back an inventive curse. "It's…complicated, Mom."

He couldn't flat-out deny it, not until he knew if Trinity had planted the story on purpose. She better not have. He'd already told her his views on a fake engagement. His temper set off at a slow boil.

"Oh. So are you engaged or not?"

He couldn't lie to his mom, either. They'd always been close, but since his dad had died, Logan made sure that his mom wanted for nothing. They'd made the agonizing decision together to sell McLaughlin Investments, the online stock trading company his dad had founded, and then split the money in half. It had bonded them in a way nothing else could have. "I'll call you later and tell you. How about that?"

"As long as the answer is yes, sure."

Of course that was what she'd say. She'd been bemoaning the lack of a daughter-in-law for going on ten years now and recently had started in on the lack of grandchildren. *You're not getting any younger*, she liked to remind him, *and I'm certainly not*.

He had a ticking clock in his head, too, and didn't need any help feeling like the life full of family and kids that he saw when he closed his eyes did not even slightly resemble the one he lived every day. The line of eligible women wrapped the block twice, but he couldn't seem to find the *right* future Ms. McLaughlin. Certainly he would not increase his chances by parading a fake one around.

A shower did not improve his mood, and neither did the images that had been flashing across his mind since the undressing of last night. Trinity's body was the stuff of legends, and he was not the nice guy she'd painted him as.

Oddly, thinking about that second kiss put more wood in his shed than visualizing her perfect breasts as he peeled off that outfit made of sofa cushion material. So horrible. But once it was gone? So beautiful.

The woman. The kiss. The way she'd made herself vulnerable to him, both on that bed as he'd stripped away all of the outer trappings that hid Trinity from the world and on that bar stool as he explored what he'd found. So amazing.

He palmed himself and took care of the worst of the aching need, but he suspected he wouldn't ever fully absolve it until he gave in to the inevitable.

Which wasn't happening.

When he got out of the shower, he hunted up something to eat in the enormous kitchen that had come with the house he'd bought in Prosper because it was close to the Mustangs training facility and the school district was one of the best in north Texas.

Yeah, it had occurred to him that the woman he eventually married might like to pick out her own house, but he'd fallen in love with the property the moment his Realtor showed it to him. Twenty rolling acres spread out around the main house with plenty of room for kids and dogs, and a stable sat up on a hill overlooking a lake that he'd stocked with fish. Now all he needed was the wife.

Apparently he'd been granted step one in that process without his consent, and since he really couldn't put it off any longer, Logan snatched his laptop from the built-in desk near the fireplace in the great room and booted it up as he mainlined coffee.

The shot spilled onto his screen, and yeah, it was hot. He was standing between Trinity's legs, back to the camera and his hand on her thigh. The photographer had captured the kiss perfectly to show Trinity's face and expression—rapturous.

Logan's entire body cued up at the memory. This wasn't a picture of two people faking it for the camera. They wanted each other more than they wanted to breathe, and it was all there in full color for the world to see.

That's what his mom should be worried about, not whether the caption had any validity, although it did say exactly what she'd said it did.

Trinity Forrester was not the woman of his dreams. Fantasies? Sure. It would be impossible not to think about finishing that kiss with all her clothes on the floor. But the idea of her being his fake fiancée did not sit well. At all. He needed to call her, but it was barely nine o'clock on a Sunday and despite all of the evidence burning up his laptop screen, he did have a small sense of decorum left.

His phone beeped with a text message from none other.

Looked like she wasn't a late sleeper, either.

Did you see? It's all over my social media. I need a ring.

That pushed far more buttons than he should have allowed, and his temper flared. A fake relationship was one thing, because frankly, it wasn't all that fake. They *were* dating, and no one had asked how serious it was, so there had been no reason to lie. Until today.

He called her. Some things couldn't be properly conveyed via text message.

"Isn't it great?" she gushed by way of answer. Clearly she'd been sitting on her phone waiting on a return text and was perfectly fine with a conversation instead. "My publicist already called me. She's thrilled with the response. One of her trackers says the picture with the proposal caption has been shared twenty-five thousand times."

The phone nearly slipped from his suddenly nerveless fingers.

"Twenty-five thousand? Really?"

God, the nightmare just kept going, didn't it? How was it possible that people cared so much about something as unimportant to their daily lives as two people they'd never met getting engaged? And it was a lie, besides.

"That's just the one with your hand on my thigh. The other one is better, but it's not getting as much traction, probably because it's not as splashy."

The other one? Wedging his phone against his ear, he did another search and so many results scrolled onto his screen, he could hardly fathom it. There. He clicked.

The photographer had gotten a one-in-a-million shot in that moment after Logan had pulled away, in between the first and second kisses, just as Trinity had started to reel him back in. They weren't kissing, not yet, but the raw desire on her face was unmistakable. This picture was worth a thousand words, perfectly encapsulating what he'd felt as he'd been sucked into her—as if flesh and bone had dissolved, leaving only their essence behind.

She'd felt it, too. And he hated sharing what should have been a private moment with the world.

He hated a lot of this.

"I'm not buying you a ring," he muttered. "Are you the one who planted that caption?"

"No, I was just as surprised as you were. It might have been my publicist, but she won't admit it."

"We have to set the record straight. That's nonnegotiable. I don't mind letting a bunch of strangers think we're dating, but it's not fair to the people in my life to let them think there might be a wedding in our future when there's not."

"Why do we have to say anything?" She waved off all of his concern with that one airy statement. "No one is asking for an interview. Let it ride. See how your numbers are Monday morning and then let's strategize some more."

Easy for her to say. If the Mustangs won today, he'd most definitely be in front of a dozen sportscasters, and he'd bet good money they'd ask him about his love life.

They didn't win.

But by noon on Monday, he had evidence in his hand that people were buying tickets regardless, in record numbers. Logan McLaughlin had become the poster boy for the Dallas Mustangs ball club, and Myra had very specific ideas for how to capitalize on it.

Logan bit his tongue and picked up the phone to call Trinity.

Five

There was literally nothing about baseball that had matched Trinity's expectations. Case in point: when Logan had called her to ask if she'd go on a road trip with him, she'd actually thought he meant a *road trip*. Like the kind every single person on the planet except Logan would interpret as two people in a car driving somewhere.

Not what he'd meant.

Fortunately, jetting off to San Francisco for a few days to watch the Mustangs take on Oakland fit her need to not be at work on Monday. She might even call herself pathetically grateful to have a valid excuse for why she couldn't be at Fyra giving the nonexistent Formula-47 presentation.

Also, Logan had failed to mention that the Mustangs had a private plane for away games, which made the trip even more fun. The entire fuselage had been fitted with first-class-size seats, which made her feel even tinier in a cabin full of large men, but she reveled in the luxury.

Shortly after takeoff, the flight crew began circulating with drinks and food. Logan casually took Trinity's hand, lacing their fingers together. Strictly for show. She knew that. But it put a little tingle in her stomach that she secretly didn't hate.

She was looking forward to a lot more *tingle* in her future. After all, this trip was the perfect opportunity to take their relationship to the next level, both on camera and off.

"Tell me again," she murmured with a nod at the middle-aged man Logan had introduced her to earlier as the Mustangs' manager. "You're the general manager and that guy is the manager with no other title in front of it?"

"Right. It's a weird baseball thing. I never think twice about it." Logan's thumb brushed over her knuckle as he spoke and she wondered if he even realized he was doing it. "Gordon is the coach and I'm the CEO."

Prior to today, Logan had been almost deliberately affectionate, as if he was only paying attention to her because their on-camera relationship required it. She was trying not to ascribe any meaning to his seemingly subconscious touch other than the obvious—he was technically at work and probably focused on that.

Besides, they weren't a real couple. There didn't have to be meaning to anything he did. In public, everything was fake. She didn't have to dissect his moods or worry if he was thinking about ditching her. None of that mattered, which was what made it great.

"CEO, huh? So everyone reports to you and you could fire them all?"

He nodded with a shrug.

That was a job she was glad Cass had signed up for at Fyra. Trinity would hate having so many people looking to her for answers.

She scooched down in her seat. Wasn't that still the case with the marketing campaign for Formula-47? Skipping town on the wave of positive publicity didn't absolve the fact that a lot of people depended on her to hit a home run on this one.

And Logan had apparently invaded her consciousness to the point where she was making baseball analogies.

She'd noticed that around Logan, her muse was inspired. She'd gotten a double dose of inspiration from that scorching-hot round of kissing Saturday night, but the dozens of half-finished sketches hadn't moved her much closer to her goal. Something much more…*encompassing* than mere kissing might be the ticket, and she had a four-day trip ahead of her to prove her theory.

The next time she got naked with Logan, there would be a whole lot more happening than a conversation, and no one would be putting on clothes for quite a while. But she didn't want to clue him in that she had a stake in taking this very public flirtation behind closed doors.

When they got to the hotel, a slew of photographers waited outside the sliding glass doors. The limo Logan had chartered slid to a stop near the valet stand, but he didn't get out right away.

"By the way, I tipped off the local press that we were coming to this series. Together," he said. "As a couple. I hope that was okay."

"Brilliant." She'd wondered if this was the typical welcome a baseball team received in a host city. But it was the general manager and his girlfriend-slash-fiancée that they'd come to see. Nice. "Maybe we should think about hiring someone to follow us around with a camera. I like the organic reach of having unbiased third parties pick up the story, but it couldn't hurt to goose things a little."

"Got it covered. My publicist does, anyway," he amended as Trinity lifted her brows in question. "She's sending someone to all three games to take photos of us in my suite."

"We have a suite?" Like with a bed? Suddenly the prospect of sitting through three baseball games got a little more interesting. "You should have mentioned that way before now. Maybe we can take an adult nap during the middle part when nothing happens."

She waggled her brows to be sure he picked up on the double entendre.

His chuckle warmed her enormously. "It's not like a hotel suite. It's a skybox with seats for people to watch the action on the field, but with air-conditioning and a bar. I also invited several acquaintances to come hang out with us. It'll be a party."

Oh. That still sounded better than being outside in the sun while watching guys in uniforms hit a ball. "I shall be attentive and adoring in front of your friends. And the photographer."

Just that morning, a new article had made the rounds with damaging allegations about Fyra's animal testing practices. Cass had already involved their lawyer to see if they could sue. But anything Trinity could do to negate that bunch of BS would only help.

He climbed from the limo and helped her out, slipping an arm around her waist to guide her inside. The porter began pulling luggage from the limo's trunk as people surged forward, cameras poised to begin snapping money shots of the couple they'd come to photograph.

"Nice shoes," he murmured in her ear as flashes went off around them.

Yeah, she'd worn her six-inch Prada heels even though her ankles got puffy when she flew. The straps were cutting into her flesh and she'd lost feeling in her toes at least three hours ago. But she liked it when he could put his arm around her, too.

"You're welcome."

He grinned, and she promptly forgot about her ankles. Maybe she could talk him into an adult nap right this minute. Just to take the edge off. Her insides had never quite cooled after that second kiss Saturday night, and she'd be quite happy to pick up where they'd left off.

But then she distinctly heard him tell the hotel clerk *two rooms*. "What?"

He glanced at her. "One sec. I'm checking in."

"I realize that." She smiled at the clerk. "Excuse us for a moment, please."

The charter bus the rest of the team had ridden in from the airport picked that moment to unload. A wave of testosterone flowed through the doors, raising the noise level to a dull roar as the athletes, coaches and staff members sorted themselves out.

Dragging Logan to an uncrowded corner of the lobby was no small feat given both her precarious balance and his resemblance to an immovable mountain. But he came willingly, which she appreciated. She raised her brows. "Are you insane? We can't have separate rooms."

"We not only can, we are." He crossed his arms. "As soon as I get the keys, that is."

Aghast, she stared at him, but he looked perfectly serious. "After you went to the trouble to hire photographers, what are the odds they'll snap a picture of us going into separate rooms? Like a hundred and ten percent."

He scowled. "So? We can be a chaste couple waiting for marriage, can't we?"

His scowl deepened the harder she laughed. When she finally got herself under control, she gingerly dabbed at her eyelashes without fear thanks to Harper's waterproof, smudge-proof, morning after–proof mascara, all of which Trinity had personally tested.

"Did you actually look at the pictures from Saturday night?" She had. A lot. And twice she'd had to finish the job he'd started herself. Her vibrator hadn't ever gotten so much action. "They had ten times the reach that the ones from Friday did. The posed red carpet thing? Not for us. The spontaneous, hotter-than-hell, can't-wait-to-screw-each-other vibe is what our fans like. What they want to see."

His expression didn't change, and her panic level started an uphill climb. She needed him. Needed to get hot and heavy away from the camera. Inspiration was in short supply, and he was hogging it all.

"No. It's not happening. I've already made huge concessions—"

"Like what?" Hands on her hips, she forced her voice back down into a lower register before someone overheard them. She didn't mind if the photographers captured a public fight, but she did not want them to splash the cause of it across the web. "I'm the one constantly changing my clothes and—"

"One time you changed, and only because I forced you—"

"You so did not force me. I let you change my clothes because it suited me. Make no mistake, you don't control me."

"I don't want to, Trinity!" He apparently had no concept of volume, and several heads swiveled in their direction.

"Shh." She jerked her head at the press, who had

definitely clued in that something was afoot and started snapping away. Hopefully they'd get some good shots. "Act like you're mad all you want, but we can't afford any prying ears."

"I'm not acting," he growled. "I've already had phone calls about our impending engagement, despite your certainty that no one was going to ask about it. I don't like being put in that position. Nor do I want to be in the position of defending my personal choices regarding sleeping arrangements."

Gee whiz. His old-fashioned streak went a whole lot deeper than she'd credited. What a fun new challenge she'd stumbled onto here. Gaze narrowed, she swept him with a once-over designed to put a few thousand degrees of heat under his skin. "You must not be aware of what I have planned, then, if you think this is about sleeping."

Instantly, wariness and a fair amount of caution snapped across his expression. Who was throwing up shields now, hmm?

"Separate rooms," he said firmly.

"Fine."

She threw up her hands, but only to make it look like she still hated the idea, when actually, she'd realized it worked in her favor. It was a much juicier story if they had separate rooms but, oh, look, someone just caught them macking down in the hall outside one of them. And then they could both duck inside to take the super-hot kiss to its natural conclusion.

It was also in her best interests to ensure it was his room…so she could accidentally on purpose let someone photograph her sneaking away from it at dawn.

"Separate rooms. But you have to take me to dinner," she insisted. "Otherwise, we'll miss a golden opportunity to get more lens time."

He nodded with a smug smile. Probably because he thought he'd won. She let him think that. By the end of the night, he'd realize they'd both won.

One thing she could say for Logan, he did not cheap out when it came to putting up his fake girlfriend-slash-fiancée in a hotel.

Trinity took a long soak in the garden tub and used every ounce of the bubble bath the hotel had provided from their signature spa, strictly for market research purposes.

One hot-and-heavy sheet session with Logan could do the trick to get her muse back in the game full-time. But she was fully prepared to go all night with him if need be. Three or four orgasms fit into her schedule just fine, especially when Logan was the one delivering them. The man got her hotter than concrete in August.

In deference to her agenda, she selected a very simple white shift dress strewn with tiny colored flowers that covered her almost to the neck. It looked spectacular on her even though it didn't advertise any skin. To make up for the conservative dress, she put a pink stripe down the side of her hair and wore lace-up heels that crisscrossed her ankles a bajillion times. It would take both an enterprising and patient man to get these shoes off, and she shivered in anticipation of the foreplay that could be involved.

Logan knocked on her door.

She answered. His gaze dropped to her dress and lingered, hot appreciation blooming on his face. Score one for Trinity.

How had she missed that he liked her *that* much better in conventional clothes? He'd been so turned on by the simple jeans and T-shirt, but she'd mistakenly believed that had been a result of him being the one to put them on her.

"I expected to have to redress you," he threw out casually, but she did not miss the undercurrent of disappointment. He not only liked her in conservative clothes, he liked picking them out. Road trips made for interesting fonts of information, that was for sure.

"I was feeling generous."

"Noted. I will return the favor by escorting you to a nice dinner."

Where she would be charming and pretend that dinner was the only photo op of the night.

As predicted, a few photographers were still hanging around in the lobby, and she and Logan dutifully stopped before continuing on to the restaurant, allowing pictures. It didn't matter that the photos were staged, because they would all pale in comparison to the ones later on tonight, anyway. These chaste pictures got them nowhere.

Dinner was surprisingly normal. And nice. Logan exhibited incredible patience as Trinity peppered him with baseball questions that he must have found tedious. But she liked listening to him talk about his passion, and baseball was clearly it. He talked with his hands, smiled, laughed. If she didn't know better, she'd think they were actually dating.

No. Slipping into a fantasy about this whole thing being real was the surest path to problems.

"Walk me to my room?" she asked casually after noting several photographers had drifted away. Only the most tenacious had hung on, which meant they would likely be the most interested in being thrown a bone.

"Sure." Logan laced his fingers with hers in what had become a very common move for him. She liked it, but that was a deep, dark secret she'd never spill.

Was this what normal couples did, how they acted with each other? Was that why so many people did the relationship deal despite the surety of things going south? If nothing else, participating in a fake relationship gave her an inkling why Cass, Alex and Harper had all jumped on the marriage bandwagon.

But none of her friends were broken. Obviously. Just because real relationships had happened for them didn't mean it would for Trinity. That's why this one was so great—it would end before anyone got attached.

Of course, they hadn't exactly established an expiration date, but he could announce one any second. Letting go of Logan suddenly felt like the very last thing she'd be okay with, and her throat tightened along with her hand.

He squeezed hers back and oh, God, she didn't want to let him go. Not tonight.

They stepped out of the elevator on her floor without any reporters following them, and she didn't care. None of this was about the press or sales. He was a man and she was a woman and she needed him. For a lot of things, some she didn't even want to articulate to herself, let alone to him.

Logan must have sensed her distress, because he lifted her hand to his lips and kissed two knuckles as they arrived at her door. "What's wrong? You're shaking."

"Nothing." *Blow it off.* Not letting a man see her weaknesses was so ingrained, she did it automatically. "Just thinking about our missed opportunity to get photographed kissing downstairs."

"We have the next three days. We'll have plenty of opportunities."

She couldn't let him leave. Desperately, she shook her head and smiled, easily falling into seduce-and-conquer mode. Because that's what she knew how to do. "Maybe we should practice."

He laughed. "Kissing? You saw the pictures from Saturday. I don't think lack of practice is our problem."

"No, it's not," she murmured. "Our problem is that we always stop."

A glint popped into his gaze that she couldn't read. But he wasn't walking away. "We stop because we're in public and our agreement doesn't extend to making X-rated films."

But not because he *wanted* to stop. She pounced on that small distinction and held up her card key, then deliberately dragged it down his torso until she hit his belt. "So don't stop."

If he didn't, it would be her one chance to pretend Logan could be hers for real. Just for one night.

The little white dress Trinity wore had been killing him since he'd first glimpsed her in it. All Logan could think about during dinner was putting his hands under it to see if she had on virginal white underwear or had gone full-bore bad girl with a racy thong, maybe in red.

Either one would work.

The mystery could be solved very easily. All he had to do was sweep her into his arms, open the door and lay her out on the hotel bed.

He didn't. There were rules in place. For a reason.

"Are you inviting me into your room?" His voice had dropped, going raw with need that he couldn't control if he tried. So he wasn't trying. "Because that would be a no-no. We're only a couple in public. A fake couple."

"Oh, right. We're still worried about your rule book." She didn't sound worried. She sounded like she was about to rip all of his rules to shreds. And maybe some of his sanity, too. "If it would make you feel better, we could leave the door open."

A technicality. It had potential. If they left the door open, they'd theoretically still be a couple. It was only behind closed doors that he'd established any sort of parameters.

"That doesn't make it real," he cautioned, and he was pretty sure she realized he was talking to himself more than her.

Kissing in public was one thing, but to take it behind closed doors meant he had to admit his fierce attraction to Trinity went far deeper than it should. She wasn't the right woman for him.

Her laugh ripped through his groin, hardening his shaft to the point of pain.

"For the love of all that's holy, Logan. Please tell me what about the sizzling-hot thing between us isn't real?"

She had a point, one he wished he didn't like so much. Real was relative.

They had a real attraction. A real interest in getting each other naked. The only fake part was how it had started. And how it would end. He'd always defined a real relationship as one with potential to be permanent, but again, perspective.

"What are you saying, that we'd become a real couple?" he asked.

What did that even mean? How would they manage the logistics of that?

"Sweetie, you're thinking about all of this way too hard." She took his hand and flipped it over, exposing his palm, where she laid her room key as some kind of offering. Or challenge. "We don't need rules or definitions. That's how things get all messed up. All we need is to know that once we step through that door, we're both going to have a lot of orgasms. Together."

Something akin to relief rushed through his body along with a very strong lick of lust that put every nerve on high alert. She was doing her best to make this all about sex. Which was working. What did it matter whether she was a woman he could marry or not? That wasn't on the table, for either of them. Why was he even struggling with this?

She closed his fingers around her room key. "This is your show, Logan. If you want to play this as a publicity angle, I'm all for it. Think about how much sizzle photographs of us will have if we're actually burning up the sheets. It's a no-brainer."

The key to everything was literally in his hand. She'd given him the choice—wisely—because then he couldn't say he hadn't made it. "You're just going to keep throwing out my rules until I give in, aren't you?"

Wickedness laced her smile. "I'm pretty sure I already have. Oh, wait. I forgot rule number one. Logan McLaughlin, I dare you to take what you want. Let me fulfill every last fantasy you've ever had but were too busy being nice to indulge in."

That was the sexiest thing a woman had ever said to him.

"Every one?" he murmured. She didn't move, but thick, dense awareness rolled between them like fog with teeth, weighting his words. "I'm afraid even you couldn't keep up with my vivid imagination. It's been in high gear pretty much since the moment you told me you had a tongue piercing."

"Try me."

The chemistry that had been building since day one exploded inside him, and he pressed her up against the door before he could think. Not thinking worked for him. She'd given him permission to feel and he planned to.

Mouth on hers, he angled her head in a fiery kiss that flowed through him, hot, molten. When she added her tongue, he sucked it in greedily. Sensation cleaved across his flesh as she worked that steel bar.

He had so many fantasies about that thing. Where to start?

Her lush little body didn't fit against his the way he wanted, so he wedged a hand under her thigh and boosted her higher against the door until his raging erection slid into the valley between her thighs.

She moaned in a register that drove him insane. When she felt pleasure, she let him know. That was powerful, and it burst open something inside him. He wanted more of that, more of her under his mouth, more of her crying out his name.

But they were still in the hall. Because he hadn't yet committed.

It was time to take this behind closed doors.

Scrabbling with the plastic in his hand, he somehow got it into the slot without letting go of her. The door swung open, and just so there was no opportunity for either of them to throw down another roadblock, he picked her up to carry her across the threshold. It was symbolic, maybe more for him than her, but her feminine sigh unfolded something inside him as he kicked the door shut.

When he laid her out on the bed, he meant to immediately dive back into the kiss he'd had to cut short with the room entrance logistics. But he paused for a half second to drink her in, because she was a stunning sight, lounging there on the bedspread wearing that simple white dress. She'd put it on for no other reason than because she wanted to please him.

She had. She did. Constantly, even when they were crossing swords. A lot of times, he didn't even care if he won the battle because the act of fighting it turned him on. It should bother him. How messed up was that? But everything about her turned him on, and he was done resisting it.

But before he could get started on the million or so fantasies he'd lined up in his mind, she rolled to her knees and reached for his belt buckle, drawing him closer as she peered up through her lashes. "I can't wait to taste you."

His shaft grew impossibly harder, and it took a supreme amount of will to gather his faculties enough to still her hands. She'd already gotten his belt unbuckled and had started to pull it from its mooring.

"No," he said hoarsely. "That's not what I want."

Obviously his meaning did not compute, because she cocked a brow and broke free of his hold to yank the belt completely off. "In case I'm not being clear, I'm going down on you. Right now."

"I wasn't confused."

His eyelids shuttered closed as she trailed her fingers across his erection. Her touch through his clothes felt like liquid fire, and he nearly came at the thought of her mouth on his flesh. The real thing would probably be the death of him, but he wasn't going to find out. Not at this moment, anyway.

What she wanted was to stay in control. She wasn't going to get her wish.

The sound of his zipper sliding open put a little more urgency in that thought. Encircling her wrists, he drew her quick fingers away from his body. "Stop, Trinity. As good as I'm sure that would be, that's not what I fantasize about."

Bewilderment marred her face. "Really? Not ever?"

He groaned. "Of course I've thought about it. I'm not the Goody Two-shoes you seem to think I am. But neither am I a selfish ass who only thinks about how great it would be to have a woman go down on me."

"You'd be in a small minority of one," she muttered. "I have to ask. What in the world do you fantasize about then?"

Now they were talking. He eased her backward on the bed, still holding her wrists, until they hit the bedspread. Nuzzling her neck, he held her hands captive as he lightly sucked on her skin, diabolically pleased with the gasp that burst from her throat.

"I fantasize about being the man you moan for," he murmured against her skin. "The one who makes you come so many times, you don't remember what it's like to be with anyone else. I'm guessing you've had a lot of sex in your life, Trinity. But you've never been with me before, and I guarantee you this will be nothing like any of those times."

"So it's a competition thing?"

That was so not it. But neither did he know how to be someone other than who he was. He liked to feel something inside when he made love to a woman. A connection. His gut told him the surest way to get that with Trinity was to not let her do things the way she always did.

"Is it so difficult to believe that I want to give you a unique experience?"

"When it comes down to a choice between me pleasuring you or the other way around, yeah." The disbelief in her voice sliced through him, and it scored a place inside he wouldn't have said she could reach.

As many times as she'd surely gotten naked with a

man, had she never had *one* who cared about her pleasure above his own?

That was not okay.

He lifted his head and released her wrists at the same time in favor of threading her inky hair through his fingers. The thumb he brushed across her cheek put a note of tenderness in the moment that he hadn't intended... but there it was. "So then I have to ask. What do *you* fantasize about?"

Something akin to shock zipped across her expression, but she covered it almost immediately. "Making a man come with my mouth."

He grinned. "How many times have you said that? You must practice in the mirror, because it was impressive how you spit it out without having to think about it. Now give me the real answer. Otherwise, I'm going to have to work my way through all the things I can think of until I figure it out for myself."

"Maybe that's what I want," she said flippantly. "Maybe that's what I was after all along."

Yeah, he didn't think so. The wild uncertainty in her gaze told a different story, one that he should be ashamed he liked so much. But Trinity unsettled and off-kilter might be the sexiest she'd been yet. That was a state he could get into a whole hell of lot more.

He wanted her naked and writhing under him as he gave her orgasm after orgasm until she was so spent, she forgot all about her need for control.

And she was going to like it.

Six

Trinity swallowed as Logan's big palms engulfed her face. The kiss he laid on her lips had far too much sweetness in it. Like he wanted this thing between them to be real as much as she did.

I want to see the real you.

The request—demand—he'd made when he'd changed her clothes suddenly took on new meaning. Maybe she'd let him see her for reasons she hadn't fully admitted to herself. Her chest quivered with some nameless, unfathomable emotions. Which was not supposed to be the deal.

She'd given him permission to make this about nothing more than sex. Tried to stick to that herself. She'd practically had his zipper down and her hands on his rock-hard shaft, which she wanted to see with her own two eyes but hadn't yet, because he'd shifted gears so hard in the other direction, she still didn't know what had happened.

He'd *stopped* her from giving him the first of many climaxes.

What was he trying to do to her?

"I've been wondering," he murmured, "about what you have on under that dress."

"I've been wondering how long it would take you to find out," she shot back. Except the sassy note she'd tried to slip into her tone hadn't come out like she'd wanted.

Instead, it had sounded wistful.

With a wicked smile that shouldn't have tripped so many alarms in her head, he put his hands on her knees to situate her the way he seemed to want: shoes on the ground, bottom nearly to the edge of the bed, thighs open wide. He knelt between her legs and slid both palms along her skin, his rough hands thrilling her as he gathered the fabric in a slow reveal that hitched her lungs.

The ivy tattoo appeared. He settled his mouth on the first green leaf and dragged his tongue across it. Gasping, she bowed off the bed and levered herself up on her elbows, because she didn't want to miss anything.

The sight of his beautiful mouth on her thigh did it for her like nothing else.

"More where that came from," he murmured.

He licked her tattoo clear up to her panties, shoving back her dress and fingering the fabric of her white thong. "I'm going to take this off."

"You don't have to check in with me," she informed him breathlessly. Now that he'd so thoroughly turned the tables, she couldn't get air into her lungs. She ached for him to touch her intimately, and she wanted it now. "Really, I'm game for whatever you have in mind."

He glanced up, his expression hooded and implacable. "It would be best if you'd clue in right up front that I do things my own way. Therefore, I will be telling you what I'm doing to you as I do it. For example, I'm about to put my tongue between your legs."

The promise raked heat through her core. Logan McLaughlin had a dirty mouth, and she was a huge fan of it.

Hooking his fingers at the waistband of her thong, he slid it off and tossed it over his shoulder. His gaze went hot as he looked his fill at her uncovered sex. No one had ever done anything like that before. Sure, she'd had men go down on her, but usually in the dark, and most of the time it had a mechanical, scripted vibe as if there was some unwritten rule that she had to get off before her partner got his turn. In short, not very romantic.

This...was.

Logan had already eliminated his pleasure from this equation, and it was as unsettling as it was exciting. It was easy to take what she wanted from a man after he'd done the same to her, but she had no idea how to accept pleasure freely given.

"Trinity," he murmured, and her name floated across her skin like a prayer. "You're so gorgeously made. I want to taste all of you at once. I hardly know where to start."

She fought the urge to say something outrageous, to deflect, to ease her discomfort. She didn't know how to deal with a man who wasn't letting her run the show. He took away her dilemma by easing his thumbs up her thighs until he hit her slick center, where he went on an exploring mission that instantly lit her up.

Eventually, he replaced his thumbs with his lips.

Her core flooded with heat, and she gasped as he draped one of her knees over his shoulder, moving closer to her, increasing the pressure, the hot, wet sensation that had her crying out as she soared toward the ceiling. His tongue—it felt like it was everywhere at once, thanks to the sheer power of suggestion.

His big, solid hands held her in place as her hips bucked against his mouth. He welcomed it, going deeper, harder, faster until her skin incinerated under his onslaught and she came with his name on her lips.

"Again," he murmured, his lips grazing her core as he spoke. "Don't hold back. I want to watch you."

He fingered her pulsing channel, catching the faint echoes of her orgasm and whipping her into a frenzy instantly. Her back lifted from the bed as he shot sparks through her entire body, shoving her over the cliff a second time. She crashed into the release with something akin to shock, letting it play out in a way she never had before. In a way she'd never been able to before.

Bleary eyed, she stared up at him as he covered her, dipping his head to take her mouth, sharing the earthy taste of herself on his tongue. It was as arousing as it was intimate.

Good sex stems from intimacy. It wasn't just a throwaway comment he'd made. The man meant what he said. Always. Instead of enticing the all-American boy to take a walk on the wild side, he'd yanked her firmly over to his side. But she had no time to reflect on the irony of that as he shifted her to her stomach so he could unzip her dress.

This time, he offered no explanation as he stripped her of her dress and bra. When she was naked, he laid her back on the pillow and picked up one foot. He took one look at the tangled mess of strings and grinned. Wickedly.

"Is this some kind of Mensa test?" He yanked on one

firmly tangled string. "Let's see if the good ole Texas boy is smart enough to figure out how to get this off."

"Maybe." She shrugged and matched his smile. "Maybe it's an opportunity to prove how badly you want it."

"Sweetheart, you underestimate me." With that, he dropped her shoe to the bed. "I can do all sorts of things to you without taking them off, which I don't mind one bit, and you're the one who has to wear them during, so…we'll have a discussion later about our individual intellects."

With that, he rolled from the bed and did the most provocative striptease she'd ever seen in her life. First he slipped all his shirt's buttons from their moorings and inch by inch revealed the torso she'd felt plenty of times but was only now getting her first glimpse of.

There might have been drooling.

Then he took off his shirt, first from one broad shoulder, then the other, and the final product dried up her mouth to the point where drooling was definitely not in her future, along with not breathing. The man was magnificent, hard, sinewy, clearly not an executive who spent a lot of time behind a desk. Or wearing a shirt. He had a tan line where the sleeves of his many and varied T-shirts hit his biceps, but he must do something outside with his chest bared because it was deliciously sun kissed, highlighting what blew past a six-pack into uncharted territory.

She'd have to count the indentions across his abs. With her tongue.

The prospect unleashed a shiver. He undid his pants and let them drop to the floor along with whatever underwear he might have had on, and then she was really glad she was already lying down, because holy hell.

Powerful thighs. Thick erection. Too much to take in. No words.

But she didn't need any as he retrieved a handful of condoms from his pants pocket, which she scarcely had time to register. Though they'd circle back to the fact that he'd had condoms *in his pocket* the entire time.

And then there was no more thinking as he gathered her up and settled her into the grooves of his body. The hard, brutal planes of his physique had no give, and she thrilled at the feel of it against her bare skin.

He tipped up her head with both hands and she fell into the kiss, instantly drowning in Logan. Their legs entwined and his muscular thigh came up between hers, seeking her sweet spot…and finding it, rubbing hard at her still-sensitive bits until gray blurred her vision and a gasp tore from her throat.

Her skin heated so quickly she feared she might burn to ash. His hot hands spanned her waist, rolling her to her back. Taking one nipple in his talented mouth, he nipped and sucked until her back arched, and she had enough brain cells to realize he was doing exactly as he'd promised—pleasuring her with no thought to himself. He'd already made her come twice and seemed in no rush to stop.

What do you fantasize about?

She'd done precious little of that in her life. Her creativity was usually drained by the end of the day, and by the time she got naked with a man, it was never about what she wanted.

Why was it never about what she wanted?

Logan's teeth hit a spot on her nipple that barreled through her like a freight train, and she cried out.

"I love it when you do that," he murmured. "It's like an aphrodisiac."

Since aphrodisiac should be his middle name, she liked it, too. "Maybe you should see what switching to the other side gets you."

He chuckled and did exactly that, dragging his tongue across the valley between her breasts as he went, and then sucked her other nipple into his hot mouth. But he coupled that with a very well-placed finger between her legs, and the dual sensations spun her off into oblivion again. Breathless, she clenched her way through another spectacular orgasm that encompassed her whole body.

Logan had a condom rolled on and was poised at her entrance, pushing inside before her vision cleared. Mewling sounds tore from her throat as the pressure built, and it was so good, so unbelievable on the heels of a release. He grabbed one stiletto and tugged her knee nearly to her shoulder as he widened her.

"Relax," he murmured. "I'm…big."

Yeah, she'd noted that for herself. "You say that like I should be disappointed. That's usually on the pro side of a girl's checklist."

Oh, yes, he *was* big. Her whole body went liquid as the exquisite feel of his length slid along her sensitized flesh.

But not too big. Perfect. Especially after he'd primed her to the point where she was so swollen and wet that he slid in easily. And she didn't miss that he'd done so. Even in this, he was thinking about her pleasure instead of taking his own.

When he'd buried himself inside completely, he sucked in a breath and froze, bliss stealing across his features. "You feel so amazing."

How was he forming coherent sentences? Her own body had wheeled off into the stratosphere, greedily sucking in all the new sensations as he began to move, circling his hips as he thrust. She couldn't have stopped the moans pouring from her throat at gunpoint and she didn't want to. He murmured his encouragement with well-placed phrases as they came together again and again.

The test was when he wrapped her leg around his waist and let go of her stiletto in favor of cupping her jaw. But he didn't kiss her, just watched her as he plunged deep inside, his eyes dark and focused. Fingers tangled in his hair, she couldn't look away, even when his face tightened and turned tender with release. It was so powerful to witness such a strong man showing his vulnerability that she nearly came apart inside.

When was the last time she'd done it missionary style? It was her least favorite position—or at least it had been until Logan.

He made it exquisite, an experience. Not just sex, but pleasure combined with connection, both beautiful and precious.

This was what she fantasized about. A man who would be the same in bed or out, day in and day out. Still there in the morning. Strong, capable. Honest. One who cared about her over his own selfish needs.

She fantasized about being loved.

And she'd spent the last few years of her life systematically ensuring she'd never have to think about the fact that she didn't have that, wasn't capable of having that.

Which meant she had to shove that particular fantasy back into the deep. Where it belonged.

The pictures from outside Trinity's door the night before shot their fake relationship into the stratosphere.

Apparently some of the photographers from the lobby had followed them after all.

Logan downed the first of what would likely be many cups of coffee that morning as he ate breakfast in the small dining room of the hotel restaurant and reread the email from Myra crowing about his brilliant strategy to be photographed kissing Trinity outside her hotel room.

If you could call it that. Strategy hadn't been forefront in his mind. And it was hard to label it something as innocuous as a kiss.

The scene was almost pornographic, raw and sensual, and the photographer had timed it perfectly to show Trinity's card key clutched in his fingers as he searched blindly for the slot without even lifting his mouth from hers. The urgency burned visibly between them.

He almost couldn't look at the picture. It was too much truth, too intimate. Had Trinity known a photographer had followed them upstairs? Was that the only reason she'd given him the green light?

Last night had been real—to him, anyway. As real as the ache in his elbow from the vigorous activity, which had caused his old injury to flare up. And it didn't sit well that something so personal had been captured and then turned into a marketing gimmick by his and Trinity's respective publicists.

But that's what they'd been doing all along. Why was this picture different? He didn't like the answer. Or the kick to his stomach as he glanced up to see Trinity breeze into the restaurant and take a seat at his table without so much as a hello.

God, she was gorgeous. Even with an inch-wide green stripe running down the nonshaved side of her hair. He was almost accustomed to the heavy hand she used to apply her cosmetics, and honestly, it was part of the overt style that bled from her pores. She wore a flowy, hair-stripe-matching grass-green dress that covered her to her calves and tied up around her neck. She looked so sizzling hot that he had his suit jacket unbuttoned before he realized he'd been about to take it off so he could cover her up with it.

Moron. She'd shredded his brain cells last night.

It was a very respectable dress. It was what was under the dress that got him, and he didn't just mean the body. Trinity was fierce on the outside, but when he'd gotten her behind closed doors, she'd melted into his arms, becoming so sweet and impassioned he could hardly fathom it.

That had been a huge surprise. And all he wanted to do this morning was pull her into his lap and stick his nose into that juncture of her neck and shoulder, where it most smelled like her. Then he'd start peeling back her outrageous shell again.

"Lara called me already," Trinity said as she smiled at the waitress and ordered coffee. "My publicist. She's thrilled with the traffic on our website. I have a couple of calls in to Alex to get some prelim sales numbers now that it's close enough to the end of the month to have the data."

"Good morning to you, too," he said and almost didn't choke on it.

Trinity shot him a look. "Get up on the wrong side of the bed? Or maybe in the wrong bed entirely? I told you to stay. You were the one who insisted on propriety and left."

Because he'd had to. Sleeping in the same bed with her put a stamp of permanence on this association that he couldn't afford. Not as far as the outside world was concerned; it was already too late for that. But in his mind. They were a real couple now, for better or worse, and he wasn't sorry they'd taken things to the next level. But it was *temporarily* real.

He couldn't forget that. Sleeping with her, wrapped up in each other all night long, would be a mistake.

Instead of letting the unsettled restlessness in his chest take over his mood, he lifted her hand from the table and kissed her palm. "My publicist is happy with the results as well. Act like you're enjoying yourself. There's a slew of photographers across the way."

She peered in the direction of his subtle head jerk from the corner of her eye to where a crowd of people lined the lobby, visible over the low wall separating the restaurant from the rest of the ground floor. "They're here early. And I don't have to act like I'm having fun with you. I just do."

Really? He eyed her. "You're in Oakland, California, at a hotel eating crappy breakfast food, and I'm about to make you watch a baseball game that you don't want to sit through. You should have higher standards."

Her smile heated him so fast, his vision grayed. "It's what will happen after the game that's keeping my spirits up."

And now he was thinking about that, too. He'd been trying not to, because they hadn't really established any morning-after rules, like how frequently they'd take their relationship behind closed doors. Given that they'd be doing deliberate on-camera work today as well, maybe she'd want a break. What did he know about what went on in her head?

"The endless interviews and postgame strategy sessions?" he commented. "Yeah, that'll be a blast for you."

She'd agreed to do the whole nine yards' worth of

press junkets in hopes of getting some extra exposure, which had seemed necessary at the time but now felt excessive given that they were already burning up the internet with their presex activities in the hall.

"You're so sweet to worry about me." Her hand was still in his, and she thumbed his knuckle almost affectionately. "But I can amuse myself. All I have to do is think about how much it'll be killing you to stand next to me, knowing that I'm completely naked under this dress."

Hot coffee scalded his throat as he choked on it.

Clearly nowhere nearly as concerned as she should be—since his inability to breathe or swallow was her fault—she arched a brow. "Are you okay?"

"What do you think?" he growled. "Are you really commando? Like, one hundred percent?"

She nodded with a sly smile. "And I plan to sit really close to you during the game. Maybe there will be a table that might cover a wandering hand or two?"

That dress took on a whole new definition of shock value—and now he definitely wanted to cover her up. With his naked body.

Going commando under a simple dress should definitely be a morning-after rule. He just couldn't decide if the rule should state *never* or *always*.

Trinity chatted some more about strategy and photo ops while drinking her coffee and refusing to eat anything, a female tendency he could never understand. The team had already left for the stadium so they could get started on their pregame rituals. Ballplayers were a superstitious lot, and you couldn't pry their customs from their cold, dead fingers. They always ate at the ballpark, mostly so Gordon could watch the players like a hawk, but also because hotel food sucked.

Normally, he'd be with them, angsting alongside the coaches. But instead of doing his job, Logan was still at the hotel, listening to his fake girlfriend–slash–real lover talk about how great it was that this partnership was paying off.

"Fyra was featured in a cosmetic review on *Allure's* website," she gushed. "And it was so positive that our northeast distribution warehouse is out of stock of Bahama Sunset eye shadow and the mascara they mentioned. They panned us last time, claiming the products they tried were overpriced. Like anyone cares about value when it comes to whether your mascara clumps or not."

"Uh-huh." Her lips moved constantly and he couldn't help but think about how quiet she got when it counted. When talking wasn't necessary because they were communicating perfectly with their bodies.

He wasn't done with his fantasies, that was for sure. And for the first time in his life, he resented the fact that he couldn't just watch a baseball game with a gorgeous woman and then take her back to his room for some postgame activities. Maybe he could cut things shorter than normal. He was already making concessions by not being on the field at this moment.

"We'll leave in about an hour," he told her as they left the restaurant after breakfast.

"Oh. Isn't the game at one o'clock?"

He hid a smile. "Yeah, but the team usually gets there about six hours early. I'm cutting you a break since it's your first time."

She hit the lobby an hour later, exactly on time. The day was perfect for baseball—cloudy with a slight breeze off the bay, which put the temperature near sixty degrees. Logan loved this area, especially in the summer, when it routinely reached 110 in their home stadium in Texas. Trinity shivered as they stepped outside the glass doors to the valet stand.

Without hesitation, he stripped off his jacket and draped it around her shoulders. Gratefully, she smiled and slipped her arms into the sleeves. He didn't feel guilty at all about getting extra clothes on her and bit his tongue instead of asking if she owned a sweater.

He was pretty sure he already knew the answer to that.

Somehow he resisted putting his hands on her during the limo ride to the field. The stadium sat overlooking the bay with a great view of the Oakland bridge. Across the bay, San Francisco gleamed in the low light of the morning, and he was extraordinarily glad they didn't have to venture to that side of the bridge. The traffic in the Bay Area rivaled Dallas, and he was not a fan of sitting in the car for hours.

Of course, he'd never done it with Trinity. That might make a long commute worth it.

The stadium was less grand than some others, but he got a rush walking through the gates regardless. The smell of popcorn lingered in the air, something almost all stadiums had in common, even the open-air ones. He'd never lost the sense of being on sacred ground, and no matter what time it was, he could hear the thunk of the ball against his glove, the shush as it sailed through the air, the roar of the crowd in his head. God, he could still feel the energy even though it had been nine years since the last time he'd pitched here.

Some days it felt like his life had ended when his career had.

Trinity slipped her hand into his, squeezing it. More strategy? If she'd noticed he'd slipped into a funk, she didn't say anything, but the timing couldn't be a coincidence. She'd somehow tuned in to him and he didn't hate it, no matter how weird it felt to be here with a woman, especially one wearing his suit jacket. Weird, but nice.

Trinity oohed and ahhed over the skybox he'd borrowed from a friend. He tried to see it through the eyes of someone who'd never been in one before, but he'd grown up in the box his dad owned, often hanging out for hours on random Saturdays during the season.

It was odd to be above the field when his team was on it. The players were warming up, and he automatically assessed each one.

Trinity's unique feminine scent hit him a moment before the woman did. She joined him at the glass overlooking the field. "Are you okay? You seem distant."

He shrugged, mystified how she could do that when he hadn't clued in on her moods to the same degree. "I'm an in-the-trenches guy. It's very unusual for me to watch my team play from this vantage point."

"Why are you here, then?"

It was a valid question. No one else was here yet. The party wouldn't start for a couple of hours, closer to game time. And there certainly weren't any photographers around. "I don't know."

He literally had no idea how to integrate a woman—fake, real or otherwise—into the rest of his life. Sure, he'd dated a few women here and there since buying the Mustangs. But they'd never been serious enough relationships to bring the lady to a game.

Which of course begged the question—how serious was this one?

There might have been a hundred other things he

could have taken his fake girlfriend to besides an away game, where they'd be stuck together for three more days until they went home late Thursday night. Yet he'd pounced on Myra's suggestion. Why, because he'd wanted to see how Trinity fit in here?

Trinity cocked her head, contemplating him. "If you're normally down on the field, the only conclusion I can draw is that you're here for me."

He made the mistake of meeting her ice-blue eyes, which had gained a great deal of warmth as she watched him.

"I am." No point in lying about it. "I didn't want you to be alone. This is a big stadium, and you don't know anything about baseball."

Okay, that part might not have been the whole truth. But he wasn't sure what was.

She laughed. "I'm a big girl, Logan. I can find things to do no matter where I am. But since you've made such an excellent point, tell me about baseball."

Eyeing the green dress and sandals she wore, he crossed his arms. "Really? Like all of it?"

"Sure." She uncrossed his arms for him without his permission and guided him to the long leather couch on the front row of the seating in the box. "We have time, right?"

He settled onto the cushion next to her, but only because he'd just realized the benefits of having this suite to themselves with no danger of her undergarments going missing.

The protective one-way film on the glass suddenly seemed like genius on the part of the stadium planners. No one could see in. No one could enter the suite without the lock code, and all the people who were privy to it wouldn't arrive for quite some time.

He had a temporary pass to have real sex with his fake girlfriend. That was the only thing he should—could—focus on right now. It was all they had between them that was real. All he could allow to be real.

Things had just gotten a hell of a lot more interesting.

Seven

"We have a couple of hours," Logan told her and picked up Trinity's hand to raise it to his lips, nibbling on her fingertips because he wanted to and he could. "What do you want to know about baseball?"

"I want to know everything."

Her voice had dropped into that register that somehow plugged straight into his groin, lighting it up. She pulled her hand from his grasp deliberately, with a little tsk. Without taking her eyes off him, she hiked up her skirt to flash him a very quick peek at her naked sex and levered one gorgeous leg over his lap, settling herself astride him.

Oh, God, yes.

Her heat ravaged his instant erection, burning him thoroughly even through his clothes. She leaned forward, rolling her hips to increase the contact between their bodies, and nuzzled his ear as she murmured, "Tell me what baseball means to you."

His pulse went into a free fall.

"Baseball is like breathing," he said hoarsely as her fingers went to work on his buttons.

He should stop her for...some reason. Because she was taking control. That was a bad thing. But he couldn't find any fault in the way she worked her hips against his length, and he groaned as she laved at his exposed collarbone.

"Breathing?" she prompted, tonguing her way up his throat.

He liked her out of control, when he was the one calling the shots. But his head tipped back easily as she cupped his jaw to move him into a position she liked better, and he was pretty sure he wasn't going to stop her. "I don't have to remind myself how much I enjoy the way my lungs function. They just do. I step on the mound and my body automatically cues up into the right stance to throw."

"What else?" She opened his shirt, her clever hands sliding down his torso to explore every inch of it, and her touch enflamed him. His thoughts fragmented as he fell into a sensuous haze, and words just spilled out from somewhere inside.

"My mind turns the ball over and over, examining it, hearing the way it sounds in the air. In my peripheral vision, I'm checking out first base to see if the guy has a little too much of a leadoff. The sun is usually high in the sky and I have to adjust my cap. But that guy at bat? He's not getting a piece of my arm."

"Logan, that's beautiful," she murmured and cupped his face with her hot hands, laying a kiss on his lips that he felt deep inside. When she pulled back, her eyes glowed with something he couldn't name, an appreciation, maybe, for what he'd shared without really meaning to. "You're a pitcher."

It wasn't a question, but he nodded as his throat worked, and he couldn't swallow all at once. None of that should have come so automatically, and she'd clued in that it was significant. Somehow. He'd never told her that he'd played professionally. That it still killed him on a regular basis that he wasn't down on the field at this moment warming up.

Sometimes being in the dugout with the team let him pretend for a few moments that he would actually don a uniform. Up here in a box? No way to maintain that illusion.

So here he was perpetuating another one. With Trinity.

When had he become so dependent on fantasy?

And how had she figured that out about him?

Before he could gather his scattered wits, she kissed him again, but this time, it had far more intent. Her mouth slanted against his, growing more heated and deliberate. Her tongue wound against his, seeking more, going deeper, and he helplessly fell into her, because he didn't care if it was supposed to be fake.

He wanted this woman as bare to him as he'd just been to her.

The tangle of their bodies pressed intimately together and her hips circled harder, faster against him. He reacted instantly, his insides turning molten until he couldn't feel his bones any longer. *Closer.* He needed her, ached to be inside her, and put his hands on her waist to hold her in place as he ground into her core, his shaft so hard between them it was a wonder he didn't bruise her tender flesh.

"Logan," she murmured. "Let me pleasure you."

And then she easily broke his hold, dropping to the ground between his legs. Her lithe hands went to work on his belt buckle, and before he could think of a reason to stop her, she yanked down his zipper, burrowing into his clothes to hit bare flesh.

He sucked in a breath as she peered up at him and simultaneously cupped him in her hot hands, running his tip along the line of her lips. He jerked involuntarily as sensation rocketed up his length.

The raw mood she'd uncovered twined with the physical reaction, making everything feel ten times more powerful.

"You're so beautiful," she crooned. "I'm going to take care of you. Let me show you how good this tongue piercing can make you feel."

So much blood rushed south he didn't understand how his heart could still be beating, but his pulse thundered in his ears, so things must still be in working order.

And then the entire world slid sideways as she dragged her tongue up his length. The bite of the steel coupled with her hot, rough lick nearly separated his bones from his skin. Then she sucked him fully into her mouth and he was lost to the dual sensations of cold and heat.

The emotional vortex inside him heightened everything.

Higher and higher she spun him. It was so good that his hips bucked automatically, shoving him deeper into her mouth, but she took him, *all of him*, and it felt unbelievable. So amazing that he couldn't hold back, couldn't stop the flood of Trinity through his blood, and his thighs tensed with the effort it took to simply keep breathing.

The release pounded through his entire body, ripping

a cry from his throat that was one hundred percent primal, and it was easily the hardest he'd ever come in his life. She finished him off expertly and he fell back on the couch, nerveless and so spent he couldn't feel his toes.

But the sated serenity that stole over him was so very right.

The sight of her on her knees before him, with her lips wrapped around him, had burned into his mind indelibly. She tucked him away and disappeared for a moment, then came back to settle into his side on the couch, lifting his arm so she could snuggle against his chest with his arm around her.

It was so nice, his eyes closed automatically as he soaked in the feel of her warm body bleeding through his. "You know I won't ever think about pitching again without thinking of your tongue piercing, right?"

She laughed, her fingers toying with one of the buttons hanging from his shirt. "I wanted to give you a unique experience. Since you did that for me. Last night."

The information she'd just shared filtered through his poor, beleaguered brain. "You mean I was successful?"

Of course, their conversation had been extremely limited last night because their mouths had been on each other, not talking.

Her smile was a little misty. "Let's just say I have a lot of selfish men in my past and I'm not sorry they're in my rearview mirror. Plus, I'm looking forward to how you're going to repay me for that."

"Yeah?" he growled. "Lucky for you I've got hours and hours to come up with something spectacular."

Unfortunately, it would have to wait, because what he had in mind would not work in their current environment, given that people might start arriving at any time. And that he'd stupidly left all the condoms back at the hotel. But honestly, he'd never have considered a baseball stadium ripe ground for a sexual encounter.

He would not make that mistake twice.

Once he had all his clothes in order, Trinity stood with him at the glass and listened intently as he explained the mechanics of the game—at her request. She asked intelligent questions and genuinely sought to understand the rules, of which there were a lot.

"No wonder you're such a fan of rules." She rolled her eyes good-naturedly. "My eyes glazed over ten minutes ago."

No, they hadn't. She'd absorbed every word, even when he'd gotten entirely too impassioned in his defense of the concept of a designated hitter, which he should hate as a pitcher. Former pitcher.

But all at once, he didn't feel like he had to make the distinction. He was still a pitcher even though he didn't do it professionally any longer. He didn't have to pretend it wasn't a part of him. Trinity hadn't labeled him as a former pitcher or asked if he used to pitch. She'd just understood that baseball wasn't a job, it was his essence.

And then gave him the most amazing sexual experience he could imagine.

How in the hell was he supposed to go back to a one-color, lackluster, *boring* woman after that?

Short answer—he had to. Trinity was temporary. He couldn't be constantly distracted from his life by a sex-on-a-stick marketing executive. Especially not one who'd just demonstrated a remarkable ability to entice him down a rabbit hole of fantasy, which was apparently an Achilles' heel he'd just discovered. They should start talking about exit strategies, stage a public fight. Surely their fake affair had done all the good it was going to do.

But the universe wasn't finished knocking his plans around.

The Mustangs won. And Trinity instantly became a good-luck charm. What was he going to do now, drag her to every game from now until the end of the season?

It was not cool how great that suddenly sounded.

Logan had not been kidding about the interminable rounds of interviews that happened after the game. Trinity lost count of the number of times she heard him repeat the same phrases to yet another reporter.

"Johnson can absolutely repeat that three ninety tomorrow," Logan said easily, which was always followed by, "O'Hare is still on the DL, but we're calling up a reliever from Round Rock who will knock your socks off."

Three ninety—that might have been a reference to the mysterious stat called a batting average that Logan had mentioned earlier. But she wouldn't put money on it at this point. DL meant nothing to her.

It was like a secret code that only the kids in the know could crack, and by the time dinner rolled around, she was jonesing for a glass of wine. Spending an hour on her stuffed-to-the-gills email inbox wouldn't be out of line, either. Her face hurt from smiling as she stood by Logan's side, but his arm never left her waist, and the photos would be brilliant, especially since she'd worn this green dress that would pop on camera.

Several of the reporters asked about her, and Logan eagerly introduced her without a label, but the adoring look he gave her told the story vividly and none of the eagle-eyed cameramen missed that shot.

"You're a much better actor than I would have given you credit for," she murmured as they held hands and dashed for the limo after Logan had finally deemed them both done. "Even I almost believed we were headed for the altar soon."

She'd meant it as a joke, but it twisted at her heart painfully because it was frighteningly easy to pretend the adoring looks weren't faked.

He laughed and kissed her cheek playfully. "Wasn't an act. I'm very fond of you right now."

"Um...really?" She glanced at him askance.

"Did you not see the scoreboard at the end?" He picked up her hand and kissed her fingers, a habit she could get very used to. "Mustangs put one up in the win column. Thanks to you."

"Me?" Had she blown his brains out earlier? She wasn't bad in the pleasure department, but no one had ever actually lost their mind afterward. "Pretty sure I never picked up a bat the whole game."

"You didn't have to. You're good luck. Obviously."

The stress he put on the word *obviously* was like a verbal eye roll, except she still didn't get it. "What, like I'm your Blarney stone now?"

That piqued his interest, and he swept her with a once-over. "Yep, which means I have to kiss you in order to get my dose of luck."

"Now that has possibilities." She let him pull her into his lap to get started on that, which effectively dropped the subject. Fine by her.

By the time the limo reached the hotel, they were both breathless and she'd nearly hit a high C twice as he fingered her under her dress, dipping his talented fingers into the pool between her legs again and again.

"Have dinner with me," he murmured as they hustled through the lobby, ignoring the coaches and players she vaguely recognized. Some of them called out to Logan, but his gaze was trained on her. Deliciously so.

"Think there will be more photographers here later?"

She glanced around, but the lobby was bare of the press. For once. Had they finally gotten tired of the story? Her spine stiffened and a cold chill crept along each vertebra. If there wasn't a story, what did that mean for this fake relationship?

"Trinity." He waited until she glanced at him to continue. "I'm asking you to eat with me. Not because it's good for my ticket sales or to get people to buy more mascara. Because you have to eat, and why not do it with me?"

That was too much like a date. Which was a ridiculous thing to be wary of. They'd been on plenty of dates already. Seen each other naked and put their mouths on each other in places that would get them arrested if they'd done it in public.

All at once, she realized—it *wasn't* like a date. She'd been conveniently standing there when he'd decided he was hungry, that was all. He wasn't asking her to spend time with him because he liked her. What if he had? Would that make a difference? It didn't matter. He wasn't supposed to like her. She didn't like *him*. This wasn't real.

Maybe she'd blown her own brains out earlier. Furious with herself for turning into a waffling, idiotic crybaby, she shook her head, totally unable to fathom why she couldn't get rid of the crawly feeling on the back of her neck.

"I need to catch up on work after spending all day at a baseball game."

"Okay." He nodded like it was no big deal, and why

wouldn't he? It wasn't a big deal. Convenient dining companion was unavailable. So what?

But then he pulled her into his arms by the elevator and gave her a scorching-hot kiss that curled her toes. His tongue talked to hers in a timeless mating ritual that her body responded to in ways no man had ever evoked. He'd literally just made her come in the limo before they'd arrived, and already she was hot for him again, wishing she'd given him a different answer when he'd asked her to dinner.

That's why it was so much better that she'd said no. She didn't need a man to entertain her, and she'd already gotten a couple of orgasms out of the deal. What more did she want?

They weren't dating. This wasn't real. The more she had to remind herself of that, the farther away from Logan she needed to stay.

When she got back to her room, her face still stinging from his stubble, she sat down at the desk to boot up her laptop. The long list of bolded unread emails flashed onto the screen and she nearly cried. Choosing emails over Logan McLaughlin. She was certifiable.

But the job of the chief marketing officer did not stop simply because the woman with the title spent the day watching a bunch of guys in tight pants whack some balls around. The only reason she'd met Logan was because she'd been doing her job, and she needed to keep focusing on that.

An email from Alex with the title Preliminary Sales Numbers jumped out from the screen. She clicked on it.

And blinked. The first line of Alex's email had fourteen exclamation points. For a numbers girl, that was so out of character. Trinity's eye immediately scrolled to the bottom line of the profit/loss statement.

"Holy crap."

It was three hours later in Washington, where Alex lived, but this was too important to wait until tomorrow. Trinity thumbed up Alex on her phone and hit Call.

"Seriously?" she said when Alex answered. "A seven percent increase in sales this month?"

"Would I lie to you?" Alex's indignation spat over the network. "No. I would not, especially not about something as sacred as my balance sheet. You are a star, my dear. Whatever you're doing, don't stop. You've almost singlehandedly halted this smear campaign in its tracks."

Trinity sank down in her seat and shut her eyes. Figured. This had been personal for so long and she'd put her all into reversing the tide. Did this mean she and Logan had to keep going no matter what?

And how long could she actually keep it up without dissolving into a puddle of feminine confusion? Didn't matter. She couldn't quit now.

She plied Alex with a few platitudes, asked after Phillip and the twins her friend was carrying, avoided the topic of Logan like a champ and hung up, determined to make some headway on the campaign for Formula-47 now that everything in her life was on track.

The design program she pulled up sat there mocking her, and her mind drifted to who else? Logan. The way his hair always fell into his face and he shoved it back—she loved touching his hair, threading it through her fingers. Which of course reminded her of his big, solid body over hers...

Funny how that was the strongest image she had of him. But Logan was a closet romantic, and she sighed a little over how he expressed it. Like the single long-stemmed rose he'd given her on their first date, which she might have pressed into a book simply because no one had ever given her a rose that matched the outfit she'd been wearing the day they'd met.

The rose popped out in her mind. And twirled loose some other images. In a flash, the entire Formula-47 campaign unrolled with a million and five different bursts of inspiration.

Her fingers flew to the keyboard and when she next looked up, two hours had passed and she had a crick in her neck.

Bloom. The product was going to be called Bloom.

What better image to sell people on the idea of a cream that regenerated skin cells? *Fyra's Bloom promises to make your skin do exactly that. You'll bloom; your youthful self will bloom; your skin will bloom.* The concept had so many applications, she still had new ad copy and packaging ideas zipping through her mind despite having just devoted two hours to dumping the contents of her brain onto the screen.

It was so perfect, even she was impressed, and once she had the name, the whole thing exploded into exactly the multimillion-dollar marketing push it needed to be—and she had Logan to thank for it.

Before she could think of the ten million reasons it was a horrible plan, she ordered a bottle of the most expensive champagne on the hotel's room service menu. Then she changed into the most seductive black bra and thong she owned, threw on a little black dress that showcased her legs and went to find the only person she had any interest in celebrating with.

When she knocked on his door, he answered with his shirt unbuttoned and hanging loose over his gorgeous chest, as if he'd shrugged it on. His blank expression melted into one of easy appreciation as he swept her with a look that burned her nerve endings.

"Wasn't expecting you. I like the wardrobe change. As long as we're not going out."

She held up the champagne bottle, choosing to ignore his comment about her wardrobe. "I might be convinced to share this with the owner of today's winning baseball team."

"No more work tonight?" He still hadn't moved from the door, blocking the entrance as if to say he had every intention of determining her intent before he let her in. But the sizzling look in his eyes told her he'd clued in pretty fast to why she was here, and it wasn't to ask him to dinner.

"None. I had a breakthrough on a sticky problem and Alex told me we have a seven percent increase in sales this month. I thought you might be up for a celebration."

He stepped back and held the door wide, allowing her to brush past him, but she didn't get far. Snagging her arm, he took the champagne bottle and set it down on the dresser near the door, then whirled her into his arms for a kiss that rivaled the one by the elevator earlier.

Her body went up in flames. Hungrily, she kissed him back as he stripped away every ounce of doubt about what they were doing here with nothing more than his hot mouth on hers.

She moaned and he backed her up against the door, his hard body pinning hers. The contact sang through her and she didn't even mind that they hadn't gotten to the champagne yet. It would keep. And it had been an excuse to seek him out anyway.

She wanted *him*. Against all reason.

Her fingers found the edges of his shirt, and in a flash, she yanked it off to let it drift to the floor, letting her palms delight in the feel of his back, which never ceased to thrill her to the marrow.

"You're barefoot," he growled. "You're too short now."

She laughed as he circled his erection against her stomach, which was so very far north of where they both wanted it. But she could be flexible. "I don't have to be wearing shoes for this."

He groaned as she spun him and pressed him against the door so she could mouth her way down his beautiful abs. That part was like an extra-special treat, perfect for her tongue. The steel bar dipped in and out of the crevices, exploring, tasting. Dipping below the waistband of his pants. But when she reached for the zipper, he stopped her with his hand to her chin, tipping it up.

"Trinity."

All at once, her feet left the floor as he picked her up and carried her to the bed, throwing her down on it. He rolled onto it next to her and immediately picked up that kiss, but now that they were horizontal, it took on new urgency. Their legs tangled together and his fingers tugged on the zipper of her dress, yanking it down until he could peel the fabric from her shoulders, which he followed with his mouth, kissing down the curve of her back as he revealed her skin inch by inch.

When he got the fabric to her waist, he sucked in a breath as he took in her lacy black shelf bra. "That's the most gorgeous sight I've seen all day."

"Better even than the scoreboard?" she teased.

He glanced up at her from under his lashes. "Sure you wanna go there?"

"I, um... It was just a joke."

"That was no joke." He laid her back against the pillow and kissed the valley between her breasts, hooking the straps of her bra with both thumbs to drag them down her arms. "The Mustangs play one hundred and sixty-two games a year. Every win counts, but it's just another day at the office. You can't dwell on one win. We have another game tomorrow with a blank scoreboard."

Transfixed, she watched as he threaded the straps of her bra through his fingers, winding them up until his hands were bound to her arms.

"You, on the other hand," he continued. "Are exquisite. Every time I see you, there's something new to explore. And I was expecting you to be naked under that dress. Because you were earlier. It was a surprise to find this bra. I like that."

Her throat froze as he bent his head to trace the top swell of one breast with his tongue and then dipped behind the wall of lace to curl the tip around her covered nipple. The visual of him licking her underneath her bra put a shower of sparks at her core.

He was telling her that she was indeed the most gorgeous thing to him and he valued her above his team's winning score. What was she supposed to do with that?

All at once, he yanked on the straps, revealing her breasts to his ravenous gaze, and with his fingers still tangled against her arms, it effectively trapped her. Mercilessly, his hot mouth descended on her, licking her, sucking at her sensitive flesh. Moaning his name, she writhed under the sensuous onslaught.

She was supposed to let herself go, obviously.

The little cries she gasped out increased his urgency. He liked it when she made noise, and she liked the result of it. In a matter of moments, he had her clothes on the floor and her naked body decked out on the bed for his blistering perusal. She squirmed a little as his gaze traveled over her and his arousal bulged in his pants, clearly advertising how much he liked what he saw. But he didn't undress, suit up and plunge in. Instead, he rolled her to her stomach and knelt over her, the whisper of his bare torso skating up her back.

The first exploratory touch of his lips on her spine tightened her whole body. He lifted her hair away and licked at her neck, traveling in lazy, delicious circles as if in no hurry to quench the flames he'd ignited under his lips. He kissed the small of her back and kept going across her buttocks, down one leg until he reached her foot, where he sucked at the arch.

The pressure lit her up as he explored an erogenous zone she hadn't been aware she possessed. Gasping as he added his tongue to the party, she nearly came up off the bed.

Apparently he was going for some kind of record in how many new experiences he could find to give her. She did not have a problem with that.

Fabric rustled, and she turned her head to see him finally shedding his clothes. Since that was her favorite show, she watched with unabashed glee. His body was so beautiful. Powerful, sinewy, solid—she could perfectly imagine him in another age as a model for an Italian sculptor.

"Just getting comfortable," he told her with raised eyebrows, but still he didn't seem to be in a hurry to get to the main course.

No arguments on that front, either.

He knelt back in place and licked his way up her leg, lingering around her knee as if he had all the time in the world and was not in fact driving her insane with the combination of his mouth and whiskers on skin that rarely saw more action than a razor blade in the shower. Under the blitzkrieg of Logan's brand of seduction, however, her core exploded with unfulfilled promise, aching to have that same treatment.

He gave it to her. Slowly, he worked his way north until he hit the crease between her legs, and before she had time to wonder about the logistics involved when she was still facedown, he demonstrated by tonguing her from top to bottom, teasing the flesh of her rear with his fingertips at the same time. White lightning forked through her, and automatically, her hips rolled, seeking more, grinding her nub against the mattress so hard, pinwheels of sharp desire exploded everywhere at once.

His fingers worked magic in tandem with his tongue, and she came so fast she scarcely had time to register it was happening before it ripped her apart inside.

Midquake, Logan covered her with his big, solid body, lifted up her thigh and slid home in one fluid, exquisite shot that had them both groaning. His mouth latched on to her neck as he levered out and pushed back in slowly. It was so amazing that she shut her eyes, sinking into the mattress as he sank into her.

It was a long, slow slide into perfection, and she reveled in it, savored each sharp intake of his breath. The feel of him was like nothing she'd ever experienced, lush and tight. He pushed her closer and closer to the edge, one tiny step at a time, and she'd be fine if this lasted for an eternity.

But his urgency increased, driving hers until she couldn't stand it. Pleas fell from her lips as she met him with backward hip thrusts, desperate for more of him, aching for him to fill her faster, harder, deeper. His fingers slid down between the mattress and her stomach to find her center, doubling her pleasure until she came so hard that she had to bite back the scream he'd ripped from her throat.

His teeth bit into her shoulder as he groaned through his own climax, and his undulations set off another round of ripples in her core until she couldn't feel where she ended and he began.

Collapsing to the mattress, he pulled her tight against him, raining weak little kisses on her shoulder where he'd nipped her, apparently in apology, but she didn't care because her body was in a state of bliss.

But then he stiffened and swore. The string of curses was far more explicit than anything she'd ever heard from him, so she half rolled to check in with him when the gush of wetness against her thigh clued her in on the source of his consternation.

"The condom broke," he said tersely. "Extra strength, my ass."

She bit back a curse of her own. But she managed to choke out, "I'm on the pill. It should be fine."

He didn't look relieved. "I appreciate the pass, but it's not fine. I shouldn't have tried that position. I can't even say I'm sorry, because it can't possibly cover how crappy I feel right now."

"It's not your fault," she insisted. "It was an accident."

Just like the first time she'd gotten pregnant. But she hadn't been on the pill then. In all the years since then, she'd never had so much as a scare. It *would* be fine.

His tentative smile went leagues toward quelling her panic, as did the way he held her like he never intended to let go.

"You're very forgiving," he murmured, his voice gruff with an emotion she wasn't sure she understood. "And don't take this the wrong way, but as accidents go, that was an amazing way to have one."

She nodded against his chest because, yeah. The condom had broken for a reason—the sex had been earth-shattering.

Before she was fully ready to lose his body heat, he

rolled from the bed to dispose of the condom remains, then snagged the bottle of champagne, tore off the foil seal and expertly pried it open. "Shall we drink to how real this relationship just got?"

Her pulse jumped into her throat. "What are you talking about?"

Scouting around near the mini fridge, Logan came up with two flutes and poured the champagne. "If you get pregnant, I'll want to be involved. One hundred percent. Can't get more real than the reality of failed birth control."

She took the flute from his outstretched hand and downed it in one gulp, then held it out for more.

"Nothing has failed." And wouldn't. She could not handle another miscarriage, another guy who was fine with sex but not the responsibility that came with it. Sure, men got in line for orgasms, but midnight feedings? Forget it.

Except that wasn't Logan. He'd just said so.

He glanced at her and tossed back his own champagne. "Would a positive pregnancy test be so bad? I mean, let's play it out. I'd be the baby's father, no matter what. We'd have to be coparents, which is a relationship in and of itself. Why not make it official and just coparent as a couple?"

Her heart ached as the sentiment pinged around inside her, seeking a place to land. She wished all at once that he'd meant he wanted to be with her because he'd developed feelings for her. Because he couldn't stand the thought of being apart. But of course he was just talking about the reality of the consequences, not happily-ever-after tied up with a bow.

Fine. She didn't want that. Or at least she was going to convince herself she didn't. Really soon.

Besides, her confusion didn't matter, because there wasn't going to be a pregnancy. Secretly, she'd always assumed that the horrific nature of her miscarriage had rendered her infertile, but she'd never had it officially checked out.

"I can't possibly tell you how much I appreciate that," she said slowly, keeping the rest of her swirl of thoughts under wraps.

His expression warmed. "I've always dreamed of having a family."

"But we don't have any idea if that's what's going to happen," she countered firmly. "Nor will we for some time. Can't we just put it away for now?"

"Sure." He dinged his newly full champagne glass to hers. "For now."

With all of this academic talk about babies and families and a future with Logan in it, a yearning she'd never allowed to gain traction reared its head, settling into a place in her heart. She was pretty sure it wasn't going away any time soon.

Regardless, she was not the right woman to fulfill his dreams, which meant she *should* find a way to stay far away from Logan McLaughlin.

Except she didn't want to.

Eight

Trinity left to go back to her room, but Logan couldn't sleep. The whole day had been wild, and the conversation they'd just had put the crazy sauce on the sundae.

He couldn't stop thinking about the definition of real and how easily he could envision trying to create something that sounded a lot like that with Trinity.

This whole situation had unraveled alarmingly fast.

He'd always thought he'd get married first, then he and his wife would eagerly get on with baby making. They'd take their first pregnancy test together and she'd throw herself into his arms when it turned positive. Happiness would ensue.

Obviously the broken condom had presented another possibility that he might have to get used to—being with Trinity long-term as coparents and maybe more.

Was that what he wanted? Was that what *she* wanted? They hadn't really finished the conversation, not to his satisfaction, but he'd been willing to shelve it for the time being, since there was little reason to discuss it at this point.

Except for the fact that he *liked* the idea of having something real more than he should.

His chest hurt as he reminded himself that he and Trinity weren't at all suited for anything that smacked of real, no matter how he defined it. He'd known from the beginning that they weren't right for each other. Nothing had changed.

And yet everything had changed.

By unspoken agreement, they continued the rest of the trip as planned. Trinity came to the games, his guys played baseball and reporters took pictures afterward of the general manager and his girlfriend. Every time Logan felt like pulling her into his arms to lay a kiss on her that would communicate how much he still wanted her, she came willingly, and he liked her in his bed better than he should as well.

The heat between them sizzled for the camera and sizzled behind closed doors. It was like they couldn't quit each other now that the boundaries had evaporated.

The Mustangs won both games. Naturally. Because of Trinity, he was convinced. His team was convinced, too, and treated her like royalty, sending her flowers and chocolate, cards with funny cartoons. The Mustangs' shortstop, the one who was dating the supermodel against Logan's wishes, convinced his girlfriend to call Trinity about doing ad work for Fyra Cosmetics as a token of goodwill.

When Logan asked her about it, Trinity grinned and told him she had a meeting with the model's manager next week. All in all, it felt like a great match, she said. At night, she worked on a campaign for a new product that she chattered about endlessly during her midnight treks to his hotel room. He loved listening to her talk about the things that mattered to her.

On the plane ride home to Dallas, Trinity sat next to him and they held hands like they had on the way to the West Coast. Somehow it was different. As if the broken condom had created an unspoken agreement that they were testing out how things might go if they did slap a "real" label on their relationship.

If anyone had asked him how he'd like the concept of Trinity Forrester as a permanent lover, he'd have said there was no way it would work. But the last few days proved that was a lie.

What was he supposed to do about that? Unless she got pregnant, there was no call to have any sort of discussion about labels.

Maybe he didn't have to do anything. Maybe he could just let it ride, see how things played out. No one had breathed a word about stopping what they were doing.

Before he could think of a reason not to, he reached out and brushed her jaw with a thumb. Intimately. She didn't miss it and raised her brows at him.

"I wanted to touch you," he murmured. "Sue me."

She laughed. "You don't have to apologize for touching me. I like it. So no lawyers needed."

"Then you should know I plan to keep doing it once we're home," he advised her.

"Oh? I'll be curious how that's going to work when we both have jobs."

"Yeah. We'll have to adjust. Give some things up, maybe." When she made a noise in her throat, he did a double take. "What, you can't make our relationship a priority? We're still trying to generate publicity. Right?"

"Lest you forget, I'm an executive running a multi-million-dollar cosmetics company." She spiked her tone with enough irony to get her point across. "I told you I was working on a new product campaign. I have a strict deadline. Some of us don't get to take trips to the Bay Area and stay in fancy hotels for our work. And when we accompany those of you who do, we have to burn the midnight oil to make up for it."

"I want to spend time with you."

That had not been what he'd meant to say. But now that it was out there…he couldn't help but be curious what she'd do with it.

She scowled as the plane flew through a thick bunch of clouds, temporarily throwing the cabin into shadow. "My career is more important than breezing by your bed to pick up a couple of orgasms."

That wasn't all they had between them, and she knew that wasn't what he'd meant. Her refusal to admit things had shifted between them rankled more than he'd like, but he couldn't force her to be honest. He could only be smart enough to outwit her.

And she hadn't pulled her hand from his, a telling point that he had no problem exploiting.

"Your career is definitely more important than orgasms," he agreed smoothly. "But they shouldn't be exclusive of one another. After all, you found a way to seamlessly integrate one with my job. Let me do the same for you."

"I do like the way you think." There was still a note of caution in her voice. "What do you have in mind?"

"You know the guys need you, right? You're their Blarney stone." He pulled her hand to his mouth for what should have been a quick kiss to her fingertips, but he liked the taste of them so much, he kept them there and talked around them. "Come to the home games with me. I'll pick you up. It's on the way."

"That's not putting my career first, Logan. What happens to your luck if I say no?" Her fingertips curled against his lips in a deliberate caress that immediately made him sorry they were on a plane with a hundred other people.

"You can't. They need you." He was pretty sure she heard the unspoken *I need you* in that as well, but he didn't care. "I'll make it worth your while. Look what I've already done for your career. Seven percent increase in sales isn't anything to sneeze at. I'll figure out a way to blend work and orgasms to your satisfaction. Trust me."

"Okay." She snuggled down in the seat. "It's good for us to keep being seen together anyway."

"Absolutely," he agreed and didn't bother to hide his smile. He'd definitely won that round, and if she wanted to pretend like they were still seeing each other for publicity reasons, he could live with that.

Ticket sales were at an all-time high after a three-game winning streak and the extra boost from the publicity surrounding the road trip he'd taken with Trinity. When he got back to his office at the ballpark, he dived headfirst into his job, which he'd sorely neglected lately. Trinity wasn't the only one with deadlines. Some crucial trade agreements had finally landed on his desk—also thanks to the positive publicity his team had recently seen—and he worked through those without pausing to think about her laugh more than about a dozen times. A personal best.

Trinity came to the games and the Mustangs didn't lose. Their winning streak stretched to five games. Then eight. They were on fire, a flame eclipsed only by the one between Logan and Trinity as they burned up the sheets after games. Sometimes she brought her laptop and worked while the team tore the competition to shreds. Sometimes she put it away and cheered alongside him, occasionally coming up with relevant comments about the action on the field, which showed that she was learning baseball whether she'd meant to or not.

With his fake girlfriend by his side, Logan hadn't watched a game from the dugout since the Mustangs played Oakland. It was a huge shift in his managerial style, one that his coaches hadn't failed to comment on. He let them think it was because Trinity had caught him by the neck and wouldn't let go. Secretly, he was convinced it was part of the good luck that she'd brought them. It was simple math. If he went down to the field, they'd lose. So he stuck to his box and sometimes used the seventh-inning stretch to make sure Trinity felt like she was getting her share of orgasms out of the deal.

The subject of the broken condom hadn't come up, and he trusted she'd tell him if there was something to report. Everyone was getting what they wanted.

A call from the commissioner's office burst Logan's bubble. Cal Johnson, his star player, was the subject of a doping investigation and would likely be suspended pending a long string of meetings that Logan had just been cordially invited to attend. The devastation this news would create could not be overstated. He'd go to the meetings and then see what was what.

Without pausing to question the decision, he drove from his office to Trinity's condo, parked and texted her.

I'm outside. Can I come up?

Her response was immediate.

Of course.

When she opened the door, he forgot everything he'd been about to say, even though he'd seen her yesterday.

She looked so good, gorgeous in a pair of jeans and a T-shirt, which signified she'd had no plans to go anywhere this evening. Of course she had on her facial armor, but her eye makeup was more subtle than normal. But even if she had done her Cleopatra thing, it was part of her whole package, one that he could secretly admit he liked on her. She was bold, outrageous, and he couldn't get enough of her.

"What's up?" she asked, and it was obvious from her expectant expression that she'd assumed the reason for his visit had something to do with their publicity campaign.

"I wanted to see you."

Suddenly, he felt foolish showing up unannounced when in reality, he didn't know what was up. He'd done more wicked things with this woman than with any other woman of his acquaintance, but that didn't give him any better ability to understand how to communicate with her. What was he supposed to do, come right out and admit that he'd been dealt a devastating blow and she was the only one he wanted to be with right now? Because that felt way too real for what they were doing here.

Something shifted in her expression. "Then come in."

He must be more transparent than he thought. He'd never just dropped by like this. Their association started and ended with being seen together for publicity purposes, which he was using as an excuse to continue having sex without committing to anything else.

This was crossing a line. An irreversible line.

He came in.

"I brought you something." Before he changed his

mind, he fished the jewelry box from his coat pocket. "To say thank you."

"For what?" She eyed the long flat box like he'd pulled out a tarantula. "There aren't any reporters here to capture this moment for all posterity. Sure you don't want to wait and give that to me later?"

"No," he growled. "I don't want to wait. This is personal and I don't want it on camera. I..."

Have no idea what I'm doing here.

Instead of floundering around like a moron, he snapped the lid open and showed her the eight-carat diamond necklace he'd painstakingly picked out at the jeweler earlier that day. Before he'd gotten the call from the commissioner's office, finding something to commemorate the Mustangs' eight-game winning streak— a club record—had been his top priority.

"What the hell, Logan." Fire flashed from her gaze, which was not the reaction he'd been looking for. "You can't give me something like that. It's gorgeous."

He couldn't help the laugh that bubbled out. "You have a funny way of showing your appreciation."

Cautiously, as if afraid it might bite her, she held out one finger and touched the teardrop stone. "It's pink. Like the flower you gave me."

Yeah, because the instant he'd seen it, he'd thought of her and how it would look against her beautiful skin. "Does that mean you like it?"

"It's too much for a thank-you." But she nodded. "I like it."

"Shut up and let me put it on you then."

She held up her hair and presented her back without further argument, thank God. He drew the fine chain around her neck to clasp it, then took advantage of the absence of hair to kiss her exposed flesh. She didn't move away. One second against her skin became two, and that was the extent of his self-control.

He mouthed his way to her ear and yanked her backward into his embrace so he could thoroughly ravage her. She melted into his arms and he walked her toward her bedroom, a path he knew from the handful of times they'd ended up naked after games.

But this was the first time they weren't high on the public displays of affection they'd indulged in. The first time he had no excuse to be here other than the obvious—he couldn't stay away.

When he hit the edge of the bed, he lifted his mouth from her neck long enough to strip her and himself, then rolled her to the coverlet. He reached for the condoms she kept in her bedside drawer and then pleased them both by sucking at every one of her erogenous zones until she was wet and swollen enough to take him fully. And she did, with a little gasp that thrilled him.

That pink diamond sparkled in the low light from the neon outside her floor-to-ceiling view of downtown Dallas. He'd never given a woman jewelry before, and the sight of the chain around her neck when she had nothing else on her body except him put a glow in his chest that felt a hell of lot like something that shouldn't be there. As he sank into Trinity again and again, building the fire until they were both moaning with it, the significance of what was happening here overwhelmed him.

This relationship was as real as it got. And he liked that.

He refused to take time to sort that out as she bowed up, thrusting her breasts high. This, he understood, and he took one of those rosy nipples between his teeth, rolling it almost savagely as he thrust faster, spiraling his hips the way he knew drove her insane, silently powering her to a climax that would trigger his. Because they knew each other's bodies, how to please, how to gratify. Physically, they were a perfect match, but not in any other way.

So why was he so wrapped up in her?

They exploded together, and he bit his lip to keep the wash of emotions inside, where they belonged. Afterward, he spooned her into his body the way they both liked it, and she curled into his embrace.

"What's the real reason you came over tonight?" she murmured.

His eyes shuttered automatically. Would she ever *not* be so good at reading him? He couldn't do that with her. It wasn't fair. But that didn't give him any better ability to lie to her, either.

"Johnson is probably going to be suspended. I'm..." What was he? Disappointed? Frustrated? Furious? "Not sure what's going to happen to the team as a result."

"That's crappy." She squeezed his arm with her soft hand. "What did he do?"

"Performance-enhancing drugs, or so they say. They're against the rules. I'm cooperating with the investigation, but I have to go to New York for some meetings."

With neither of them at the away games, the Mustangs' winning streak would most likely come to an end. A brutal but inescapable truth.

"Do you want me to come with you?" she asked, and the note of genuine concern in her voice unfolded all the emotion inside that he'd been trying to keep under wraps.

Silently, he kissed her shoulder, worried something inappropriate—like *yes*—would slip out if he tried to speak. The fact that she'd offered meant more to him than he could say.

Because she deserved an answer, he finally choked out, "No need."

She rolled in his arms and glanced at him, her eyes warm and huge. "This is really bothering you, isn't it?"

He shook his head. Why he'd denied it, when it was obvious she'd already figured that out, was a mystery to him. "I don't know. Yeah. Maybe. I feel like I should have known or something."

Of course doping went on. It was no different today than when he'd been pitching. Everyone knew who was doing it and who wasn't. Logan had never touched the stuff. Fortunately, he'd been good enough that he'd never been pressured like some of the guys.

Maybe Johnson had felt some of that pressure. Had Logan inadvertently been one of those pressure points?

"You didn't do this, darling. It's not on you."

"I'm the boss," he said simply. "And I feel like I failed at keeping my team strong. My dad ran a billion-dollar company for years and years, and he never let anything like this happen to him."

"You're not your dad, Logan. And this is a totally different industry with different rules and strategies. You have to lead like you." She fanned her fingers across his cheek, lightly caressing as she spoke the gospel according to Trinity. "You can't compare yourself to someone who's gone, either. You don't know what might have happened if he'd lived. Maybe someone in his organization would have been brought up on insider trading. Would that have been his fault for hiring someone who made bad choices?"

No. Of course not.

"You're not allowed to make me feel better with logic," he grumbled.

But her point was not lost on him, and some of the

weight lifted. Exactly what he'd hoped would happen when he'd gotten into his car to come over here. Somehow, she made life…brighter.

She laughed and kissed him sweetly. "What if I make you feel better a whole other way?"

Her legs tangled with his, and her wandering hands left no doubt how she intended to make good on that. Since he was pretty sure she could deliver, he let her.

But the whole time he was pondering some huge questions of his own—like, if he wasn't his dad and it was okay to do things his own way, did that mean he could admit he didn't want a nice, unassuming woman? And that maybe the reason he'd never met the right woman had to do with the fact that he hadn't met Trinity yet?

But the most important question of all was, what would she say if he told her that despite all of his objections to the contrary, he was falling for her?

Logan left to go to New York, and Trinity spent a lot of time pretending she didn't miss him.

Funny how she'd never watched sports in her life, would have claimed under oath she hated the concept of grown men throwing balls around in some macho contest. But for God knew what reason, she couldn't go to sleep at night unless a baseball game was on in the background.

The Mustangs' winning streak ended as Logan had predicted that night before he'd gone to the meetings. But they won the next one even though she wasn't at the game to provide good luck, which was such a silly concept. Of course she'd never say that to Logan's face, since he took his superstition so seriously.

He texted her occasionally with updates, but there

was nothing in the messages that indicated his state of mind or whether he was thinking about her like she thought about him. Days stretched into a week, but neither of them approached the subject about when he was coming home or if they'd pick up where they left off when he did.

The Formula-47 marketing presentation had been rescheduled a couple of times due to everyone's crazy travel schedules, but finally, Cass threw a dart at a day and told everyone they better attend or else.

That morning, Trinity had a nearly impossible time dragging herself out of bed. Despite having subscribed to her cable channel's baseball package—which she would deny if anyone called her on it—there hadn't been one game on the night before, and sleep had come fitfully.

While she was busy not sleeping, her mind kept turning over whether Logan was using this trip to New York as a break—from her. Fyra's numbers were up. Logan's ticket sales had gone through the roof. There was little reason to continue seeing each other. But she didn't want to be done. Selfishly, she'd used their publicity campaign to pretend their relationship was real, and she'd liked it far more than she'd expected, especially given that it had been a very long time since she'd spent time with a man outside of bed.

As she dressed in a teal-green suit and did her makeup, she tried on the idea of casually mentioning to Logan that maybe they could still see each other occasionally, if their schedules permitted. Which sounded crappy in her head and probably wouldn't be improved by saying out loud. The problem was that she didn't know how to tell him that she wanted something more, something real, when she had no clue how to do either one.

When she got to the boardroom, Cass was already there, keying in the virtual meeting details on her laptop. Alex and Harper popped up on the split screen TV.

Harper blinked. "Holy crap. What is that around your neck, Trin?"

Fingering the pink diamond that she couldn't bear to take off, Trinity frowned and opened her mouth to say it was a loaner, and to her absolute mortification, she burst into tears instead.

Cass shoved her chair back and rounded the table to pull Trinity into an embrace, a trick and a half since her expanding belly got in the way. But Cass pulled it off with her typical togetherness, murmuring soothing words until the waterworks subsided somewhat.

"I'm sorry," Trinity sputtered. "I don't know what that was about."

Alex and Harper made noises and talked at the same time until Cass shushed them.

"I think I speak for everyone," Cass said with a smirk, "when I say we've all been there. Let me guess. Things with Logan aren't so fake after all."

"That obvious?" Trinity thought about putting her head down on the boardroom table, right on top of the printed materials she'd brought for the campaign. "I don't know what's real and what's fake and why I'm upset about it or what to do about it. I can't sleep and I'm exhausted all the time."

Cass cocked her head. "Have you talked to him about what you're feeling?"

"I can't," she wailed. "He's in New York at meetings about a very big problem for his team and I just want him to come home and sleep with me, like really sleep. I want to wake up with him in the morning and have coffee and just be together. We've never done that. I don't do that with anyone. I don't know why I want that now. It's ridiculous to feel so clingy and out of sorts and—"

"Trinity." Alex's voice rang out from the TV. "Breathe. That sounds like hormones talking. Maybe after your cycle, you'll feel better."

"I'm not on my period," Trinity snapped. Like Alex knew anything about that. She'd only been pregnant for forever. "I'm not even due to start until—"

The first. What was today? Trinity glanced at her phone. The sixth. *Oh, my God.* It was the *sixth.* And she was always so regular.

Panic slammed through her chest as she did the math. It had been almost three weeks since the broken condom incident. With all the baseball games and juggling the Bloom campaign and missing Logan, she'd totally lost track of the calendar.

"I'm sensing we're having a revelation in the works," Harper said cheerfully. "Should we reconvene another day while you go take a pregnancy test?"

A pregnancy test.

The phrase made literally no sense, as if Harper had spoken Swahili. Trinity hadn't taken a pregnancy test in eight years. Because she'd never had the slightest doubt about what the result would be.

"I have a couple of extras in my desk," Cass offered. "From when Gage and I were trying. If you want to know now."

Numbly, Trinity nodded at the woman who had been her best friend since eleventh grade. The distance that had grown between them due to their very different life circumstances vanished. There was no one else she'd want holding her hand as she verified whether her problems with Logan were exponentially greater than she'd supposed.

After an eternity that was really more like ten minutes later, she had her answer.

Amazing how she could actually see the plus sign though all the blurry tears. *Pregnant.* With Logan McLaughlin's baby.

"Should I say congratulations or I'm sorry?" Cass asked quietly.

Trinity didn't answer, just tossed the positive test onto the counter and sank to the ground to put her head on her bent knees. Her whole body shook with a cocktail of nerves and wonder and disbelief and hope. But she had to squash that. Now.

There was no way she'd carry to term. Her body didn't work like that. The little miracle inside would be snatched from her before it had a chance to form, and she'd have to deal with it. Again.

Oh, God. A new round of horror tore through her. What was she going to tell Logan? She'd promised she'd let him know if this happened, but that had been back when she'd been ridiculously certain her birth control would stick. Obviously her pills had failed her and her secret belief that she couldn't get pregnant again was false.

"I don't understand how this happened," she sniffled out brokenly to Cass through the sobs still racking her chest. "What am I going to do?"

"Do you want the baby?" Cass asked, cutting to the chase in her usual style. And of course that was the most important question, and Trinity knew the answer instantly.

"Of course. But that's not in the cards—"

"Stop. You don't know that. You're going to get the best prenatal care possible," Cass countered. "And then we're going to stage sticky-baby sit-ins, ply you with peanut butter, whatever it takes to make this work for you this time. Your womb has had eight years to develop, to mature."

The words filtered through the crushing pain in Trinity's chest but did nothing to absolve it. She couldn't do this, couldn't bear the idea of eventually—soon—having absolute confirmation that she was indeed as broken as she'd always assumed.

But what if Cass was right? What if the baby actually stuck? What if this was the start of the most amazing chapter in her life? For today, right now, she was pregnant with Logan's baby.

Fledgling emotions that she'd never allowed herself to embrace welled up and over with the realization that she had a piece of him inside her, that the universe had conspired to make their relationship real in the most wonderful way possible.

She could admit that when he talked about having a family, she wanted that, too.

And then she realized. She couldn't tell him.

Instead of fearing that he'd take off, the opposite would be true. He'd want to be there every step, to go to the doctor's appointments, pick out a crib. That's who he was, and he'd be devastated if—when—she miscarried. And then she'd have to deal with it alone, because what else would bind them together? He'd be done with her at that point, forever.

She could not take the double loss.

They had nothing between them except a successful publicity campaign and a mass of cells that would never become anything but another heartbreak.

Nine

New York had been brutal. Johnson's forty-five-game suspension destroyed the Mustangs' morale, precisely as Logan had expected when he'd received the verdict.

He'd appealed, naturally, which meant extending his stay longer than he would have liked, but the appeal would take a while to work itself out. Plus, it was strictly a formality; the inquest had Johnson dead to rights, including video of him frequenting the clinic that sold the PEDs.

The whole thing was disheartening.

Once a day, he'd reached for the phone to call Trinity and beg her to fly to New York, just so he could see her. So he could touch her. Hear her laugh, lose himself in her sweet body at the end of a long day of meetings that ripped his team apart. He wanted to be with her, to let her make the horrible reality better.

He wanted more.

But he never dialed. It wasn't fair to start that discussion over the phone. So he held off until he got back to Dallas. While waiting for his luggage to appear from the bowels of the airport, he texted her.

At the airport. Can I come by Fyra to see you?

God, that was bold. Trinity had a job. *He* had a job. Jumping off a plane and driving straight to her wasn't smart. But it was the only thing he wanted to do.

She didn't text him back right away. Probably in a meeting. He went home, which was what he should have done anyway. The house smelled stale and musty from disuse, even though he'd only been gone for a few weeks. The emptiness crawled onto his last nerve, and he hated it. Why had he bought such a monstrosity of a house when he had no one to share it with?

What was today? Thursday? Maybe he'd see if Trinity would ditch work tomorrow and spend a three-day weekend at his place. He'd never brought a woman home, and he could picture Trinity draped across his bed with frightening ease. She'd like his giant marble garden tub, too, he had a feeling. Or rather, she'd like what he did to her while she was in it, which was practically the same thing.

They could order takeout, or maybe he'd cook steaks on the massive grill in the outdoor kitchen that overlooked the pool. Afterward, he'd strip her down to her bare skin, pick her up and lower her into the hot tub at the north end of the pool, cleverly tied into the design via an outcropping of natural river rock.

He checked his phone, but she hadn't texted him back yet. His plane had landed four hours ago. Maybe she hadn't seen the message. He called her this time.

No answer. Fine. She was busy. He'd been gone for a while, and they hadn't really talked much since he'd left Dallas.

Thursday stretched into Friday, and he made the long trek from Prosper to his office in Arlington. The team was in Pittsburgh playing a three-game series and getting their asses handed to them. Myra had some very depressing numbers regarding the decline in ticket sales, which of course had taken a hit with the double whammy of losing the Mustangs' marquee slugger and the lack of new, steamier pictures from the club's favorite poster boy.

But oddly, the most unsettling thing in Logan's world right now was the distinct absence of Trinity Forrester. He missed her keenly, had for weeks, and he could not seem to focus on anything but the three, maybe four, unanswered text messages he'd sent since landing yesterday.

He'd made a mistake not calling her while he'd been in New York, that much was clear. He had to fix it. But if she wasn't responding to his messages or the voice mail he'd left, it was entirely possible she'd lost her phone. It happened.

By Friday night, he couldn't stand it any longer and drove to her condo. Stupid. He couldn't get into the building unless she buzzed him in, but she didn't respond. He could see her Porsche in her designated spot in the parking garage from here.

His temper flared. She was here but not interested in seeing him? That was not cool.

The gods of security smiled on him when a well-dressed couple came out of the building and glanced at the flowers in his hand as he skulked about outside.

"Is she not answering? You must be early, then," the

elderly woman surmised with a misty smile, apparently drawing her own conclusions about the situation. "That's so nice to see."

"Yes, ma'am," he replied, because there was really no other answer.

"Come on, then." She winked and held the door open. Once he was inside…he had no idea if Trinity would even answer the door.

One way to find out. He took the elevator to the fifteenth floor and banged on the door in case she had music on. She answered almost immediately, clearly frazzled, her hair mussed and her ratty sweatshirt a marked contrast to her normal style.

And she wasn't wearing any makeup. She'd literally never been more beautiful. He could not tear his gaze from her.

All the color drained from her bare face. "Logan."

Not expecting him, obviously.

"Surprise." He held out the flowers. His pulse hammered in his throat, and he wanted to sweep her into his arms so badly his hands were shaking.

She eyed the bouquet, her expression frozen. Why wasn't she taking the flowers?

"You, um…didn't respond to any of my messages."

Which judging by the ice chips currently jetting from her eyes, she already knew. "I've been busy. You shouldn't have come by."

The long process of dealing with the PED inquest and fatigue and sheer confusion swirled together to step on Logan's temper. "I wanted to see you. Can I at least ask why the reverse isn't true?"

Warily, she shrugged, but not before he noted her expression. She wasn't as unaffected as she'd like him to think. It settled his temper a touch.

"It was a good time to break things off. I really thought you were on the same page with your lack of communication over the last few weeks."

That speared him right through the chest. She had been avoiding him. On purpose.

"My fault," he agreed smoothly, mystified why there was this distance between them. It felt like she was trying to push him out.

"Let me make it up to you," he said with a smile. "And I don't mean in bed. Unless that's what you want."

Her eyelids shuttered, hiding her thoughts from him. But then, he'd never been able to read her, and the frustration of it almost snapped the stems of the blooms in his hand before he realized the pain in his palm came from the thorns digging into his flesh.

"I'll pass, thanks."

Something was very wrong. Fatigue pulled at her eyes, and all at once, he clued in that her death grip on the door frame wasn't designed to keep him out— she was holding herself up. Alarmed, he made his own guess about why she wasn't wearing makeup. *Idiot.* When her face had drained of color, he'd assumed she'd been unhappy to see him, but in reality, she was sick.

"Is it the flu or something more serious?" he asked.

"It's...nothing," she lied when it was so clearly something. And then she weaved as her knees buckled.

Tossing the flowers, he scooped her up in his arms and shut the door with his foot, refusing to recall the last time he'd done this—when they'd ended up naked together. He couldn't even enjoy the fact that he was touching her again after an eternity apart.

She felt so insubstantial in his arms, weakly protesting as he strode to her bedroom and laid her out on the bed, then wedged in next to her to stroke her hair.

"What is it? Can I get you something? Water or—"

"No, I'm fine," she whispered but her eyes closed and her head pushed into his palm like a cat seeking affection. He was more than happy to give it to her. It pleased him to have his hands on her, even in this small way.

The longer he stroked, the more she relaxed and the less his chest hurt. If she was sick, it explained why she hadn't immediately jumped on his text messages. Probably she'd had one of those silly moments where she'd railed against having him come over and see her without makeup, like he cared about that.

Didn't she know she was beautiful to him regardless?

All at once, she moaned, and it wasn't the good kind. Helplessly, he watched as she turned over, curling in on herself. That was not going to work. But what should he do?

Leaving her on the bed, eyes still squeezed tight, he ventured into her bathroom to see if she had some kind of prescription or over-the-counter medication. And maybe if he found something, it could clue him in to what the hell was wrong with her.

There was nothing on the counter except a small mirrored tray covered with tiny, expensive-looking bottles of perfume. The drawers on the right side of the espresso wood–and–marble vanity held her cosmetics in an array of holders and shelves and various hidey-holes that made his skin crawl, so he shut them and pulled open the cabinet on the left.

Hair spray and various other female things lined the bottom. Including a small white plastic wand with a blue tip. It was face up and he could easily read the words Pregnant and Not Pregnant, next to a plus sign and a negative sign. The big circle prominently featured a blue plus sign.

Logan's brain went fuzzy as his knees gave out and he plopped onto the bathroom floor, half on the short-pile bath mat, half on the white marble tile.

Trinity was *pregnant*. That's what was wrong with her.

"I didn't want you to find out this way." Her low voice floated to him from the doorway.

He glanced up to see her standing there, leaning on the door frame as if it was the only thing keeping her from joining him on the floor.

"What way did you plan for me to find out?" It came out a little harsher than he'd intended, but she'd promised to tell him if this happened, and after ignoring all his messages—

The first tendril of blackness snaked through his stomach as he stared at her flushed face. The lack of welcome. The way she could barely look at him. The cold silence on her end of the line once he'd returned from New York.

"You weren't going to tell me, were you?" How he got that sentence out around the baseball in his throat was nothing short of miraculous.

After the longest pause in history, she shook her head. "But not because I didn't want to. Because—" Something choked off her words and she bent nearly double, scrubbing at her face with the heel of her hand.

He had no trouble filling in that blank. Because it wasn't his baby.

Dark, ugly jealousy flooded his chest as he stared at her. While he'd been falling for her and trying to reconcile all of these strange, wondrous emotions, she'd been seeing other people. Why wouldn't she? They hadn't established any exclusivity. He'd just assumed...

And look where that had gotten him. He followed

the rules and she broke them. She'd never had any interest in having a family, not the way he did. They were always going to be opposites and pregnancy was an irreversible showstopper.

Thank God he hadn't told her he wanted more like he'd half considered while in New York, or this gutting would definitely be worse. Though he had a hard time seeing how when it felt like his stomach was on fire.

How was it possible that he'd been trying to figure out how to take the next step with her while she'd been backing away as fast as she could?

The longer Logan sat on her bathroom floor by the open cabinet, the more Trinity genuinely thought she might throw up right then and there.

Morning sickness had picked a hell of a time to whack her. She'd called in sick to work, a first, but Cass had totally understood despite the fact that she'd never once done it herself.

Trinity was too miserable to care that she was not the champion pregnant woman among Fyra's executives. Now Logan had forced her to deal with him, too.

When she'd opened the door, the first thing that had slammed through her body was relief. *Thank God.* He was here and she didn't have to do this by herself. All she'd wanted to do was fall into his arms, to babble endless words about how much she'd missed him, how beautiful and strong and solid he was. How she knew he was going to make everything better.

Good thing she hadn't. As soon as she realized he was in the bathroom going through her cabinets, she'd hurled herself out of bed to stop him. But it was too late. And judging by the look on his face, this pregnancy conversation was not going to end well.

He was furious.

"You didn't want to tell me?" he ground out through clenched teeth. "You didn't think I had a right to know?"

She'd never heard his voice sound so tightly controlled, so much like he was holding himself in. It frightened her a little. Hadn't he said he wanted kids and had every intention of being in the baby's life? Or had she completely misremembered that?

"I..."

Have no defense.

Really, she didn't. It was only due to her own cowardice that she hadn't told him right away, and as a result, she'd ended up alone over the last couple of days anyway. Nausea turned her stomach over and threatened to expel the chicken noodle soup she'd eaten earlier to settle it.

"I can't do this now," she whispered and sank to the hardwood floor outside her bathroom. She'd thought... well, it didn't matter that she'd thought maybe there was a chance things might magically work out.

"Or ever?" he countered. "You didn't want to tell me because you realized our publicity campaign would be over, right?"

Stricken, she stared at him. He thought she'd kept this quiet because she was worried about *publicity*? "That makes no sense, Logan. Why would our opportunities for publicity end just because I'm pregnant?"

As if that was the most important thing to hash out. He hadn't asked how she was dealing with it, how far along she was. Whether she'd gone to the doctor. None of the things she'd expected. His reaction was almost... cold.

A shiver worked down her spine. This situation was unraveling fast. Potential for miscarriage aside, now that he knew, she'd honestly expected more of a positive reaction.

"Oh, you're right," he said silkily in a dark tone that did not sound like that of a man happy to find out he was going to be father. "Why not continue faking our relationship no matter what? Should be easy. We've been doing it this long, pretending we like each other for the camera. What's an unexpected pregnancy between *friends*?"

There was nothing friendly about his sarcasm, and his point cut through her. He'd been faking it this whole time. While she'd been fighting her feelings and trying not to fall for him, he hadn't been engaged in a similar battle. She'd created a fantasy in her head because he'd given her a few intense looks during sex.

Nothing about their relationship was real. Hadn't she learned that lesson by now? She should have. The pain radiating through her chest was exactly what she deserved for daring to pretend they'd been building something neither of them could walk away from.

"My mistake," she said, proud of how substantial her voice sounded when in reality, her insides felt hollowed out. Fitting that she could fake even this. "I misspoke. It seems as if it might be best if we ended our public relationship. The sooner the better, so we have time to work on a recovery plan."

"And our private one, too." Then he twisted the knife in farther before she had a chance to fully process that. "That's why you didn't tell me, I'm guessing. You knew it would be the end of us and opted to keep the devastation to a minimum."

Miserably, she nodded and shut her eyes against the blackness spreading across Logan's face. At the end of the day, that was the gist of it. She hadn't told him out of pure selfishness. She'd eventually miscarry anyway and there'd be nothing holding them together. But even that had been imaginary, because there was nothing holding them together now, either, apparently.

Why not let him leave now instead of then? It was a simple matter of timing.

Obviously he didn't want her or the baby. Or maybe he didn't want the baby strictly because it was hers. Hadn't he always said she wasn't his type? They were ill suited for each other. That was why he'd always asked her to dress differently, after all.

"I can't do this now, either," he growled. "Congratulations. You've successfully provoked my temper. I have to get out of here."

She scuttled out of the doorway so he could stride from the bathroom. Without a backward glance, he stormed from her condo and took the majority of her heart with him.

The only piece left was tucked in next to the fetus still growing in her womb. For now. She lived in fear of the day she'd wake up in her own blood and know that she was once again alone.

Trinity forced herself to lie in the bed she'd made, continuing to go to work and do her job, but it was far more rote than she would like to admit. Her body hurt all the time and her creativity fled along with her ability to feel anything other than miserable. Thankfully, she'd gotten far enough along in the Bloom campaign that her creative team could run with it.

Logan didn't call. She kept her phone in her hand constantly and cursed every time it buzzed and there wasn't a message from him.

Funny how when he'd been trying to reach her after

returning from New York, each contact point had sliced through her and she'd prayed he'd stop, that he'd leave her alone to figure out how to manage this huge, terrible secret between them.

Now that he had actually broken off all communication, each moment of silence cut even deeper. He really wanted nothing to do with her or the baby. Nor would he be a strong hand to hold when she miscarried. He wasn't the man she'd thought he was, and that was perhaps the worst realization of all.

Late one afternoon, Trinity roused herself out of her stupor to help Harper and Alex throw a baby shower for Cass. It was good for her to stop stewing over things she couldn't change, and it was definitely better to quit dwelling on what had not yet happened, which she had zero control over. Plus, Cass was her best friend, no matter how distant they'd been lately.

Maybe it was time to change that.

Harper flew in from Zurich for the occasion and coupled the trip with some on-site meetings with her lab staff. Alex's twin girls weren't technically due for another six weeks, but her doctor in Washington was convinced she'd deliver any day now, so she participated remotely. As soon as she had her babies, Fyra's CFO would take six months maternity leave.

Once, Trinity would have labeled that ludicrous and pretended a woman's career should trump everything else. When really, it was solely Trinity who had grabbed on to her job with both hands in lieu of seeking what her friends seemed to fall into so easily—a supportive relationship with a husband who loved his wife and couldn't wait to be a father.

Now she could readily admit she was so jealous she couldn't stand it.

As the four pregnant executives gathered in one of the conference rooms at the company they'd built from the ground up, Trinity had enough energy to hug Harper, whom she hadn't seen in person in quite some time. Never would Trinity have thought they'd all have pregnancy in common a few weeks ago. Fyra's chief science officer had finally developed a belly, which she patted when Trinity commented on it.

"Dante calls him Amoeba. I tried to get him to quit, but he thinks it's hilarious." Harper rolled her eyes at her absent husband, whom she'd left behind in Zurich, but only because he was filming his television show about the science of attraction. Otherwise, he'd have been following his wife around like an overprotective caveman, wearing a goofy, adoring expression that communicated how very much he loved Harper and their baby.

Obviously Trinity could use some pointers on how to find a man like that—she should have been watching Dr. Gates's show all along. Then it wouldn't have been such a shock to find out Logan hadn't been falling for her all along like she'd been for him.

Tears pricked at her eyelids and she let them fall. Didn't matter how hard she tried to hold it all in, everything came gushing out anyway. Why fight it?

"Oh, honey." Harper rubbed a sympathetic hand along Trinity's forearm. "It gets better."

Cass settled into the chair on Trinity's other side and drew her into a hug, bopping the balloons tied to nearly every surface of the room. "You still haven't talked to Logan?"

Trinity shook her head against Cass's shoulder without fear, because Harper's combo foundation and powder was bulletproof against smearing. Maybe that could be the genesis of a new ad campaign. But her thoughts refused to jell, like everything else in her life. Her creativity had left the moment Logan walked out of her condo. Which was of course appropriate, because he'd become her muse along with her reason to breathe, the father of her baby and the sole thing that occupied her thoughts 24-7. Ironic, much?

"You have to talk to him," Alex called from the TV screen. "He has legal obligations to you and the baby regardless of whether he likes it or not. Child support, if nothing else. Phillip is texting you the name of a lawyer right now who will get you everything you deserve."

What did she deserve? Half of Logan's fortune? Season tickets to the Mustangs' home games? To be alone because she'd spent her adult life pretending she didn't want the fantasy she'd created with him?

Cass nodded as Trinity sat back in her chair. "Also, things are not always how they seem. I thought Gage and I were destined not to work. And we tried it twice. I never would have predicted that he'd storm into my office with an engagement ring in his pocket."

That was different. Everyone had known that Gage had it bad for Fyra's CEO.

"Phillip kidnapped me on the way home from the hospital, after that time I passed out, so he could talk me out of divorcing him," Alex threw in. "Men can be very unpredictable when they decide they want something."

Harper laughed. "Dante flew from Zurich to Los Angeles, then to Dallas almost back-to-back to tell me he'd screwed up when he left. I've been in love with the man for ten years. I would have taken a phone call. But it was nice to feel like I was his number-one priority."

"You all deserve the happiness you've found," Trinity sniffed. "But you married men who wanted to have children—"

The gales of laughter interrupted her as all three women wiped tears of mirth from their eyes.

"I cannot even begin to tell you how wrong that is," Cass said when she'd gained a small measure of control. "Becoming a father to a one-year-old was probably the hardest thing Gage ever did. He looks like a pro now, but trust me when I say it took a lot of soul-searching on his part to get where he is today."

Harper laced her fingers with Trinity's and smiled. "You do remember that Dante is not the biological father of my baby, right? It took me forever to convince him to go to the doctor with me as my *friend*, let alone for him to decide he wanted to be the baby's father. It nearly broke us apart, but we figured it out. If it's meant to be, you and Logan will, too."

"And if it's not," Alex countered, "you're a strong, independent woman. We'll be there for you as you raise your baby."

"If the pregnancy sticks," Trinity reminded everyone. Because that was the biggest hurdle. It didn't matter what she *wanted*. It mattered what her body decided to do with the baby, which she had no control over. That was probably messing her up the most.

But the love in her friends' words filtered through all the misery anyway, and Trinity smiled for the first time in a long time. "Thanks. You guys mean the world to me, and I appreciate your support. You would have been well within your rights to tell me to stick my self-righteousness where the sun don't shine when I got pregnant."

Harper grinned. "I thought about it. You were pretty smug when you swore you'd never get knocked up. I should get a medal for not blabbing that fifty percent of all pregnancies are unplanned."

"Statistically speaking," Cass said drily, "I think the four of us proved that in spades."

"Yet we still manage to run a multimillion-dollar company." Trinity smiled because that was still amazing. "Even though we apparently suck at launching a secret revolutionary product."

"Hey." Cass scowled. "Your marketing proposal for Bloom is brilliant. We're launching the formula on schedule despite numerous setbacks with first the leak to the industry about our unannounced product, then the legalities of the FDA approval process nightmare. We navigated the tainted samples and triumphed over the public smear campaign. Each of us according to our strengths. That's how we started this business and that's how we'll keep on doing it."

Flinging her red hair over her shoulder, Harper leaned forward with her pit-bull face on. "I wasn't going to mention it since this is supposed to be a party, but since we're on the subject, when I met with my staff earlier, I had an idea for how to catch our culprit. I'm pretty sure I know who it is. But I need everyone's help to close the deal."

"Like a sting operation?" Alex's raised eyebrows reflected in her tone loud and clear. "We're executives, not Charlie's Angels."

"But our lawyer already advised us we couldn't go to the police because we didn't have enough evidence," Trinity argued. Honestly, the whole thing sounded like exactly what she needed to get her mind off everything else. Alex didn't have to ruin all the fun with her logic and reason. "At least hear what Harper has to say."

They bent their heads together and talked through

Harper's thoughts, which Cass insisted was more productive and beneficial than opening gifts containing clothes the baby couldn't even wear until it was born.

Finally, they had a solid plan for how to deal with the hits their company had taken over the last year as they dared branch into a new product line. They were still four strong and would prevail.

Right after they made their plan, Cass, Harper and Trinity devoured the finger sandwiches and cakes Melinda, Fyra's receptionist, had ordered for the party. They were all eating for two, after all.

Ten

Logan groaned and put a pillow over his head as his phone rang at the god-awful hour of…9:45 a.m.

How was it already almost ten? Did he have a game today? Was someone calling to see where he was? His brain would not connect any dots.

Juggling the phone into his hand, he launched out of bed. His big toe collided with the heavy wood nightstand, and when his foot jerked back automatically, his ankle crashed into the bed frame.

The curse he bit out wasn't fit for a dive bar, let alone the caller on the other end of the phone.

"Logan Duncan McLaughlin." His mother's voice had that no-nonsense thing down pat. "I will personally come over there and wash your mouth out with soap if that's how you're going to talk to me."

"Mom, please. I'm really not in the mood."

His head hurt from the copious amounts of alcohol he'd poured down his throat last night after the Mustangs lost their third game in a row. And now he had matching aches on the other end of his body. Rubbing his throbbing toe, he sank back onto the bed and fought the wave of agony inside that was far worse than the physical discomforts.

No amount of alcohol could fix how miserable he was without Trinity.

"Well, I'm sorry, but I don't enjoy learning things about my son's life from the internet." Her tone softened a tad. "I saw an unconfirmed rumor that you and your maybe fiancée broke up. Is it true? Because if it's not over, I still want to meet her."

Wasn't that the million-dollar question? It *should* be over. But he couldn't stop thinking about her, missing her, wanting her.

He flung himself backward to stare at the ceiling in his master bedroom that was far too masculine for his tastes, but the decorator he'd hired had insisted that he'd like the heavy, depressing jewel tones and dark wood. Honestly, he suspected the only thing that would fix it was a woman with a penchant for bold fabrics and colors, who wasn't afraid of slinging her particular brand of style around.

One woman in particular.

He sighed. "The thing with Trinity never really started in the first place. The whole relationship was staged to generate positive publicity for our respective companies."

He braced for censure, shock, something. Who knew what? What he'd just confessed was no doubt blasphemy of the highest order to someone who'd had a great relationship with a man for nearly forty years.

"Oh, please." His mother gave a very unladylike snort. "It might have started out that way, but anyone can take one look at those photographs and see that you care for her."

"Well, *she* doesn't fall in that category, unfortunately." And Trinity was the most important one in that equation. If he wasn't so wrecked, he'd have the energy to get really pissed about it all over again. But all he could muster up was a dose of profound sadness.

"I think you're too close to the situation. She's got it as badly for you as the reverse is true. So why don't you tell me what's really going on?"

He almost smiled at that, but only because his mom sounded like Trinity, reading his mind and his moods with ease. "How do you know anything is going on? We had a fake relationship and now it's over. What more could there be?"

Everything. And nothing. Because he'd been naive enough to think what they'd had was special. Real. Instead, it was all an illusion, and he'd walked right into it without even realizing it was vanishing around him until it was gone.

"Please. I was married to your father, wasn't I? The day I can't understand a man with McLaughlin DNA is the day I gladly go to meet my maker. Spill. Or I'm coming over there."

Which was not an idle threat. She'd do it, too, and drag the whole story out of him while cooking him something full of fat and calories and love.

Suddenly that sounded so nice, his throat went tight. "I'd be okay with that."

"Oh, sweetie. Is it that bad?"

"She's pregnant." Why had he blurted that out? It was too early for this kind of ambush.

"What? Give me that girl's phone number right now!" His mother's outrage nearly burned up Logan's phone, his fingers and his ear. "I cannot believe that woman would try to use you to extort money—"

"Mom, she didn't try to get money out of me."

"She...tried to pass the baby off as yours?" Obviously that was the more delicate issue in her mind.

"No, she didn't do that, either."

"So. Let me get this straight. You had a fake relationship with her but you had an agreement to not see other people?" When he muttered *no*, she blurted, "I'm drawing a blank here, then. It's like you gave up within sight of the finish line. What did she do that was so horrible that you can't tell her how you feel?"

"The baby is not mine!"

"So? What does that matter?"

The phrases echoed through his head, condemning him, because suddenly, he didn't know the answer. It felt like there should be some kind of rule that said you didn't stay with a woman who'd gotten pregnant by another man. But Trinity had never conformed to the rules, and she'd certainly proven her ability to get him to break them often enough as well.

"I—"

"Have a temper and let it ruin your relationship?" she guessed easily. But his mom wasn't done icing that cake. "Do you love her?"

"Of course I do." He blinked. "I mean...I don't know. Yeah. I thought I was moving in that direction, but it all fell apart."

"Honey, you basically just told me that a pregnant woman had a billionaire on the hook and chose to be honest with you about what was going on. Sounds like a keeper to me. Get off your butt and go get what you want."

Was his mother *daring* him to be with Trinity anyway? "It's not that simple."

"Then move on," she advised. "Put this chapter behind you. There's this really nice girl I want to introduce you to. She just joined my church. That's why I called, actually—"

"Thanks, Mom, but no."

He stood up as conviction roared through his chest. He didn't want a nice woman. He wanted a shocking one who didn't put up with his crap and dared him to take what he wanted. A woman like his mom.

Maybe he was more like his father than he'd credited.

For the first time since he'd left Trinity's condo, his world made sense. He was in love with Trinity and he'd screwed up by walking out on her. Period. Everything else was just incidental.

Now he had to convince her that while they were busy faking it, reality had crept up and changed everything.

The sting operation—such as it was—had been a huge success. Fyra's four executives had delivered Harper's lab manager into the hands of the police, along with her venom-filled confession recorded digitally on Trinity's phone.

It was so great to have finally taken control of *something*.

"That woman deserves to burn," Harper spat as the detective the Dallas police department had sent finally left. "Imagine the nerve. Assuming she deserved any credit for Formula-47. That was my baby. I gave up my life for two years to develop it. All she did was take notes. *Dante* did more than she did when he created the new FDA samples after *she* ruined the first ones."

The woman had been so angry about the perceived lack of credit that she'd confessed to causing all of their problems in hopes of ruining Harper for the snub. In reality, the lab manager had little to do with the creation of Bloom. Psychological screening was definitely in order.

"It's over now," Cass said soothingly and glanced at Trinity's phone, which was still on the table in front of her after she'd played the recording for the detective. "We should go celebrate."

Trinity sank into a swivel chair in the conference room where they'd met with the police, clutching her weak stomach. "That doesn't look like the face of a CEO who just plugged the leak in her company."

"I, um…think you should see this." Cass held out Trinity's phone to show her a text message. From Logan. "I didn't mean to read it, but it popped up with the preview."

"It's okay."

Numb, she tapped up the whole message. She probably wouldn't have read it now—or ever—if Cass and Harper hadn't been sitting there staring at her. But she had to talk to him sometime. Avoidance wasn't a good coping mechanism.

The text jumped off the screen.

We need to stage a public breakup. I left a ticket to today's game at will call. Come by before the seventh inning and we'll get it on camera.

It was a good idea. Brilliant, in fact. Maybe they could still generate some publicity with another fight. Except her stomach heaved so much that she genuinely feared she might throw up.

So this was it then. Logan was really lost to her. In

keeping with the painful theme of their relationship, it didn't seem real.

"Want me to drive you?" Cass asked quietly.

Disoriented, Trinity nodded. Cass didn't try to talk to her on the way to the stadium, a blessing because she didn't know what she'd say. At will call, Cass insisted on buying her own ticket, even though Trinity tried to pay for it as a thank-you for driving her. She couldn't have done this alone. For a woman who claimed to value independence, she'd grown remarkably unable to stand on her own two feet lately.

Per the additional instructions Logan had texted her en route, Trinity found the security guard expecting her, and he led both women through a warren of hallways and out onto the field where Logan was supposed to meet her. They hung back, well out of the way of the cameramen and other personnel.

The game was in progress. Top of the seventh, so she'd made it before the stretch as instructed. The Mustangs were up to bat, two men on base and two outs. She eyed the lineup. The next batter couldn't afford a sacrifice fly because the runner on second wasn't fast enough to tag up—God, what was she doing? Where did all that stuff even come from?

Well, no mystery there. Logan had infused her with his passion so easily because she'd loved hearing him talk about baseball.

LA's left-handed pitcher took out the right-handed batter in three easy strikes and the inning was over. The players streamed from the field, and a woman in a US Air Force dress uniform sang "God Bless America." Trinity had seen this routine several times now, but never from the field. The perspective was dizzying.

As the last notes faded, a figure shadowed the stadium lights, and Trinity glanced up.

Logan. Big, beautiful and such a hit to her already strung-out nerves. How dare he stand there with that killer smile, looking so amazing that her knees actually buckled before she could catch herself? Apparently her body hadn't gotten the memo that she didn't go for men who bailed when the going got tough.

"You rang?" she called out sarcastically and crossed her arms before he noticed her hands were shaking. "Looks like even I couldn't save Walker's RBI, so your plan to get your good-luck charm on the field failed. LA's reliever is hot."

He shrugged good-naturedly. "Win some, lose some."

"Close your mouth, Trinity," Cass muttered from behind her. "There's a camera on you. And it's streaming your conversation to the big screen."

Somehow Trinity hinged her jaw back into place, but not because of the camera. The whole point of her being here was to put this madness behind her once and for all, and she had to actually talk in order to get this argument started.

No matter how much it hurt.

"Win some, lose some?" she repeated incredulously. "Who are you and what have you done with Logan McLaughlin?"

Because the guy she'd known would never say that. Maybe that was part of the point. She hadn't ever really known him.

His brow arched. "I told you, the scoreboard is not the most beautiful thing in my world. You are."

Something was off here. They were supposed to be staging a public breakup, not rehashing stupid things they'd said to each other. Hands jammed down on her hips, she scowled. "You hate my clothes."

"I do like you better naked," he agreed readily. "But I don't hate your clothes. I just like the ones I pick out above the ones you pick out. But we can compromise."

"Compromise?" Now she felt like a parrot. "Can you even spell that? You're dictatorial, inflexible and frankly, I have no idea how you walk around under the weight of all the rules you've got slung over your shoulder."

Now they'd get into the knock-down, drag-out part of the agenda. He hated it when she made fun of the stick up his butt.

But instead, he nodded. "That does sound like me. That's why I need a woman like you in my life to shake things up and point out when I'm being too narrow-minded. I lost the best thing that ever happened to me when I walked away. So this is your public apology. I'm sorry."

The stadium lights swirled into a big blob as her vision tunneled and the roar of the crowd's approval swelled up and over the sudden pounding of her pulse. This wasn't an argument. He'd lured her here under false pretenses so he could *apologize*?

"What are you doing?" she whispered. "We're supposed to be breaking up."

"But that's not what I want." Logan inched forward on the grass, capturing her hand in his and bringing it to his lips like he'd done so many times. "Forgive me. I didn't handle our last discussion well and I'm asking you for another chance. Publicly. I'm also giving you the opportunity to humiliate me, because I deserve that far more than I deserve you."

Her throat clogged with unshed tears that shouldn't

be there. None of this could be real. "Why will this time be any different?"

Which was not at all what she should have said.

There was an angle here that she wasn't getting.

That's when he smiled and the tenderness in his expression washed over her. "Because this time, I'm admitting right up front that I'm in love with you."

Blood rushed from her head so fast that she nearly passed out. When she wobbled, Logan's expression shifted instantly to concern and he waved the camera off, scooping her up in his arms.

This time, she wholeheartedly agreed with his tactics, because holy hell. "Did you just tell me that you're in love with me?"

"It's okay," he murmured as he carried her through the warren of halls. They passed people getting ready for the eighth inning now that the team owner's theatrics were over, but no one stopped them and finally he found a private, unlocked room. "I'm not totally used to it yet, either."

He settled her into a chair and knelt by her feet, caressing her face with questing fingers, likely to verify whether she was about to face-plant on the floor. His heat faded from her body far too fast. All she could do was drink in his precious face, hair falling into it and all. God, she'd missed him, missed the feel of him under her fingers, missed the rush of him through her blood.

"Why would you say something like that?" she burst out. Now that they were alone, all her emotional consternation over the last few days squished her chest. Which wasn't going to work. She needed to be calm and rational instead of a hairbreadth from flinging herself back into his arms, where she felt safe and beautiful and loved. "None of what we had was real."

"Because I'm trying to make it crystal clear that what we had before might have been fake, but what I want to have going forward isn't." Quietly, he surveyed her. "We're starting off with no misunderstandings. The way I feel about you *is* real. I should have told you before now."

"But I don't understand." Her voice gained a little strength as some of what he was saying filtered through the ache in her heart. "You didn't want anything to do with me or the baby. What changed?"

He didn't so much as blink. "I realized that I was being shortsighted by letting something like a past relationship stand in our way. I can accept a baby that isn't mine. As long as you come along with it."

The ground slid away at an alarming rate. Words. Buzzing in her ears. No context.

"What past relationship?" And then *isn't mine* registered. "Are you accusing me of having *slept* with someone else while we were dating?"

Before she could stop herself, she slugged him on the arm. Her knuckles glanced away and started smarting like she'd hit a brick wall. Which wasn't far off.

"It's okay," he said soothingly. "We didn't have an exclusive agreement. I was being a Neanderthal about it."

"The baby is yours, idiot," she ground out through clenched teeth as his face went ghost white. "*Men.* Oh, my God. Really? When would I have had time, Logan? Of *all* things. I went to four million baseball games with you. I went to *Oakland.* What do I have to do to prove that I was invested in us? If you've made me miserable for the last few days because you didn't bother to ask me one of the most basic questions—"

Air whooshed from her lungs as he snatched her into

his arms, holding her so tightly she couldn't breathe. But she could still hear him repeating *sorry* over and over.

Squeaking, she shoved at his rock-hard pecs until he eased up a bit. "Seriously? You thought the baby wasn't yours?"

Oh, God. All of this started making a wonderful, terrible sort of sense.

"I...made my own assumptions about why you didn't tell me right away," he confessed miserably. "I'm so sorry. I should have clarified before storming out. It's really mine? I'm going to be a father?"

As she nodded, the clearest sense of wonder stole over his features and his smile spread through her veins, warming her. "Really. No question."

He wanted the baby. Raw, gorgeous emotion beamed from deep inside him so clearly that those unshed tears inside her welled up and over, falling down her cheeks unchecked. This was what it *should* look like when you told a man you were having his child. Beautiful. Bonding. Amazing.

His smile turned a little misty. "You're right. I'm an idiot. And you can feel free to call me one for the rest of your life."

"Are you going to be around that long?" she murmured, her eyes widening as he pulled a square box from his pocket and unhinged the lid. "What are you doing?"

Exactly what she'd dreamed of, obviously. Giving her the one thing he'd never given anyone else, because he thought she deserved the unique experience reserved for the future Mrs. McLaughlin.

"Proposing," he verified as her stomach twisted. "But not on camera. Because this is for me and you only."

The ring sparkled in the light, shooting pink flares into her eyes and nearly blinding her to all the huge problems with what he was about to do. Everything came to a head in one horrific shot. She swallowed and shook her head. "No, you can't."

He eyed her. "Why not?"

I might say yes.

He deserved better than a defective bride. Her frozen hands wouldn't move, wouldn't stanch the flow of pain. "You didn't ask why I kept such a big secret. I have a history of miscarriages. This baby might not ever be born. Then where will we be?"

His eyelids shuttered for a moment, and when he opened them, the compassion there nearly crushed her anew.

"Let's start over." His voice broke as he held out his hand, which she didn't hesitate to take, letting his big palm cover hers. "My name is Logan McLaughlin and I own a baseball team that I bought because I thought it was going to fill a void in my life that throwing out my elbow had created. I was wrong. *You* fill the void. I love you. Whether you can carry a baby to term or not."

Finally, she'd stripped him of his conservative armor and gotten to the real man underneath. Her heart filled so full of him that she could hardly speak. But she had to as she pumped his hand slightly for good measure. "My name is Trinity Forrester and I married my job as a marketing executive because I thought I was too broken to ever have what I really wanted. *You*," she clarified as he raised a brow in question. "I want you. For real. Forever."

And he'd uncovered the woman behind the outrageousness. Probably he'd done that the first day. Because he was exactly her type, a strong, solid man who stuck around no matter what.

Whether she lost this baby or it decided to grace them with its presence after all, Logan would be there by her side, holding her hand. Loving her. He was her every fantasy come to life, and she was holding on tight. Not because she feared he'd vanish. But because she never wanted to let him go.

Epilogue

Four local TV stations, two TMZ correspondents and a liaison from *Entertainment Weekly* covered the wedding of the year between Trinity Forrester and Logan McLaughlin. The mother of the groom told anyone who would listen that she was going to be a grandmother.

Bloom launched the very next day, but Trinity and Logan were busy cheering the Mustangs as they won their seventh straight game. They planned to take a honeymoon somewhere exotic and expensive after the season was over and before Trinity got too big. At twelve weeks, Dr. Dean had proclaimed Trinity's pregnancy mostly out of the woods. There was still a chance she'd miscarry, but the odds went down significantly enough that Trinity stopped walking around on pins and needles.

Her condo in Dallas sold in one day and she moved to Logan's Prosper estate, which she'd fallen in love with the moment she'd laid eyes on it. Slowly, her style permeated the property until it became theirs. They bought two dogs, a male and a female, and named them Nolan and Estée.

Best of all, Logan had an extra closet built off the master bedroom for Trinity's clothes and shoes and almost never complained about what she wore from it— as long as she let him take it off her at the end of the day. Win-win in her book.

The positive publicity from the apology heard round the world, which went viral nearly instantaneously, guaranteed the launch of Bloom would go well, and it did. Its success far exceeded the expectations of Fyra Cosmetics' C suite, and Alex celebrated by giving birth to healthy twin girls. Phillip, the proud father, sent his private plane to Dallas to collect her friends, and Cass and Trinity in turn collected their husbands to travel with them. Harper flew into Washington, DC, from Zurich with Dante, and the six of them gathered at the hospital to meet the babies.

Logan's big hand never let go of Trinity's as they stood at the end of the bed. Her face hurt from smiling. The babies were so precious, and Phillip's and Alex's expressions as they each held one were priceless. *Awestruck* barely covered it.

"That's going to be us soon," Logan murmured in her ear.

"We don't know for sure," she whispered back, because this was Alex's day, not hers, and negative talk had no place here. "I'll be okay either way."

And she would be. Logan had told her several times that if the worst happened, they'd look into adoption. Or wait and try again. Or buy a horse. All of the above. Whatever she wanted. That fit perfectly with her plans, because she wanted it all—a family with a man who loved her by her side.

As she glanced around the hospital room at the three women with whom she'd built a cosmetics empire, their husbands, children, babies to come…it didn't matter what happened with her own pregnancy. She had it all already.

* * * * *

MILLS & BOON®

PASSIONATE AND DRAMATIC LOVE STORIES

A sneak peek at next month's titles...

In stores from 9th February 2017:

- **Billionaire's Baby Promise** – Sarah M. Anderson *and*
  Seduce Me, Cowboy – Maisey Yates

- **Reunited with the Rancher** – Sara Orwig *and*
  Paper Wedding, Best-Friend Bride – Sheri WhiteFeather

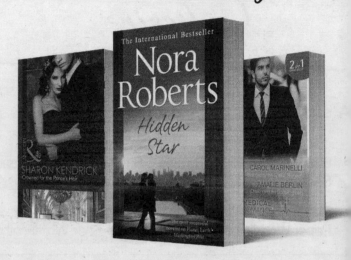

Join Britain's BIGGEST Romance Book Club

- **EXCLUSIVE offers every month**
- **FREE delivery direct to your door**
- **NEVER MISS a title**
- **EARN Bonus Book points**

Call Customer Services
0844 844 1358*
or visit
illsandboon.co.uk/subscriptions